Books by Leonard Sanders

The Emperor's Shield
The Hamlet Ultimatum
The Hamlet Warning

Published by POCKET BOOKS

THE HAMLET ULTIMATUM

LEONARD SANDERS

POCKET BOOKS

New York   London   Toronto   Sydney   Tokyo   Singapore

This book is a work of fiction. Names, characters, places and incidents are either the product of the author's imagination or are used fictitiously. Any resemblance to actual events or locales or persons, living or dead, is entirely coincidental.

POCKET BOOKS, a division of Simon & Schuster Inc.
1230 Avenue of the Americas, New York, NY 10020

ISBN: 0-671-67271-1

First Pocket Books printing July 1991

10 9 8 7 6 5 4 3 2 1

POCKET and colophon are registered trademarks of
Simon & Schuster Inc.

Cover art by David Mann

Printed in the U.S.A.

For Florene

It is my considered judgment that there is no longer a question of whether or not there will be world government by the year 2000. As I see it, the questions we should be addressing to ourselves are: how it will come into being—by cataclysm, drift, more or less rational design—and whether it will be totalitarian, benignly elitist, or participatory (the probabilities being in that order).

—Saul Mendlovitz,
president,
Institute for World Order

We nuclear people have made a Faustian bargain with society.

—Alvin Weinbert,
nuclear scientist

Nuclear terrorism is the wave of the future.

—Ovid Demaris,
Brothers in Blood

PART
ONE

Chapter

1

The Hamlet team came in darkness. Quietly, one by one, they scaled the high stone walls of El Jefe's villa with cloth-wrapped grapnels. At the massive, ornate iron gate to the flagstone courtyard, they garroted the two Andalusian watchmen in silence. Loomis did not hear them until they started up the stairs to kill him.

The soft, gentle rain that had fallen earlier in the night had ceased. Water no longer dripped from the ancient tile on the roof to murmur through the gutters of the terrace. The faint, furtive metallic click from the landing below was distinct in the stillness, bringing Loomis back abruptly from vivid dreams of old wars, of terrors survived, of friends long dead. Confused by the mingled hazards of past and present, he lay motionless for a moment, half convinced that he had imagined the distant yet insidious sound. Then, unmistakably, he again heard the firm snick of metal on metal as the second weapon was made ready for use. Through a sixth sense shaped by decades of similar deadly games, Loomis knew who they were, and what they had come to

3

do. Despite his rising fear, he was overwhelmed by anger. Hamlet would not leave him the fuck alone.

Always the surprises. No matter how much caution, how much attention to security, there inevitably came the relaxed moment—and the deadly surprises. It was a pattern Loomis had seen in every combat situation—in Cuba, Vietnam, Uganda, Guatemala, Biafra. . . .

And now, when he was totally out of it, completely relaxed, the biggest surprise of all—and maybe his last.

No light came from the terrace window, or from the lamp he had left turned low in the adjoining room. Beside him, he could hear Maria Elena breathing in the measured rhythm of deep sleep. Loomis resisted his impulse to awaken her, to send her fleeing to safety.

The killers were now on the landing. There wasn't enough time.

He knew that his only chance was to stop them before they reached the bedroom.

Sliding to the edge of the bed, he eased onto the floor, landing cat-fashion on the deep-piled carpet. He waited just long enough to make certain that he had not awakened Maria Elena. Then he moved toward the bedroom door, hoping to reach his .380 Browning automatic in the coat closet near the hall. But through the open door, there came the brief, firefly flash of a penlight in the adjoining room, and Loomis knew that time had run out.

He backed against the wall, his hand on the doorframe, and waited.

For a long moment, there were no further sounds. He began to wonder if he were wrong, if the assassins might be hunting the way to the room of the old warrior, El Jefe. But logic told him otherwise. The deposed Dominican Republic dictator, exiled and powerless, had made peace with his enemies. The revolution there was over. El Jefe no longer posed a threat to anyone. Loomis knew himself to be the target. He was the one who had stopped Hamlet in Santo Domingo. He should have known that Hamlet would not quit, nor forget. But in the peaceful, timeless surroundings

4

of El Jefe's villa, high in the mountainous Tibidabo section overlooking the ancient city of Barcelona, he had been lulled into a misjudgment.

And now, he might pay with his life.

Through the doorway came a soft, one-word whisper, another flicker of light. Loomis tensed, straining to hear the slightest hint of movement.

Unarmed, practically naked in thin pajama bottoms, he thought he might have two advantages. One was the darkness. If the killers had more than a vague knowledge of the villa's layout, they would not have hesitated on the landing, and they would not be hesitating now.

The other edge was his experience, his understanding of the patterns of assassination. In all probability, two killers had mounted the stairs, leaving the others below as a rear guard to cover retreat. All logic dictated two men had climbed the stairs. One would be too vulnerable on such an operation. Three would be too many; they would tend to get in each other's way. And Loomis was certain that he had heard the safety latches thrown on two weapons.

Two men.

A rustle of clothing came through the darkness. Loomis crouched, prepared to gamble his life on his assumption that he faced two men.

He stopped breathing as a shadow of deeper darkness moved past the door. The penlight flashed beyond him, checking the bedroom, locating the bed. Loomis was now behind the killer, within easy reach. He resisted temptation. He knew he had to wait. He put all his concentration on the doorway.

The second man entered the room without using a light. Loomis could see only a huge, indefinite shape.

But that was enough.

Loomis lashed out with forearm and elbow, aiming for the man's neck, giving his anger full vent with the blow. The connection was solid. Loomis felt the shock of contact, momentarily numbing his arm. He followed through with his full weight. He had no way of knowing where the blow

5

landed, but the killer went down, his weapon falling free in the darkness. Loomis wasted no time hunting for it.

As the other man's penlight swung toward him, he dived, driving his right shoulder into the man's chest, giving him no room or time to use his weapon. As they fell, Loomis heard Maria Elena's awakening scream. Loomis grappled, seeking a solid hold. He found the killer's chin, and quickly moved his left forearm across the killer's throat, his right at the back of the man's head. Twisting desperately, savagely, Loomis put all his strength into his arms, aware that the one he had hit might be recovering, hunting his weapon in the darkness.

With a sickening crunch, the neck snapped. Loomis rolled free, searching on the floor for one of the fallen weapons. His hands closed over the familiar shape of a 9-mm. Israeli Uzi. The safety was off. The select lever was on full automatic.

"Loomis?" Maria Elena whispered frantically from the bed.

"Stay put," he said softly.

He waited more than half a minute, listening, scarcely breathing. Nothing moved. He then groped on the floor and found the penlight. He turned its faint glow on the doorway. The man he had hit was dead. The blow apparently had landed exactly where Loomis had hoped, squarely on the larynx, crushing the windpipe and hyoid bone.

The killer with the broken neck was now in extremis. After one glance, Loomis turned the light away from him.

"Loomis?" Maria Elena whispered again.

"It's okay," he said softly. He switched to Spanish. *"Un momento, solamente."*

He lowered his head to the carpet and forced himself to relax, regaining control. It was an old trick, learned in Vietnam, taught by a sergeant whose ribbons had reflected most of the history of the Corps. The theory was simple. When the adrenal glands are dispensing nature's potent drug, resistance is futile. A man must roll with its punch, absorbing, harnessing its power, instead of allowing it to use him.

Loomis had put the theory into practice through more than twenty years of combat. Now, under his enforced concentration, he felt his muscles relax. The tremor in his hands ceased.

He picked up the other Uzi, moved across the room to Maria Elena, and whispered close to her ear. "There're probably more of them," he said. "I'm going downstairs."

"No!" Maria Elena whispered fiercely. "Call the *policía!*"

"Can't," Loomis told her. "The wiring is cut."

He was guessing. But the matter was moot. There was not enough time for police response in the mountainous Tibidabo.

"I'm coming with you," Maria Elena whispered.

"No," he insisted. "In the dark, it's safer alone."

"Please!" she said.

"No!" he answered, more sharply than he had intended. He did not want to leave her alone. But he must. Did she not understand that?

"What about El Jefe?"

She still tended to worry over the safety of her uncle. Normally, Loomis also would have been concerned; he still was considered chief of security to El Jefe's household-in-exile. With the end of the Caribbean revolution, all threats to El Jefe faded, relegating Loomis to the role of houseguest, adviser, and friend.

"He's okay," Loomis said. "If not, we would have heard something."

Faintly silhouetted against the terrace windows, Maria Elena looked past him to where the bodies lay in the darkness. "Hamlet?" she asked.

"My guess," he said. He checked the bolts of the weapons, making certain that rounds were chambered. He put one of the machine pistols on the bed beside Maria Elena. "Stay here," he said. "If they get past me, use this. Be careful. The safety's off. Just grip the handle, pull the trigger."

He moved away before she could protest.

Still in pajama bottoms, and barefoot, he walked cautiously out through the adjacent room and into the hall.

As he had suspected, all interior lights were out. Either the wiring had been cut, or the power switched off. He inched his way across to the stairway, one hand holding the weapon, the other outstretched to find the railing. At the top of the stairs, he stopped. He waited for two long minutes, hearing his own heart beat, listening to the complete silence of the house. Then, holding the penlight at arm's length, he blinked it twice at the foyer below. After a moment, a tentative query came in a low whisper.

"Pedro? *Qué pasa?*"

Loomis fired, aiming at the source of the sound. The burst from the Uzi on full automatic was deafening in the confined space, the muzzle blast momentarily blinding. Loomis traversed the foyer with bullets. He then abruptly dropped to the floor.

There was no return fire.

Convinced he had connected, Loomis went down the stairs fast, holding the Uzi ready. He crossed the foyer, knelt, and waited, listening. He heard only gasping, labored breathing. Bracing the Uzi, he flicked on the penlight.

A crumpled body lay in the center of the foyer. The man's lifeblood was spreading slowly on the marble floor. Loomis turned off the penlight. Although he was certain the rest of the team had fled, he was taking no chances.

He felt his way through the dining room, into the kitchen, and down the basement stairs to the fuse box. He flipped the switches, restoring power to the villa.

Moving with care, he then searched the entire compound.

The other members of the team had fled.

At the front gate, he found the bodies of the two watchmen. Kneeling to feel for any sign of pulse, Loomis found evidence they had been eliminated by competent professionals. The wire snares were still in place, cutting deeply into the flesh at the throat.

When he returned to the house, El Jefe was standing over

the body in the foyer, one arm around Maria Elena, a huge old 9-mm. broomhandle Mauser cradled in the other. El Jefe, now in his late sixties, was still a handsome man, big, almost as tall as Loomis, and of heavier build. He remained athletic, and there was little fat on him. The deposed dictator, freed of all responsibilities, seemed to be enjoying his life in exile. But now his deep tan from many hours in the pool failed to hide the pallor of shock. He spoke to Loomis in Spanish, using the familiar *"tu."*

"Are you all right?"

Loomis put a firm hand on El Jefe's shoulder. He felt genuine, close affection for few men. El Jefe was one of the few.

"Physically, yes," Loomis told him. "Mentally, no. It was a close thing, Jefe."

Maria Elena was still in her favorite red silk coolie pajamas, her long dark hair loose. Those large, intelligent, enigmatic eyes were now filled with fright. And her lips trembled as she fought to hold her emotions in check. She came to Loomis. He held her for a moment, fighting back his frustration, anger. He had thought that in Spain they would be safe.

Now he knew that neither he nor Maria Elena would be able to find refuge as long as Hamlet existed.

El Jefe gestured with the Mauser toward the body on the marble floor. "Do you know him?" he asked in Spanish.

"No," Loomis said. "His name's probably not important. He was only hired to do a job."

Loomis knelt and searched the body. He found no papers, labels, or jewelry, aside from a standard, inexpensive watch. Three slugs from the Uzi had passed through the chest. Small, swarthy, and definitely Latin, the killer did not in any way seem familiar. There were no obvious scars or marks. Loomis studied the face. Twenty-five, perhaps. Certainly no more than thirty. Young, and incredibly foolish for a man in his profession. Loomis could not believe that he himself had ever been so foolish.

9

"They will try again," El Jefe said. "Next time, we will be ready."

"No," Loomis said. "I almost got the two of you killed tonight. I can't take that chance again. I'll have to get away from here, until this is over."

"No!" Maria Elena said.

"We'll arm the compound," El Jefe promised. "This won't happen again."

Loomis pointed to the body. "The Spanish authorities are going to take a dim view of this, Jefe. I can't let you jeopardize your situation as a guest in this country."

"I have friends, even in the new regime," El Jefe insisted. "I can make the proper arrangements."

Loomis did not answer. He would win no argument with the old revolutionary. There was only one solution, painful and difficult. To go away.

Maria Elena asked questions plaguing Loomis. "What does Hamlet want? Why are they trying to kill you?"

"I don't know," Loomis said. "Maybe it's time I found out."

Maria Elena turned and gave him a steady, unflinching stare, letting him know that she would battle him all the way.

Loomis walked away. He had a difficult decision to make— one he might regret the rest of his life.

The Spanish authorities arrived at daylight and spent the entire morning in the compound, searching. For what, no one seemed to know, including them.

Loomis was questioned twice, each time before a different audience of *policía,* who seemed more intrigued by the entertainment value of his account than by the facts it contained. Shortly before noon, a phone call came from Madrid, bringing an abrupt change in the atmosphere, and the first signs of any positive action. After listening intently to Madrid for a quarter of an hour, the chief inspector seemed tremendously relieved that decisions had been taken out of his hands. He became almost jovial.

"Clearly, you acted in self-defense," he told Loomis in flowing, formal Spanish. "There will be no complications. The matter will be kept as confidential as possible."

"Have you learned any more about the dead men?" Loomis asked.

The inspector gave an elaborate shrug. "They were of little consequence," he said. "The two you killed upstairs, we have dealt with before. Criminals known for smuggling, robbery, a killing or two. Both were from Madrid. The other was from Valencia. He has been arrested from time to time for various crimes."

"Any idea who hired them?" Loomis asked.

Again, the elaborate shrug. "Who knows?" He paused, carefully choosing the right phraseology. "We are aware, of course, of your recent exploits in the Caribbean. We must assume that you remain in a certain degree of danger. We can, if you wish, assign men to the villa for a limited time."

"That won't be necessary," Loomis said. El Jefe did not like to have strange people around his villa, especially if they were carrying guns.

"If we have further information, we will notify you," the inspector said.

After the *policía* had gone, Loomis went to his quarters for a shower. When he emerged, Maria Elena was waiting. She was wearing a rose-colored floral print bikini and matching terry robe. She handed him a drink without comment.

When Maria Elena was upset, she had a way of erecting barriers, of closing herself off from the world. The only effective way to deal with the mood, he had learned, was to draw her back with normalcy.

"The police are gone," he told her. "Apparently there will be no problems."

"Have you made up your mind?" she asked.

He sat on the edge of the bed and continued to towel himself while he considered how to answer. The matter of Sir Reginald still lay heavily between them, the first real disagreement in their relationship.

"I'm still thinking about it," he said.

11

"But you know how I feel."

"Yes."

"Then there's nothing more I can say," she said. "I will be in the pool." She turned and walked toward the stairs.

Loomis took his drink into the salon and stretched out on a sofa. He had not slept after the attack. At the moment, he felt every one of his forty-six years. His energy had been drained considerably by the battle, but even more by the resentment, the rage he felt against the injustice of his position. Why should he be forced back into his old line of work?

He was weary of danger, of the kind of life he had led.

He wondered, briefly, how many men he now had killed. Long ago, he had stopped counting. But the burden always remained.

Three more on his conscience did not help.

Again, he marveled over his survival, as he had for more than two decades. The odds had grown phenomenal. But he was still alive after high-risk CIA operations in Cuba and Vietnam, after fighting as a mercenary in Uganda, Nicaragua, Chile, and the Dominican Republic.

For more than twenty years, killing had been his way of life.

Now, when everything seemed to be perfect, could he leave all of this, and Maria Elena, to go back to that life?

Maria Elena, never one to dodge an issue, had made her position clear. She had recognized immediately that the visit of Sir Reginald Heath of the United Nations three days ago had brought the first serious danger to their relationship.

And now he would have to choose between Maria Elena and Sir Reginald, between his deepest desires and his strong sense of duty.

He thought back to the meeting, going over it again, seeking clues to what he should do.

Loomis and Maria Elena had received Sir Reginald in the mahogany-paneled library of El Jefe's villa. The tall, lean Britisher affected that ramrod military courtesy that the British army seems to assume as its exclusive domain.

Towering over Maria Elena, Sir Reginald had turned his full charm on her, apparently recognizing her as the major threat to his mission.

He managed the continental hand ceremony with casual grace.

"I am one of your greatest admirers," he told Maria Elena. "I have seen every film you have made—some many times."

Maria Elena accepted the compliment with the detachment she usually adopted when her movie career was mentioned.

With obvious effort, Sir Reginald turned his attention to Loomis.

"And you," he said. "I trust you are recovering satisfactorily from the incident in Santo Domingo."

Loomis preferred not to think of the wild, sixteen-minute helicopter ride with Johnson, out to the open sea with Hamlet's atomic bomb—sixteen terrifying minutes in which he and Johnson had saved the city of Santo Domingo from nuclear destruction. The purple radiation burns that remained on his neck, ears, and forehead after two months were no longer painful, but they seemed difficult for others to ignore.

"No problem," he said. "The outer layers of skin were cooked. But they tell me the effects will go away in time."

"A brave, brave thing," Sir Reginald said, taking the chair Loomis indicated, facing the open courtyard. "I hope all the attention you have received from the press has not been overly taxing."

"I've managed to avoid it here," Loomis said.

Sir Reginald persisted in small talk while El Jefe's houseman served drinks. Later, after Maria Elena made excuses and left them alone, Sir Reginald turned to Loomis and spoke with the intensity and abruptness of a man accustomed to moving straight to the point.

"What I am about to tell you is confidential. My reasons for making it known to you will be obvious. But first, I should give you some background. As you may know, the

13

organization I head is usually referred to as the United Nations International Atomic Energy Agency. What is not generally known is the fact that the agency is not a true unit of the UN, but is linked only by a relationship agreement. The headquarters of my agency is in Vienna, not New York. Another fact not generally known: the agency is committed not only to promoting peaceful uses of atomic energy, which admittedly is its primary function, but also to making certain that materials and facilities under the agency's supervision are not subverted to military or political purposes."

Sir Reginald hesitated, as if determining how best to phrase his next thought. "What greatly concerns us now, we have in hand strong evidence that the Hamlet organization has acquired considerable nuclear material under my agency's jurisdiction."

Loomis anticipated where Sir Reginald was headed. He began to wish he had found excuses to avoid the meeting.

"How much material?" he asked.

"We are not certain," Sir Reginald said. "Unfortunately, the EurAtom countries—Belgium, France, Italy, the Netherlands, and Germany—have refused to allow inspection either by my agency, or by the United States agencies. And India, China, Israel, and Egypt also remain outside the system. Since the United States has altered its position on the breeder reactor, vendor companies in Germany, Japan, Sweden, France, Italy, and Belgium have become vigorous in proliferating nuclear capabilities in other countries. Our facilities are limited. We have only sixty-seven inspectors, at the moment. However, our preliminary estimate has given us sufficient reason to become alarmed. When the matter came to light, I immediately called an emergency meeting of the agency's board of governors—all thirty-four members. At that meeting, with your nuclear incident at Santo Domingo fresh in the minds of the members, I obtained unanimous support. I'm authorized to take extraordinary measures to track down the missing materials, to identify the Hamlet Group, and to bring the members to justice."

"Wouldn't that be a job for someone other than your agency?" Loomis asked.

"Who?" Sir Reginald asked. "That has been the question from the beginning. Our critics say that the agency was stillborn at its creation. In a way, they are correct. When we find a violation, our only course is to file a complaint with the UN General Assembly. However, no other agency has *more* authority. Interpol is limited largely to action among member nations. The CIA and similar agencies are limited to establishing elaborate scenarios, which would require time to construct and to implement. And there would be limiting political aspects with each country involved. That is why we requested, and obtained, special sanctions. We at least hold portfolio."

"Wouldn't your agency be limited in the same ways?" Loomis asked.

"Not necessarily," Sir Reginald said. "I have been assured that the full weight of the entire United Nations is behind us in this matter. Our difficulty, however, is obvious. We are staffed with information specialists, scientists, diplomats, administrators. We are not accustomed to performing police work. That is why I have come to you. We need you to find out what has happened to this material, and what use is being made of it, and by whom."

"Why me?" Loomis asked. He found his reluctance total. Surely, he had paid his dues. And he saw insurmountable drawbacks. "You need someone who can work quietly," he said. "With all the uproar over Santo Domingo, there would be no way I could work from a low profile."

"The publicity you received *could* be turned to our advantage," Sir Reginald countered. "Your experience and expertise are now known and respected among all police organizations. You could work with and through them. In that regard, you would be the ideal person. And, to use a good English schoolboy term, you've already had a scrum with these Hamlet fellows. You know what we face."

"So far, I've only dealt with Hamlet's mercenaries," Loomis pointed out. "I know nothing about Hamlet itself."

"Still, you've been in on the problem since its inception," Sir Reginald insisted. "We need to assimilate all information obtained on Hamlet by various police and intelligence agencies. You might recognize clues where others would not."

Loomis was not flattered. But he was intrigued. "How would I go about it?" he asked.

"That would be for you to say. You would be a free agent. You could conduct operations any way you think best. If you elect to direct a staff, from our headquarters in Vienna, that would be fine. If you think you should go into the field, alone, that would be satisfactory. Ostensibly, you would be in an investigative capacity, not combative. But as you of all people would know, this is an extraordinary matter. I assume extraordinary measures might be necessary."

"Weaponry would be a problem."

Sir Reginald nodded agreement. "Presumably, you will work closely, and coordinate efforts, with various national security groups. You probably will be able to work out some arrangements with host countries."

"I can't believe I'm the man you want," Loomis said.

"Frankly, I can think of no one better qualified," Sir Reginald said. "And every other man anywhere near your caliber is engaged or untrustworthy."

Despite himself, Loomis was tempted. Sir Reginald was right in one respect: the job had to be done.

But leaving Barcelona, and Maria Elena . . .

"Could I have a few days to think about it?" Loomis asked.

Sir Reginald hesitated. "We need you urgently. However, I can understand your reservation. The terrible risks you took in Santo Domingo were beyond anything one man should be expected to do. And now, here I am asking you to do more. I hope you will take into consideration our desperate straits."

With that, Loomis and Sir Reginald had rejoined El Jefe and Maria Elena for dinner. Throughout the evening, Loomis marveled over Sir Reginald's ability to return to light talk, considering all that was on his mind.

But Maria Elena was not fooled. All through dinner, she cast long, studious glances at Loomis. Later that night, she asked him, point-blank.

"What was that all about?"

He told her.

"Are you going to accept?"

"I told him I'd think about it."

"Which means you will accept."

"Not necessarily," he said. "Maybe I should. They need me."

"You promised," she reminded him.

"I know. I know. But this is something different."

Maria Elena stared at him for a moment. "There always will be something different," she said. "Someone always will be coming to you with something like this."

"But this *is* different," he said. He tried to explain. "I owe Hamlet something. I feel . . . well, that I have just half completed a job. It is not a good feeling."

She remained silent for a time. When she spoke, her voice was heavy with emotion. "You know, don't you, that if you take this job, you will wreck what we have together?"

"No. I don't *know* that," he said. "I only know you think that."

She rolled over in bed and faced him. "I've thought a lot about this," she said. "And I know now why I am so certain. It's because if you go back to that life, to the killing, to the danger, then you are not what I thought you were—someone who has been *through* those experiences, and who emerged a better man. You will be like an alcoholic going back to the bottle, an addict back to the needle. You will be showing that you don't know me, and that I only thought I knew you."

"It isn't like that," he told her. "Lord knows, I don't *want* to go back."

"Then don't," she pleaded. "We are living a good life. The best we've ever known. We've both said that. I don't

17

want it to end. But if you do this, it's over. I know this is true. You know this is true."

For the next three days, Loomis delayed calling Sir Reginald. He had felt he should accept. He had been miserable, and his relationship with Maria Elena had been strained. He could not bring himself to face the inevitable.

He knew that Maria Elena was right on one point: if he accepted, the good life would end.

And it *was* a good life. Barcelona was a fantastic city, old, and yet modern. There was always something to do, even if it was a simple stroll along Las Ramblas in the Gothic quarter. Sometimes they visited the nearby mountains for the spectacular views. Or they would drive down to the Mediterranean beaches. Loomis and Maria Elena had planned, at the first hint of boredom, to explore the hundred or more restored castles and monasteries in Spain and, eventually, all of Europe at their leisure.

Now that apparently was not to be.

Hamlet had made the decision for him.

That was the most galling thing of all.

But he would have to face Hamlet eventually. The alternative was beyond consideration: hiding, constantly looking over his shoulder, waiting for the moment when Hamlet would try again.

The only way was to go after them, to end the thing once and for all.

The official post Sir Reginald was offering him would be ideal for his purposes. With United Nations connections, and full credentials to work with the CIA, Interpol, and whatever other agency he felt necessary, he would have the tools he needed.

He rose from the sofa. Sleep was impossible.

He picked up a film script Maria Elena had been reading and leafed through it, idly, thinking.

The more he considered the matter, the clearer became a basic fact: he was only delaying the inevitable.

And there was much to do.

He went to a phone and put through a call to Sir Reginald

in Vienna. Within seconds after Loomis gave a secretary his name, Sir Reginald was on the line.

"I've thought it over," Loomis said. "If the job's still open, I'll take it."

He heard Sir Reginald's intake of breath. "Excellent, excellent. When can you start?"

"I've started," Loomis said. "I have a plan I would like to try on you."

Sir Reginald hesitated. "I'm not certain this line is secure," he said.

"Nothing is, anymore," Loomis said. "What I'm about to say is not exactly a state secret. It just happens that not many people know of it. You have a certain wedge with the U.S. government at a high level. I think we should put it into use."

The line was silent for a moment. "Maybe you should come here," Sir Reginald said. "We could talk about it."

"I'd like to get moving," Loomis said. He could have added that he regretted having squandered three days in indecision.

Sir Reginald remained cautious. "What would you have me do?"

"I need to establish strong liaison with the United States. I have a friend in place. We need him named coordinator of our project, with all the authority he'll need to cut through bureaucratic problems. I think your friend could help my friend."

Sir Reginald thought for a few seconds before answering. "That might be possible," he said. "Give me twenty-four hours. If you wish, you might go ahead and make preliminary contact with your friend."

Loomis agreed to the suggestion. Twenty-four hours also would give him time to do a few things in Spain.

"You may reach me through the Secretariat in New York," Sir Reginald said in signing off. "Just ask for me, and give them your name."

Loomis left the phone somewhat relieved. Sir Reginald had not needed to ask the names of their respective friends.

After mixing another drink, Loomis returned to the phone and put through a call to the residence of Richard Allen Johnson in Alexandria, Virginia. An operator came on the line to say that the phone had been disconnected temporarily at the customer's request.

Puzzled, Loomis called CIA headquarters at Langley. After being passed from one disembodied voice to another, he at last managed to talk with someone who claimed to be in charge of the operations desk.

"Johnson is unavailable at the moment," the slightly prissy male voice said. "We will be glad to pass on any message."

With an effort, Loomis put aside his dislike of people who clothe themselves with plural, first-person pronouns. He had found the affliction most prevalent among governmental agencies.

"Please tell Johnson that Hamlet has just made an attempt to do what nobody has done yet," he said. "Tell him Loomis called to remind him that he is also on their shit list. Please quote me verbatim."

After a pause, the effeminate, overly officious voice came across the Atlantic. "We will see that Johnson gets the message."

Loomis broke the connection, disturbed. He knew bureaucratic procedure. He had no confidence whatsoever that Johnson would receive the message.

And Johnson now might be the key to the first solid link to Hamlet.

Wheels were in motion. Sir Reginald would be busy with his staff, making the necessary preparations.

Loomis was committed. He had to get moving.

There was no way he could avoid what he now must do.

He pulled on tan trousers and a matching knit shirt. He clipped the .380 Browning automatic to his belt, allowing the shirt to hang over the weapon.

Never again would he be caught without a gun in reach.

He went downstairs and through the salon to the sunlit pool. Maria Elena had just left the high board, and was turning a half gainer. She sliced neatly into the water and swam submerged the length of the pool, surfacing at the ladder. As she climbed out, he handed her a towel and eased into one of the wrought-iron chairs.

"Pretty good," he said.

She used the towel, then spread it on a chair beside him.

"Why don't you get out of those clothes and try it?" she asked, seating herself carefully on the towel.

"I've got to go up and pack," he said. "Miles to go."

That was one way to break the news.

Maria Elena said nothing for a moment. "You've made the call," she said. She reached for her big sun hat and adjusted the brim low, hiding her eyes from him.

Loomis turned to face her. He *had* to make her understand. "Look, I had no choice. As long as I stay here, I'm putting *you* in danger. I'm putting El Jefe in danger. I'm putting myself in danger. The only thing I can do is to get into it, and get it over with."

Maria Elena turned away, facing the pool, not answering.

"I wish I had a pretty speech ready," Loomis said. " 'I could not love thee so much, loved I not honor more,' or something like that."

"Actions are what count," she said.

"I'm thinking—I'm hoping—that some of your reaction is only because you're upset—over the raid last night," he said. "That makes two of us. I don't mind admitting it. I'm scared. This is the first time I've ever fought anyone I couldn't see."

"You've been lucky," she said. She glanced at him. "My worst fears have never had faces. That's the way it is now. I don't know what's coming, but I think I could face anything Hamlet could dish out. What I can't face is that I know things between us will never be the same again."

"They will," he said. He tried to put conviction into his words. "They've got to be."

"No," she said. "If you go back to your work, I'll go back to mine. In two months, I've turned down three scripts

21

I wanted to do, scripts Paul begged me to do. I'll call him tonight, and tell him I'll take the new one."

"That part's not right for you," he said.

He was surprised by her flare of anger. "Well, thank you, Mr. Cinematic Expert," she said. "What you mean is, it has substance. You don't think I can handle it."

"You can handle it," he said quietly. He felt keenly that the role was wrong for her. He tried to explain. "I suppose I just don't want to see you change your screen image so completely. This woman has a built-in animosity to everyone around her."

Maria Elena looked at him with that level, cool disdain that had driven the film critics ecstatic.

"Since when have you fallen in love with the world?" she asked.

He made another effort. "It's just that this character strikes me as a perfect four-wheeled bitch. And that's not you at all."

Maria Elena picked up the towel as she left the chair, and gathered up her robe. "To the contrary. The part should be perfect for me," she said. "Because that's exactly how I'm beginning to feel." She turned and walked rapidly across the courtyard and disappeared into the salon.

Numb inside, Loomis returned to his quarters and packed his bags.

He did not bother to say good-bye.

Two hours later, he was en route to Valencia, the home of one of the assassins, hunting any clue he could find.

It was the start of a long journey.

Chapter

2

Through a tiresome evening President Travis J. Robertson made every effort to keep his attention focused on his duties as host to the largest gathering of performing artists ever assembled in the White House. The best-known faces and talents of theater, music, film, and dance were jammed into the huge, imposing oak-paneled State Dining Room.

A large French bronze purchased by President Monroe in 1817 served as the centerpiece at the head table and the major topic of polite conversation. The tables were circular, to circumvent that Washington obsession, protocol. The china service was from the Lyndon Johnson Administration. Although Robertson was not an expert on White House history, he knew enough facts to keep the talk flowing around him. He was much better acquainted with the decor and appointments than with the guests.

But when the time arrived for him to speak, he managed to overcome his limited expertise in the beaux arts—with the help of his speech writers, aided considerably by his own dry wit and deadpan delivery. He paid tribute to theater, ballet, opera, music, and the screen without a bobble. When he acknowledged certain individuals present, he successfully nodded in the right direction, thanks to detailed notes in his prompter text.

He received a standing ovation as he returned to his seat. His wife seemed pleased, and he was gratified to note that the svelte, ravishing woman seated on his left, who happened to be director of the National Endowment for the Humanities, was ecstatic.

His official duties completed, Robertson found his mind wandering from the remainder of the program, emceed by a popular comedian. As the Endowment director took the podium to respond to Robertson's remarks, and to outline the Administration's goals for the future, Robertson gradually became totally immersed in more pressing problems.

By the time the world's greatest living tenor ended his second encore with a selection from *Figaro,* Robertson had made several crucial decisions that would affect everyone in the room, and quite possibly the entire world.

Later, as he escorted his wife toward the elevator, his attention was brought back to lesser concerns by her effusive praise for his brief speech.

"I lost count of the people who told me tonight that you've already done more for the arts than any president since Kennedy," she said.

Robertson waited until the elevator door closed before answering. "That's more flattering than true," he told her. "Considering that Lyndon Johnson did a hell of a lot more." He lit a cigar, the first he had allowed himself in more than three hours.

"At least Kennedy had more style," his wife said.

Robertson chomped hard on his cigar and said nothing. He and his wife would never agree on Jack Kennedy.

He walked her to the bedroom door in the west sitting hall. "Are you coming to bed now?" she asked.

"I have a couple of late meetings," he said. "I'll be back up in a little while."

His wife turned and gave him a flirtatious smile. "Travis, sometimes I almost suspect you're playing poker again."

Once, long ago, his passion for all-night poker games had endangered their marriage. Now, they could joke about it.

"You'd be right," he said. "That's exactly what this is."

24

In a sweeping gesture, he took in the White House, the presidency. "The whole thing is just one big poker game."

He returned to the elevator, the thought lingering.

The stakes kept going up. The pot grew larger. A president could only hang onto his best cards, and hope for luck in the draw.

Tonight, while most of the nation slept, he would make an effort to get a peek at some hole cards.

Robertson descended to the lower level and the almost-deserted Situation Room in the White House basement, silent now except for the occasional scraping sound of the high-speed printers next door, bringing some tidbit of information from outposts around the world.

Robertson pulled out a chair, sat down at the conference table, reached for an ashtray, and waited.

Outside the room, in the quiet halls, he could hear his retinue efficiently changing stations, adjusting to the shift of presidential power from floor to floor, room to room. Three minutes later, he heard the faint, muffled clatter of doors as his aides emerged from the seldom-used, secret tunnel from Treasury. Installed as part of the six-million-dollar renovation during the Truman Administration, as a potential escape route for a beleaguered president, the tunnel had been virtually forgotten, a curious and ever-surprising alternative in Secret Service contingency plans. Previously, only Nixon had slipped at least one potential nominee into the White House for a clandestine conference, evading the White House press corps. Robertson now found himself resenting the fact that Sir Reginald had made this subterfuge necessary.

He could not understand why Sir Reginald had not gone through channels. For one of the world's most respected diplomats, the visit was a curious departure from commonly accepted procedures. But years ago, Robertson had worked closely with Sir Reginald in Lisbon, where they had served as military attachés for their respective embassies.

He had learned to appreciate Sir Reginald's judgment. They had remained friends through the intervening years, frequently exchanging personal notes. Sir Reginald obviously wanted this meeting kept absolutely secret. Robertson could think of only one possible reason.

Yet the secrecy went against Robertson's grain. He would have been happy to welcome Sir Reginald, publicly, as an old friend.

Robertson's chief of staff had recommended use of the tunnel for the clandestine midnight meeting. Robertson grudgingly had agreed.

Sir Reginald was escorted into the room. Tall, gray, and distinguished, the now-aging British diplomat always reminded Robertson of a walking advertisement for scotch whiskey and tweeds. Robertson stood, shook hands, and, after a brief exchange of small talk, walked his visitor down the hall and into the now-deserted office of the Presidential Assistant on National Security.

"I hope you don't mind the inconvenience," Robertson said as they were seated. "If we went upstairs, the wrong person might see you."

"No inconvenience, Travis," Sir Reginald said. "And after all, I'm the one who insisted that we meet like thieves in the night. I really think, with the matters at hand, it is by far the best. If no one knows that we are working together, perhaps we can steal a march on our enemies."

"No new enemies, I hope," Robertson said. "Frankly, I have about all I need."

"Not new," Sir Reginald said. "But I think they rate a reevaluation."

"Hamlet?"

Sir Reginald lifted his bushy eyebrows. "I assume our time here is limited, so I'll be blunt, old friend. How much do you know? You may be ahead of me."

Robertson usually kept his own information in reserve for use as needed. But he caught the urgency in Sir Reginald's voice. He decided to employ what a previous administration would have termed "a limited hangout."

26

"Not much," he said. "I've only had reports from here and there, nothing conclusive. I know that an attempt was made to assassinate Loomis in Barcelona twenty-four hours ago, and that the effort failed. I know that you met with Loomis four days ago. My sources are not as extensive as you might think. I don't know what you talked about. I only know that you conferred with him alone for fifty-three minutes. I know that shortly after the attempt on his life, Loomis was on the phone to you, and that your phone conversation was brief. Later, Loomis attempted repeatedly to reach Johnson at CIA and, failing that, asked for an appointment with our director of Clandestine Services, or whatever Dirty Tricks is called these days. The people at Langley passed the buck to me. I gave my approval for him to enter the country, with certain limitations. He has a file a foot thick, you know. Ordinarily, it would take an act of Congress, or some similar idiocy, to get him through Immigration. I authorized an administrative cloak over his file, temporarily. And there you have it."

Sir Reginald nodded. "I'll be brief, and as candid. My mission is twofold. First, I must apprise you of a situation. Secondly, I will give you the steps I have taken so far to meet it, and ask for your cooperation. Are your agencies aware of the vast amount of plutonium stolen throughout the world?"

"Only in a general way," Robertson said, poker-faced. "We hear rumors of some gone here, some gone there. But we haven't been able to put a hard number on it. The inventory shortages are for the most part overseas, under other governments and, unfortunately, out of our hands."

"We have a fairly accurate estimate, I believe," Sir Reginald said. "We have just completed an examination of all facilities. We suspected, from the start, that the shortages were widespread. But we were absolutely stunned by the total. At the moment, from the more than one hundred and fifty nuclear reactors in twenty-four countries, we estimate that more than three thousand pounds of plutonium are missing.''

Robertson nodded. Sir Reginald's total closely matched the estimates made by U.S. agencies.

"Have you definitely linked the shortages to Hamlet?" Robertson asked.

That was the one thing his agencies had been unable to do.

"No, we haven't," Sir Reginald said. "At this point, Hamlet is only the best educated guess. And this brings us to my main problem. As you no doubt know, we have no police facilities to speak of. We must depend on the assistance of member nations. And that is why I went to Loomis. My trip to Barcelona was to ask him to undertake a personal investigation, in the hope that he can determine where this material is going, and the use being made of it.''

"What do you suspect? More bombs?" Robertson asked.

"A prime possibility, certainly," Sir Reginald said. "But we're now wondering if it could not be something else. I'm told that is enough material for more than one hundred atomic bombs. Quite a production problem. The quality of the device Hamlet tried to detonate in Santo Domingo was high. But the designer is now dead. The expertise and facilities to turn out bombs in quantity might be difficult to acquire. And if Hamlet were only wanting to build another half-dozen bombs, why would they need so much material?''

"Any ideas?" Robertson asked, fishing.

"My associates have speculated that Hamlet might be planning something crude, but more deadly," Sir Reginald said.

"What would that be?" Robertson asked, knowing, but wanting to determine how much information Sir Reginald had in hand.

"Pollution," Sir Reginald said. "If plutonium is truly one of the most poisonous substances known to man, I suppose one can derive all sorts of horrors from that basic fact.''

Robertson sat and rolled his cigar for a moment, thinking.

Upstairs, locked in his safe in the Oval Office, was a report. Earlier in the day, he had spent more than two hours absorbing what he could of the extremely complex information. Much of the study had dwelled on the dangers posed by plutonium emitted into the atmosphere. Although Robertson had known most of the general facts before reading the volume, the specifics had given him cold chills.

"I gather you suspect we may be facing a new type of nuclear terrorism," Robertson said.

"Not really," Sir Reginald said. "In fact, you might even say that the threat of pollution predates the bomb. I remember that during the war—World War Two, maybe you remember that one—the matter came up. At the time, I was aide to General Whiteley, who was Assistant Chief of Staff, G-2, to Eisenhower. In April of '44, two months before the Normandy invasion, a theory was advanced by your people at Los Alamos that Germany might be preparing to salt the beaches along the French and Belgian coasts with radioactive materials. Or even to use some sort of radioactivity against England. Your General Groves sent a delegation over from the Manhattan Project to brief Eisenhower. For a time, there was considerable concern about it. An entire program was put into motion—Geiger counters, sensitive-film packets, survey meters, the whole works. Operation Peppermint, it was called. Hundreds of people were given emergency training. When the invasion came off, and there was no radioactivity, everyone forgot about it. Operation Peppermint. I hadn't thought of that name in years."

Robertson did not intend to sit up nights refighting old wars. He pulled Sir Reginald back to the subject. "Have you had any indication who Hamlet is? Anything at all?"

Sir Reginald smiled. "You're the man with armies of spooks at your disposal. I was hoping you might be able to tell *me* something."

"Theories," Robertson said. "That's all I have."

"It's a fertile field for speculation," Sir Reginald agreed. "One of my colleagues, a respected medical researcher, is convinced that we are embarked on the Carcinogenic

Century—the Age of Cancer—even without further atmospheric pollution. He has offered some interesting figures.''

"You obviously want to scare me," Robertson said. "Go ahead."

"My friend tells me that one-millionth of a gram of plutonium inhaled into the lungs can cause cancer. One ten-thousandth of a gram would kill a person within days—a horrible death, incidentally. One-thousandth of a gram would be fatal, almost instantaneously, through massive fibrosis of the lungs. These are arbitrary figures, of course. Effects would vary with individuals. For instance, even moderate cigarette smoking destroys cilia, the fine, hairlike projections that clean the lungs, making the heavy cigarette smoker far more susceptible."

"That's why I stick to cigars," Robertson said.

"There's another theory that will get you anyway," Sir Reginald said. "Dr. John Gofman, who used to be in medical physics at Berkeley, calculates that every pound of power plant grade plutonium introduced into the atmosphere could cause twenty-one billion cases of lung cancer. That's billion. Not million."

"He shouldn't be alarming people with figures like that," Robertson said. "It's all speculation. My people claim he could be wrong by half."

"Some reputable scientists believe his figures to be conservative," Sir Reginald said.

"And others say he's full of shit," Robertson pointed out. "Let's admit that most of this is only theory."

"Granted," Sir Reginald said. "Still, all in all, I'm impressed with the credentials of those who have spoken out against the proliferation of nuclear materials—scores of men like John Gofman, including Nobel laureates and respected leaders in many fields of science. In almost every instance, they have spoken their convictions at personal sacrifice. They have jeopardized their careers. And they have convinced me that we must at least listen."

"And there are other scientists, just as impressive, who call those people alarmists," Robertson told him. "When men of such impeccable credentials disagree so completely, how are we to decide?"

"It's difficult," Sir Reginald admitted. "But I can't resist projecting some figures. If Dr. Gofman is correct, and if Hamlet has stolen those three thousand pounds of plutonium, then Hamlet possesses the potential to cause sixty-three thousand billion deaths."

"I still say Gofman could be off by half," Robertson said. "But you've made your point. What do you want me to do?"

"I need your help, desperately. I have only sixty-seven inspectors to investigate nuclear facilities throughout the world. My budget is a little less than thirty million dollars. Out of that, I must support laboratories, a center for theoretical physics, the publication of hundreds of scientific texts, and the operation of an international organization, communicating with almost every country. Truly, I am expected to do the impossible. When Argentina removed fifty kilograms of plutonium waste from her Atucha station some time back, obviously with the hope of acquiring nuclear bomb capability, we were criticized severely because we did not report the violation. But we are virtually impotent in matters of enforcement. For the most part, we have to accept the figures offered by the nation involved. When we do find a violation, our only recourse is to notify the UN Security Council, where the matter is usually ignored, out of political considerations."

"I'm not sure I will be able to help," Robertson warned him. "I know that the United States presidency is generally termed the most powerful office in the world. And maybe it is. But those powers are paradoxical. For instance, Russia has two hundred and eighteen cities with a population of more than a hundred thousand people. It's no secret that in the next thirty minutes, given proper provocation, I could detonate thirty-six nuclear weapons over *each* of those cities. Now, that's power. But I can't fix your parking ticket, stop some drunken, idiotic congressman from embarrassing the country—or spend a penny that Congress has not allocated."

"You misunderstand me," Sir Reginald said. "I'm not asking for funds. I'm asking for the use of your facilities."

"That may be the same thing," Robertson said.

"Mutual use," Sir Reginald said. "If we have a common goal, then there would be no conflict."

"Try me," Robertson said.

"I have asked Loomis to make a personal investigation, to determine what has happened to those missing materials. I have obtained carte blanche from the Secretary General. I have passed that carte blanche to Loomis."

"And now you want carte blanche from me."

"In a sense. Loomis will have to work with the approval of participating governments. Your overseas structure of surveillance is the best in the world. And certainly, you have the best technical facilities—the communications network, the agents in place, computer files, and so forth. I would like for Loomis to work from or through Langley, utilizing those facilities during this emergency situation. Remember, we are working toward the same ends—we've *got* to find, and destroy, Hamlet."

Robertson rolled his cigar for a moment in thought. "I can't do it," he said. "There is no way that I can farm out an essential portion of our government to the United Nations. Or to any of its allied agencies. There are ramifications, political and legal, that simply remove the matter from consideration. The best I can do is to offer my limited cooperation."

"How limited?"

"Within certain guidelines I mentioned. In short, we would conduct our own operation. If at all possible, we would coordinate our activities with yours. I would have to authorize the Intelligence Director to limit Loomis's participation, if he believes discretion advisable in certain instances. And you must understand that I cannot be bound to policies and procedures originating on the East River, or in Bern, or in Vienna."

"That's plain enough," Sir Reginald said. "Does the fact that Loomis is a former CIA intelligence officer, now in bad graces, affect your decision?"

"Not necessarily. But his record does complicate matters. There are people at Langley who remember Loomis and the whole affair. As you may know, they twice tried to kill him. And he killed two U.S. intelligence officers sent against him. Those two men are still remembered by many friends in the agency. I suppose I could lean on those who object. We can walk around that problem. My major objection to Loomis is philosophical. I'll admit I liked the way he handled that affair in Santo Domingo. Certainly, he saved the lives of several hundred thousand people. But I'm not certain he is the right man for *your* job."

Sir Reginald smiled. "Travis, for the last twenty years, I have been a career diplomat. I think as a diplomat, act as a diplomat, effecting changes through tact, negotiation, the proper atmosphere. You are a politician. You have been a politician throughout your whole life. You are adept at manipulating power through reason, persuasion, and occasional, productive compromise. We both possess the skills necessary to our jobs. I believe Loomis has capabilities essential to us at the moment."

"Even if he leans toward the physical solution to problems?"

Sir Reginald nodded emphatically. "Travis, my government sent a seasoned diplomat to talk to Hitler at Munich in 1938. Neville Chamberlain came back with what he considered to be a diplomatic victory. He almost led us to disaster. We sent the wrong man. Hitler was beyond diplomacy, beyond politics. There are times when diplomacy, politics are dangerous. We should have sent to talk to Hitler a man who spoke his language—violence."

"If I may coin a phrase, that's the last resort," Robertson said.

"Or maybe the first, most logical choice," Sir Reginald snapped. "No, Travis, I can't accept the cliché, 'violence is never the answer.' If you accept that, you in one breath remove our moral stance for World War Two, and, I might add, yours for the revolt in the colonies."

Robertson chuckled. He often missed the long sessions of debate he once enjoyed with Sir Reginald.

"The problem is that sometimes intelligent violence is the *only* answer," Sir Reginald continued. "We absolutely have to recognize that fact, and act accordingly. That is why I chose Loomis. And that is why I gave him free rein. He understands the type of people we're dealing with. He speaks their language. He would be hampered if he had to clear matters through my diplomat's mind."

"Or through my politician's mind?"

"You said that. I didn't."

Robertson carefully considered Sir Reginald's argument. He sensed a valid reason for objection to Sir Reginald's choice of Loomis. But as yet, he had not had time to define his vague feeling of unease.

"I can only pledge to do all I can, within my limitations," he said.

"I suppose I shall have to be satisfied with that," Sir Reginald said. "I'll test you with two requests. First, Loomis has asked that his friend Johnson be named liaison between himself and the operation at Langley."

Robertson considered the request. Moving Johnson into such a position, where he could deal with certain people at their own level, would require a promotion. That would ruffle a few feathers. But perhaps those feathers needed ruffling.

"That could be arranged," he said. "Second?"

"We will need a channel of confidential communication, between my agency in Austria and Loomis, wherever he happens to be. Also, possibly a confidential link between you and myself. I am on first-name basis with your chief of station in Vienna. He probably does not know I am aware of his dual status. Perhaps our messages could be sent through the CIA communications network, if your man in Vienna were apprised of the necessity."

Robertson again was rolling his cigar. He pondered possible repercussions. Neither Loomis nor Sir Reginald would have direct access to the network. No secrecy standards would be violated.

"As long as communication is limited to confidential

information that couldn't be handled otherwise, I can see no objection," Robertson said.

"Excellent. I'm glad I came to see you. I'm not ordinarily given to premonitions, but this Hamlet thing has disturbed me greatly. I feel that we at least are now taking some positive steps. I think we still have a long way to go. I fear that this matter may be far more serious than we have suspected."

Robertson nodded, accepting the statement without comment. He saw no reason to alarm his old friends further by revealing that his own fears were remarkably parallel.

Robertson escorted Sir Reginald to the tunnel for the trip back to Treasury, a State Department limousine, and a quick dash to Andrews for a special plane. Robertson went back to the Oval Office to await his second personal appointment of the night.

He preferred less imposing surroundings for routine work. But the awesome atmosphere of the Oval Office made Robertson feel the full weight of his responsibilities. It was here he did his most serious thinking. At the Oval Office desk, he was more inclined to set aside personal and party considerations, and to perform as a president.

He ordered coffee and sat in semidarkness for a long time, not working, merely turning over in his mind all the known facts concerning Hamlet. From those facts, he felt, he should be able to arrive at certain conclusions.

In his presidential files were copies of hundreds of diabolical scenarios, the products of think tanks hired by the government to anticipate every conceivable potential danger.

All of those imaginative schemes added up to one solid premise: the means to accomplish extensive mischief always exists.

The rare qualities are the genius, dedication, perseverance, ruthlessness, and self-sacrifice required to put them into operation.

Somewhere, a set of brains was directing Hamlet, plotting, devising, maneuvering the whole elaborate intrigue. Robertson believed that if he would really put his mind to work, he might fathom what kind of enemy he faced.

He sighed, poured another cup of coffee, and pulled a legal-sized scratch pad onto his desk. He uncapped a felt-tipped pen. Speculating, he began a list.

In order to function, Hamlet needed certain things. One was organizational structure. Administrative officers would be needed in various sections of the world, and minions to do their bidding. Second, Hamlet would require at least minimal physical facilities; all those people would need places to do their jobs. Third, some means of effective and confidential communication would have to exist, a rapid, clear-cut system, with no bureaucratic bottlenecks or security leaks. And fourth, Hamlet would need—and obviously had—vast financial resources.

Reviewing his list, Robertson began to see a fallacy in Sir Reginald's apparent assumption, and in almost all speculation by his own people concerning Hamlet.

Everyone had taken for granted that the Hamlet structure was hidden.

Robertson could see no way that Hamlet could operate on such an elaborate scale without evident profile. An invisible organization of that size simply could not exist.

Hamlet undoubtedly was using a network already in existence, one that the world recognized and accepted.

The supposition opened a wide realm of possibilities.

Robertson began making a new list.

The United Nations?

He put the UN down as a remote candidate. The structure was too fragmented to provide many of the requisites. Yet, a network within the UN structure remained a slight possibility. He gave it a one-star rating.

The U.S. military?

A stronger contender, perhaps. But Robertson could see one obvious flaw: the military contained enough weaponry to wipe out two or three ordinary-sized planets. If members of a clandestine group were working from within the military, they would need only to divert a small part of the nation's nuclear stockpiles. A nuclear submarine or a few sophisticated warheads would do. They would not need to steal from civilian stockpiles of bulk nuclear materials. Robertson gave the military a two-star rating.

The CIA?

A much stronger possibility. In the past, factions within the CIA had made efforts to manipulate the government. A splinter group at Langley had assumed awesome power at one time—enough to assassinate a president, some people believed. And like most closed institutions, Langley was a hotbed of constant internal intrigue. Yet, there was one saving factor: each bunch of spooks usually knew what the other factions were doing. In any event, all major communications were handled through a central desk. Extensive private exchange within that framework would be difficult to arrange. Robertson gave the CIA a three-star rating.

Business? Multinationals?

Robertson felt that the field deserved at least four stars. The parent corporation would have to be huge. The inner clandestine group would need tight control. Such an operation would be difficult. But many companies maintained a high level of secrecy in some sectors because of rampant industrial espionage. In fact, some corporations now maintained intelligence networks larger and more efficient than those of many nations. A clandestine group could use those security measures as a cover. Hamlet could be buried within "research and development" of any firm that maintained global facilities.

Robertson put down five stars.

Airlines? Shipping?

Extensive communications and exceptional mobility definitely would be plus factors. But the smaller staffs of those companies, compared to the investment, would make surreptitious operations difficult. Robertson accorded that possibility three stars.

He scanned the list, pondering the odds.

The most efficient organization, he concluded, would be a combination.

Robertson ripped the sheet from the pad, folded it, and

stuck it in his shirt pocket. He would use the notes later in the approaching day to start a brainstorm program.

He then turned his mind to the elusive sense of unease he felt over Sir Reginald's selection of Loomis.

He sat quietly, turning the cigar slowly, thinking. Fifteen minutes later, he had the answer. He went over it again, just to make certain.

He had spent considerable time with Loomis's file during the incident in Santo Domingo. With Loomis en route to confer with the people at Langley, Robertson again had pulled the file. It now lay within easy reach. But he had absorbed all the details.

He could not find fault with Loomis's record.

The problem was that Loomis's greatest strength also was his greatest weakness.

Sir Reginald was correct on one point: Loomis had acquired an impressive amount of experience with violence.

In Vietnam and Laos, Loomis and Johnson had performed as a legendary team. Growing unhappy with U.S. policy in the Far East, Loomis had complained to his superiors. When his complaints did not achieve results, he had taken direct action, blocking some U.S. operations, leading the administration at Langley to conclude that he was a double agent. Loomis had been dismissed from service with extreme prejudice. But no one was able to fulfill the contract. Loomis had killed the two men Langley sent to assassinate him.

With the skills he had acquired in conventional and guerrilla warfare, Loomis later had commanded mercenaries in Uganda, Guatemala, Chile, Nicaragua, and the Dominican Republic.

Through all of that, he had followed a definite pattern.

Loomis was an individualist. In every instance, he had exhibited a firm resistance to authority.

Loomis was not a team man.

That was the flaw that Robertson had sensed, but could not find.

In Vietnam, Loomis had thrown a monkey wrench into

an important field operation, solely because he disagreed with it in principle. No evidence ever had been found that Loomis had been on another payroll. The eventual conclusion was that Loomis had resisted the orders simply because he did not like them.

No one told Loomis what to do, and made it stick. Not if Loomis decided to do otherwise.

Robertson intended to keep that fact firmly in mind.

The soft buzzer sounded on Robertson's desk. He picked up his phone.

"Secretary Parker is on the line, Mr. President," the night shift switchboard operator informed him. "He said that if you were awake, he'd like to speak with you."

"Of course, of course," Robertson said. He heard the click that indicated he had been connected.

"Sam, what the hell?" Robertson said. "I thought you were coming by."

"I said I'd be by if you were restless, up prowling around, and felt like talking," Parker reminded him.

"Who can sleep these days?" Robertson asked.

"Not me," Parker said. "That's what I want to see you about. Give me twenty minutes."

Robertson hung up the phone feeling a measure of relief from the unusual loneliness of this night. He and Parker had been freshmen in Congress together, years ago, sharing interests on several pieces of legislation, and often serving on the same committees and subcommittees. A close rapport had developed. After Parker left Congress to return to banking, they had remained close friends. On Robertson's election to the presidency, Parker had been the first Cabinet selection. Of all his appointments, Robertson considered Sam Parker his most astute. Robertson had thought he knew Parker well. But the veteran banker and politician had performed even better as Secretary of Commerce than Robertson had expected.

Robertson received Parker at the door of the Oval Office and escorted him to the striped couch by the small fireplace. Facing Parker from one of the wing chairs, Robertson took the secretary's measure while coffee and brandy were poured. He noted with concern the deep lines in Sam's face, the hint of bags under the eyes, the unaccustomed solemnity. Robertson, whose success was derived from sensing what was in other men's minds, recognized that Sam Parker was a man on the verge of exhaustion. The fact gave him a sobering dash of foreboding. Sam Parker, tall, lean, with an impressive shock of silver hair and a firm jaw a movie star might envy, was a man who could smoothly run huge corporations with plenty of time left over for golf, poker, and a full social schedule. He was not a man given to worry or panic.

Before him, Robertson saw a deeply disturbed man.

He made an effort to put Parker at ease.

"Glad you could come by, Sam. I need your company. I get pretty lonesome, rattling around by myself in this old house at night."

Parker gave a distracted nod. "I really don't know what I'm doing here, Travis," he said. "I'm not certain that what I'm going to say will make sense."

"That's about par for the course around here," Robertson told him. "But you may be the first man who has ever made such an admission in the Oval Office."

Parker grinned. "I've been intending for several days to come see you. I just didn't want to burden you until I had something more concrete. I still don't have anything solid, but I'm going to unload it on you anyway."

"I can take anything except an Administration sex scandal," Robertson said. "What's on your mind?"

"Many things," Parker said. "If you take them one by one, they don't sound like much. But when you put them all together, I wonder what the hell is happening. Sometimes, I think maybe I'm crazy, that I'm just imagining these things. That's why I wanted to see you alone. I didn't feel that this is a matter for the Cabinet. But I did think I should share my concern with you."

"Shoot," Robertson said.

"I'll give you examples, and maybe we can go from there," Parker said. "First, as you may know, each year our Bureau of Economic Analysis does a complete projection and profile on international companies and on foreign affiliates, supplementing our monthly and quarterly reports."

"Sam, I'll have to confess I didn't know that," Robertson said. "But on the other hand, I can honestly say that I'm not a damned bit surprised."

Parker went on, ignoring Robertson's wit. "In addition, the Bureau of the Census also issues a quarterly summary of foreign commerce in the United States. I've never understood exactly why, but they do. And our Bureau of International Commerce also issues regular Overseas Business Reports."

"I'm beginning to get the picture," Robertson said. "But you'd better hurry. I may lose it."

"All of these studies, done independently, have shown some strange fluctuations lately—especially during the last year. In themselves, they don't mean much. But the odd aspect is that there are drastic alterations in all sectors."

"Like what?"

"Minor things. But puzzling. I have examined a few. You may recall that the stock market plunged drastically for a few days immediately after the last Mideast crisis."

"I remember the Mideast crisis," Robertson said. "But I didn't pay much attention to the market. They made me sell all my stocks before they'd let me have this job."

Parker reached into his coat pocket for a sheaf of papers. "I had the analysts in the BEA run a profile of the heaviest transactions during that period, of people and firms who bought huge blocks when the stocks bottomed out. I found something very peculiar. A surprising percentage of those stocks were bought by companies and institutions that are no longer in existence."

"I don't follow you," Robertson said.

"Each buyer took a quick profit on the rising market, then was merged, acquired, or phased out. In short, those companies apparently were created for a special, short-term purpose—perhaps to serve as a front in making a quick killing on the stock market, one that normally would not be traced."

"You're suggesting prior knowledge," Robertson said. "But who would have prior knowledge of events in the Middle East? As I recall, that crisis made asses out of all the experts, Russians included."

"That, Travis, is my point. What I'm saying is, maybe someone set off the whole thing. The possibility boggles my mind. But it's there."

"Let's see, that crisis was triggered, initially, by a Palestine terrorist group, a new one," Robertson recalled. "Are you suggesting that terrorist action was staged, in order to manipulate Wall Street?"

"The thought has occurred to me, Travis."

"Unfortunately, it never occurred to me. Do we have anything tangible to hang your theory on?"

"Just this list of defunct firms," Parker said, handing the sheaf of papers to Robertson. "In effect, all of these companies ceased to exist shortly after dumping the stocks they owned."

Robertson scanned the list. More than a hundred companies were involved. "Wait a minute, Sam," Robertson said. "Lord knows, I'm not a businessman. But I do know it's not all that easy to set up a company, and phase it out. Aren't there people you can trace?"

"Of course. And that's the most interesting part. Each of those companies—those we investigated are marked by an asterisk—ostensibly had a legitimate function. Solid, sound reasons were behind each merger or phaseout. The men involved were for the most part responsible, established businessmen. We have complete profiles on them. Yet, without exception, none knew that for a brief period a large portion of his company's liquid assets was converted to stocks. I'm convinced that not one of those men is lying. In each instance, the loose, volatile nature of conglomerate finance was utilized by someone who managed to mask his movements."

Robertson rolled his cigar, sipped his brandy, and considered the possibilities. "In other words, you're saying that the companies also were manipulated."

Parker sighed. "I can't bring myself to believe anything of this scope is possible. Yet, logic tells me there is no other explanation. My God, Travis, I've been in business almost forty years. I've seen a lot of things happen. But nothing like this!"

Robertson thought for a moment. "Assuming that these companies *were* being manipulated, how would it be done?" he asked.

"Carrot-and-stick principle, I suppose," Parker said. "We have some evidence. In each instance, the executive officer, or the board, was presented with an opportunity too good to resist. The action they took was the most logical under the circumstances. And here, we get into another puzzling factor. There has been unusual foment recently in the area of mergers and conglomerate transactions."

"In volume?"

"Yes. As I said, logic seems to be involved in each instance. But the point is that the statistics have changed drastically. Where we once could project X number of business mergers during each quarter, we now may have twice or three times that number one quarter. Then, without rhyme or reason, we may have half the projected number the next quarter, and no factors to indicate why. I warned you that all this might not make sense."

"Would there be any way to manipulate things in that sector, to that extent?"

"I wouldn't think so. But damn it, these things apparently are happening."

"Any theories?"

"We first suspected some elaborate tax dodge. But if a new scheme were being practiced so widely, we would have heard about it. We do have eyes and ears in the business community."

"I'm sure you do."

"I asked some of my people to project some possibilities. A couple of my brighter analysts have produced a scenario that might be conceivable. We have long noticed that for all practical purposes, two or three competing corporations may perform as one. This is not surprising. They're in the same business. They think the same way. But this scenario suggests that a league of multinationals has been formed—a sort of conglomerate of conglomerates—in order to control world economy. But the implications there are staggering. And I keep arriving back at the certainty that if anything of that scope were afoot—meetings, talks, and so forth—we would have had at least some inkling of it."

"We may yet," Robertson said. "You mentioned several things. What else?"

"There's a pattern to American business that disturbs me. You've seen it. Now it's routine. A talented man starts a business—bakes a better cookie, cooks a better hamburger, puts together an imaginative line of merchandise. He gets his business going against all odds, and makes a small fortune. Then along comes a big outfit that makes him an offer he can't refuse—one that sets him up for life. He usually gets a wad of cash with a good tax spread and a large continuing income to stay on as a figurehead. More specifically and insidiously, what happens next is that the outstanding cookie is tossed out and replaced with the standard. Also, you find indications of connections between corporate suppliers and corporate consumers—but again, nothing that can be nailed down."

"Justice into this?"

"I've talked to Don, in a very informal way. He promised to look into it."

Robertson rolled his cigar and thought for a time in silence. He weighed the total of hard information. Sam was right. There was nothing here he could take into the Cabinet Room and lay on the big table.

"What you have brought me, then, is your gut feeling that something is wrong, but you can't find the handle," Robertson said.

Parker nodded. "That's the sum of it."

"Well, don't sell yourself short," Robertson said. "I've learned to trust gut feelings. Sometimes I think they may be more reliable than all the statistics put together. Especially on something like this, where experience counts. I'm glad you brought this to me. There are other things going on. This may fit."

"Could this be related to that thing in Santo Domingo? The Hamlet Group?"

Robertson hesitated. "What in the blue-eyed world made you ask that?"

"That gut feeling."

Robertson studied Parker's face for a moment. "Well, maybe intuition is all we have to go on, anymore. To look at the federal employee roster, you'd think half the country is involved in intelligence. But when the chips are down, you can't find out a goddamned thing for certain."

Parker sighed. "The world has grown too complex, Travis. Time was, you could walk into a bank, or any company, glance over their books, and in a couple of hours you had a good idea of how things were. In hunting an error, or any skulduggery, there was a cardinal rule: find the original, and trace it through. Now, with everything in computers, there *is* no original. You have nothing on paper, unless you ask for an after-the-fact printout. There's nothing to pin down. Everything's up in the air, nebulous."

"Sounds like Congress," Robertson said.

After Parker had gone, Robertson finished his cigar, along with another snifter of brandy.

Shortly after 3 A.M., he took the elevator up to the presidential quarters. His wife rolled over in bed and glanced at the clock.

"How was the poker game?" she asked.

"All the fun's gone out of it," he said. "Too many wild cards. I'm beginning to suspect they don't even play my kind of game."

Chapter

3

José Martinez arrived ten minutes early for his appointment at the Piedras Negras. Not a punctual man by nature, Martinez always forced himself to make a special effort when he felt at a disadvantage in a situation. He preferred to arrive first, study the surroundings with infinite care, and make certain that all was safe. In that way, he could dismiss this matter from his mind and concentrate on the other person, and upon the subject of the meeting.

The Piedras Negras, only a block from the scenic Paseo del Rio in downtown San Antonio, was quiet, dark, and cool. As José entered, he could see three beer drinkers in the gloom toward the back. They were regulars who came to soak up beer and discuss various plans for getting rich. Toward the front, a white whore and her black pimp were involved in a sullen argument. The sounds of street traffic came through the open door, muffling voices. That was good.

No one looked up as José entered except the bartender, which was as it should be. José walked across the concrete floor to a rear booth and sat, facing the open door and the street. *"Bacardi y Coca-Cola,"* he told the bartender. José eased down into his seat, making himself as inconspicuous as possible.

When the drink came, he sat watching the door, waiting for Henryk the Pole, thinking ahead to the meeting.

In José's trade, face-to-face conferences usually indicated

something unusual. Routine assignments were handled at a distance, through a cryptic telephone call, a coded classified in a newspaper. Personal contact was risked only when a job demanded José's most expensive skills. Glancing around to make certain he was not observed, José carefully adjusted the stainless-steel .357 magnum International Police revolver in his shoulder holster.

The gun made him nervous. Texas was full of crazy laws. A man could carry a concealed pistol on the streets without undue worry. If he were caught, he could expect a light fine, at worst. At best, a man would be able to talk his way clear, because the gun laws were full of loopholes. Anyone who habitually carried large sums of money could go armed to protect his valuables. A traveler was permitted to have a pistol in his possession, and anyone who professed intention to cross county lines might be considered a traveler. A man could transport a gun from his home to his place of business, or to the pistol range. Anyone beyond a half-wit could find some logical excuse to be packing a pistol.

But in an eccentric moment of brilliance, Texas legislators had now made the carrying of weaponry into bars and taverns *prima facie* evidence for a felony conviction.

Consequently, José spent little time in bars. For he was always armed.

At three o'clock, the big Pole that José knew only as Henryk entered the Piedras Negras. He walked straight to José's booth without hesitation, nodding a greeting.

Sweating profusely, Henryk was breathing with difficulty. Apparently he had hurried a considerable distance. He slid into the booth, facing José, and mopped his red, round face with a white handkerchief.

"What's that swill you're drinking?" he asked.

"Rum."

Henryk winced. "That stuff will pickle your gut." He turned to the approaching bartender. *"Tiene usted Heineken's?"*

47

"Lone Star, Pearl, Bud, Coors, *solamente*," the bartender said.

"Lone Star *es bien*," Henryk said.

"In the sense you mean it, '*Está bien*,' " José corrected.

Henryk waited until the bartender walked away. "I didn't come here for a Spanish lesson," he said. "In fact, the less I see of you, the better. You've had a string of luck. But if you fuck up on this one, you're gonna be one hot tamale in a day or two."

José felt his pulse quicken. The job obviously was even bigger than he had anticipated. He said nothing, and carefully kept his face expressionless.

"You get your team together?" Henryk asked.

José looked at Henryk three heartbeats before replying. José was known for his chilling, blank stare. Killer's eyes, they said, and truthfully. José often let his eyes unnerve people. He now let them unnerve Henryk.

"I have the team," he said. "What is the job?"

Henryk pulled a two-month-old *Newsweek* from the inside pocket of his gray-striped, wash-and-wear sports coat. He spread the magazine on the scarred formica-topped table so José could see the cover. "You are to eliminate Johnson," Henryk said, pointing.

José remembered the cover, and the story about the *bomba atómica* in the Caribbean. The newspapers and television had been concerned with little else for days. José had read the *Newsweek* story. He had an interest in such things. He remembered all the magazine had said about the two men, Loomis and Johnson. They had hauled a nuclear bomb out to sea with a helicopter, jumping out with parachutes just seconds before the thing went off. José studied the idealized portrait of Johnson, trying to hide the myriad thoughts coming into his mind. He waited until he was certain his voice would not betray his surprise. He had anticipated an unusual assignment, but certainly nothing of this scope.

"How is it to be done?" he asked.

48

"How in hell would I know?" Henryk asked. "You're the specialist." He studied José's face for a moment, then grinned. "Does this one scare you?"

José ignored the question. He would not let Henryk goad him into anger. "How much?" he asked.

Henryk leaned closer. "I'm told that there's to be no bickering, no bargaining. My people want the job done. There is no time to spare. Actually, it was supposed to be done earlier, but Johnson has been out of pocket."

"How much?" José insisted.

"My people are willing to pay in proportion to the risks. They realize that you'll have to hire help. They recognize that there'll be plenty of heat. You may have to get out of the country for a while. Taking all this into consideration, I'm authorized to pay you twenty times your usual price, plus whatever expenses you incur for equipment, transportation, and so forth."

José was not good at arithmetic. He had been bored throughout his academic career—all eight years of it. But these were fat, round numbers. Five thousand times twenty was one hundred thousand dollars for one day's work. If he hired four men at five thousand each, he could still clear eighty thousand dollars, tax free, plus whatever he could knock down on expenses. Henryk had always paid well, much better than José's other clients. A simple job of looting a boxcar or of driving a sealed truck across country might net a thousand dollars. José had never spent much time wondering about the identity of Henryk's employers. He had always assumed that the money came from a branch of the Mafia or some other facet of organized crime.

But now he knew.

"Your people," José said. "Hamlet." He pointed to the newsmagazine.

"You said that. I didn't. Me, I never mention that name. I want to go on living. If you are interested in the job, just keep your mind on the money. You don't know anything about where it comes from. Believe me, it's healthier."

"Okay. Where and when?" José asked.

"Here is a map, and a diagram. Memorize and burn. The necessary equipment is waiting in Colorado. Have your team ready to leave tonight. Johnson will arrive at the site sometime tomorrow afternoon. You'll have to be in place. It's remote, rough country. Surprise is on your side. I can't see how you could have any trouble. It looks like a simple job."

José studied the diagram, hesitating. Henryk had said there was to be no bargaining. But he instantly could see how a job like this could go wrong.

"I'm taking four men for backup," he said. "I will pay them well. But they won't like this. The map shows only one road into the place. If anything happens, we'll be trapped there in the mountains. Don't kid me. This job is a high-risk business."

"All right. I was saving this," Henryk said, leaning closer until his face was near José's ear. "If all goes well, as it should, with a clean kill and no complications, I'm authorized to pay you a personal bonus of fifty thousand. You don't have to tell your men. It seems to me that bundle should take care of any qualms you have."

José toyed with his empty glass, picturing in his mind the way the job would be done. He examined the map in detail. He did not like the terrain. Although José had never hunted any animal smaller than a man, he once had gone into the mountains of southwest Colorado to steal some dynamite from a mine shack. That had been years ago, early in his career. Some of the main roads probably would be better now. But not those old mining roads in the mountains.

The risks were enormous. In his line of work, they usually were. If anything went wrong on this job, if the way should be blocked, they would have to leave their vehicle and go out over the mountains. And there was no place to go. All the surrounding towns were small. If five rough-looking Chicanos came walking out of the woods, the natives no doubt would blow the whistle.

But Henryk had offered an impressive incentive. A clear profit of a hundred and thirty thousand tax-free dollars would put him on ice for a while. He and Juanita could travel—around the world, if they wanted—until the heat cooled.

"Okay. I will take the job," he said. "But let's understand. I don't want to be tied completely to this plan. Maybe Johnson will show up with friends. Maybe I will have to do it another way."

Henryk hesitated. "That wasn't discussed," he said.

"Don't get me wrong," José said. "It's a good plan. It looks fine, here on paper. But there in the mountains, things may look different."

"There could be a reason for wanting it done this way," Henryk said doubtfully.

"Johnson dead is Johnson dead," José insisted. "Look, remember the express office job in Seattle? I was told the goods would be on the dock. But they weren't. So I looked around, and I found them, already loaded onto a truck. If I hadn't said to hell with the plan, I would have come away with nothing. But I figured the goods were like the stuff we stole in Oklahoma City, Cleveland, Atlanta, Phoenix. So when I found the crates, I took them. But they fucking sure weren't where they were supposed to be."

"All right," Henryk said. "As long as you do the job, I can't see where they would complain."

"How do I make contact?"

"When you get to Denver, call this number," Henryk said, sliding a card across the table. "Identify yourself as Pedro Ramirez. You are a salesman from Gulf Coast Novelties in Houston. You will be fed a line of chatter, interoffice gossip. Listen for two names. Johnson will be Tom. If he has a backup, or anyone tailing, he will be called Sam. So if they say Tom and Sam have gone on up to the campsite, you know Johnson's got someone riding shotgun. Understand?"

José nodded.

"You will be told where Tom and Sam are, what they are doing, possibly what they plan to do."

"Okay," José said.

"If you have any difficulty, call the other number there, on the back. Collect. Just mention the name Henryk. I will meet you, when and where you say, if we have to pull your ass out of the fire. I would prefer, of course, that this does not happen."

José nodded again.

"A suggestion. One of my own. If I were you, I'd stick to the plan, and then get the hell out of those mountains. And I wouldn't leave any witnesses."

"Let me take care of that," José said, irritated. He didn't need anyone to tell him how to kill people.

Henryk reached into his coat pocket and placed a fat manila envelope on the table. "Here's twenty-five thousand. That should handle current expenses. We can settle, later. Tomorrow, fifty thousand will be deposited to your account. The rest will be there when the job is done."

Henryk finished his beer, eased out of the booth, and adjusted his belt. "Good luck," he said. "My people will be very disappointed if they don't have reason to make final payment, with bonus."

"I'll be more than disappointed," José said, giving Henryk the eye treatment. Henryk grinned, raised a hand in farewell, and walked out of the bar.

José ordered another drink. It would be his last until the job was done.

He wondered, briefly, why Hamlet wanted Johnson dead. Were they settling old scores, wiping out information, playing for more headlines, or just buying insurance against the future?

José remembered the many jobs he had done for Henryk, and apparently for Hamlet. Mysterious sealed trucks had been moved from here to there, with elaborate precautions on the ignition keys, routes, and timing. He had committed more than two dozen burglaries for Henryk, always for specific items. Each time, he had received a detailed layout.

Were all of those jobs connected? Were there other free-lance professionals, all over the country, maybe all over the world, working for Hamlet?

Who were those people? What were they planning?

José fought to subdue his mounting excitement. All his life, he had looked for the big score. He had known that some day he would find a way to use his talents to move onto a new level of operation.

He now had a strong hunch that the opportunity had arrived.

Clearly, the Hamlet Group had tested him on minor things. He had performed well. Now they were trusting him with a major assignment. If he eliminated Johnson, he no doubt would be trusted with even bigger things.

Maybe they would accept him into the inner circle.

When that moment came, José wanted to be ready. He had to know more about Hamlet if he was to take full advantage of any offer that came his way. He would not learn through Henryk, his sole contact with Hamlet, who obviously was only a trusted messenger.

Who was Henryk?

And who stood behind him?

José had to know. He had to learn more about Henryk, so that if anything happened to Henryk, or if José needed to go over Henryk's head, he would have a clue as to where to start searching in order to make contact.

On a whim, he quickly downed his drink and left the Piedras Negras. Walking rapidly, he headed east. In a few minutes, he had Henryk in sight, strolling across the Commerce Street Bridge, pausing occasionally to look down on the Paseo del Rio. Slowing his pace, José followed Henryk on across Broadway to North Alamo. Henryk then turned left toward the Menger Hotel.

As Henryk entered the hotel, never looking back, José strolled on to Alamo Plaza, satisfied for the moment. José knew ways to check the hotel registry to determine the identity Henryk was using.

Tourists were lined up before the entrance to the chapel. José walked past them to the corner of the Long Barracks, where he lit a cigarette and leaned against the rough, ancient stones, mildly amused.

Henryk did not understand what he was messing with. José could see it in Henryk's Anglo eyes; Henryk looked at José as he would look at any wetback. Henryk did not understand the true situation.

José's family had been living in San Antonio de Bexar a hundred years before there was a fucking Anglo in Texas.

José had connections no Anglo knew anything about.

He had decided before his twenty-first birthday that he would collect some long-overdue debts. There was no reason he should be pissed on—as he had been since he was a child. He refused to accept things as they were, or to turn bitter, as had his father, and his father before him. José had set out to do something about it.

And he had.

A word from José, and Henryk could die, the victim of a surprising variety of lethal techniques in the repertoire of local talent.

José did not control that talent. But he worked with the power entrenched in the underworlds of San Antonio, Laredo, El Paso, the whole border country. He had far-reaching connections. If José wished, jail doors could be opened as far south as Mexico City. A knife could be slipped between specified ribs at the state prison at Huntsville, even the federal prison at La Tuna.

José's position was unusual. He had achieved it as the result of much thought and hard work.

He had remained aloof from the fratricidal gang wars of the late sixties and early seventies. Early in his career, he had let it be known that his chief concern was monetary. He would do a job for anyone, if the price was right. A truckload of marijuana from Mexico, a military payroll robbery, a well-planned hit with no embarrassing consequences— the job would be done.

And a curious thing happened. Those who hired José became frightened of him.

José always left them guessing as to who had submitted the top bid.

José did not rule the underworld. But those who did took great care to walk softly around José.

When he had an important job to do, such as the one in Colorado, he could pick and choose. The best backup men available would hop at his summons.

For the job on Johnson, he had chosen well. Each was an experienced, natural-born killer.

José was certain that when the Hamlet people saw how efficiently he operated, they would be impressed. More jobs would come his way. In time, he would create his own niche in the Hamlet organization, just as he had in San Antonio and Laredo.

Tossing his cigarette aside, José crossed North Alamo and headed back toward the Paseo del Rio and a telephone booth. He had six calls to make.

By midnight, he would have his assassination team assembled.

And by daylight, they would be in Colorado.

Chapter

4

Shortly after dawn, Robert Mangrum slipped from the pier at Houston Yacht Club in Shore Acres and steered for the Bayport Channel. Savoring the smooth, calm water and the gently diffused sunrise amidst the haze over Baytown, Mangrum left the forty-foot Chris-Craft at one-third throttle. At the Houston Ship Channel, quiet as was usual at this hour on a Sunday morning, he made a gradual turn to starboard, advanced the throttle, and headed toward the open Gulf.

After he had made the first dogleg to port, he looped a line over the wheel and pulled out his charts. Working steadily, keeping an eye out for the light channel traffic, he patiently plotted his course for a point sixty miles off Matagorda Island. As he cleared San Leon and Smith Point at the entrance to Galveston Bay, he carefully checked his position against the chronometer. He crossed East Bay, cleared Point Bolivar, and soon was alone on blue water.

Sometimes, while fishing, Mangrum took along a one- or two-man crew. But on mornings like this, with the Gulf calm and the Chris-Craft engine purring confidently, he preferred his own company. At times, under the prevalent lazy, cottony clouds, with wide stretches of the sea all to himself, Mangrum almost forgot the elaborate masquerade that had brought him to Houston, and his present, precarious position. At odd moments, he sometimes regretted his weakness in falling into the situation.

But when he was out on the ocean, in his own boat, he tended to wonder: Could he have done otherwise?

He had been a second-string executive in a Philadelphia brokerage firm when a client invited him on the fishing trip that had changed his life. From the moment he had boarded the hospitable attorney's yacht, Mangrum had become an insatiable admirer of lavishly appointed powerboats, deep water, and big fish.

He made a concerted effort, but he never succeeded in moving himself into the financial league that could afford the type of seagoing craft he wanted. Nor could he achieve financial independence from his nine-to-five rut. What little money he managed to put aside usually went into week-long charters during his infrequent vacations. On those trips Mangrum learned everything he could about boats, navigation, fishing, and equipment, hoping that some day a miracle would happen, and he would be able to afford his own boat.

Then on a trip to the Bahamas, the miracle happened. A mysterious man named Henryk was registered at Mangrum's hotel. As usual, Mangrum had been fishing every day, skipping meals, dodging the bar, hoarding every penny for one more half a day at sea. Henryk seemed to share his interest. He invited Mangrum to come along on his own chartered boat. They spent a pleasant day on the water.

A week later, back in Philadelphia, Mangrum was surprised by a visit from the jovial Pole, who invited him on a weekend trip out of Miami, all expenses paid. Henryk explained that he could not manage the boat by himself, and needed Mangrum to help. Mangrum did not believe him. Boat captains were a dime a dozen. But Mangrum went, both for the fishing and because he was curious about what Henryk wanted.

On the second day out, after watching Mangrum's boat-handling, Henryk made his pitch. He explained that he represented a firm that needed someone to do errands in the Gulf of Mexico, operating mostly out of Houston and Corpus Christi. The company needed someone who could pose as a wealthy pleasure fisherman, someone who could live that life, who could look the other way at the right moment. Most of the time, he would be free to fish to his heart's content. Only once every few weeks would he perform a simple errand. And even that errand would not cut drastically into his fishing.

Mangrum had measured risk against desire. Clearly, Henryk wanted him for something illegal. Yet, there was the promise of endless fishing.

The mental turmoil had lasted less than thirty minutes.

Almost as an afterthought, Henryk had mentioned that in leaving one life for another Mangrum would need a convincing cover.

"I'll give you a stake of twenty thousand or so," he said. "Make up a story—an inheritance, an insurance policy cashed in, anything. During the next several weeks you'll receive certain tips on stocks. Invest all your money according to the information you receive. Within a few months, you'll be the talk of Philadelphia. People tend to exaggerate. When you resign from your firm, the word will be out that you are retiring as a wealthy man."

The first investment tip concerned a small firm manufacturing computer components—so small that Mangrum had some difficulty locating the over-the-counter stock. It was selling for fourteen cents a share. A few weeks later, the stock hit six dollars. Mangrum was then advised to sell, and to put the money in another small electronics firm.

Within six months, Mangrum had pyramided a small fortune. He knew, from the attitude of those around him, that the word had spread.

Two SEC investigators came around and asked Mangrum questions. He managed to convince them that he was a careful investor, making prudent purchases based on solid research.

Henryk was amused. "We've planted a few rumors," he said. "It seems you've been doing this for years, and keeping quiet about it. You'll be going to Houston with all the reputation you'll need."

Mangrum arrived in Houston with the cover story that he was retiring from the Philadelphia brokerage firm to pursue his all-consuming passion of deep-sea fishing. He established sizable accounts in three Houston banks. His bid for membership at the yacht club was handled adroitly and effectively. Mangrum knew that his charade was aided immeasurably by his appearance. Small and trim, with a good head of hair and an athletic build, Mangrum had a flair for clothes. He had seemed to be a successful businessman even back when he was not. In Houston, where a man tends to be accepted at face value, and where the affluent society is even more mobile than most, Mangrum was soon firmly ensconced.

Around the bar at the yacht club, Mangrum revealed to a carefully selected few his artfully contrived philosophy. He explained that he simply had awakened one morning wondering why he continued the financial rat race, when he had gathered enough money to live comfortably for the rest of his life. He was a widower, he explained, and his two children were grown and out on their own. He had no worries about them. That much was true. His son was a drummer in a rock band. Mangrum had not heard from him in two years. But he never worried about him. His daughter had married an ecology freak who had renounced civilization for the wilds of Canada. Mangrum had heard from his daughter only twice in the last six years—brief notes informing him that he was a grandfather.

A month after his arrival in Houston, Mangrum was involved in an accident that was the talk of the club for weeks. His new cruiser had struck a submerged log fifty miles out to sea. The entire bottom was ripped open, and the boat sank in seconds, allowing Mangrum only time enough to inflate a small emergency raft. Fortunately, he had been rescued by a passing tanker. Mangrum knew that he had gained considerable respect through his prompt purchase of another, identical boat. He had outfitted it with identical equipment, and continued to spend much of his time on the Gulf. Often he ranged down past Padre Island to the Mexican coast. At other times he turned eastward, heading into Louisiana and on to Florida waters. His sailfish, bono, and marlin catches were being recorded in local record books.

In his first year with the boat, Mangrum had made fewer than two dozen trips for Henryk. In recent months, the trips had grown further and further apart. Mangrum was beginning to wonder if his mission was near completion.

The water shifted to a deeper shade of blue as Mangrum steered southwest. No storms had marred the shallow Gulf yet this season, and the water was free of the kelp and trash brought in almost every summer by hurricanes. Mangrum maintained a steady fifteen knots, wishing that he could throttle back and troll a line. But he knew he did not have the time. The rendezvous was figured to the split second.

Thirty miles south of Freeport, he sighted a large ship hull-down on the horizon off his port quarter. Mangrum doubted that the vessel was Coast Guard, but he eased the wheel toward the coast, passing the ship at a greater distance. He then turned back seaward, advancing the throttle slightly to make up for the lost time.

As he neared the entrance to Port O'Connor and Port Lavaca, the amount of shipping increased. Mangrum cautiously maneuvered to keep his distance from all craft. Off Cavallo Pass, he made final landfall to make certain of his position, then headed south toward the rendezvous.

Two hours later, he sighted the freighter, ostensibly bound for Corpus Christi. Mangrum closed to within five hundred yards, then turned onto a parallel course. On a signal from the freighter that all was clear, he steered toward it, pulling in under the overhanging cargo boom as the freighter lost way, coasting to a dead stop. Sprinting forward, Mangrum grabbed the dangling cables and made them secure to the boat. A seaman came down a jacob's ladder and helped him secure the cables aft. A few seconds later, Mangrum and his boat were swung over the ship's side, on across the deck to midships, and lowered gently into a cradle along-side Mangrum's first boat—the one supposedly sunk. The two boats were so alike in detail that not even Mangrum could tell them apart. All registration marks, serial num-bers, and paint had been duplicated perfectly. Each was kept in excellent shape to prevent any identifying scratches or stains.

As soon as the boat was secure, a protective canvas was rolled over both boats. Mangrum climbed over the side and dropped to the deck. The ship's captain was waiting at the foot of the ladder. Originally from Australia, the captain was huge, almost six feet two, and big-boned, a fact he stressed by shaving his skull naked.

"Welcome aboard," Captain Ayers said. "Any trouble?"

"None that I know of," Mangrum said. "You?"

"All quiet," Ayers said. "Of course, these days you never know; you've got to assume some fucking satellite is monitoring your every move. I suppose our salvation is the sheer number of ships they've got to watch. The only way they'd ever get on to us, I think, would be if they had reason to get suspicious, and started turning back through old records."

"And of course we've got to see that doesn't happen."

"Right. Drink?"

"Why not?"

He followed the captain forward to his cabin. The drink had become something of a ritual.

"We've plotted your speed and fuel consumption," Ayers

said. "Our guess should be pretty close. But the crew will make certain."

"Same load?"

"As far as I know. It's in six cartons this time. Each weighs seventy-five pounds, or thereabouts. The word is that they're not to be opened under any circumstances. But after you get them off my ship, I don't care. Be my guest."

"I'm certain I don't want to know," Mangrum said.

Ayers dropped ice into two tumblers, dumped in some whiskey, and filled them with soda. He handed one to Mangrum and motioned him into a chair.

The captain sat at his desk, put one foot up, and grinned at Mangrum. "Don't you ever wonder what it's all about?"

Mangrum shrugged. "Sometimes. But not often. Mostly, I think about my boat, my fishing, the good things those packages bring."

"I used to think it was dope," Ayers said. "But I'm now convinced it's not."

Mangrum felt somewhat relieved at the news. He had always assumed the packages contained heroin or cocaine. "How do you know?" he asked.

"Little things. First, we've made fourteen trips now, right? Several hundred pounds each trip. There's not that much hard stuff in the world. And hash wouldn't be worth all this effort. Also, I'm thinking about what happened a few days ago in Lisbon. The people who bring the stuff aboard did something different this time. They went over the ship with some kind of gadgets. They looked like Geiger counters to me."

Mangrum sipped his drink while he toyed with that information. "Did they say why?"

"No. They made no explanation. And I fucking sure didn't ask."

"Well, nothing surprises me anymore. What are my instructions?"

"Take out the same panels as before, like you're going into the engine from the bottom. You'll find the goods. A key hanging in your cockpit will unlock a panel truck in a parking garage in downtown Houston. Here's the address, and the license number of the truck. Memorize and burn. Don't you ever get tired of that one? Memorize and burn. Put the gear in the truck. Destroy the key with your blowtorch. And that's it."

Mangrum nodded. He could assume that someone had a duplicate to the key and would take the truck to wherever it was supposed to go. The organization seemed to think of everything.

The phone on Ayers's desk buzzed. Mangrum knew the message even before the captain conveyed it.

"Your boat is ready. Radar indicates all clear. We'll put you back in the drink."

They walked aft to the boats. The ladder had been moved to the starboard boat. At the foot of the ladder, Mangrum shook hands with the captain.

"Good luck," Ayers said. "Until next time."

"If there is a next time," Mangrum said.

"There's always that problem," Ayers said.

Mangrum climbed into his boat. The winch promptly took a strain, and Mangrum was lifted from the cradle and swung gently over the side of the ship. As the winch brake squealed, Mangrum and his boat were lowered into the water.

He hurried aft and released the cables. The forward hooks were more difficult, but he soon had them clear. He returned to the cockpit and started the engines. Pulling rapidly away from the freighter, he headed for Corpus Christi.

The whole operation had taken less than half an hour. Mangrum noted with satisfaction that the fuel tanks were more than half-depleted, making his stop in Corpus seem natural, in case anyone noticed. Looping a line around a spoke of the wheel, Mangrum plotted his return course against the clock.

With any luck, he should be able to get in a couple of hours of fishing before he was scheduled to dock in Houston.

Chapter
5

Forty-five miles beyond Creede the road narrowed to vague ruts that climbed through sun-laced forests and green meadows, and plunged ever deeper into ravines, seeking ridges that rose higher and higher. Before easing the Bronco into a bright, clear, swift-flowing creek, Johnson paused to engage the four-wheel drive. His four passengers held their breath as the mountain stream rumbled solidly against the floorboards, threatening to sweep them downstream into weathered boulders. Gunning the engine, Johnson carefully guided the vehicle out of the water. He climbed the other bank and followed the road as it ascended steeply through a rank stand of lodgepole pines so perfect that the children rode in open-mouthed awe. Johnson watched their faces in the rearview mirror. Christopher, perhaps too solemn, thoughtful, and reserved for a four-year-old. Lita, at three a small, angelic bundle of restless energy, for the moment untypically subdued by her surroundings. Michael, at seven too tolerant of his own limitations, overly sensitive to slights, real or imagined, flawed, yet in many ways the most lovable of the three. Johnson could not remember when he had seen them so engrossed. As he had told them repeatedly, the Rockies beat hell out of television. And today, no one had suggested flipping channels.

Only Melana was unhappy. Mountains and heights made her nervous. She had not wanted to make the trip. She came only because of the children. Tense and silent, she rode ramrod straight on the seat beside Johnson, her long black hair circled into a chignon, the dark almond eyes now locked on the canyon floor far below. In the rearview mirror Johnson could see that Lita again had turned to make certain the small two-wheeled trailer was still bobbing along behind them.

As the Bronco topped a ridge and started down again, Christopher leaned forward and yelled into Johnson's ear. "What'll we do if we meet a bear?"

Johnson downshifted, using the engine as a brake for the descent. He raised his voice over the metallic whine of the gearbox. "Bear? Gee, I don't know what we'd do. I hadn't thought about it. What do *you* think we should do?"

Melana glanced questioningly, perhaps warningly, at him. She tended to be overly protective of the children. Johnson fumed at her in mock defense.

"Well, holy cow! Chris is four-and-a-half years old!" he said. "It's about time he started making *some* of the decisions around here. We've got to have a plan ready. What if we *do* meet a bear? That'd be a great time to sit around and make plans."

In the rearview mirror, Michael was grinning widely at his father's sport. Their eyes met. Johnson winked at him.

"Maybe we could yell and scare him," Chris said.

"Might work," Johnson agreed solemnly. "But I bet it'd just be our luck to meet a deaf bear."

Michael laughed, hugging himself, consumed with glee.

"We probably couldn't scare him anyway," Chris said.

Johnson slowed the Bronco to a crawl before crossing another stream. "We might let him chew on Lita while the rest of us run," he said.

"No!" Lita said.

"No," Chris agreed.

"Well, that's out, then. I'm sure not going to hang around. And I don't think we'd want to leave Mom or Michael for him to chew on."

"No!" the younger children said in chorus.

Melana glanced again at Johnson. Her Oriental countenance was not inscrutable at the moment. Those dark eyes were telling him to knock it off.

"Have you got your gun?" Chris asked abruptly.

Johnson did not hesitate. Early on, he and Melana had agreed to be totally honest with the children, always. Honesty would not damage their sensitive little radar. "Sure," he said. If the truth were known, Daddy always had a gun within reach, even when he went to the can.

"Then you could shoot him," Chris said.

"That wouldn't be very nice," Johnson pointed out. "This is the bear's home. We're his guests up here."

The road was now winding around the edge of a deep ravine. A few feet of soft earth separated them from a sheer drop. Johnson concentrated for a few minutes on his driving.

"What *would* you do?" Chris asked.

"I'd give him a choice," Johnson said. "I'd try my best to be friends with him. If he didn't want to be peaceable, *then* I'd shoot him."

Never let it be said that Richard Allen Johnson did not instill within his children a strong sense of morality.

"We're not going to meet any bears," Melana interrupted, emphatically putting an end to the discussion. "And if we did, he'd probably be more frightened of us than we would be of him." Her hand went instinctively to the dash as the canyon below deepened. "How much farther is this place, anyway?"

"Another two or three miles," Johnson said. "We'll know it when we get there."

"Why?" Chris asked.

"We can't miss it," Johnson told him. "It's at the end of the road."

And with that remark came his first vague feeling that something was wrong.

Johnson was not a believer in hunches. He had a theory that what most people termed premonition stemmed from inadequate pursuit of logic on the conscious level. He believed that the subconscious merely shoved into the open what the conscious was too lazy to notice, and people called it "a hunch." Johnson put his full faith in logic. Yet, he drove a few more minutes before he could trace his nagging sense of danger to its source.

Tire tracks.

If the campsite were at the end of the road, only two miles away, the route should be seldom traveled.

But on the bare earth of the road, three sets of tracks had been made since last night's rain. On a short level stretch, Johnson braked to a stop.

"I want to check the map and get a kink out of my legs," he said. "You people stay put."

He walked several yards to the front of the Bronco, holding the map before him, but looking above it to study the tire tracks.

A set of snow tires had made one trip up the trail, then back. The knobby tread had left a wide set of tracks each way. He was certain of the direction of travel from the way the mud was thrown from the ruts.

Apparently the tires were attached to a truck, or large panel job. A smaller vehicle, possibly jeep-sized, also had gone up the trail, overlapping the first set of snow-tire tracks. So both vehicles had been up toward the old cabin at the same time.

And the smaller vehicle had not returned.

Johnson walked back to the Bronco. He ignored a questioning glance from Melana. "We're almost there," he said.

He drove on, mildly troubled. There were many explanations that might fit. Late August was too early for deer hunters, but not for mountain climbers, hikers, spelunkers, rock hounds, amateur prospectors, birdwatchers, campers . . .

One vehicle up and back. Another still up there in one of the most remote regions of the Rockies.

"You won't be bothered," Tycoon had said. "Nobody ever goes up there."

But somebody *had* gone up there.

At least two somebodies, and within the span of a few hours.

For the hundredth time in four days, Johnson wondered if he should have created more of a flap over the decision at

Langley to take him off the Hamlet operation. The assistant director had left little room for argument.

"You're out of it," the AD had said, with copies of *Time* and *Newsweek* prominent on his desk. "You've blown your cover, and your nation's carefully nurtured pose of neutrality. Get lost."

Johnson had protested heatedly. He had pointed out that he was the logical person to direct field operations against Hamlet. The AD did not agree.

"For every move you'd make, we might as well send them a telegram. You are of no use to us at the moment. All we can do is make it obvious that you are off the case. You've got your presidential commendation, your departmental reprimand. You really should take time to contemplate the incongruity of your situation. Please take your lovely family, and go on a long, long vacation."

"I've already used all my vacation time," Johnson said.

"We'll call it extended sick leave, then," the AD said. "The radiation burns on your hands, received in heroic service of your country, haven't healed yet. Nobody can argue with that. And when you come back, we'll see. Maybe the congressional watchdog committees will have forgotten that you have a disagreeable penchant for disobeying orders and shooting people without your government's permission."

Further protests had seemed useless. Johnson had remembered that his old friend, Ralph Webb, once had mentioned owning a place high in the Rockies. He had invited Johnson to make use of it. Webb was an old hand in the trade, dating back to World War II and the Office of Strategic Services, Allen Dulles, and all that. After the war, during the formative years of the CIA, Webb had been bankrolled by the agency for an export-import firm that was to serve as his cover. The firm prospered beyond all expectations. Webb's cover soon tripled and quadrupled his CIA salary, and he became known as the Tycoon. Johnson and Loomis had worked with him in Vietnam and Laos, where his firm had branched out to include an airline and—some sources claimed—drugs.

Now ostensibly retired from service, Tycoon remained available to the company on short-term contract basis. He sometimes worked out of Johnson's desk—often enough that with orders to get out of Washington, Johnson's first thoughts had been of Tycoon and his mention of a retreat he owned, high in the Rockies.

Johnson had phoned Tycoon. A map, directions, and the keys to a Bronco arrived in the first mail. Considerable camping gear, a large sturdy tent, and a small, two-wheeled trailer were stored with the Bronco in Creede. There Johnson had bought sleeping bags and additional equipment he thought they might need.

He had started the trip with enthusiasm. He felt the mountains might offer a chance to show the children that something else existed besides concrete, steel, manicured parks, and television. And he had assumed that the remoteness of Tycoon's campsite would offer a certain amount of privacy and security.

Now he was not so certain.

"There's Marmot!" Lita yelled, pointing.

Johnson slowed. A small brown animal was scurrying into the trees, seeking cover. Johnson glanced in the rearview mirror at his precocious three-year-old. "How do you know that's a marmot?" he asked.

"I saw him on TV," Lita said, triumphant.

Johnson saw that Melana was grinning.

"How did the pioneers win the West without television?" Johnson asked.

The campsite was everything Tycoon had promised. A clear, swift-flowing creek looped around the ruins of the old mining cabin, now overgrown with weeds and wild flowers. A smooth meadow sloped down to the creek. Behind the cabin, a sheer wall of granite rose more than two hundred feet, blocking the view to the north. To the south and west, the horizon rested on mountain peaks thirty to fifty miles away. Tycoon had underplayed the scenery.

The children first ran to investigate the old cabin. Most of the roof had caved in, but the log walls and huge granite chimney were still standing. After a preliminary circuit of the cabin, the children then raced for the stand of pines above the creek on the other side of the clearing. Melana stood on the porch, watching them.

"What about snakes?" she asked.

"Lita probably has seen the zoo people handle them on television," Johnson said. "She can cope."

"Well, they might meet Chris's bear."

"That's the bear's problem," Johnson said. He walked down the slope to the Bronco and began unloading the camping gear. He made four trips back up to the level place by the side of the cabin. After stacking the bedrolls and cooking gear on the cabin porch, Johnson caught his breath, and carefully examined the trees to the south and east, watching for movement.

Melana leaned against a cedar pillar of the old porch, studying him. "Is something wrong?" she asked.

He reached for the post and pulled himself up onto the porch. He locked his arms around her, and looked over her head toward the distant trees. "Not really," he said. "I was led to believe that no one lived up here but Lita's marmot. Tycoon said this is a mining lease, the road's not on most maps, and he hardly ever saw anyone up here. But there were two vehicles up here this morning."

Melana turned her head to study his face. "Here?"

Johnson nodded. "One turned around there in the clearing. You can see tire marks in the grass. It came back down the road, but we didn't meet it, which means it was here early, probably not long after daybreak. Or else . . ."

A new thought came.

"Or else?" Melana said.

"Or else they turned into the woods before I noted the tracks," he said. "Maybe they just came up here to see where the road went."

"Then why are you jumpy?"

"I hate puzzles," he said. "Also, the other car turned off into the woods about a half mile back. And it's still there."

"How do you know?"

"If it had left, we'd have heard it," he explained. "Sound travels a long way up here."

He released Melana. "I think I'll walk down there and take a look around," he said. "If we've got a neighbor, we better find out who in hell he is."

Johnson walked down the mountainside, following the two faint ruts that served as a road. The sun had dropped beneath the distant peaks to the west, but he estimated that at least another hour of daylight remained.

When he found where the tire tracks turned off into the woods, Johnson knelt and examined the tread marks. No hesitation or indecision was evident in the tracks. The driver apparently had known where he was headed. Johnson began to feel easier about the situation. The driver probably had been here before, and was not merely awaiting a guy named Johnson.

Leaving the road, he followed the tracks into the woods. He had no difficulty finding the route. The vehicle had avoided the larger trees, but had flattened saplings and brush. Obviously, the driver had made good use of a four-wheel-drive vehicle. Johnson found himself climbing a ridge that soon depleted his wind in the rarefied air of the mountains.

He was standing, regaining his breath, when a machine gun opened up less than two hundred yards away.

Dropping flat, Johnson had his .357 Python out and pointed up the slope before he realized that no bullets were coming his way. As the machine gun continued to fire short bursts, he could hear the impact of the bullets, far up the mountainside.

In a crouch, his Python in hand, Johnson climbed through the trees toward the gunfire. He soon found the jeep. Beyond it, six vintage machine guns were placed in a row, facing uphill. A heavyset bald man was seated behind a tripod-mounted gun, firing brief bursts. As Johnson watched, he fired the last rounds in the pan, laughed, patted the machine gun affectionately on the breech, and got to his feet. Johnson hurriedly returned his Python to its holster.

"I thought the war was over," Johnson called, expecting the man to be startled.

The man turned with a broad grin and raised a hand in greeting. He was of stocky build, with a fringe of gray hair, a white goatee, and old-styled wire-framed glasses. He seemed pudgy in the middle, but moved with surprising agility across the rough ground as he came toward Johnson.

"Hello," he said. "I saw you driving up toward the old DeLoach cabin. I *thought* somebody might come down here to see what all the noise was about."

Johnson looked at the machine guns. "Quite a collection you've got there."

"It's a hobby," the man said. "If they outlaw hobbies, only outlaws will have hobbies."

Johnson could not quarrel with the logic in that. He leaned over, hands on knees, to inspect one of the guns.

"That's an interesting one," the man said. "That's an old Lewis. It came from the Metro-Goldwyn-Mayer auction a few years back. Remember the last scene in *For Whom the Bell Tolls?* When the rebels were taking Ingrid Bergman away, and they faded out with Cooper firing? That might be the very one Gary Cooper was shooting." He laughed, knelt beside the gun, and began reloading.

"Here. Try it out."

Johnson studied the man. He was dressed in faded Levis and a beat-up bush jacket, yet the shirt and boots seemed expensive. His face was solid, pleasant, with an engaging grin and heavy crow's-feet of humor around the eyes. His skin was tanned, yet without the heavy weathering of a man who spends all his time outdoors.

"There," the man said, working the bolt. "Go ahead and burn a few rounds at that old dead tree up there."

Johnson squatted and examined the old gun. He had never seen anything like it. Sighting through the leaf aperture, he fired two carefully timed bursts.

"Right on the money," the man said as Johnson got to his feet. "I'm Jim Burke," he added, sticking out his hand. "And you're Richard Allen Johnson."

Surprised, Johnson felt a wave of caution sweep over him as he shook hands. "How did you know that?" he asked.

Burke laughed. "Elementary. One, I'm a medical doctor. Not the best in the world, maybe, but I recognize radiation burns when I see them. Along with most of the world, I know what you did in Santo Domingo. So I might have figured out who you were, even if I hadn't seen your picture twenty or thirty times in newspapers and magazines during the last two months."

Johnson pointed to the machine guns. "You scared the shit out of me," he said.

"I can see why," Burke said. "Maybe I can put your mind at ease. I'm a surgeon in Albuquerque. My wife died three years ago." He waved a hand toward the guns. "This is indeed no more than a hobby. I simply marvel at the precision, the exquisite machinery. A lot of people can't understand that."

"I can," Johnson said.

"I could never fire one in anger," Burke said. "I was a combat army surgeon. I saw what those things can do. But there's no denying their fascination. They're perfectly legal, of course, although I'd hate to have to explain that fact to some small-town deputy. Most people don't know that in many states you can own a machine gun as long as you pay the two-hundred-dollar federal transfer tax. And they're a good investment. That one there, I bought for fifteen hundred dollars a year ago. I could sell it now for three or four thousand."

"But you won't."

"No," Burke agreed. "I hope I've convinced you I'm not a complete kook—or someone out to do you in."

"You have," Johnson said. He noticed Burke's bedroll and camping equipment. The doctor was planning to camp overnight. Johnson realized that the ball was now in his court. "Why don't you come on over to the cabin about dark, after we get set up?" he said. "We'll put on an extra steak."

"I'd like that, if I wouldn't be intruding," Burke said.

"Not at all. We'll be expecting you. While we're on the subject, have you seen anyone else up here today?"

Burke pointed toward the road. "Two men in a large Rover. They went up toward the cabin, stayed a little more than an hour, then came back. I don't think they saw me, or noticed my tracks. They drove quite slowly, and stopped several times to look around with binoculars. They might have been birdwatchers."

Johnson again felt a growing apprehension. "Did you get a good look at them?"

"They were some way off," Burke said. "I had the impression that the one driving was a Latin. But I had hoped you wouldn't have to ask about them."

"Why?"

"Because after I recognized you, I hoped *you* knew who they were. I hoped they were government men, checking things out for you."

"Maybe they were," Johnson said, not that he believed it.

That evening, Johnson built a huge bonfire. At night the mountain air was surprisingly crisp. After dinner they sat in a circle around the fire, enjoying its warmth, while Jim Burke did most of the talking.

From the first, Michael and Burke developed a special rapport. The doctor quickly won Lita and Chris with his charm, humor, and imaginative stories, but in him Michael found a strong ally.

Lita, never the diplomat, forever the prime dispenser of family secrets, inadvertently founded the close relationship.

"Mike's a scaredy cat," she said.

Dr. Burke studied Michael solemnly. "What makes you think that?" he asked Lita.

"He won't fight boys half his size," Lita said.

"Maybe he has good reasons," Burke said gently.

"No, he's afraid," Lita assured him. "At school, he hides."

Michael squirmed, his face hot with embarrassment. Burke did not seem to notice.

"Maybe Mike knows something they don't," he said.

"What?"

"That fighting is stupid unless you're fighting for something really important. Is that the way you feel about it, Mike?"

Michael nodded.

"See?" Burke told Lita. "Maybe your brother is just smarter than those other guys."

As Burke spun stories, posed riddles, and popped child-oriented jokes throughout the evening, Michael's eyes seldom left his face. Mike seemed to sense he had found help in his battle against the world.

While Melana put the children to bed, Johnson drove Burke back down the trail to his campsite. Burke was still laughing over Lita's antics.

"What a wonderful family," Burke said. "I've never seen such marvelous children. You must be very proud of them."

"I am," Johnson said.

Burke paused for a moment, as if fishing for words. "I hope you'll forgive me for asking. But has Mike had medical attention?"

"We've taken him to a number of specialists," Johnson told him.

"I shouldn't have asked," Burke said. "Most doctors learn to live with our more stupid ethics. I never have. When I see someone I think I might help, I can't keep from sticking my fucking nose in."

"No offense," Johnson said. "In fact, I appreciate your interest. The consensus seems to be that his problems are emotional. I was gone a lot during a crucial time in his life. An occupational hazard. His mother hadn't learned much English. She was having trouble coping. Mike's Oriental features make him feel different in an Anglo situation. He went into a shell, and almost didn't come out again."

"I suspected something like that," Burke said. "I also

have the feeling he's exceptionally intelligent. I believe he's keeping his intelligence under a shell, too, as a protective device."

"He's certainly been successful in hiding it from his teachers," Johnson said.

"I think there may be a way to reach him," Burke said, climbing out of the Bronco. "He needs to be brought out of that shell, given some self-confidence. Why don't you bring him over in the morning? He'll be the only kid in his class who has fired six different machine guns."

At first, frightened by the noise, Michael remained at a respectful distance, covering his ears with his hands. But under Burke's gentle encouragement, he soon learned to load and to fire a huge German MG-42, mounted on a massive field tripod. By noon, he was spacing and placing his shots like an expert.

After lunch at the cabin, and on Burke's suggestion, they all hiked to an abandoned ghost town three miles away. With the children racing on ahead, Burke, Johnson, and Melana leisurely followed the trail through the heavy forest.

"This is one of my favorite hikes," Burke said. "There's something about it that reminds me of the Ardennes—a feeling of permanence, of timelessness."

"The Ardennes?" Melana asked. Most of her geography was half a world away.

"Belgium, Luxembourg," Burke explained. "I was there during what we old folks call 'the war.' "

"Battle of the Bulge?" Johnson asked.

"In a manner of speaking," Burke said. "I was a young army surgeon assigned to a green division supposedly held in reserve. Patton borrowed us for his thrust to relieve the Hundred and First Airborne at Bastogne. He simply forgot to give us back until after we'd crossed the Rhine. Ancient history."

To Burke's surprise, most of the ghost town was gone. Only the ruins of two stores remained.

"Last time I was here, a couple of years ago, there were still a half-dozen buildings," he said. "I guess they've been carried off by scavengers, piece by piece."

"How'd they manage that?" Melana asked.

"There are several ways in here, from this side of the range," Burke explained. "These mountains are honeycombed with jeep roads. This whole section was heavily mined, and still is. It just seems total wilderness because it hasn't had the commercial development of other sections yet, thank God."

While Melana and the children explored the remains of the ghost town, Burke and Johnson climbed the side of the mountain to examine an old mine shaft. The timbers were rotten, and a portion of the shaft had collapsed.

When they returned to the remains of the town below, the children were attempting to unearth a mysterious piece of metal.

"That's an old andiron," Burke explained. "It's used to hold the logs in a fireplace."

"We need it," Lita said. "We don't have one."

"It would make a good souvenir," Melana agreed.

Johnson and Burke worked almost an hour freeing the souvenir from the hard-packed ground. Almost four feet long, the huge andiron had been standing vertically in the earth, with only the tip showing. After their labors, Johnson and Burke refused to be daunted by the fact that the thing weighed eighty pounds or more. They carried it between them, all the way back to the cabin. They arrived sweaty and exhausted.

"If you two will take some cold beer and get out from underfoot, I'll see about fixing some dinner," Melana said.

"That sounds like a fair trade," Burke said.

The sun had disappeared behind the peaks to the west. Johnson and Burke walked down to the Bronco and sprawled in the grass with a cold six-pack from the cooler. The children began a game of one-eyed cat with a softball. Burke watched them for a time in silence, apparently lost in thought.

"Sometimes, I think I'd like to say to hell with the world, and just stay up here in the mountains," he said. "In fact, I wish I had done it twenty years ago, with my family."

"I've had thoughts along those lines," Johnson admitted.

Burke was silent again for a moment. "My daughters turned out fairly well, I suppose, by today's standards. The youngest is now in graduate school, studying archeology. She's taken up with a guy who never finished high school. I can't see what she sees in him, but there must be something there I don't see. My other daughter left college in her sophomore year. She works here and there, at odd jobs, parties a lot, and seems to have no roots or permanent attachments. I don't understand her life-style. She says that's the way she wants to live. I haven't tried to stop her. Am I wrong?"

"I don't have the answers anymore," Johnson said. "It's a different world from the one I grew up in."

"It is indeed," Burke said. "I've gone back, trying to determine where everything began to go to hell. I remember, when I came back from the war, all things seemed possible. God, but we were cocky. We'd whipped Hitler, Tojo, the greatest war machines ever assembled, with only a little bit of help from the Russians and the British. We were the saviors of the universe. My generation! Hell, we had it all—energy, ideals, know-how. But we blew it!"

"Maybe it wasn't your generation that blew it."

"Yes it was. And I'll tell you how and where. We had seen Roosevelt—the government—battle us out of the Depression and through a world war that boggled the imagination. We kept on expecting the government to solve every problem that came up. But there was one thing we didn't know. I've done a lot of thinking about this, and I believe I've found a fundamental truth. You have to understand it to understand anything. And that truth is this: A government, any government, tends to work contrary to the general welfare of the people."

"I'm not sure I follow you," Johnson said.

"Well, look at it this way. The business of the government is to govern. Nobody could argue with that. So long as the government responds to pressure, it is functioning, responsive to the people. The problem is, most of the pressure is applied by the people who want something. Why should anyone work, when all he has to do is petition the government? If he is out of work, wants to write poetry, start a business, buy a house, find out how many times a bumblebee flaps its wings, all he has to do is get the government to support him. So we have the government bestowing all this munificent bounty on the cities, the arts, the sciences, the shiftless, businessmen, farmers, poets, everyone you can imagine. On the surface, the government appears to be functioning beautifully. But in truth most of what it is doing is contrary to the general welfare. It removes a large segment of society and national resources from production, lowering the gross national product, destroying free enterprise, killing initiative. The burden, of course, is borne by the poor deluded assholes like me, who have fought for the government, believed in it, and if you want to know the shameful fact, championed its boldest programs.''

"There's nothing sadder than a fallen liberal," Johnson said.

"I suppose not," Burke said. "I'm simply amazed by the absurdity of it all. There seems to be no limits to what the American taxpayer will endure without protest. We're now so thoroughly attuned to bureaucracy, we'd feel right at home under Hitler or Stalin. We live in one of the most restrictive governments on earth, and don't even know it."

"Oh, come on now," Johnson said.

"You don't believe me? Try to farm. They'll tell you what and how much you can plant. Start a small business. You'll spend most of your time keeping records. Buy a bottle of aspirin. There is a federal law as to what kind of top it's supposed to have on it. Need megavitamins? You have to eat a pound of gelatin every day to get them, because the drug administration, in its infinite wisdom, has decreed the limits of your daily requirements. And I'm sure

I don't need to tell you about Social Security and income tax."

"I'm beginning to understand why you've got all those machine guns," Johnson said.

Burke laughed. "As my history teacher told me, 'That government is best which governs least.' 'The tree of liberty is watered with the blood of tyrants.' And so forth."

"Well don't count on me," Johnson said. "I'm pure Civil Service, GS-16."

"Oh, I'm not advocating violent overthrow," Burke said. "Think I'd talk like this if I were? It just galls the hell out of me what they've done to this country. Used to be, the keenest competition was at the top, in search of excellence. Now it's at the bottom, scrambling for a handout."

"I majored in football," Johnson said. "But they did make us go to class every once in a while. You sound like what one professor used to call an anarchist."

"No, anarchists are destroyers, bomb-throwers. I just want to disassemble this monstrous machine we've built, a wheel here, a gear there, quietly, without anyone noticing, exactly the same way it was assembled. It's the absurdities! Four times a year, my tax consultant and I sit down and plot like thieves. Me, a medical doctor! Truly, I don't understand it."

"I have the feeling that if I talked to you long enough, I might not understand anything anymore," Johnson said. "You should come to Washington. I'll take you on a tour of all those big government buildings. It's real inspiring to see the hundreds of thousands of government employees streaming out at the end of the day. I think it'd do your heart good."

Burke grinned ruefully. "I probably couldn't stand it " he said.

In the first light of dawn, Johnson was awakened by Melana's hand on his shoulder, shaking him gently. "It's turned colder," she said. "The fire's gone out. Lita's teeth are chattering. Where are the extra blankets?"

"In the Bronco," Johnson said.

He slipped into his jeans and moccasins. Picking up his .357 Python, he slipped it into his belt. Michael's eyes were open, watching. Johnson winked at him, and stepped out of the tent. He was surprised to find a thin layer of frost on the canvas, and on the grass. The dawn was crisp and clear. The sun had not yet emerged on the eastern horizon, but to the west he could see the first rays striking the distant peaks.

He walked down toward the Bronco and dug out the blankets. He turned, and was starting back toward the tent when a tremendous blow to his head knocked him sprawling. Numb, dreamlike helplessness overwhelmed him. He knew he was falling, but he was unable to do anything about it. A wave of blackness came that he could not fight off.

He regained consciousness to Melana's screams. Blinded, stunned, dizzy, he fought to stand, but fell again, heavily. Melana's arms closed around him, and she was screaming his name, holding him flat. His head cleared enough for him to make sense out of the words.

"They're still shooting!"

Reflex took over. Rolling onto his stomach, he felt for his revolver. He could not find it. A strange flap and a sticky wetness covered his eyes. He pushed the flap aside with one hand, and was clearing the red haze away when a gun boomed, not more than thirty or forty feet away—the deep, no-nonsense boom of a magnum.

"Mike!" Melana screamed. "No! Mike! Come back!"

Raking aside the red curtain for a moment, Johnson saw Michael running across the clearing toward the distant trees, Johnson's .357 magnum clutched in both hands. And in that moment Michael stopped, raised the gun, and fired again at the edge of the woods. Johnson tried to stand, but the blindness and dizziness swept over him. Even with partial support from Melana, he went to his knees, hearing his own gun fire again. And for the first time, he heard the other gun, a heavy-caliber rifle, apparently a semi-automatic. Three evenly spaced shots rang out across the clearing. And with the third, Melana left Johnson, running toward the shots, screaming.

"Mike! Mike! Oh, you sons-a-bitches!"

Crawling, Johnson clawed at the red film and saw Melana running toward Michael, now crumpled in the grass. A new sound, the roar of an engine and the whine of a jeep's four-wheel drive, came from below, along with the unmistakable hammering of a machine gun. Johnson looked back and caught a glimpse of Burke tearing up the hill, actually standing in the open jeep, with the Lewis propped on the windshield, firing measured bursts as he roared toward them. He swept by, still firing, swinging southwest toward the far side of the clearing. Then Johnson was on his feet, running, holding the strange flap away from his eyes with his left hand. Michael lay crumpled, motionless, on the ground. Melana was on her knees beside him.

"He's hit! He's hit! Oh, God, he's shot!"

Tearing off his T-shirt, Johnson wiped his own eyes clear. By wrapping the cloth around his head, sweatband fashion, he at last was able to see.

A crimson stain was spreading below Michael's belt. Lifting the boy's hip gently, Johnson examined the exit wound. Michael was still holding the .357. He handed it to Johnson.

"I got one of them, Daddy," he said.

Johnson was too overcome for a moment to answer. He loosened Michael's belt. The bullet, thank God, apparently had been copper-jacketed, going through neatly without much expansion. With a man, there was a good chance such a wound would not be fatal. But what about a small boy?

"I thought they had killed you, Daddy," Michael said.

"They made a mistake," Johnson said. "Imagine, trying for a head shot—on my hard head! We're both going to be all right. They're going to have to do better than this to get these Johnsons."

Michael grinned.

Burke had now stopped his jeep at the edge of the creek. Johnson could see him cautiously approaching the rim. He raised the Lewis and fired three short bursts.

"I better go help Burke," Johnson said.

Still unsteady on his feet, Johnson trotted dizzily down the hill toward Burke, who had lowered the Lewis. Burke glanced around as Johnson reached the jeep.

"They're down there around that bend, headed downstream," he said. "Just as well. I'm about out of ammo. How bad are you hit?"

"I'm okay," Johnson said. "But they hit Mike in the gut."

"Oh God," Burke said. "Get in."

Johnson climbed into the passenger seat as Burke wheeled the jeep around, and gunned up the hill toward Michael and Melana. Lita and Chris came running from the tent.

"How many were there?" Johnson asked.

"I saw four," Burke said. "I think they all went on downstream. But maybe we better get everyone inside that old cabin."

"You take them," Johnson said. "We're still exposed. And Mike thinks he hit one. Maybe I better check the perimeter."

Burke nodded as he braked the jeep. He paused only to give Michael a quick check, then took him up in his arms and hurried toward the old fallen-down cabin. Melana, Chris, and Lita trotted after him.

Acutely aware that only two cartridges remained in his pistol, Johnson moved rapidly toward the trees. He paused beside a large pine and listened for a moment before entering the woods. He then circled, hurriedly heading toward the area where Michael had been aiming.

Beneath a thick stand of quaking aspen, he found tracks. They were too vague and diffused for him to ascertain the number of men who had made them. Moving more cautiously, Johnson completed his circle.

The man was seated, leaning against a tree so naturally that for a moment Johnson thought he was merely resting.

But then he saw the neat round stain in the center of the man's chest. The man was no longer breathing.

He was small and dark, apparently a Mexican-American. The clothing was standard army-navy store castoff, but there seemed to be something of quality to the man's features. Johnson could find no identification papers. Nor could he find a weapon. A dozen .30-06 cartridges in his jacket were the only indication that the man had been armed.

Johnson backed slowly toward the clearing, then turned and trotted back to the cabin.

Burke already had moved some equipment from the tent into the old roofless cabin. He had placed Michael on the folding picnic table. With applied psychology, he had put Melana to work, heating water over the portable stove, and ripping sheets into bandages. Lita and Chris were watching, wide-eyed.

"What do you think of your scaredy-cat brother now, Lita?" Burke asked. "What'd I tell you. Just let somebody mess with his family, and he'll charge hell with a bucket of water."

Michael was still conscious, pale but grinning. Lita and Chris seemed even paler.

"Chris, why don't you and Lita be our lookouts?" Burke asked. "If you see anything moving around out front, yell, and we'll come running."

Dodging the holes in the rough wooden floor, Chris and Lita went to the logs at the front of the cabin and peered out between the chinks. Johnson walked over to Michael.

"How you doing?" he asked.

"Okay," Michael said. "Did I get him?"

Johnson's hesitation was brief. Why the hell not tell him? Michael was old enough to know that this was no game.

"You got him," he said. "And I think it was the same guy that got me."

"When you warriors get through comparing notes, I'd like to look at your head," Burke told Johnson.

"I'm all right," Johnson said. "I'll wait till you get through with Mike."

"I'm growing tired of people with bullets through them telling me they're all right," Burke said. "I'm the doctor around here. I'll tell you if you're all right or not. Come over here and sit down."

Johnson followed Burke to the back wall. Burke seated him on a campstool, leaned his head back, and unwrapped the bloody T-shirt.

"How is Mike?" Johnson asked quietly.

"I think the bullet missed the descending colon," Burke said. "That's in our favor. As you probably know, bowel shots can be messy. My big worry right now is that he seems to be losing too much blood internally. I'm afraid the femoral artery is nicked. I'd like to go in and see."

"Here?"

"Here. It'd be exploratory, and to do temporary patchwork. As soon as we get him to a hospital, we can do it as it should be done."

"If you think it best," Johnson said.

"I do."

Melana came with a pan of hot water and bandages. Burke cleaned Johnson's forehead.

"What's loose up there?" Johnson asked.

"Something for the medical journals," Burke said. "This may be the first scalping in Colorado since Chivington's Massacre. The bullet apparently hit your hard skull, flattened, then ripped the scalp, just like you'd tear a blanket, from temple to temple."

"Can you fix it?"

"Can and will," Burke said. "I hope you don't mind if I don't use an anesthetic. I like to see government employees earn their pay."

Johnson got the message. Burke wanted to save what anesthetic he had for Michael.

"Why don't you fix Michael up first?" Johnson asked. "I can wait."

"I'm truly impressed by the stoicism exhibited by the whole Johnson family," Burke said. "But the fact of the matter is, I'm trying to get you patched up so you can stand guard while I work on Mike. I'm more worried about those guys coming back than I am anything else. Mike may not feel like running them off, next time."

"Okay," Johnson said.

Burke searched in his bag a moment. "I might as well use my best high-test line," he said. "Doesn't look as if I'll get in any fishing, this trip." He prepared a needle, and leaned over Johnson. "I'm not going to do anything fancy," he said. "I'm just a run-of-the-mill, two-hundred-dollar-an-hour surgeon. If you're worried about your looks, you can go to some high-priced plastic surgeon later. He may be able to undo the damage I do. On the other hand, he might not."

"I'll risk it," Johnson said.

The stitching went easier, and faster, than Johnson would have thought possible. With Melana's help, Burke wrapped Johnson's head in a large turban-style bandage.

"You've lost some blood," Burke said. "You may feel weak and dizzy for a while. Ordinarily, I'd give a patient in your shape a pint of blood. In your case, a slug of Jack Daniel's might do. You'll find it under the front seat of the jeep. Leave a little. I'm going to need it."

"What about ammo?" Johnson asked.

Burke looked at him for a moment, apparently assessing his condition. "There's a footlocker in my tent," he said. "If you think you can manage, you can load it and the machine guns and bring them up here. I don't think they know the exact location of my camp. It's well hidden. But they might start poking around."

"I have a theory," Johnson said. "They didn't see you. But they heard our practice shooting. Not knowing what the hell else to think, they figured *you* were my federal bodyguard. They've been trying for two days to figure out what to do. They decided to circle around you and nail me this morning. They damned near did it."

"But they didn't count on Mike," Burke said. "Take the jeep. It's easier to load." He tossed Johnson the keys.

The Lewis still held a few rounds. Johnson put the gun across his lap and drove down to Burke's camp. He was able to drive quietly until leaving the main road, but for the next fifty yards he had to use engine and gears, climbing, alerting every ear in the canyon.

Hurriedly, he carried the footlocker to the jeep and lifted it into the backseat. The effort brought on a wave of giddiness. He hung on to the door of the jeep until his head cleared. He listened for a moment, and heard nothing he could identify as human. Yet, the memory of that shot without warning remained strong. He quickly carried the machine guns, one at a time, and stacked them in the vehicle, leaving the awkward tripods, belts, and other trappings to be picked up later. He listened again, cautiously, before starting the jeep and leaving the shelter of the trees. When he reached the road, he gunned the engine and drove straight to the old cabin.

Burke met him on the front porch.

"I'll need some help," he said. "Who would be best as a surgical nurse? You or your wife?"

"Melana," Johnson said, thinking of his own oversized, awkward hands.

"Can she take it?"

"She's seen worse in Nam."

Burke nodded. "Good. I'll feel safer with you ready to repel boarders."

They walked through to the table where Michael had been stripped and washed. Burke put a hand on his shoulder.

"Mike, I'm going to have to put you to sleep, so I can do some work."

"You're going to operate on me?"

"Right. Nothing serious. During the war, I did surgery on hundreds of young men with worse wounds than yours. None was braver than you. So I'm not worried."

"He filled them with sawdust, and sent them right back into battle," Johnson said.

Mike grinned.

"You've read too much Hemingway," Burke said.

Fitting an ether cone over Michael's nose, Burke began dripping liquid into the absorbent cotton. Johnson watched until Michael's eyes closed. Through stethoscope and pulse, Burke was carefully monitoring Michael's vital signs.

"Call me if you need me," Johnson told him.

He went back to the front of the cabin and gathered Lita and Chris close to him. "Let's watch those trees," he said. "If those guys come back, we sure want to see them first."

Forty minutes later, Burke came and squatted down beside Johnson.

"He's all right, for the time being," he said. "It's damned lucky I went in. The femoral *was* nicked. He's healthy, and he'll take the loss of blood all right. My main concern now is with complications during the next several hours."

"Peritonitis?"

"That, and some chipped bone floating around in there. The pelvis was nicked. Not seriously, but bone fragments can be dangerous. If we can get him to a hospital, I'd put his chances at a hundred percent. If we don't make it within five or six hours, I'd make it fifty-fifty at best."

"Are there any other roads into this place?"

"None. There are a few jeep trails off in various directions once you reach the mouth of the canyon. But from here to there, only the one road. They could be waiting any place on that road."

"What about over the ridge to the old ghost town, and out that way?"

"We could do it on foot. But it'd take a week. There's no way of getting a vehicle through."

"So it's got to be down the mountain."

"Unless you can think of something better. God, I wish to hell I'd gotten a CB. I thought about buying one. But I decided I couldn't put up with all the idiot talk."

"I think we've got one advantage," Johnson said. "These are city people, not used to open country."

"What's your reasoning?" Burke asked.

"Think about it," Johnson said. "They didn't see your jeep tracks cutting off into the woods. They didn't have the woodscraft to nose around and find out what the hell was going on with the machine guns. And the attack on me was city—a hit and a quick getaway. An outdoorsman, a hunter, would have set me up better, made certain of his shots."

"Out of their element," Burke said. "When things went wrong, they panicked."

"Right. That may be our edge. I've fought in the boonies before."

"I gather, then, that you have a plan."

"Not much of one, but it may be the only one we've got. They'll probably be waiting for us to come down the road in one of our vehicles. I'll sneak down there, on foot, and try to surprise them."

"Count me in," Burke said. "Remember, I said I could never fire a machine gun in anger? Well, I was wrong. I can now."

"No," Johnson said. "We need you here with Mike."

"But there's at least four of them," Burke said. "What if they take you?"

"They won't," Johnson said. "Because I can't let it happen."

José led his crew down the creek, frantically searching for the spot where he had left the big Land Rover. Armendaraz and Ibarra were both in bad shape, nauseated from the altitude and heavy exertion, near complete exhaustion. Ruiz was younger and in better condition. But he seemed badly scared. At a sharp curve in the creek, José called a halt.

"Ruiz, you watch. Make sure nobody comes up behind us," he said. He turned to Armendaraz and Ibarra. "You two lie down a little bit, see if you can pull your stomachs together."

Ibarra went to the creek and leaned over the water, trying to vomit. Thoroughly sick from running such a distance at such high altitude, he had emptied his stomach earlier. Now he could only manage some dry heaves. José walked into the water and put a hand on his shoulder. "Lie down a minute," he said. "You'll feel better."

"What you goan do?" Ruiz asked from behind him, suspicious.

José whirled on him. "You just keep watch, like I told you to do. Let me worry about what I'm going to do." But then he relented. Puzzled and miserable, Ruiz just stood looking at him. "I'm going to look around a little," José said.

He did not want to admit that he was lost.

"I'll be back in a few minutes," José told him. "Rest up."

He walked up out of the creek bottom, hunting high ground, so he could see where the fuck he was in relation to the road, maybe even in relation to the Land Rover.

The whole operation had seemed simple on the map. The road went here, the creek went there. On the ground, things were different. A whole forest of trees would get in the way, or a high ridge of rock that had no business being there. The underbrush restricted a man on foot mostly to the creek.

José knew what had been his first mistake: he should have found out more about the terrain.

He was still mystified over the guy with the machine guns. Nothing about him made sense.

How had they failed to see the guy when they first went up and looked around? If he was a federal man, guarding Johnson, as most of José's crew believed, why had he burned hundreds of rounds of ammunition, letting everyone on the whole mountain know where he was?

Yet, if he was not guarding Johnson, what in hell was he doing with machine guns? And if he was a federal man, on official business, why did he not have a radio on his jeep?

That was one stroke of luck. Apparently no one in the canyon had communication with the outside world.

José still believed his decision to circle around the guy with the machine guns was the right one. How could five men, armed only with rifles, take a machine gun without heavy losses? If Salinas had blown Johnson's head off on the first shot, they would not have had to hang around for a second shot, the boy would not have entered the picture, and Salinas would still be alive.

If he managed to find the Land Rover, and they attempted to drive back down the road, the possibility existed that they would meet someone on his way in to see Johnson. He had to keep that in mind. Yet . . .

The only alternative was worse. He looked up at the sheer ridges above him, the mountains beyond. Ibarra and Armendaraz would never be able to go over the mountains on foot. And if they did reach some mountain village, the fun would start. By then the whole state would be looking for four Mexican-American males.

Breaking through a curtain of underbrush, José saw the road. But he did not know if he was above or below the Land Rover. He examined the tire tracks. He found plenty. But he could not remember the Land Rover treads. He had not paid enough attention. The network of tracks was a meaningless hodgepodge.

He walked down the road a quarter of a mile and came to a hairpin turn he remembered. Kneeling in the grass, he spread the map and traced the road with a finger until he found the sharp curve.

The Land Rover was at least another mile downstream.

José turned and started back to his men. But again, things looked different. He could not remember the exact spot where he had found the road. He did not know where to turn off toward the creek. He lowered himself onto the ground for a moment, resting, while he decided what to do.

The answer, of course, was to find the creek. He could then walk up the creek until he came to his men, proud of his solution. Yet, even finding the creek was not so simple. He had to fight his way through underbrush and low-hanging limbs. And when he reached the creek, he had no choice but to step into the knee-deep, swiftly flowing water and struggle against the current.

When he found his men, Ibarra and Armendaraz were asleep. Ruiz had taken his boots off, and was using strips of cloth from his shirttail in an effort to make padding for the blisters on his heels.

José kicked the feet of Ibarra and Armendaraz. "Let's go," he told them. "I found the truck."

"What we goan do?" Ruiz asked.

"Johnson and the man with the machine guns are still up there," José said. "They've got to come down sometime. When they do, we'll be ready."

"There was effocking lot of blod," Ruiz said. "Maybe he ees dead, already."

"No," José said. "I looked back. He was on his feet, running. I don't think he was even bad hurt."

"We doan know for *seguro*," Ruiz argued. "Maybe he *naqueado*." His voice rose. "I doan wan another *chuteo*."

José sighed. *Naqueado* was a word trapped between two languages, meaning knocked out. *Chuteo* meant shoot-out.

"Ruiz, you have lived in the country all your life," José said. "If you are going to speak English, speak English. If you are going to speak Spanish, speak Spanish."

"Okay," Ruiz said. "But eef you theek I'm goan stay here, you're effocking *craqueado*. I saw the blod. Johnson ees *muerto*."

"We can't count on it," José said. "And unless he *is* dead, we don't get the money."

Ruiz pulled his boots on cautiously. "Rat now, money ees the last of my effocking worries," he said.

Ibarra was studying José. "So we're going to set up an ambush, huh?"

José nodded.

"Why don't we just go back and tell the people who hired us that we fucked up?" Ibarra asked.

José did not bother to answer.

Ibarra prodded. "You seem more afraid of them than you are of Johnson and the guy with the funny gun."

"I want the money," José said. "But I want to keep on living. That's something we damned sure better think about."

The three looked at José for a moment, then looked away.

"That stupid Salinas," Ibarra said. "If he had just taken more care. All these bad things would not have happened."

José knew the "bad thing" foremost in Ibarra's mind— the shooting of the boy. The matter weighed so heavily on their minds that it had not been discussed.

"Let's go," he said.

The walk downstream was easier. José made a fairly accurate estimation of the exact point to leave the stream. When they found the Land Rover, José distributed the food, water, and extra ammunition. He then led them into a pile of rocks that provided an excellent view of several hundred yards of road. He positioned his men, making certain they covered a wide field of fire.

Then there was nothing to do but wait.

Chapter

6

Fiddling idly with the badly tuned television set, Herman Grindstaff waited impatiently for the limousine to return from Dulles International Airport. He patiently checked all channels, but found nothing worth watching. He turned the set off. Crossing to the front window, he monitored what he could see of the motel parking area. He was growing more irritated with each passing minute. Galton and Kochman were almost an hour overdue. Keenly aware of his area of responsibilities, Grindstaff for a moment considered calling Dulles and having his assistants paged. His reluctance stemmed from the strong possibility that the paging of his two bumbling undercover agents at Dulles would become a choice hoot in the halls at Langley.

In years past, Grindstaff had ridiculed his own superiors. He knew he was not immune.

He had to be patient. For the moment, there was nothing he could do.

The assignment was, for Christ's sake, so simple that Abbott and Costello could have carried it off: meet Loomis, whisk him through Immigration and Customs with no hassle, and bring him straight to the motel for a briefing.

Obviously, something had gone wrong.

Grindstaff considered his options. More than a dozen National Security Agency goons were stationed in and around the motel, and along the road to Dulles. All were equipped with radios—their own radios and their own frequency. Through lack of planning, Grindstaff had no direct contact with his own men. The director had been firm in his insistence that no radios be used unless absolutely necessary.

As Grindstaff watched the parking lot, the head of the NSA detail, Thompson, strolled out onto the blacktop, looked up at the window, and shrugged elaborately. Grindstaff forced himself to be calm. If the radios were silent, surely nothing serious had happened.

Behind him, the phone rang. Grindstaff walked across the room, picked up the receiver, and held it to his ear without speaking.

"Galton here," said Galton. "That you, Herman?"

"Who'd you expect?" Grindstaff asked. "Kochman?"

Galton laughed. "That's what I called to tell you. Kochman's getting the baggage now. They lost it."

Grindstaff did not understand. "Who lost what?"

"The airline. They lost the baggage. But they found it. That's why I'm calling. To let you know everything's okay."

Grindstaff held his temper. Everything was *not* okay. He doubted that the baggage was misplaced by accident. Some other agency must be holding up the works, checking on Loomis. Some agency that was violating a direct order of the president of the United States.

"Did you tell them there were supposed to be no delays?" Grindstaff asked.

"Well, you know how it goes," Galton said. "There's always some shitbird that doesn't get the word."

But maybe someone *had* gotten the word, Grindstaff thought. Someone in some other agency. The delay no doubt meant that someone was fucking in his territory. He intended to find out who that someone was. But first, he had to make certain he got Loomis squared away.

"Our man okay?" Grindstaff asked.

"Oh, sure. No problem. We should be on over there in a few minutes."

Grindstaff hung up the phone, furious, wondering who had the audacity to block an agency operation. Someone, somewhere, had wanted to peek into Loomis's luggage. Customs had been informed that Loomis's possessions were flagged, to be expedited through all formalities. Grindstaff doubted that anyone in Customs would have dared violate that order. He considered other possibilities. The FBI was always nosing around in CIA affairs. Or the someone could be from NSA, or one of the military intelligence branches, or even some congressional watchdog committee. Once one began thinking about it, the possibilities became endless. Tracking down the source of the delay might take time. Grindstaff damned sure intended to put forth that effort. He had too much at stake.

He had received far more important assignments during his career. But never before had one been handed to him personally by the Intelligence Director. Langley was compartmentalized to the point of absurdity. Although Grindstaff often had suspected that he had been singled out for special assignments, the details always had come to him through three or four levels of supervisors. But for his operation, the director had personally summoned him into his inner sanctum.

"We can't afford to screw up on this one, Grindstaff," the director had said. "We've got to walk a narrow line. We want to do our job so there'll be no repercussions, now or later. And we want to keep the president happy. That may require some delicate decisions. I want you to work closely with me on this."

The director had given Grindstaff specific verbal instructions. "Take Loomis to a motel, and keep him there overnight, under tight security. Don't let him contact anyone—the president, Johnson, anyone connected with the government in any way. Tell him that, technically, he hasn't arrived yet, not until he checks in through Langley. Bring him here first thing in the morning. Brief him at the motel, but for the most part, you stay in the background. We want to keep him guessing about what's happening."

So Grindstaff had remained at the Howard Johnson's, trusting that idiot Galton to oversee procedure inside the terminal. He had no direct control over the NSA goon squad, now spread over several miles of road.

And this was an operation that could make or break his career.

He thought of all the long hours he had devoted through more than twenty-five years to what David Atlee Phillips called "the night watch." He had risked his life repeatedly in a cold war when most people were not even aware any danger existed.

Grindstaff did not expect medals for his career as a cold warrior. But the current fad of criticizing and ridiculing the CIA made him furious. The criticism negated all his accomplishments. The bastards simply did not know what had happened. And under the Secrecy Act, there was no way he could tell them.

He was certain that he had contributed as much to his country as any soldier, in work often more deadly. And now this, at the highest point of his career, on direct orders from the White House . . .

Three or four cars roared to life in the parking lot below. Grindstaff hurried to the window as tires squealed. He looked out in time to see a string of cars still burning rubber as they entered the ramp onto the expressway.

The NSA goons guarding the motel had left.

Something had happened.

The phone rang. Grindstaff crossed the room and grabbed the receiver on the second ring.

"Herman?" Galton asked, panting for breath. "He's gone."

Grindstaff felt a constriction around his heart. "What do you mean, gone? Who's gone?"

"Our man," Galton said, fighting for breath. "He went to the can. He didn't come out."

Grindstaff heard himself shouting. "Get hold of yourself. Slow down. Tell me."

He could hear Galton inhaling deeply. When Galton spoke, he had his voice under control. "Kochman went to get the baggage, see. After it was found, I was waiting with . . . with our man. He said he had to piss. I didn't know what the fuck else to do. I didn't want to go into the can with him. That'd be too obvious that we were sticking to him like glue. And I knew there was no other way out of the can. I'd checked. So I let him go by himself."

That was standard procedure. "You did right," Grindstaff assured him.

"And I watched that goddamned door like a hawk," Galton said. "Nobody anywhere near his size came out. I'd swear to it. He's a great big guy, you know."

"I know," Grindstaff said. "Go on."

"When he didn't come out after a few minutes, I went in to check. And he wasn't there."

"Where were the goons there at the airport while all this was going on?"

"They'd moved to the front of the terminal, to set up a screen for us to get from the door to the car."

"Great," Grindstaff said. "What's happening now?"

"We've looked everywhere. The airport police, the goons, they're running a check—taxis, limousines, rental cars. They might turn up something. But boss, I got to tell you something. I don't think we're going to find him. It was too well planned. He's gone."

"Okay," Grindstaff said. "Let the goons do the checking. That's their area of responsibility. You come on back here. We've got a report to make."

He hung up the phone.

He wished he could handle matters himself, and keep the fiasco hidden until he could as least partially make amends. But he knew the scope of the operation that would now have to be put into effect. Dozens of agencies, perhaps thousands of men—federal, state, and local—would be put to work.

Only one man in the Company could get an operation of that magnitude started immediately—the director.

He picked up the phone and dialed the director's private, direct line at home.

The shit was about to hit the fan.

Chapter

7

Late in the evening, the party began to disconnect. The rowdier elements moved out, beyond the terrace, to the pool. Through the sliding glass doors no one ever bothered to close, Maria Elena could hear shouts and laughter from drunken horseplay. In the sunken living room, on the tiered sofas of the conversation pit, talk had fragmented into three heated discussions. A pornographic film was being screened in the study. Some party guests had drifted, by twos, threes, and fours, into the bedrooms down the hall. Maria Elena remained aware of all this, even while listening to the young director.

"I mean, you have to retain your integrity," he was saying with his curious, distant self-preoccupation. "If you let the producer, the writers, everyone, have their way, even on little things, you wind up with a pile of shit. You know what I mean?"

The young director was seated at her feet, his arm resting lightly across her knees. He had made two films, each sufficiently vague to be termed brilliant by the critics, yet entertaining enough to turn the corner at the box office. In looks, and in manner, he strongly reminded Maria Elena of a guerrilla leader she had known in Uruguay—the same black, feverish eyes, the same angelic, almost babyish face. The resemblance was disturbing. Maria Elena had seen the guerrilla bleed to death in an alley from a gunshot wound.

Maria Elena chose her words carefully. She knew this was not an abstract monologue. Through his clichés, he was telling her he had his own concept of the role her producer-host had invited her to America to discuss.

"Yes, I understand all that," she said. "And to a certain point, I agree. But the director isn't alone. The actor must have a clear concept of character, and remain true to that concept, or his performance will not be convincing. It's that simple."

Clichés could work both ways.

The young director nodded sagely, his eyes focused on a Jackson Pollock painting on the opposite wall. "I agree with *you* to a certain point," he said. "But let me explain to you what happens."

He began, then, a long description of his difficulty with the male star on his last film. Maria Elena only half listened. She had heard the story before, from the actor. The incidents leading toward Hollywood's current outstanding feud were not especially interesting.

Maria Elena was tired and bored from the long evening. She had not recovered from her sudden separation from Loomis, her vindictive decision to accept the role, and her abrupt, disorienting trip across an ocean and a continent.

She wished she could leave the party and go to her guesthouse to rest, but she could not do that to her producer-host. She understood Hollywood, the way it worked. Although the guests were a varied lot, each had been invited for a reason. Her long-anticipated return to the Coast, and presumably to filmmaking, had caused enough of a stir that she now served as the *raison d'être* for the party. To leave now would be rude. Yet, she wondered if she would last the evening.

Listening to the director, she allowed her attention to wander. She studied a couple across the room. She had noticed them earlier, as both were rather striking in appearance. He was smaller than average, but of lean, muscular build. The woman was obviously a natural blonde, tall and athletic. Both were deeply bronzed with the weathering that comes from much exposure to wind and sun, unaided by tanning lotions. Seated on a love seat, they formed an island of calm amidst the chaos around them. Again, Maria Elena wondered who they were; she had not been introduced.

A passing actress stopped to speak to the director, interrupting his story. Her party gown was even more outré than most, with generous cleavage to her waist. She leaned to catch the director's reply over the noise and, mildly drunk, almost fell. Maria Elena moved quickly to take advantage of the situation.

"Here, take my chair," she said, gently disengaging the director's arm from her knee. "And if you'll excuse me, we can take this up later."

The director nodded. His focus of interest had already shifted. The actress fell into the chair.

Maria Elena crossed the room to the couple. They glanced up and smiled, expectant.

"I thought I would come over and learn your secret," she said. "How do you manage such serenity in all this?"

With effortless physical grace, the man offered Maria Elena his seat, moving to a hassock. "That's an easy question," he said. "We're scientists. After years of looking through a microscope, you arrive at a marked disassociation. You tend to see everything as though through a microscope."

"Are you researching Hollywood mores?" Maria Elena asked.

"No, we're *marine* biologists," the man said. "We've been watching, but as yet, nothing has happened in the pool."

"That comes later," Maria Elena said.

"Then we absolutely *must* stay," the man said to his wife. "It's been a while since I've observed vertebrates."

"I'm Betty Parrish, and this is my husband, Donald," the woman said. "We're technical advisers on the film our host is planning to make. It seems that some problems with an underwater sequence may seriously affect the plot some way. We were summoned to a story conference. Our host sent a plane. It didn't occur to me to pack a party dress."

Maria Elena offered her name, shook hands with the couple, and told Betty her basic black dress looked fine.

"And what do you do?" Donald asked Maria Elena.

Betty blushed scarlet. "Oh my God, Don! The whole world knows that Maria Elena de la Torre has returned to Hollywood to make a film. And you ask a question like that!"

Donald remained unruffled. "Quiet, woman. This is my technique with beautiful young women, as you should know."

"If I remember right, when I was young you had no technique," Betty said.

"The absence of a technique may in itself be a technique," Donald said, winking at Maria Elena.

"Well, in that case, you *were* a whiz," Betty said.

"Could I get you a drink?" Donald asked.

While he was gone, Maria Elena sought to learn more about them. "Have you worked in films before?" she asked.

"Only a documentary," Betty said. "Donald became involved with it, hoping to use the film to help land a research grant. He didn't get the grant, but that film led to this."

"If I'm not being too inquisitive, what kind of research?" Maria Elena asked.

Betty paused a moment, assessing Maria Elena, before answering. "Donald believes that plankton, kelp, and other marine life can be grown, harvested, and packaged into palatable food. He has been trying for ten years to set up a laboratory to put his theories into practice."

Donald returned with the drinks. "What have you two found so interesting to discuss?" he asked. "Me?"

"I think Hollywood's beginning to affect you," Betty said.

"Your wife was telling me about your work, your theories," Maria Elena explained.

"Not theories," Donald said emphatically. "Solid fact. Enough food goes to waste each year in the oceans to feed the world population several times over. All we have to do is find a way to recover it."

"And to make it edible," Betty said. "I do hope you don't forget that problem."

"First things first," Donald said. "You've got to catch a fish before you can fry him."

Betty winced. "Would you believe this man has two Ph.D.'s?" she asked.

"You can laugh, but that bromide won one of my Ph.D.'s," Donald said. "It served as the essence of my doctoral dissertation. Of course, in the academic world, you have to couch it in more esoteric language, imbue it with a patina of scholarship. . . ."

"In Hollywood, you only have to have integrity," Maria Elena said.

"Integrity?" Donald asked, feigning puzzlement, pretending he had never before heard the word.

"Artistic integrity," Maria Elena said. "That's the prime requisite to Hollywood success. At least that's what I've just been told by one of Hollywood's most successful directors."

"I'll never make it, then," Donald said. "I would lie, steal, cheat, do anything short of murder to get the bread I need. Hell, I'm forty-two years old. Almost a third of my life is over. I've got to hurry, if I'm going to get anything done. I'll take any shortcut."

Maria Elena laughed. Suddenly, the ludicrousness of the

situation overwhelmed her, and for a moment she was convulsed.

"That was funny?" Donald asked.

Maria Elena attempted to explain.

"It *is* funny," she insisted. "Here you are, in tinsel town, at the dream factory, where all reality is reduced to dreams, and here you sit, in the middle of it, with the biggest dream of all, trying to get the money to turn it into a reality."

Donald looked at his wife and raised his eyebrows. "Well, so much for shallow actresses," he said.

Later, despite her exhaustion, Maria Elena was unable to sleep. She watched old films on television. Occasionally, she could hear sounds from the party, still in progress across the green from her guest cottage.

She lay awake for hours, wondering if she had made a mistake. She missed Loomis, sometimes more than she thought she could bear. But underneath all lay the deep ache of betrayal. Loomis had led her into believing he was through with fighting and killing. He did not have to go back to it. She knew that. He had accepted Sir Reginald's job only because his need for danger was greater than his feelings for her.

As the sounds of the party died, two hours before dawn, she began thinking back over the evening.

The scientists and their marriage intrigued her. Their easy way with each other, their confidence in each other, filled her with warmth. Donald reminded her somewhat of Loomis, not physically, but in his complete self-control, and in his unmistakable intensity, energy, and drive.

And as she compared the two, she began to suspect what was at the core of her disappointment in Loomis.

Chapter

8

With the first hint of dawn, they were well beyond Creede and, Loomis was certain, still climbing. Tycoon handled the jeep with the same effortless abandon he had shown at the controls of the Lear jet. And now, in second gear with all four wheels engaged, he seemed oblivious to the sheer drops of hundreds of feet that frequently bordered the road.

"How much farther?" Loomis asked.

"Thirty, maybe thirty-five miles," Tycoon said. "Trouble is, we've got to climb to the pass, better than eleven thousand feet. The road gets worse. We're at least a couple of hours away yet."

Loomis gripped the handle on the dash as Tycoon sent the jeep down a long grade and around a sharp turn. Then they were climbing again. Far below, the tops of pines rose eerily above the mists that enshrouded the canyon floor.

Loomis had managed to sleep some on the transatlantic flight. Yet he was tired. He had traveled all over the world, in all kinds of circumstance, but never before had he been so disoriented. A short time ago, he had been at peace with the world. Now he was back, hunting trouble before it found him. And again he felt the old familiar tension rising in his groin. After running down several leads in Spain, then a marathon trip across the Atlantic and the United States, he sensed he was nearing action.

But where he once approached battle with mounting excitement, even enthusiasm, now there was only a growing reluctance, a jaded weariness.

He missed Maria Elena, and Spain, more than he would

have thought possible. But in thinking back over the last few hours, he could not see how he could have acted differently.

So far, he had taken the right steps, he believed. Fortunately, he had remembered that Johnson once had mentioned Tycoon's campsite in the Rockies. On a hunch, Loomis called Tycoon in Acapulco. Tycoon had confirmed that Johnson was in Colorado. When Loomis described Hamlet's attack on El Jefe's villa, and conveyed his concern about Johnson's safety, Tycoon had quickly volunteered to meet him in Washington.

Once, in what now seemed a lifetime ago, they had all been very close—Loomis, Johnson, and Tycoon—fighting the war in Southeast Asia, back when the CIA seemed to be on the side of the angels.

Loomis marveled at Tycoon's endurance. Tycoon had gained some weight, but he carried his years well. He obviously still had plenty of piss and vinegar left in him. After flying from Acapulco to Washington on sudden notice, and arranging to spring Loomis from the clutches of the CIA at Dulles, Tycoon had then flown from Washington to Colorado, regaling Loomis with stories all the way. He had radioed ahead for the jeep. They had now been on the road more than two hours.

"Tired?" Loomis asked, half hoping Tycoon would surrender the wheel.

"Just hungry," Tycoon said. "There's supposed to be some sandwiches and stuff behind the seat. And a bottle. Why don't we dig in?"

Loomis found the box behind his seat. He opened it on his lap and checked the contents—cold hamburgers, ham sandwiches, and a fifth of Jack Daniel's.

Tycoon downed a slug of whiskey, then tackled a hamburger, handling the jeep with one hand.

"You never want to go into these mountains without food, no matter how you travel," Tycoon said between bites, obviously launching into another one of his stories. "This is Al Packer country. Some of these passes are twelve thousand feet or more. Snow hits you up here, you may be here till spring. That's what happened to Ol' Al. He was guiding a party of miners across the mountains. They got snowed in. When spring came, Al strolled out alone, fat as a coon. They backtracked him and learned why. Story goes that the judge sentenced him by saying, 'There was only seven Democrats in all of Hinsdale County, and you, you man-eatin' son-of-a-bitch, you et five of them. I sentence you to be hanged by the neck until you are dead, dead, dead.' "

Loomis waited until Tycoon's laughter subsided. He remembered how he used to bait Tycoon. "Did he?" he asked.

"Did he what?"

"Hang."

"Loomis, you always did have a talent for ruining a perfectly good story. No. Al Packer spent most of his life in prison. Hand me that bottle."

With stronger daylight, the mists were gradually disappearing from the canyons. Loomis now could see the distant peaks. Spain and Maria Elena already seemed remote, untouchable, a part of another world. That life now seemed to be ended, just as Maria Elena had predicted. Now he was deep into another job. He remembered the confidence he had felt when he talked to Sir Reginald a few days ago. Now he already was on the run, a fugitive from the CIA, the NSA, the FBI, and whatever other agencies they were using to chase him.

Yet, he could not help but feel some satisfaction over the mess he and Tycoon had left behind at Dulles.

On first contact, Loomis had sensed that Langley planned to keep him under wraps. Later dialogue confirmed his suspicions. No one he had talked to seemed worried about Johnson.

Fortunately, Tycoon had performed brilliantly. Although Tycoon now was only a contract CIA agent—subject to call for special assignments—he obviously retained excellent contacts. After he helped Loomis elude his escort at

Dulles, they dashed to Tycoon's waiting Lear, waiting at National, and Tycoon had kept the throttles near the stops all the way to Colorado.

Still, Loomis felt a growing concern that they might be too late in reaching Johnson.

Tycoon apparently was now having the same thoughts.

"I should have realized what might happen," Tycoon said. "But Johnson had mentioned earlier that he might use the lease sometime. And when he called, I just didn't think . . ."

"I wasn't thinking either," Loomis said. "Hamlet damned near nailed me, in Spain."

"I guess we're getting older, more vulnerable," Tycoon said.

"Speak for yourself," Loomis told him.

Tycoon grinned. "We're nearly there," he said. "We've got to make some decisions before long," he said.

"What are our options?" Loomis asked.

"We could circle around to an old ghost town and approach the cabin from the far side. The drawback to that is that we'd have to leave the jeep and finish the last three or four miles on foot. It'd be noon before we'd get there."

"That's out, then," Loomis said.

"Don't jump to conclusions. There's only one way up to the cabin from this side. The road, or what there is of it, follows the creek, crossing it a dozen times. The old cabin is at the end of a box canyon. It's rough, rough country. The point is, you can hear a jeep coming for five miles. Ten, maybe, if the wind is right. There's no way to sneak in quietly, unless we walk."

"You know the country. Assuming that we're not here on a wild-goose chase, what do you think they'll do?"

Tycoon shifted down to brake the jeep on a long descent. He waited until they crossed the bottom of a ravine and were climbing again. "We don't know who they are, so we don't know how they'll act. But if I were running the show, and if I knew where Johnson was headed, I'd get up there first and look around, get the lay of the land. Then I'd pull my vehicle off the road two or three miles away, and hide out a half day or so, until his guard was down. I'd walk in quietly, and wait for a clean sniper shot. That'd be the safest way to get Johnson. If anyone should hear the shot, no one would think anything about it. Lots of people burn a round or two occasionally, for target practice or sighting in. A game warden might come around, if there happened to be one nearby. But up there, the odds are mighty slim against that."

"After the shot, then what?"

"Then back to your vehicle, and a quick trip out."

"So we might meet them, coming out."

"We might. But there's something else. They may have an ambush set up, waiting for him to come out. We may drive into the back end of their ambush."

"If there's anybody up there at all besides Johnson."

"If there's anybody up there at all," Tycoon agreed. "The joke may be on us."

Loomis studied the options for several minutes. "I elect to go straight in, hell for leather. What do you think?"

Tycoon laughed. "Hell, is there any other way?"

Tycoon had brought two heavy-caliber rifles—a .35 Remington automatic and an old .30–06 Garand. As they turned onto the jeep trail up the canyon, Loomis loaded the weapons. And for the first time, he began to comprehend fully the hazards of the terrain. Sheer rock walls rose on each side of the creek, which came down from higher ridges occasionally glimpsed in the distance. Spruce and pine clung to every available patch of dirt. The road, what there was of it, precariously followed first one side of the creek, then the other.

Loomis watched the road ahead, trying to determine likely spots for ambush. Hardly an open stretch existed that did not offer a good site. The cliffs above them, and even the opposite side of the canyon, provided plenty of cover for snipers.

Tycoon geared down as they crossed the creek once more. "You mentioned on the phone that you might have a job for me," he said. "What makes you think you could pay my kind of wages?"

"Who said anything about wages?" Loomis said. "I'm just offering you a chance to make the world safe for your far-flung empire."

"I didn't even know I had a cloud on my horizon," Tycoon said. "Save my empire from what?"

Loomis told him about Sir Reginald's visit.

"They've given me a free hand," he summed up. "And you're my first recruit."

"Why me?"

"I need your wisdom, your expertise, your handsome face."

"And my jet, my ability to cross borders, grease palms, and find weaponry."

"That, too."

Tycoon remained silent for a time, apparently thinking over the situation. "How come the folks at Langley aren't cooperating?"

"I don't know," Loomis said. "But it was quite plain they were putting me on ice."

"Well, with that caper at Dulles, we've probably fixed my wagon with Langley," Tycoon said. "Not that it matters. But tell me, does the Company know what's going on anymore?"

"I hear you're still under contract," Loomis said. "I thought you could tell me."

"All I know is, I was called in on that operation in Lisbon. Hamlet burned our ass good. I have the feeling the Company has slipped badly in handling Hamlet. That need-to-know shit doesn't exactly contribute to a well-informed, alert intelligence community."

"You haven't heard talk about all this?"

"Oh, lots of talk. I think they're shook. They know Hamlet's big—perhaps bigger than anyone had suspected. The thing that has impressed everyone is that in all the operations Hamlet has conducted, all they've shown us is their hired folk—mostly cheap mercenaries."

"Watch your mouth," Loomis said.

Tycoon grinned. "Well, that's probably what we're going up against now, assuming there's anybody up there at all."

"Assuming there is anybody up there at all, who would they be? Where would Hamlet do the recruiting in this country?" Loomis asked.

"Oh Lord, that depends. You could name your type. There are your run-of-the-mill New York and Chicago hit men. Arizona has blossomed out, especially around Phoenix. There are enough Cubans-for-hire in Miami to start a full-scale war, and they probably will, eventually. You can find good local talent in bars in Fort Worth, Dallas, Houston, El Paso, Denver, you name it. Then there are the exotics—the New Orleans mafia, the Chicano mafia, the border dope runners, the California crazies."

"If you were Hamlet, who would you hire?"

Tycoon thought for a moment. "For a one-shot operation, an out-of-state cop."

"Why?"

"The mafia—which of course doesn't exist—is too clannish, riddled with politics. Too many Cubans in this business tend to have a screw loose. And I distrust anything you find in a bar. No, if you want someone killed, no one can do a better job than a real, genuine son-of-a-bitch—a renegade policeman."

"You think that's what we face?" Loomis asked.

"No. Hamlet's probably not as smart as me," Tycoon said.

They forded the creek several more times, crisscrossing to take every advantage of the terrain as they climbed higher and higher.

The morning mists had cleared, and Loomis could now see the far-off peaks in sharp relief against a bright blue sky.

As they drove up a steep grade, through a perfect stand of lodgepole pines, Loomis began to feel apprehensive. He moved the two rifles from his lap to port arms with the knowledge that if they hit an ambush, every split second would count.

"How much farther?" he asked.

"Four or five miles," Tycoon said.

As they emerged from the trees, the road skirted a clump of boulders, high above the jeep trail.

Studying them, Loomis saw a blur of movement. At first, he thought he might have glimpsed a small, scurrying animal. Then he saw the glint of metal.

He was putting out a hand to signal Tycoon when the windshield burst into cobwebs.

Loomis rolled out the right side of the jeep, still holding the rifles. As he left the vehicle, he saw Tycoon switch off the ignition and bail out the other side.

Taking the full force of the fall on his right shoulder, protecting the rifles, Loomis was momentarily stunned. Looking up, he saw the jeep chug to a stop thirty yards away. It then began rolling backward. Tycoon leaped to his feet and ran toward it, picking up a rock en route. He chocked the right rear wheel and raced back to cover.

He flopped into the ditch beside Loomis.

"Good show," Loomis said.

"Damned if I'm going to walk out of here," Tycoon said. "Give me a rifle."

"Which one?"

"Well, we could fuck around and draw straws. But I really don't care all that much. The Remington will do. An old Gyrene like you should feel at home with a Garand."

A half-dozen more shots sounded from the rocks above. Loomis and Tycoon ducked, but no bullets came their way.

"They don't know who the hell we are," Tycoon said.

"And we don't know who they are," Loomis pointed out. "We may have stumbled into somebody else's fight."

"I have a theory that has always stood me in good stead," Tycoon said. "Anybody who shoots at me must be wearing a black hat." He swiveled around on the ground to see more of the terrain. "We've got to maneuver. How are we going to work this?"

Before Loomis could answer, a machine gun opened up, firing staccato bursts. But it was like no other gun Loomis had ever heard. Too heavy for a machine pistol, the gun was too light for a Browning.

"What the hell was that?" Tycoon asked.

"I don't know," Loomis said. "But he's shooting at your black hats. I heard lead hitting up there."

Tycoon was moving his head, trying to get better perspective of distance. "Where is he, anyway?"

"Above, the other side, and slightly to the left of that outcrop. He's keeping their heads down, so he's doing us a favor. Let's do him one. Let's climb to the top of that ridge."

"I thought all you true leaders always said 'follow me,' " Tycoon said.

"All right. Have it your way," Loomis said. "Follow me."

Crouching, cradling the rifle, Loomis dashed across the road and hurriedly climbed the ridge beyond. He was to some degree protected until he reached the top. But the crest of the ridge was on a level with the rocks. As Loomis sought cover, one of the gunmen saw him and began shooting. Loomis returned the fire. There was no time to aim. He squeezed off four quick shots and put the man's head down.

Loomis dropped behind a fallen log. Tycoon came up and fell beside him.

"What now, leader?" Tycoon asked.

"Let's try something," Loomis said. Reloading, he fired three quick rounds into the cluster of rocks. After a moment's hesitation, the strange machine gun fired a brief answering burst. Loomis saw the bullets hit, chipping rocks close to where he'd last seen the gunman.

Loomis fired two quick rounds into the same spot. The machine gun answered with a trigger-tapping reply.

"What the hell?" Tycoon asked.

"That's Johnson up there," Loomis said.

Loomis and Johnson once had been the best fire team in Southeast Asia. Now they were back together, working again. Loomis hoped he remembered all the signals, all the tricks. He tensed, waiting for Johnson's next move. When it came, he was ready.

Johnson's machine gun opened up in a sustained burst, providing cover. Loomis ran across the open stretch to higher ground and the protection of the trees. Dropping to the grass, he stacked three spare clips beside him. He then took over, giving Johnson cover, firing rapidly, allowing the gunmen no chance to shoot. Johnson moved closer and to a better position. When Johnson resumed firing, Loomis ran for the outcropping of rock directly above the gunmen.

He had almost reached cover when he saw movement. A gun was swinging toward him. Loomis fired on the run, a one-handed, desperate shot. He was rewarded by the sound of a bullet thunking solidly into flesh. Loomis rolled to the ground and waited for a moment. He cautiously raised his head; a second gunman was in the open, attempting to pull the wounded man to cover.

Loomis calmly shot him.

Johnson came into the open, shooting, his head wrapped in a white turban bandage. He was cradling a twenty-six-pound Lewis light machine gun.

Loomis gave his full attention to giving Johnson cover, but he could not see what was happening on the other side of the rocks.

Johnson abruptly ceased firing.

"That's it," he called. "You can come on down."

Loomis walked down the steep grade to the rocky knoll. Johnson had already reached the scene. He turned the bodies over with a toe. Apparently satisfied with what he found, he looked up and grinned as Johnson and Tycoon approached.

"Well, it sure took you guys long enough," he said. "What the hell kept you?"

The same Johnson. Too cocky, overconfident, and fearless for his own good.

Suddenly all the tension Loomis had built through his five-thousand-mile-rescue dash burst into righteous anger.

"You stupid shithead!" he yelled, closing the distance between them. "What'd you come up in these mountains for? You just asking for it?"

"What the fuck was I supposed to do?" Johnson yelled back. "Hold press conferences every day on my lawn?"

"You could have found a quiet place to hide out without making a target of yourself," Loomis pointed out heatedly.

"Well, you weren't any fucking help," Johnson shouted back. "If you had taken the job the Company offered, we'd be out in the field now, working. They wouldn't have dared to put me on the shelf like this. It's all your goddamned fault."

Tycoon collapsed on a rock and laughed until tears came to his eyes. "Come on," he said. "Let's get to the part where you two start pounding the piss out of each other. That's the part I always liked best."

"I'd be glad to oblige you," Johnson said. "In fact, there's nothing I'd like better. But right now I don't have the time. Those sons-a-bitches shot my oldest boy. He's in bad shape. I've got to get him to a hospital, fast."

He explained briefly about the attack at the campsite, Michael's wound, and Dr. Burke.

"Take our jeep," Tycoon said. "We'll wait here. You can pick us up on your way out."

After Johnson left, Loomis and Tycoon methodically searched the four bodies. They found nothing in the way of identification.

"What do you think?" Tycoon asked.

Loomis summed up. "Boot heels look like they're used to pavement. No calluses on the hands. They're city people, and not laborers. Fairly expensive guns. There's money behind them. No needle marks, so they're not junkies making a quick score. Beyond that, it beats the shit out of me."

"That dark guy over there was the leader," Tycoon said. "I heard him yelling orders, before Johnson creamed him."

"We'll know more after the federal people get here," Loomis said.

"What makes you think the agencies might be chasing them?" Tycoon asked.

"They're not chasing *them*," Loomis said. "They're chasing *us*."

* * *

Johnson returned a few minutes later with his family and Dr. Burke. Michael's condition had deteriorated. His heart was fibrillating.

Traveling in two cars, they rushed Michael to the hospital in Durango. After hurried X rays, Burke reported to Johnson.

"It's what I was afraid of. A piece of bone has traveled to his heart. Fortunately, it's lodged there. He's all right for the moment, but if it breaks loose, it could go to the lungs, and cause a massive infarction."

"Can you operate here?"

"This calls for open-heart surgery," Burke said. "He has to go on a machine that circulates the blood while the heart is stopped. I've pulled some strings with my army connections. We can rush him to Brooke in San Antonio. It's probably the best anywhere."

"I can get him there in little more than an hour," Tycoon said.

Twenty minutes later, they were airborne. Burke remained at Michael's side throughout the trip. The younger children slept. Tycoon radioed ahead. When they landed, a medivac helicopter was waiting to fly Michael and Burke straight to the quadrangle at Fort Sam Houston. Loomis, Tycoon, and the Johnsons were driven by an army corporal through the arched entry of old Fort Sam Houston, and past the turn-of-the-century buildings to the hospital. By the time they arrived, Michael had already been taken to surgery on the second floor of Beach Pavilion Annex. They were asked to wait on the first floor, in a small lounge partitioned off the main hall by translucent plastic.

The lounge was filled with people who looked as if they had done a lot of waiting.

Chapter

9

Shortly after four in the afternoon, George Hampton crossed Shell Plaza to the lobby of One Shell Place and descended into the opulent world of underground Houston. The elevator he shared with four other executives was lined in seamless leather. A story persisted that the Shell people, determined to have elevators without seams, had searched the world for cattle with hides sufficiently large. Eventually, a herd was located in Belgium. Hampton liked that story. It fitted his philosophy of life. He believed that when one was faced with a problem, one could always find a solution, if one tried long enough and hard enough. Hampton did not like failure.

Today, he was placed in the uncharacteristic position of being forced to admit to a failure.

The necessity left him consumed with anger, even though he considered the failure a temporary condition he damned well intended to remedy.

Hampton walked into the subterranean bar and ordered a one-oh-one—a double martini—and a pimiento cheese sandwich. He had not eaten since breakfast, waiting all day for that crucial phone call. Although the warmth of the martini spread through his system with surprising speed, Hampton immediately ordered another.

He sat for a time, thinking. He knew most of the executives in the crowded room. Some nodded in his direction, and some spoke, but none approached him. That was the way Hampton wanted it. There was a pecking order involved. He was at the top. No one was to approach him unless he indicated they should do so. He knew his reputation: a ruthless son-of-a-bitch of the first water, most would say. And they were right—a fact that did not disturb Hampton in the least.

Hampton not only knew the executives, he also knew what each was worth, and his chief area of operation—the Gulf, west Texas, North Sea, Middle East, Alaska north slope, or Venezuela. He knew their strengths, their weaknesses, their wives, their mistresses.

That was *his* strength.

He checked his reflection in the bar. His three-piece, top-of-the-line suit remained neat and unwrinkled. His gray sideburns and heavy black hair needed a trim. But his solid, James Garner face remained unlined at forty-four. He knew he created an impressive image—one of Houston's most handsome, and richest, millionaires, and certainly the most eccentric. Hampton looked away from the mirror; he was satisfied with the image.

He waited impatiently until shortly before five. Then he called for a phone and dialed his office.

"Any calls?" he asked Sheila.

"Which first, local or LD?"

"LD."

"Mark in New York asked that you return his call, no matter how late. He sounded worried. Harvey in Atlanta, ditto. Ashley in LA said it'd keep, that he'll get back to you in the morning. Your number-three ex called—Marcia— or was she number four? Shit, I forget. She's in the Virgin Islands. Isn't that hilarious?"

"You're being impertinent," Hampton said.

"And you love it," Sheila said. "You can always find a secretary that says 'Yes, sir.' But you'll never find one that gives you what I give you. Right?"

There was a grain of truth in that, Hampton reflected. "Not tonight," he said. "I have work to do. That all the calls?"

"All the LDs. Want the locals?"

Hampton was now certain. Something had gone wrong in Colorado. No news was bad news.

"Put them on my desk," he said. "I'll be up in a few minutes."

"Should I wait?"

"No need," he said.

Sheila was silent a moment. "Well, don't work too hard," she said. "But if you do, you know how to reach me."

"Sheila . . ." he said.

She laughed and broke the connection. He ordered another drink and waited for the buildings and the underground corridors to clear.

At five o'clock each working day, twelve thousand office workers from the skyscrapers above poured down through sixteen banks of elevators into six miles of tunnels under downtown Houston, heading for their cars through a maze of shopping centers, bars, and tile-lined corridors—a world few other people knew existed. Atlanta had turned underground Atlanta into a tourist mecca. Houston, being Houston, apparently did not care whether anyone knew that a $195 million marvel lay beneath the city's streets, linking sixteen skyscrapers.

Where Hampton now sat cost thirty-six thousand dollars a square foot. He had acquired that odd fact somewhere.

Thirty minutes and two martinis later, the catacomb city had emptied. Hampton signed for his belated lunch and headed back for the Shell elevators. He returned to his suite of offices, deserted now except for the security guard at his station beside the PBX.

"Working late, Mr. Hampton?" the guard asked.

Hampton never responded to the obvious.

"I'll be here a couple of hours," he said. "I don't want to be disturbed."

"Yes, sir," the guard said.

Hampton used his passkey to enter his private office, vaguely gratified to know that there were people in the world who still said "Yes, sir." He locked the door behind him.

He switched on a lamp at his desk, leaving the rest of the room in darkness. He badly needed time to think, to analyze his position.

His next move would determine not only his fate, but also that of Hamlet, and possibly the future of the world.

After ten minutes of careful consideration, he determined that no effort should be made to contact the Pole, Henryk.

Silence meant that the mission had turned sour.

Yet, before he could act, Hampton had to know exactly what had happened. He picked up the phone and dialed the paging service. Within two minutes, Carl responded to his beeper, phoning in on the special, sanitized phone.

"What the fuck's happening?" Hampton demanded.

"José blew it," Carl said quietly. "José and his team are dead."

"Why didn't you let me know?" Hampton asked.

"I just learned," Carl said. "Henryk *still* doesn't know. He's climbing the walls. Should I tell him?"

"How'd you find out?" Hampton asked.

"Faked a call to the sheriff's office up there."

"Risky," Hampton said. "Can it be traced?"

"No problem," Carl said. "I routed it through the Houston Police Department switchboard. If anybody bothers to check, it'll check back there."

"All right," Hampton said. "What happened in Colorado?"

"Johnson apparently had some extra help. Loomis and Tycoon showed up and helped snuff what was left of José and his crew."

"Loomis? He's supposed to be in Washington."

"The deputy I talked to made a positive eyeball. There was no doubt in his mind."

What the hell was happening? Did Hamlet not know what was going on? Why had he not been informed that Loomis was on the way to Colorado?

"What's the situation now?"

"Johnson's boy was hurt. They're flying him to Brooke in San Antonio."

"Think they've made José and his crew?"

118

"Not yet," Carl said. "But it's only a matter of time."

Hampton thought the matter out carefully. The Hamlet Group had agreed to act always on the side of caution. He did not need to ask the proper course to take now.

"Henryk will have to go," he said.

The line was silent for several seconds. When Carl spoke, his voice had dropped to a whisper. His words came with measured urgency.

"Look. We don't know there's any link to Henryk. He has worked hard. He has always been dependable. Let's give him the benefit of the doubt. Let's wait and see."

"We can't afford the risk," Hampton said. "Maybe I need to remind you that Henryk stands next to you. If they tie José to Henryk, they might make the connection to you."

And then I might be next, Hampton thought. But he left that thought unstated.

"I think you should take care of Henryk yourself," Hampton said.

"Jesus," Carl breathed. "I don't know . . ."

"This whole thing is growing too hot," Hampton said. "If Henryk goes, it ends there. With him dead, there's no way they could make the connection to you, is there?"

"I've been very careful," Carl said.

"But with Henryk alive . . . Well, you see the problem. He has to go. And it has to be you. There's no one else we can depend on."

"It's been a long time," Carl said.

"It's like riding a bicycle," Hampton said. "It'll come back to you. Do you have some gear?"

"Sure. No problem there. But, well, it'd be easier if it was some asshole I didn't know."

"Henryk has been dumb," Hampton insisted. "There's no room in our trade for stupidity. He's endangered us and the whole operation. Think about that. You should be able to work up a little anger."

"I'll try," Carl said.

"What about Mangrum? Did he deliver?"

119

"He docked yesterday with the last shipment. It's on the way to Jersey now. I should get a call tomorrow morning that it's in place."

"Good. Let me know. And you *will* take care of Henryk?"

"I'll take care of Henryk."

"All right," Hampton said. "There'll be a bonus in it. And while you're at it . . ."

He hesitated, thinking things through, making certain that this was the right decision.

"Yes?"

"Take care of Mangrum, too. We're through with him."

Carl again was silent for a moment. "Won't that be pushing our luck?" he asked.

"I don't think so," Hampton said. "What's one more murder in Houston?"

Hampton walked to a window, opened the curtains, and looked out over the lights of downtown Houston, toward the distant ship channel, a constant reminder of the city's dynamic ways. He once knew a man who made a career of delivering lectures explaining how Houston, although not on the sea, became the nation's third largest seaport by bringing the sea to Houston. Hampton could not imagine himself living anywhere else. Houston had provided him with the means for becoming a member of Hamlet. He intended to show his appreciation.

Within the next few months, he would make Houston the capital of North America.

His ties with Houston were close. His father, Ham Hampton, had become an exceptional legend in a city filled with legends. Reared in poverty in the piney woods of northeast Texas, Ham Hampton had worked the early boomtowns that became hallowed names in the oil industry—Burkburnett, Electra, Ranger, Desdemona, Borger, Sugar Land, Humble . . .

Ham Hampton made and lost several fortunes before his son was born. But respectability and permanent wealth finally came with his invention of a sophisticated seismographic device that vastly aided the fledgling science of subsurface geology. Ham had started his own Houston-based company, leasing his skill and seismographic equipment to the major oil firms centered there. But to the end, he remained a gambler, sinking huge sums into the deep wells of far west Texas, Mexico, Venezuela, and California.

Hampton never saw much of his father. As a child in Houston's affluent River Oaks section, he accepted the fact that most families had absentee fathers. Oil was a demanding game. The prevalent explanation that his father was "out sitting on a well" conjured an image in George's childish mind of his father perched, henlike, over an oil well. After he was grown, he learned that his interpretation was not far off. When a well neared pay strata, the geologist literally hovered over the hole around the clock for days on end, studying and testing drilling mud and each core sample, poring over his charts.

To ease the long hours and tension, there frequently were booze and women, who shared the backseat of his father's Cadillac. In his father's papers, George had been only mildly surprised to find evidence of an illegitimate half-brother, now a car salesman in Odessa, and a half-sister, now a cocktail waitress in Levelland. He had no way of knowing if they were aware of their origins, or if there were others.

George's mother died in his twelfth year, an event that left him curiously unmoved. He had been no better acquainted with her than with his father. She was a haunted woman, given to loneliness, liquor, and her own private hells. The autopsy attributed her death to nephritis, but George overheard a family friend express the opinion that the true cause was neglect. She was denied a share in his father's interests, and she had none of her own.

After his mother's death, George divided his time between military schools and summers in the oil fields. In those surroundings, George acquired the most priceless legacy he received from his father, a gift that proved to be even more valuable than money—a tough mind. At fifteen, George Hampton was assigned to drive a nitro truck for one of his father's crews—a job Ham Hampton seemed to view as a rite of passage. When a foreman protested that George might be too young for such dangerous work, Ham had merely laughed and said, "Pete, if he's too damned dumb to dodge a few bumps in the road, he'll never amount to a country fart anyway." The story was added to the many told about Ham Hampton in bars, whorehouses, and corporate boardrooms throughout the oil industry.

George Hampton survived. His father did not. In George's second year of college, the phone call came from his father's lawyer in Houston. Ham Hampton had been killed by the discovery well that, ironically, eventually doubled the value of his estate. In his gambler fashion, Ham had checkerboarded the surrounding land with leases before sinking his deepest well. The result was successful beyond his wildest dreams. Fifteen thousand feet beneath the surface, Ham's drill found a tremendous pocket of natural gas that came roaring to the wellhead. The crew managed to cap the hole, but pressures that stagger the imagination stripped the threads, turning the huge chunk of metal into a supersized bullet that struck his father just above the belt buckle.

Ham Hampton apparently knew his son better than George suspected. A codicil to the will stipulated that George would receive his inheritance only after completing work for his degree in petroleum engineering.

So for two more years, George battled pop quizzes and slide-rule deductions while the trust administrators maintained the status quo on Ham's fortune.

During those years, George became a member of Hamlet.

Now, he was one of Hamlet's most influential members. Yet he had to keep in mind that he was the one member who was different.

His actions, at all times, had to be exactly right.

His inclination at the moment was to use the scrambler phone, in case Hamlet wished a firsthand report, and possibly further information for immediate action. But the scrambler was to be used only in emergency situations. If he used the phone he would in effect be declaring an emergency—panicking. He did not want to convey that impression of weakness. Long ago, the members of Hamlet had agreed that a few setbacks, a few mistakes, could be considered routine. A few errors were compatible with the overall plan.

Hampton turned from the window and crossed to a locked console by his desk. He fitted a special key into the lock, swung back the top, and exposed a small computer terminal. Pulling his swivel chair into position, he switched on the power and dialed for access to the mainframe computer. High over the Atlantic, a communications satellite received his request for relay to its destination. Within seconds, Hampton received a visual invitation on his screen to proceed.

On the keyboard, he carefully typed in his complex sign-in code. In Europe, the mainframe computer politely asked for further verification. Hampton supplied it. After a moment's delay, the computer requested verification reinforcement. Hampton answered with another code. His typing, fortunately, was accurate. With only a brief hesitation, the video screen answered *ready*.

Hampton then switched on the black box. He informed the mainframe computer that the black box was engaged. The computer responded with a signal that its own black box was connected. Hampton began typing his message in the clear, confident that the black boxes were mangling the words beyond recognition: "Colorado caper failed. Assault team dead. Possible link being eliminated. Loomis, Johnson, Tycoon en route San Antonio. Advise. Last Gulf shipment received, transmitted to place. Folding Gulf operation as per plan."

Hampton reread his message before punching the key combination that would send it through an elaborate electronic process that only one person in all the world truly understood. Hampton was not satisfied with the tone of the message inherent in the words *failed, dead, advise.*

After a brief hesitation, he elected to take the initiative.

He typed a final sentence: "Strongly urge Hamlet Ultimatum be issued soonest."

He reread the full text with a feeling of satisfaction, and keyed the message on its way.

Hampton waited, confident that the screen would not long remain blank.

Chapter

10

Trane Thornsen had not left the computer rooms in three days. Above, life went on as usual in the castle. People came, left, and performed the required routines. Trane Thornsen remained below in his own world, of his own making.

Bernardo found him there, even more emaciated than ever, pale, and filthy. Bernardo was appalled.

"God, Trane, what are you doing to yourself?" he demanded. He glanced around pointedly at the trash on the floor, the debris from thousands of printouts. "Christ, look at this!" he shouted. "And look at yourself! You look like you haven't eaten in a month! And if you want to know the absolute truth, you stink!"

Thornsen was seated at his main console. Under the lash of Bernardo's words, he reached up and raked a hand across the stubble on his face. He was surprised to find it much longer than he would have thought. Thornsen tended to measure the passage of time by his beard. He shaved with each shower. Bernardo was right. He had not had a shower in some time. He glanced at the digital clock in the corner of the terminal and realized he had not moved from his chair in more than twelve hours. And he *was* hungry. He simply had forgotten to stop and eat.

"I've been busy," he tried to explain to Bernardo. "There's so much to do."

Bernardo became calmer. "Trane, I don't want to upset you. But the other guys are depending on me to take care of you. You're killing yourself. And we need you! Why don't you knock off, shave and shower, and get some food into you? I'll bet you're constipated again."

Thornsen shook his head negatively, meaning he really did not know. He was not offended. He long ago had accepted the fact that other people had to look after him. He became so lost in his work that he neglected minor things, such as eating and sleeping and going to the bathroom. Bernardo had been taking care of him for almost twenty years.

"You should let us get you some help down here," Bernardo said. "There's no reason for you to do it all yourself. God, you look like something that crawled out from under a rock."

Thornsen filed Bernardo's comment for the moment. Something else had to be done. He turned to the keyboard and signed off from the scan of economic conditions in Japan. A lingering fragment of worry remained. He made a mental note to pursue the matter. Something had happened with the Japanese fishing trade that might be of significance.

He then played back Bernardo's last comment in his mind. It merited a reply.

"We can't trust anyone else down here, Bernardo," he said. "If any of you guys want to help, I'd be glad to show you what to do."

"Trane, it isn't our fault that we're not computer freaks," Bernardo said. "We all do what we can."

Thornsen did not answer. Always alert to the machines, he heard a faint click as a printer engaged. After a pause, the daisy wheel ripped out a brief message. The extra millisecond between the click and the message informed him that the incoming signal had been routed through the black box. Bernardo had not noticed. Thornsen crossed the room and ripped off the message.

"It's gone sour," he said.

"What?" Bernardo asked. "What's gone sour?"

"The Colorado operation." Thornsen sighed. "I wish we could program the machines to kill. Why do we have to depend on people?"

"What's the situation?" Bernardo asked. When action was required, he was all business.

"The assassination crew is dead," Thornsen told him. "Hampton is eliminating Henryk the Pole, as a matter of caution. The last of the ploot has landed, and is on its way to the East. Hampton is closing out the Gulf operation, according to plan. But there's something here I don't understand. Loomis showed up in Colorado. He was supposed to be in Washington. I don't understand that at all."

Thornsen went back to his console. Bernardo moved closer to watch. Thornsen flipped some switches, altering his terminal hookup. Dialing a number pasted on the plastic face of the terminal, he sat back and waited for the response from the CIA communications network at Langley.

"Trane," Bernardo said. "What are you doing?"

"Quiet," Thornsen said. "This takes concentration."

Connected with Langley, he entered a user code. The terminal impulse—an electronic fingerprint carefully monitored at Langley—was so perfectly faked that the Langley computer did not question it. Thornsen then asked for connection with the Interface Message Processor. The IMP linked him to the entire net. He asked for a dump of high-priority messages in the interconnected systems. Within minutes, Thornsen had the readout. He poured it into a memory store, then switched it to a printer. By the time he walked over to the high-speed device, it had turned out a dozen folds of tracked computer paper. Spreading the material out on a long table, Thornsen quickly scanned all extraneous material to extract what he wanted. From the bits and pieces here and there, he saw the big picture.

He was impressed by the scope of Langley's panic.

"Loomis made fools of them," he told Bernardo. "He got permission to enter the country, then gave them the slip at the airport."

Bernardo was accustomed to Thornsen's electronic miracles. Given a few minutes, Thornsen could enter almost any communication-linked electronic system in the world. But the quick readout left him stunned.

"My God, I don't know how you do it," he said. "Those machines . . ."

"Don't make a big thing of it," Thornsen warned. "If there's one thing I can't stand, it's someone who personifies computers, giving them animation. They're just a tool, a storage box." He reexamined the readout, making certain of the agencies involved. "That Loomis must be quite a guy," he said.

He then reread the final note on Hampton's message.

"Hamp wants to issue the Ultimatum," he added.

Bernardo looked up, surprised. "Are we anywhere near ready?"

Thornsen weighed his answer. He knew Bernardo would be affected by his opinion. Bernardo was a realist. He could function well on day-to-day matters. But when the bold step was needed, Bernardo tended to be too cautious.

"We're ready," Thornsen told him. "I'm for doing it, as soon as we can put things into motion."

"God, Trane," Bernardo said. "I don't know. . . . I mean, we've got to be certain!"

After twenty years of talking, planning, thinking, Bernardo was hesitating on the point of action. Bernardo's constant wavering frequently left Thornsen in a fury of frustration.

"Look, Bernardo," he said desperately. "We've always known that this decision would come. There's nothing new about it. We've always agreed then that when conditions were right, we wouldn't wait."

Bernardo hesitated. "I only wanted to make sure you were certain," he said.

"I'm certain," Thornsen said.

"What I mean is, this is something the whole group has to decide."

"But any one of us has the option of calling an emergency meeting," Thornsen reminded him.

Bernardo looked at the readout. "Well, I wasn't arguing against it, understand," he said doubtfully. "I'm just saying that we must look at it from all angles."

"I think Hamp is right," Thornsen said again, firmly.

"I guess we *will* have to discuss it," Bernardo said. He glanced around in discomfort at the banks of computers, printers, and terminals. Bernardo did not like to spend time in the computer rooms. "Come on," he added. "Let's go upstairs. If all the guys are going to be coming here, we'll have to get ready."

"You go ahead," Thornsen said. "I have a few things I have to do. I'll be up in a few minutes."

"Promise?" Bernardo asked.

"I'll be up in a few minutes," Thornsen said again.

Irritated by the interruption, he returned to his console. He had much ground to cover, and not much time remained before some corporations and institutions closed for the day. Signing on in real time, Thornsen activated a preprogrammed sequence, and began monitoring the results.

Tapping the memory stores and on-line electronic activity among selected corporations, governments, and even a few wealthy individuals, Thornsen soon had answers from Japan, Germany, England, Switzerland, the United States, Canada, Saudi Arabia, France, Austria, and a half-dozen capitals in South America. As the answers came in, one by one, Thornsen transferred them into an analytic mode.

The Austrian schilling had closed the day in a weakened condition. By considering the other data, Thornsen could see that the deterioration would continue through the next two days, under the stress of seasonal exchange imbalance. He pondered the possibilities for a moment, then ordered a shift in various Vienna bank holdings to accelerate the imbalance. He then projected an elaborate scenario: when the Austrian schilling adjusted, buy and sell orders would automatically be issued on certain goods held by Hamlet-owned corporations over half the earth.

Thornsen learned, from carefully encoded inquiries, that steel production was overtaking demand in the United States, in the European Coal and Steel Community, and in Argentina and Canada. He promptly issued commands that would adjust Hamlet's coal holdings.

He obtained a readout on the wheat harvest nearing completion in the northern United States and in Canada. A check showed that within days, a serious shortage of grain cars would develop. He altered Hamlet's grain elevator and milling position accordingly and, just for sport, entered some railway computers and diverted more than two hundred grain cars to Florida. He found little change in the oil situation in the Middle East, but shipping seemed to pose a problem for certain parts of Europe. Thornsen decided to delay action; he encoded a note for the system to replay the situation for him in three days—or earlier, if conditions warranted.

One by one, Thornsen examined aspects of the world economy. Most of the computer's actions on such matters were automatic, but in some instances human analysis was needed.

Thornsen became so absorbed that he forgot about dinner and his promise to Bernardo. He spent another two hours at the terminal.

At last, he pushed his chair back, walked over to a couch, and collapsed, exhausted.

He was indeed certain: Hampton was right.

The time had come to issue the Ultimatum.

More than twenty years of planning and effort were coming to fruition.

Hamlet was ready.

The nuclear incident in the Dominican Republic had been an effective—and brilliant—diversion.

The crude atomic bomb planted in Santo Domingo had served notice on the world that the Hamlet Group existed.

But more important, the full attention of the world's intelligence community had been focused on the search for the bomb and—later—on the heroism of Loomis and Johnson in rushing the device out to sea before its inevitable detonation.

While the CIA and other intelligence agencies were preoccupied, shipments of industrial plutonium had been rerouted by Thornsen's computers, intercepted, and stolen.

Now Hamlet had assembled more than two tons of the deadliest material known to man.

This material was now in place, ready to back Hamlet's Ultimatum.

The most elaborate scenario ever devised by man was about to be put into execution.

PART
TWO

Chapter

11

Every hospital has a certain, inescapable rhythm. Beach Pavilion Annex at Brooke Army Medical Center in San Antonio was no exception. Within a few hours, Loomis felt as if he had been there forever. Aside from the surgical recovery room, the facilities seemed woefully understaffed. In the large, open wards, the patients looked after each other. From their beds, they watched each other's EKG monitors, summoning the nurses when erratic blips indicated a heart was not functioning properly. Relatives and visitors assumed the minor duties of dealing with bedpans, blankets, and bed adjustments.

For the most part, the patients and visitors were military people, accustomed to being regimented.

And regimented they were.

Within hours after Michael's emergency surgery, Melana became acquainted with a colonel's wife who apparently knew everything anyone would need to know about procedures at Brooke Army Medical Center. Her husband, recently retired, was recuperating from a double bypass operation. The colonel's lady clearly was in the habit of taking charge in any surroundings. She was horrified to learn that the Johnsons and their friends had gone to the expense of checking into a nearby motel.

"You can stay in the guesthouse across the Quadrangle and save money," she said. "What you do, you get some food at the PX, fix your own breakfast, and you can have lunch and dinner in the cafeteria here. It's cheaper. I'll arrange your transportation."

Gray-haired, short, and terribly earnest, she dispensed constant advice from a peculiar stance—leaning forward, her arms dangling, her head cocked to one side while she frowned up into the listener's face. The frown, Loomis decided, derived from her effort to determine how much of her abundant information the listener was capable of absorbing.

"There's a post office down that way," she said. "Red Cross is in the basement. And there is a day-care facility for your other children. I'll find out where it is."

Melana called her "The Information Lady." Johnson seemed relieved that Melana seemed to be in good hands.

"Half of Washingon is on their way down here," he told Loomis. "They're really pissed over the trick you pulled on them at Dulles. You left a paid-for motel room empty. You don't have any sense of propriety, Loomis. Did you ever try to explain something like that to a congressional appropriations committee, or the General Accounting Office? And Langley sure wants an explanation about that mess we left back in Colorado."

"I'm still waiting for somebody to explain it to me," Loomis said.

"They want us to go back to Washington with them for a debriefing."

"No," Loomis said emphatically. "You can tell them the trail to Hamlet starts right here in San Antonio, with a guy named José. There's no need for us to go play grab-ass in Washington."

"It's time we agreed on something," Johnson said.

The army surgeons reported that Michael was recovering satisfactorily. Dr. Burke put the details into plain English.

"A bone chip from his pelvis was lodged in the mitral valve," he explained. "But the heart is in good shape, and he's a healthy boy. There's no reason to think he's not going to be all right."

Johnson and Melana were allowed brief visits to the recovery room on the second floor. They spent the remainder of the time in a small lounge near the chaplain's office on the first floor.

As soon as they received the good news about Michael, Tycoon and Burke left.

"I've got to get back to my practice," Burke said. "I have patients scheduled for surgery. And you know, after you've conned a patient into surgery, it's awfully difficult to tell him something more important has come up."

"I'd just as soon not hang around for this so-called debriefing," Tycoon said. "As far as I'm concerned, you two guys were in charge. If you two weren't such famous heroes, we'd probably be decorating a Colorado jail cell. We may yet. And that worries me. I think I better mosey on back to Acapulco."

The delegation from Washington arrived early the next morning. The CIA faction was led by Deputy Director Cyrus Ogden, a short, heavyset, pipe-smoking antithesis of the James Bond school. He might have been mistaken for a professor of philosophy at some remote college. But Loomis happened to know that Ogden directed the CIA's Clandestine Services, dedicated to toppling governments, murdering potential Hitlers, and making the world safe for American business.

Accompanying Ogden was a tall, habitually worried career intelligence officer, Herman Grindstaff.

Traveling with them was Deputy Director Andrew Bell of the National Security Agency, apparently along in tacit recognition of the fact that the CIA was not empowered to conduct domestic operations—and that there had been considerable criticism over the many times the agency had done so.

Neither Ogden nor Bell seemed especially pleased with

one another's company. But if prizes had been given for bluntness, Ogden would have won, hands-down.

He led Loomis, Johnson, and the Washington delegation across the street from Beach Pavilion to a parking lot. There he turned on Loomis.

"I'll speak plainly, Loomis," he said. "You're on my personal shit list. If it was up to me, I would kick your ass right out of the country."

Johnson laughed. "Don't pay any attention to him, Loomis," he said. "He talks tough, but he's a sweet, lovable person. He really is. Just ask anybody at Langley."

"And you shut your fucking mouth, Johnson," Ogden said. "You're in enough trouble."

"*I'm* in trouble!" Johnson said, towering over Ogden. "Just answer me one thing. What the fuck were you people doing while Hamlet fielded that hit team on me? I *told* you those guys wouldn't give up. But no one would listen. So now my boy's up there, paying for *your* mistakes. I'm telling you right now, Ogden. I'm going to raise the biggest stink Langley's ever seen. I don't give a shit who knows it."

Ogden glared at him. "We're all going back to Washington," he said. "We'll talk there."

"Officially, I'm on sick leave," Johnson reminded him. "Until I know my boy's all right, I'm staying here."

Bell, the sole NSA man present, remained impassively aloof from the intramural argument. He stared straight ahead, to where a half-dozen soldiers were preparing to fire a howitzer, blow a bugle, and raise the flag. Loomis noticed that the howitzer was pointed across the Quadrangle, toward Officers' Row. He wondered if any disgruntled soldier had ever attempted to load the bore with scrap iron.

The cannon boomed across the Quadrangle. The Stars and Stripes were raised as the bugle sounded "To the Colors." Bell seemed impressed with the ceremony. He waited until it was over before motioning Loomis and Johnson into the government car for a conference. Loomis, Johnson, and Grindstaff climbed into the backseat. Bell and Ogden sat in front. Loomis lowered a window a few inches for air.

Loomis had forgotten the continual bureaucratic infighting

that prevailed in Washington. He wondered how best to handle his situation with Ogden. He did not intend to return to Washington. But he needed information about José's background and connections. He sensed that the best way might be to work through the NSA man.

"Any new information on José?" Loomis asked Bell.

Bell's impersonal gray eyes looked at him for a moment in the rearview mirror, coolly assessing him. "We can go over all this in Washington," he said. "So far, you've shown us no sign you intend to cooperate. In fact, you have demonstrated that you do *not* intend to do so."

"I didn't cross the Atlantic to watch platoons of bureaucratic spooks get in each other's way at Langley," Loomis told him.

"Why *did* you come to this country?" Bell asked quietly.

"Hamlet tried to kill me a few nights ago," Loomis said. "It took no brains to see that Johnson was next. But I couldn't convince anyone at Langley. So I arranged my own transportation."

Grindstaff entered the conversation for the first time. "One thing I want to know. How did you manage to give my people the slip at Dulles?"

Johnson laughed. Tycoon had given him a vivid description.

"I usually charge for tradecraft," Loomis said.

"Bill me," Grindstaff said.

"Do you know Dulles?" Loomis asked.

"Of course."

"The rest rooms off the main concourse?"

"I've seen them," Grindstaff said.

"Your man was standing beside the partition that screens the rest rooms," Loomis said. "I simply walked out."

"He claims he never took his eyes off the rest-room door," Grindstaff said.

"He honestly may think that," Loomis said. "But if you ask him, he may remember a terrific blonde who had trouble with her luggage, fifteen or twenty feet away. She was recruited by Tycoon. She gave your man a lingering beaver shot."

"That son-of-a-bitch," Grindstaff said.

Loomis was not certain whether he meant Tycoon, or the CIA man they had tricked. He did not ask.

Bell laughed.

Loomis caught Bell's eye again in the rearview mirror.

"I still want to know. Is there any new information on José?"

After a moment's hesitation, Bell glanced at Ogden.

"We'll have no discussion here," Ogden said to Bell's unasked question. "We'll establish an operational procedure in Washington. Until then, we can't divulge any confidential information."

"Come on," Loomis said. "Let's cut through the shit. Hamlet is not going to wait for us to draw up a dozen contingency plans."

Bell was still looking at Ogden in indecision. "We have an alternative, Cyrus," he said.

Ogden lifted his eyebrows. "I beg your pardon?"

"There's a decision tree, you remember," Bell said. "If we deem it necessary, we can deal with Loomis in the field."

"I don't deem it necessary," Ogden said emphatically.

"That's my boy," said Johnson. "He always comes through in the clutch."

"You shut your fucking mouth, Johnson," Ogden said. He glanced at Johnson's bandaged head. "I'm beginning to think that bullet scrambled your brain."

Bell remained unruffled. "Time is running out on us, Cyrus," he said. "I think Loomis is right. We don't have time to lose. We can cut through the shit. Let's go ahead and swap information with him here and now."

"What kind of swap?" Loomis asked.

"We trade our information for everything you know, or suspect, about Hamlet."

Loomis hesitated, thinking. He was amazed that Langley had so little hard information that they were coming to him. Bell, watching him in the mirror, apparently had anticipated his line of thought.

"You've dealt directly with Hamlet's hired guns," he explained. "You've gained some expertise with the unusual during your rather checkered career. We feel that you might have some thoughts on Hamlet's structure worthy of our consideration."

"Try me," Loomis said. The quicker this was over with, the sooner they would be getting on José's trail.

"First, tell us what you think happened in Colorado."

"No secret there," Loomis said. "Hamlet used independent, hired guns, just as they have every time."

"And what do you deduce from that?" Bell asked.

Loomis thought for a moment, looking out across the parade ground to the huge hospital building, more than a mile away.

"Only what may be obvious," he said. "The brains behind Hamlet use cutouts, all down the line. Their organization is greatly compartmentalized. And they are careful. That's why we've never been able to trace anything."

"That jibes with our experience," Bell said. "Early on, the CIA managed to infiltrate Hamlet on a certain level. The two agents, operating out of a European desk, were soon killed. But they had been allowed very limited contacts."

"Bell!" Ogden warned.

Bell glanced at him. "We're swapping information. Remember?" he told Ogden. "I like Loomis's phraseology. It's time to cut through the shit."

He turned in the seat to face Loomis. "This is for your ears alone, and for whoever happens to have this car bugged. Washington is going ape. Most people thought Hamlet bit the dust in Santo Domingo. Apparently the president was not among them. He's been on our ass night and day. Thus far, nothing is for sure. We've been through everything, time and again. Right now, we're grasping at straws." He paused, and took a deep breath. "So give me a quick assessment. Assuming we can find whoever hired José, what position do you think that man would hold in the Hamlet organization?"

"He'd be another cutout," Loomis predicted. "And expendable. The trick would be to find him alive—and then the man behind him."

"How many layers do you think lie between José and pay dirt?" Bell asked quietly.

Loomis had spent much time pondering that question. He had come up with some theories. But he did not know how to put his vague impressions into words.

"I think Hamlet is big—much bigger than the news-magazines would have had us believe," he explained. "It's certainly no ragtag band of terrorists. They're not going to tell you to hand over a million dollars in used twenties, or else they'll blow up the Statue of Liberty. I think Hamlet has been underestimated, all along. I have a feeling of . . ."

He hesitated, still uncertain how to phrase his thoughts.

"Yes?" Bell asked.

"Well, an entire philosophy behind everything they do."

Bell smiled. "Philosophy. A curious word. Philosophy. How do you arrive at that?"

"Not by logic," Loomis admitted. "But anytime you have a certain ruthlessness—the Nazi pogroms, Russian oppression, or the U.S. meddling in Southeast Asia, if you'll pardon the reference—you find a philosophy that serves as self-justification. I sense this in Hamlet. That's all."

"That might be an important point," Bell said. "And one all our soothsayers have missed. Tell me. What do you think Hamlet was doing in Santo Domingo? What was that nuclear caper all about?"

"Experimental," Loomis said. "Maybe diversionary. I'm certain they have stronger medicine."

"More nuclear bombs?"

"Or something worse."

"What could be worse?" Bell asked.

"Oh, come on," Loomis said. "Don't bullshit me. Why should I have to explain today's weaponry to an administrative officer from the National Security Agency?"

"Let's say we're interested in your thinking," Bell said blandly.

"I'm sure your files are full of doomsday scenarios," Loomis said. "Take your pick. Nerve gas isn't too difficult,

I understand. Exotic virus or bacteria could wipe out a good percentage of the population. I'm told any bright graduate student probably knows enough to come up with something along that line. And there are cruder ways. A truckload of common fertilizer could devastate several square blocks. You probably know plenty of other possibilities. My thinking is that Hamlet will use the worst thing available as a threat. And if you don't deliver, then they will. I think Hamlet is a new level of terrorism. The methods are different. The goals are different."

"What do you think those goals might be?"

"I have no idea," Loomis admitted. "But I have a feeling we're going to know soon."

Bell was silent for a moment, watching two nurses leave their car and walk across the parking lot toward Beach Pavilion Annex.

"And that's all you have to offer?" he asked.

"That's all," Loomis said. "Your turn."

Bell played dumb. "My turn?"

"We're swapping," Loomis reminded him.

"Okay, Loomis. Let's define our terms. First, let's make note of the fact that you obviously have some powerful friends. We had been ordered to make you privy to all information germane to the Hamlet investigation, prior to the caper you pulled at Dulles. For my own part, I've received no contrary instructions. So I'll continue to do so, insofar as domestic procedure is concerned. But you are to have no active role in our investigation. You may observe, and be apprised. Understood?"

"Understood," Loomis said. He expected nothing more.

"As far as the overseas operation of the government is concerned, you'll have to make your arrangements elsewhere. Presumably, other agencies received the same instructions we did. But at the risk of embarrassing anyone present, there is a faction determined to keep you at arm's length from the Hamlet investigation. Do you read me?"

"I read you," Loomis said.

Ogden said nothing.

"Your conduct since your arrival hasn't contributed greatly to your welcome, or helped what friends you have," Bell added. "There's one hell of a battle going on right now over what to do with you. I don't know what view will prevail. I was told to bring you back to Washington immediately. But I also hold more impressive orders to grant you full cooperation. At the moment, I lean toward following that line, if you'll act nice. What's your inclination?"

"Fine with me," Loomis said.

"Okay. The Colorado team checks out to police files in El Paso, Albuquerque, Phoenix, San Antonio, and Houston. I could give you a rundown on all the spear carriers. But I think they're unimportant. Obviously, José hired them to fill a commitment made to party or parties unknown."

He paused, looking out over the Quadrangle. "Strangely, José has the least impressive record. Maybe he was just smarter. He was known as a jack-of-all-trades along the border, for everything from burglary and smuggling to murder."

"No solid connections?"

"None. Two leads. A block of cash was deposited in José's bank account. We're convinced his wife knows from nothing. She swears the signature on the deposit slip is not his. The bank signature cards tend to confirm her opinion. But the best lick so far: an undercover San Antonio vice-squad officer was watching a black pimp harass one of his whores in a downtown bar three days ago. He happened to see José talking intently with another man. He wondered what José was up to, as things seemed to happen when José was around. José followed the guy. The detective followed José. The guy went to a room in a hotel down by the Alamo. The detective, in a commendable burst of curiosity, checked the hotel register. The ID, and the Houston firm the guy gave, are bogus. But we're working on it. We have a good description, and we may make him. The Houston police are giving us good cooperation, and there's a bonus. The man spoke with a slight accent."

"What kind?"

"We're not certain. The hotel clerk thought German, but the detective, from what he overheard, thought it was Czech or Polish. He didn't hear enough to say for certain."

"He could be local talent," Loomis said. "There are large German-speaking areas around San Antonio, and other, smaller, ethnic communities."

"So I found out," Bell said. "I truly find Texas a very confusing place."

"Maybe he put Houston down on the hotel register as a diversion," Johnson said.

"We're checking all cities in the Southwest, just in case," Bell said. "But we know one more thing. He did take a plane to Houston, that very night."

"Then why don't we all go to Houston?" Loomis asked.

"We have more than two dozen men down there," Bell said. "We can do nothing they're not doing. And . . ." Bell met his eyes in the rearview mirror. "Besides, you're here in an inactive capacity, remember? That's the deal. When something happens, we'll let you know."

He remained silent, indicating that the conference was concluded. Loomis and Johnson stepped out of the car. Ogden did not glance in their direction. Grindstaff seemed embarrassed.

Loomis and Johnson stood and watched as Bell drove away.

Johnson sighed. "I'm sure glad I'm Civil Service," he said. "Somehow, I got the impression your name may not be the only one on the shit list at Langley."

Loomis was consumed with a fatigue that was more than jet lag from his marathon trip. Convinced that, for the moment, he could do nothing, he went back to the motel.

More than anything else, he missed the presence, the tenderness, of Maria Elena, the sense of belonging that her hand, a gesture could bring. Clay Loomis, a loner all his life, had never before felt so alone.

He lay quiet for a long time. But the feeling of emotional emptiness simply would not go away.

After calculating time differences, he picked up the phone and called Spain. El Jefe answered.

"Maria Elena probably crossed the ocean before you left Spain," El Jefe said. "She is now in Hollywood. She is staying there with her producer friend."

He gave Loomis the number.

El Jefe paused, and lapsed into Spanish. "How is the friend you went to see?"

"He's all right," Loomis said. "But we had some fun, up in the mountains."

"How goes the work?"

"Not too well," Loomis admitted. "It's much more serious than I thought."

The line was silent a moment. "If I can be of any help, just tell me where and when," El Jefe said.

Loomis thanked him and broke the connection. He dialed the California number. A cool, clipped feminine voice said Maria Elena was not up yet, but when Loomis identified himself, he was put through. Maria Elena's voice was heavy with sleep. Loomis did not waste time with small talk.

"I'm sorry to call so early in your day," he said. "But I wanted to catch you. Things are not at all well with me. I think I made a mistake."

Maria Elena was still groggy. "What do you mean?"

"I'm miserable."

"Oh, that. Well, you *norteamericanos* have a phrase. Something about making your own bed. What time is it?"

"Twelve here. Ten there."

"Where's here?"

"San Antonio."

"There was a story on the news last night, about a shooting in Colorado. All very mysterious. Was that you?"

"Me. And a couple of other guys."

"You all right?"

He told her about Johnson's boy, and the emergency surgery. "He's quite a kid," he said. "It would really turn him on to get a card from a bona-fide film star."

"He'll get it. Maybe from two or three film stars. There seems to be a surplus out here."

144

"What's happening on the film?"

"Not much. We've talked. I have a concept of the character. The producer sees her differently. And the director thinks we're both wrong. They're talking about reworking the script. The new writer will probably have some more ideas. I don't think it's going to work."

"I'm sorry."

"So am I. How is your job going?"

"Not well. It's even bigger than I thought. At the moment, we're not getting anywhere."

"Loomis, if there's anything I can do to help . . ."

Loomis paused, vaguely disturbed.

"That's the second offer I've had in twenty minutes," he said. "I'll have to watch myself. My desperation must be showing."

"When Loomis says he's licked, it's panic time," Maria Elena said.

"Maybe I just forgot how to go it alone."

Maria Elena was silent for a moment. "Well, why don't you get in some more practice? If that doesn't work, we'll talk about it."

"I'll call you in a day or two," Loomis promised.

He hung up the phone, wondering.

Why, for the first time in his life, did he have this strong premonition of impending defeat?

Bell kept his word. Loomis spent most of the afternoon on the phone, in a vain effort to learn more from the authorities in Spain, reporting to Sir Reginald in Vienna, and talking with a few old contacts in Washington. Then Grindstaff called.

"I'm passing the word for Bell," Grindstaff said. "The Houston police think they have located our man. Henryk Mickiewicz is his name. They're tracking him down now. We might be able to get there before they close in. How soon can you leave?"

"Two minutes," Loomis said. "But Johnson's out at the hospital."

"Call him," Grindstaff said. "We can pick him up on the way to the airport."

"Where's Bell?" Loomis asked.

"Bell and Ogden flew back to Washington."

"They left you as nursemaid?" Loomis said.

"That's about the size of it," Grindstaff said.

At the hospital, Grindstaff remained in the car while Loomis went into the Beach Pavilion Annex. Johnson was making a quick visit to Michael in recovery. Loomis waited until he came downstairs.

The Information Lady met them at the door.

"Be careful," she said.

"I beg your pardon?" Loomis said, thinking of Henryk, Hamlet, the job ahead.

"Muggers," she said. "You two be careful, walking around outside in the dark."

"Muggers? On a U.S. Army post?" Johnson said, incredulous.

The Information Lady nodded emphatically.

"Three cases in two weeks." She shook her head sadly. "No one is safe anywhere, anymore."

She followed them several paces toward the door.

"Be careful," she called after them.

Chapter

12

President Robertson sat with his third glass of bourbon, trying to compose a remark that would put his marathon meeting back on the right track. He had selected the six men in the room with care. Each was a trusted adviser, used repeatedly to good advantage in past crises. He had summoned them to Camp David for a specific purpose. Yet the whole weekend would be lost if he moved too fast. He had prepared them cautiously, keeping conversation and booze flowing freely throughout the evening. There had been good stories, well told, and much laughter. Robertson knew that his guests were puzzled as to why he had arranged the meeting. He did not ease their curiosity. He knew that the crucial subject must be broached at the proper time, and in the correct manner.

The vice-president had just concluded a lengthy and priceless description of a dialogue he had overheard between the House Speaker and the Majority Leader. His recounting of the dialogue was embellished with an unerring mimickry of accents and mannerisms. Robertson was only half listening to the anecdote. He had heard the story before. He tuned in as Vice-President Threadgill reached the punch line.

"And the Speaker turned to Theron and he says, 'You know, when Ol' LeRoy said he spent all night on his knees, praying to the good Lord for guidance, I believed him. And when he claimed the Lord laid His hand on his shoulder and said, "LeRoy, run for the U.S. Senate," I still believed him. Hell, I announced my support the very next day. But what I want to know is, who did that son-of-a-bitch talk to,

147

and who was advisin' him, when he decided to bolt the Democratic Party and to run as a goddamned Republican?' "

The room roared with laughter. Robertson smiled, not so much at the story as at the vice-president's enjoyment of the reaction. Threadgill's unhurried Oklahoma drawl often gave listeners the impression of pure corn pone. But Robertson knew there was not a more adroit politician in Washington. A Rhodes scholar, an authority on Renaissance art, the vice-president never tried to be other than himself. And he was extremely astute. He proved that now as he looked at Robertson and winked.

"But I'll bet Travis didn't get us up here at the taxpayers' expense to listen to my stories," he said. "I'll bet our president has some work for us to do."

Rising to his feet, Robertson crossed the golden carpet to the large gray stone fireplace. He turned to face the room, so that the large presidential seal over the mantel was behind him. He looked down thoughtfully at his glass of bourbon for a moment, giving the room time to adjust to the shift in mood, to view him in this perspective. When he spoke, it was direct to the vice-president.

"You're right, and you're wrong, Hank," he said. "I really came up here to hear some stories, of a kind. When I was a child, we used to sit around late at night, telling ghost stories to scare each other. That's what I want to hear tonight—some professional paranoia. I want to hear about the things that bother you in your darker moods, back in Washington."

"Hell, Travis, we'll be here till fall," the vice-president said.

"Hank, I just hope we'll all still *be* around next fall," Robertson said. He paused as expressions froze around the room. He took the cigar from his mouth and looked at it thoughtfully. "My own paranoia is really working overtime these days," he said.

He hesitated, considering how to put his request into better terms.

"What I want you all to do is to outline to me your

148

wildest fears, the worst thing you could imagine that could happen in your department. You already may have seen something that has made you wonder. Normally, you wouldn't even mention this thing to your best friend, or your worst enemy, because people would assume you've suddenly lost your marbles. But I want to hear about it tonight. And anyone who laughs will have to go into the other room and play dominoes with Hank."

"I can't conceive of worse punishment," the attorney general said.

Robertson now had everyone's full attention. He debated for a moment how best to proceed. Defense was the man he wanted most to draw out. But Defense Secretary Charles M. Harlowe was a self-made man, restrained, formal, tense, continually on guard. Robertson decided to carry the ball himself for a while.

"I have had some very disturbing reports, from several sectors, during the last few days," he said. "We have some evidence that an unusual economic encroachment is being made into this country. We suspect things are happening, but we can't be certain. And if they *are* happening, we don't know how, or why."

After a moment's silence, Vice-President Threadgill probed gently. "In other words, you suspect that someone is quietly grabbing us by the balls."

"Hank, it gives me comfort to know I can always depend on your eloquence," Robertson said.

Threadgill grinned.

"Just for that, you can lead off," Robertson said. "Tell me. What is the scariest thing you believe this country is facing?"

The vice-president frowned and looked down at his hands for a moment. He then spoke with a seriousness Robertson rarely saw in him. "I assume, Travis, that we're just shooting the breeze here, that none of this is going beyond this room, at least for direct attribution."

"That's right, Hank," Robertson assured him. "I just want to get the benefit of your thinking. I want to know the worst you think might be happening, based on your observations."

"All right," Threadgill said. "I'll tell you. It's welfare. Now, I'm not talking about the economic burden. That's bad enough. What I'm talking about is what it's doing to the people. We've raised a whole generation that thinks the world owes them a living. They don't know how to work . . ."

Robertson nodded occasional agreement as Threadgill outlined the economic dangers of a nation on the dole, and what should be done about the whole welfare mess. Threadgill's contribution was not exactly what Robertson wanted. But the vice-president had set the proper mood. When he finished, Robertson tried to keep the conversation moving.

"Anyone have anything to add to Hank's thoughts?" he asked.

The attorney general leaned forward in his chair. "Well, that's all tied in closely with crime, of course—and my department," he said. "Aside from the crimes of passion, or those to support a drug habit, there's only one thing that makes a criminal. He has the mistaken idea that society owes him a living. If society doesn't provide him with the means for the standard of living to which he thinks he's entitled, he'll make up the deficiency."

Robertson nodded. He prodded gently. "What possibility scares you most in your job?" he asked the attorney general.

"Civil disorder," the attorney general said without hesitation. "Not organized rebellion. Just pure rampant disorder and widespread looting that could get out of control. We've seen it to some degree, first over Vietnam, then during the New York blackouts. If it ever became general, either through militancy for some cause, or through adept terrorist leadership, this country would be doomed. . . ."

Robertson sat and listened patiently for more than twenty minutes while his attorney general outlined the threats posed to the nation by crime and low public morality. When the attorney general concluded, the matter was further explored in a free-for-all discussion. Robertson noticed that Defense

Secretary Harlowe was not taking part. Robertson waited for a lull in the discussion, then turned to Harlowe. "We haven't heard from you, Charlie," he said. "You have anything scary over at Defense, other than the obvious?" he asked.

For two heartbeats, Robertson thought that Harlowe was not going to participate. But after staring at the carpet for a moment, Harlowe nodded his head. "There have been a few things," he said. "Nothing significant enough to hit the panic button over. Yet . . ."

Robertson now was certain he was on the right track. He prodded again, gently. "We're talking about panicky things," he said. "Come on, Charlie. What's the worst thing you can imagine that would happen in your department, aside from nuclear exchange?"

"Penetration of our computer network," Harlowe said.

Surprised, Robertson asked his next question from reflex. "Could that happen?"

Harlowe shrugged. "We take every precaution. But who knows? If you remember, a programmer, working on a terminal from his own home, penetrated the system at the Federal Energy Administration a few years ago."

Robertson remembered the case, but vaguely. "He didn't really get anything, did he?"

"Thirty-nine rolls of printouts," the Secretary said. "Including the agency's entire top-secret computer program. With that in hand, he had access to everything."

A warning flashed in Robertson's mind: Harlowe knew the details of that case well. He had been checking, and recently. Obviously, something had instigated that search.

"How was he caught?" Robertson asked.

"By accident, pure and simple. He had penetrated the system several times before, without incident. But by sheer chance, an agency employee saw that his own sign-on code had been punched into the system. He wondered what in hell was happening. If that fluke hadn't happened, the guy probably would not have been caught. A million-to-one chance."

"What was he after?"

"I don't think that was ever established to everyone's satisfaction. He may have just been piddling around, seeing what he could do. But he had access to data on offshore oil leases, secret energy contingency plans, and so forth. I suppose he could have found something profitable there."

Robertson considered the information. "If the worst happened, if someone penetrated *your* system, what could he get?"

"That would depend on the level of penetration," Secretary Harlowe said. "The system is compartmentalized, rigidly. But if a hacker signed on at a high enough priority, he could manipulate the system, enter the Interface Message Processor, which would give him access to most anything."

"Well, you take the prize, Charlie," Robertson said. "That's the scariest thing I've heard tonight. You mean that some guy could sit in his home, with a keyboard, and tap onto anything in the Defense networks?"

"In theory," Harlowe said. "Actually, he'd have to be one hell of a genius. Or else, like the guy in Maryland, enough prior knowledge to start fishing."

Robertson asked his next question carefully. "Have you had any indication anything like that is happening?"

Harlowe answered hesitantly. "Some of our electronics people seem to think so. To use their terminology, computer hackers seldom leave tracks. There has been no solid evidence. But some unusual things have happened, I'm told. A machine will be activated mysteriously, at times that do not conform with standard use. The programmers have found some odd material in the system of no known source."

Robertson did not understand. "How could that happen?"

"Apparently someone put it in. We can't determine who."

Robertson felt a chill up his backbone as he grasped what the Secretary was saying. "You mean someone from outside not only could take out, but also *put in* material?"

"Not only material, but computer commands, too," the

Secretary explained. "You see, we are at the mercy of the software. There is a classic example. A few years ago, a large bank in Texas bought a comprehensive computer system from IBM. But IBM didn't have the software they needed. So the bank leased software from another firm. Through error or bad management, the bank got behind in payments on the lease. The software firm kept complaining, but the bank continued to be late with the monthly payments. Then one day, right in the middle of business, the computers shut down. The IBM servicemen were called. They could find nothing wrong. When they took out the leased software, and put in the IBM standard program, the system worked fine. But when they took the IBM program out, and put the leased software back in, the system shut down again. Then the truth came out. The software firm had programmed the system so that if a check was not sent to the software firm by a certain date, the command automatically was issued for the system to shut down."

Robertson did not bother to join in the laughter. He could see the Secretary's point. He waited until reaction to the anecdote had faded. "Could that happen to the Defense Department computers?"

"Mr. President, if I understand what I am told, there could be a Trojan Horse in *any* computer, assuming someone who knew what he was doing had access to it."

"I asked for scary stories," Robertson said. "But Charlie, you're overdoing it."

Harlowe released one of his fleeting smiles. "I just wish I had something more definite, one way or the other," he said. "I don't like to deal in this hazardous speculation."

"Perhaps this is a case where we *should* speculate," Robertson said. "Aside from that bank in Texas, has this been done elsewhere?"

"There have been several isolated cases," Harlowe admitted. "Usually, the penetration is the result of a prank. Like a case not long ago at a Midwestern university. A graduate student inserted a sort of time-bomb, kiss-my-ass message, to be printed out on all twenty-six terminals, after his graduation. Then the system was to shut down. Fortunately, a programmer, hunting for something else, found the erratic command before it was executed."

"Assuming that someone does gain access to the Defense system, someone who knows what he is doing, what would be the worst command he could insert?"

Harlowe did not have to stop and think. To Robertson, that spoke volumes. Apparently much work had been done at Defense on the problem.

"Erasure of memory banks would be the absolute worst," Harlowe said. "That would wreck the system, at least until they could be restored. Erratic commands, substituted for authentic commands, would be difficult to detect until too late. The system could be ordered to shut down, do strange things."

"So our computer systems at Defense could become our Achilles' heel," Robertson said. "Tell me, if the big crunch came, could we do without them?"

"I can best answer that this way," Harlowe said. "The Social Security computers process and mail more than thirty million checks each month. Imagine suddenly going back to doing that by hand. Our system at Defense dwarfs the Social Security system. Of course, if such a personnel switch-over were possible, we would need top-secret clearance on a large percentage of those people."

"In other words, we're married to the computer."

"I'm afraid you're right, Mr. President."

The talk went on as the Secretary of State discussed the situation in the Middle East; the Secretary of Health, Education, and Welfare voiced his fears of world famine; and a round-robin debate evolved over the probably disastrous effects of long-range energy shortages.

Robertson only half listened. He kept rethinking what his Secretary of Commerce had said, and what his Secretary of Defense had just outlined.

He could not quite manage the connection.

But he knew instinctively that the fears of those two experienced men fitted together.

And he could not help but notice that everything he had learned of Hamlet's potential pointed toward brains, instead of physical action—the missing plutonium, the mysterious manipulations of corporations, surreptitious computer espionage.

He wondered again.

Could Sir Reginald have made a mistake in selecting Loomis—a man of action—to head his investigation?

And had his own Administration similarly been wrong in depending on cold warriors, the legacy of past generations, in dealing with new problems?

Chapter

13

George Hampton would not have thought it possible. Under Sheila's skillful ministrations, he was soon ready to go again. He really was not in the mood.

He went to work, as Sheila expected him to do. But within minutes, he knew the effort was hopeless. He had too much on his mind. He had his orders from Hamlet. His bags were packed. He had his plane tickets and itinerary. Everything that linked him to Hamlet had been destroyed. He was ready. All his bridges were burned.

All except Sheila.

He abandoned the effort but remained in place. Sheila looked up, puzzled, still in the long, deep breaths of passion.

"What's the matter?" she asked.

He waited a moment before speaking. "I've got to go away for a while," he told her.

Sheila sighed, shifting to arrange herself more comfortably

under him. "I've got to hand it to you, George," she said. "You really know when to bring up a new subject."

Somehow, he felt he owed her an explanation of what he was about to do. "I'm into something big," he said.

"I hope you're talking business," she said. "Not anatomy."

He nodded distractedly. "This is something I've been working on for many years, along with some friends."

"Well, I hope it works out for you, George," she said. "But frankly, if I were a hundredth as wealthy as you, I would forget about money for the rest of my life."

He would never be able to make her understand. "Money—big money—tends to put you in a certain category," he told her. "It becomes an obligation to do something with it."

Sheila turned her head on the pillow to look at him for a moment, puzzled. Then her expression changed. "Maybe I kind of know what you mean," she said. "I once saw some of your daddy's letters."

"You what?"

Sheila put her palms on his shoulders. "Don't get mad, now. You had me looking for a realty deed. Remember? A lease out around Odessa? I found some letters. In one of those old files. I read them before I realized what they were. Maybe I shouldn't have. But I'm glad I did. It made me understand you a little better. Your father talked to you like his personal slave. Do this! Do that! If you don't measure up, boy, I'm gonna cut you off without a penny!"

Hampton was shaken. He had not known that those letters still existed. For a moment, he thought about returning downtown, searching for that old file, and destroying them. But he did not have time. He was on a tight schedule. And the clock was moving.

He tried again. "I've got to go away, to be with these friends, who are very, very influential. You would recognize every one of their names if I told you. We have been working on this plan for many years. And what we're going to do—well, we're going to take over the world."

Hampton did not get the reaction he expected. Sheila stared at him, amazed, then burst into a fit of giggling.

"I've always figured you had big plans," she said. "But really . . ."

Hampton moved his elbows up, placing his forearms across her biceps, blocking her arms from movement. He massaged her neck, as he had done thousands of times before, his thumbs resting on her throat, lightly.

"Anyway, that is what we are going to do," he said. "Actually, we are far along with our plans. In fact, we're now ready to act. Remember the nuclear bomb in Santo Domingo?"

"Hamlet?"

He nodded. "That's us," he said. "Hamlet."

Sheila struggled to turn her head. "That was *you?* That terrorist group?"

"That is us," he corrected her. "And we're not a terrorist group. We're a cartel—an international cartel. Santo Domingo was just a ruse, an announcement of our existence, a diversion. But now, we're really ready."

Sheila's face was now devoid of expression. "Why are you telling me this?" she asked.

He put his face close to hers, hoping that he could make her understand. "I've got to go, you see. I can't take you with me. And I can't leave you behind."

She must have felt the pressure of his thumbs for the first time.

Recognition of what was about to happen came to her eyes.

"I just wanted you to understand that this really has nothing to do with us," he said.

"George, I've always known you were a cold-hearted bastard," Sheila said softly. "But this really takes the cake."

She began struggling, then. He squeezed with all his strength. They fought furiously, Sheila attempting to reach his face with her nails, thrashing wildly in an effort to toss him off her body. But he had her arms pinioned, and he rode her, securely in the saddle.

He had read, or heard, that in death throes the vagina constricts in a series of exquisite movements. He had expected something exotic to happen. But nothing happened that was remotely exotic.

Sheila's eyes bulged, permanently. Her lovely skin turned dead white, then blue. By the time she ceased struggling, she was not even pretty anymore. What little desire Hampton had retained left him.

He went into the adjoining bathroom and showered. He soaped his body several times, rinsing her scent away as thoroughly as he could.

When he returned to the bedroom, he made one hurried check to reassure himself that she was truly dead. He then pulled the sheet over her naked body. He dressed hurriedly, and in a moment of inspiration, turned the air-conditioning thermostat down to the minimum—sixty degrees.

With any luck, despite the muggy, humid Houston climate, she would not be found for two or three days.

That would give him plenty of time.

The first Rapier battery was located on the roof of an electrical-supply factory several miles south of Perth Amboy, only a few minutes off the Garden State Parkway. Hampton, alone in the Avis Ford he had rented at JFK, carefully slowed for the exit at Keansburg. He could not afford an accident. He wanted to leave no trace of his visit to New Jersey.

As he expected, the gates of the plant were closed. A tall, slim security guard heard Hampton's honk and approached the chain-link gate indifferently. He was holding back a German shepherd that seemed much more interested in earning his pay. Hampton left the car and walked up the graveled drive to the gate. The dog stuck his nose to the wire mesh, sniffed at Hampton's crotch, and growled.

"I believe you were told to be expecting me," Hampton said, gingerly poking the carefully contrived identification card through the gate, taking care to keep the rest of his body at a safe distance. "Mr. Arnold was to notify you."

The guard hitched up his heavy gun belt, loaded with a marvelous array of gear—pistol, handcuffs, nightstick, ammunition, walkie-talkie, Mace—all hanging precariously on his hipless frame. He had long, yellowed buck teeth. A dribble of tobacco juice had escaped from the corner of his mouth unnoticed, and dried on his chin. He studied the card for a time with blank incomprehension. Then he remembered.

"Oh! That was a week or so ago. Yes, sir. Mr. Arnold said you'd come by some night. To watch for you. Yes, sir. A week or so ago."

"I didn't know when I'd be able to make it down here," Hampton said. "If you'll please open the gate, and hold the dog . . ."

"Yes, sir," the guard said. Detaching a wad of keys from his gun belt, he tackled the big padlock.

By the time Hampton restarted the car, the gate was open. He drove through and circled up the drive to the high-rise, prestressed concrete structure defined on his diagram as the administrative office building. The guard hurriedly closed the gate, locked it, and trotted across the lawn to meet Hampton at the front door. The dog was now running free, sniffing at Hampton's footprints.

"Is it all right for that dog to run loose?" Hampton asked.

"Oh, yes, sir," the guard said, now searching for the key to the front door. "You see, if I let anybody in the gate, then he knows it's okay. He won't bother them. He's smart, that dog."

Hampton was glad the situations of the dog and the guard were not reversed. A smart dog might question a phony I.D.

"As Mr. Arnold probably told you, I'll be going up to the experimental unit on the roof," Hampton said. "I'll be up there about an hour. I don't want to be disturbed."

"Oh, no, sir. You won't be," the guard assured him, opening the door. "We've got tight security up there. Special doors. Special locks. No admittance, 'cept to authorized personnel. That's Mr. Arnold's orders."

Hampton grunted. All that Plant Manager Arnold knew

was that an experimental solar unit had been installed on a section of the roof, under direction of the parent company. He had been informed only that security was deemed necessary because the solar grids utilized a revolutionary new concept, and there was considerable danger of industrial espionage.

Arnold had not been told that also on the roof were thirty-six mortars, along with matching star shells of magnesium and plutonium. Although the solar unit was in place, the mortar battery remained in the packing crates. Hampton now had to uncrate and install the deadly arsenal.

He estimated that the job would take him about an hour.

"There's a dead-bolt lock on the big steel door they put in up there," the guard said as they walked toward the elevator. "I got the key to that. But there's a Prest-O-Matic."

"I have the combination," Hampton said.

Six flights up, the elevator opened on a narrow corridor, leading to a huge metal door. After five false attempts, the guard found the right key in his wad and turned the dead-bolt lock.

"Thank you," Hampton said pointedly. He waited until the guard was back in the elevator before he punched out the combination on the Prest-O-Matic.

A single bulb provided faint illumination for the entire roof. The huge solar panels loomed high in the semidarkness. In case anyone should snoop around, they were indeed functional. The elaborate gears and rachets now had the plates angled toward the east, awaiting the first rays of the sun, still more than nine hours away. Hampton walked past the panels and studied the crates.

Three contained the mortars—six-, eight-, and ten-inch barrels designed for professional fireworks displays. Each crate contained a dozen of each size.

The ratio of lift was roughly a hundred feet per inch of mortar caliber. The three mortar sizes would yield a spread of bursts at six hundred, eight hundred, and a thousand feet.

The ammunition was in the fourth crate, larger and much heavier.

A small crowbar and a large flashlight lay on top of the first crate.

Trane Thornsen thought of everything.

Hampton opened a crate. The mortars were packed firmly, the barrels fitted into notched wooden cradles.

One by one, Hampton placed the mortar barrels on the graveled roof, beneath the solar panels. He then unpacked the black-powder base charges, and distributed them beside the barrels. By the time he had all thirty-six mortars and charges unpacked and in place, he was sweating profusely. He stopped work and walked to the edge of the building to take advantage of the faint breeze. Safely away from the black powder, he lit a cigarette.

To the northeast, across Lower Bay, he could see the reflected lights of Brooklyn, Staten Island, Queens, Manhattan, the whole mess—an aurora borealis of eight million people.

Few would notice when the mortars were fired. If someone on Coney Island happened to be looking southwest at the right moment, he might see a fan of bright lights low on the distant horizon, and he might wonder.

The whole thing would be over in a little more than three minutes. After the mortars fired, the shells would arc into the air. The magnesium would ignite at the peak of the climb. The plutonium would burn. A small parachute would open, lowering the deadly, burning cargo gently to earth.

By the time the security guard collected his wits and called the police, the flares would be gone. The incident would be past history.

And so would be a lot of people.

Hampton stamped out his cigarette and returned to work. He carefully inspected the specially prepared concrete base for the mortar battery. Reinforced by heavy, structural steel I-beams, the long block would absorb most of the recoil.

After lowering each mortar tube into its designated hole,

Hampton connected the wires to the electrical detonators and made certain that each was seated properly in the tube.

He then lowered the black-powder lifting charges into place.

Gently, Hampton lifted the lid on the ammunition crate.

Each shell was nestled into its own bed of plastic worms to cushion it on the long ride from Houston. Using both hands, Hampton carried the first shell over to a mortar, lowered it into the barrel, and released it. The shell settled to the bottom with a soft hiss of escaping air.

After loading the rest of the barrels, Hampton connected the wiring. The elaborate hookup took only a few minutes. With simple jacks and colored wires, there was no way Hampton could go wrong.

The job was done.

Hampton replaced the side skirts on the solar system and stepped back, making certain all was in order.

The mortars were hidden from view, even if someone should gain access to the roof. The weaponry also was hidden from the air, in case a low-flying plane, helicopter, or surveillance satellite should make a visual check.

If all went as planned, the mortars would fire through the greenhouse-glass of the solar unit.

Plant Manager Arnold had been told that the network of special wiring and telephone terminals was required in order to feed data from the solar panels into the central office in New York. That much was true. But Arnold was not told that the Manhattan office housed a computer that conversed almost constantly with other computers in Hamlet's worldwide grid.

Hampton left the wooden crates stacked neatly under an overhang of the roof housing. He closed the metal door behind him, tested to make certain the Prest-O-Matic had reengaged, then turned his own key in the dead bolt. He pushed the button for the elevator and checked his watch.

Fifty-five minutes.

He was ahead of schedule. He had estimated that an

average of an hour and a half would be required for each site.

But this was the smallest battery, and did not offer a true test of the schedule.

He returned to the car, waved his thanks to the security guard, and drove back toward the parkway, stopping only briefly to study his map.

He drove the ten miles to the next site, a farm near Old Bridge. Once used as a dairy, the 320-acre place had been acquired by Hamlet three years or more ago.

Leaving the main, black-topped road, Hampton drove down a narrow lane to a group of low, fallen-down outbuildings that once had served as the dairy's barns and milking sheds. He stopped at the heavy wire gate. Leaving the car, he climbed the fence and walked to the buildings, where forty-eight mortars awaited assembly—along with the special device Hampton himself had designed.

Working steadily, Hampton armed the mortars—eight-, ten-, and twelve-inch tubes—and inserted the projectiles.

He then turned to his special device.

From the west Texas oil fields, Hampton had purchased several twenty-foot lengths of seamless, twenty-four-inch oil pipe. These had been cut in half. A three-inch base plate was welded onto one end of each section.

The two twenty-four-inch sections—and forty-eight others —were now buried nine and a half feet in the ground, in an arc across New Jersey and Pennsylvania, into upper New York State.

With his flashlight, Hampton checked the buried pipe, making certain that the electrical detonator was firmly fixed in place in the butt-plate.

He then rigged a small tripod over the hole.

Using extreme caution, he uncrated the one-hundred-and-seventy-five-pound projectile that would be fired two thousand feet into the air by the device.

He carried the charge over to the hole. Assuring himself that the projectile remained undamaged after shipment halfway around the world, Hampton hooked the chain hoist to the tripod, and carefully eased the projectile into the hole.

He then removed the tripod, and covered the hole with a thin sheet of plastic.

He could not help but be amused.

The six inches of pipe sticking out of the ground seemed so harmless.

No one would guess that out of that rusty old pipe would come one of the deadliest projectiles ever made by man— simple, but in its way far more effective than the sophisticated devices housed in multimillion-dollar missile silos.

The projectile was Hampton's own invention.

From his early oil-field experience driving a nitro truck, Hampton had developed an affinity for explosives.

When Trane Thornsen first suggested the use of plutonium pollution, Hampton immediately had thought of commercial fireworks. He had set out to find the best.

The blockbuster of the fireworks displays at state fairs, water carnivals, and rodeos was a huge charge commercially labeled Brocade Crown Chrysanthemum. Its Japanese name translated as "a million flowers."

Lofted by a five-pound charge of special black powder, the projectile was designed to climb two thousand feet, then burst into an awesome display of brilliant stars of every hue.

Fortunately, July Fourth celebrations had provided plenty of opportunities for testing the device. More than two hundred were fired—at $1,800 a shot.

Hampton once had attempted to photograph the burst of "a million flowers." From two miles away, he was unable to get the entire display in frame.

He knew then that he had found Hamlet's basic weapon.

Purchasing a Japanese fireworks firm, Hamlet had produced devices identical to the Hosoya Fireworks Company's Brocade Crown Chrysanthemum, with one essential difference.

Distributed among the chemicals that provided each projectile's many colors were three pounds of plutonium.

Hampton left the packing crates and other gear in place. After connecting the battery's wiring to the central cable junctions, he switched on the proximity alarm system.

He then hurried back to the car.

Almost two hours had elapsed. He was now behind schedule.

And he had two more sites to arm before midnight.

Two nights later, Hampton returned the Ford to Avis at Kennedy. He claimed his baggage and took a taxi into Manhattan for a good night's sleep at a celebrated hotel facing Central Park. There, in the ornate bathroom, he burned his map, his false identity cards, and other pocket clutter, dropped the ashes into the commode, and flushed it.

There now was no way to connect him with his tour across New Jersey, Pennsylvania, and upper New York State, even if anyone tried. But then, very likely no one would.

Sixteen sites armed with more than seven hundred and fifty mortars would soon scatter more than a thousand pounds of plutonium ash into the atmosphere, over one of the world's most densely populated regions.

Despite the uncertainties of the results, the known factors staggered the imagination.

Millions of people would die quickly, of massive fibrosis of the lungs. The exact number would depend on many variables—wind conditions, distribution, thermals, and so forth.

Those who died quickly would be the most fortunate.

Millions more would be doomed to a slower, horrendous death. The dying would not be able to bury the dead. There would be no escape, no place to hide. There would be no cure, even if facilities existed. Not even the terrible Black Plague of 1347, which destroyed one-fourth the population of Europe, could compare with the devastation Hampton had just prepared.

The destruction of the American Northeast would be virtually total.

True, some members of Hamlet believed Rapier would not have to be used.

Hampton was not among them. He was certain that the elimination of the Northeast would be a necessary first step. He did not believe that the U.S. government would heed the Ultimatum.

The entire Northeast, from New Jersey to Maine, would become a stark, afflicted land, filled with pestilence and death.

The reaction of the remainder of the country would be interesting.

Would other states respond to appeals from survivors in the Northeast? Would missionaries and medical help enter, despite remaining high levels of alpha-particle radiation? Or would the area be quarantined—fenced in, with the victims being turned back at the borders, and driven away from the doors of the more fortunate, as happened during the Black Plague of the Middle Ages?

Hampton would watch the results with interest. But what the people did really would not matter.

Within months of Hamlet's takeover, his own programs would be instituted. The nation would be regimented, organized, made productive beyond all current standards.

The Northeast would be written off.

Chapter

14

Fortunately, Henryk had dealt before with the bank teller—a large, wide-faced blonde who addressed him by his false identity even before he wrote the withdrawal check.

But she hesitated at the amount, looking up to make certain Henryk was not joking. Tellers do not hand out fifty thousand dollars in cash every day.

Not even in Houston.

"How do you want it?" she asked.

He had anticipated the question. "Hundreds would be fine," he said. "Unless you have anything bigger you want to get rid of."

He smiled to let her know the comment was an inside joke, that he was aware of the fact that bigger bills were now restricted to transactions between the Federal Reserve System and the Treasury Department. She smiled back.

"Excuse me a moment," she said. Turning to a phone at the back of the booth, she cupped the receiver into a plump right shoulder, facing away from Henryk. Although he strained to hear, he could not make out her words. As she talked, she summoned a readout on a display terminal. Henryk could not see the screen.

When she at last hung up and turned back to face him, she was not smiling.

"If you will come this way," she said.

Henryk followed her to the end of the row of tellers' cages. She emerged from behind the counter and escorted him across the bank lobby.

"The basement," she said, heading for the escalator.

Henryk walked meekly beside her. A bank guard apparently had been given a signal. He fell into step behind them.

Henryk began to panic.

"There's nothing wrong, is there?" he asked, making every effort to keep his voice conversational.

She glanced at him without expression.

"We have certain procedures on all large cash withdrawals," she said.

Henryk nodded, as if that explained everything.

It did not. He concentrated on placing his feet correctly on the escalator, his mind racing.

He forced himself to keep calm as they descended slowly into the basement.

He could not shake a growing premonition of impending doom.

Repeatedly, he had been over every detail. He was almost certain that José's death could not be traced to him.

Yet there were disturbing signs.

Carl had not called, as he had promised to do.

And Henryk knew the rules incumbent on everyone involved in assassination.

He was the only living tie between José and Carl.

Therefore, he was expendable.

He had remained in his apartment as long as he dared, awaiting Carl's call. But as his doubts grew, he began searching for alternatives.

There was only one: he would have to get the hell out of the country. And that would take money.

Then he had remembered the additional cash on deposit, awaiting transferral to José's account on completion of the Colorado job. Henryk was a signatory on the account. There was no reason he could not withdraw it.

Unless Hamlet had made other arrangements.

"This way," the teller said, leading Henryk past the Master Charge offices, the savings windows, the entrance to the safe-deposit boxes. A young, thin-haired executive was waiting.

"This is Mr. Wilson," the teller said. "He will take care of you. If you will excuse me, I must get back."

Henryk thanked her, discovering in the process that his mouth was surprisingly dry. He shook hands with Wilson and followed him into a small office. Wilson closed the door. The bank guard waited outside. Wilson walked around behind his desk, adjusted the vest of his navy pin-striped suit, hitched up his trousers, and lowered himself gently into a chair.

"As I'm sure Miss Madison explained, this is a mere formality," Wilson said. "You understand, with all that is going on these days, we must take precautions."

He smiled knowingly.

Henryk waited.

"First, we are reluctant to hand out that much money in public," Wilson said. "You know, someone might be watching, and follow you out."

He smiled again.

Henryk smiled back. He felt considerable relief. He thought he had just received an indication that he was going to get the money.

"And there are other considerations," Wilson said. He paused.

Henryk stopped breathing.

"We must make certain that you are doing this of your own volition. By that I mean someone might be holding a gun on you. Or they might be holding your family. Or something."

Henryk laughed weakly. He had not planned this far ahead. "Nothing like that," he said. "I . . . just need the money."

"Well, it is not our purpose to inquire into the necessity of cash," Wilson said. "We just want to make certain everything is all right."

"Everything is all right," Henryk said.

"And we would prefer that some protection be arranged."

"No need," Henryk said. "I mean, a simple black bag. Who would know?"

Wilson nodded, hesitated again, then pressed a button. "Send Pete in," he said.

Henryk waited with considerable apprehension to learn Pete's identity. Another guard walked in, carrying a bank satchel. Wilson dumped the contents on the desk.

"Fifty to a bundle, ten bundles," he said. "I will wait until you count it. . . ."

"No need," Henryk said, unable to take his eyes from the money.

If his death warrant had not been issued by Hamlet before, it would be now.

"We would prefer that you did," Wilson insisted.

Henryk picked up two bundles, hefting them. He glanced at his watch with studied casualness.

"I know it's nearly your closing time," he said. "I doubt that my count would be more accurate than yours."

For the first time, Wilson seemed to lose some of his self-confidence. "We will be here several hours," he said. "We close the bank doors at two, but most of us will be here until five, at least. You are perfectly welcome to use this office."

Henryk picked up the bundles, one by one, as if calculating the thickness of each bundle.

"I do have an appointment," he said.

"As you wish," Wilson said. "If you will just sign this."

Henryk signed the form, remembering at the last moment to use his assumed name. He zipped his bag closed, and shook hands with Wilson.

"A pleasure," Wilson said.

Henryk could not help but notice, as he turned to close the door, that Wilson was reaching for the phone.

Henryk rode the escalator back up to the main floor and headed across the nearly deserted bank lobby toward the front doors.

As he left the bank he had reason to suspect, for the first time, that he had made a serious mistake.

A tall, gangling youth was standing just outside the bank

entrance, staring at Henryk. Their glances met, and locked. Then the youth looked away. But he continued to stand beside the building.

Henryk saw an empty taxi approaching. On his frantic signal, the driver reluctantly cut across two lanes and stopped, angled in toward the curb. He regarded Henryk with undisguised ill humor.

"Where to, buddy?" he asked.

"Post Oak Galleria," Henryk said. He resented the driver's attitude. But he was in no mood to make an issue of it.

As the cab pulled away from the curb, he looked back, studying the downtown streets. The tall youth was gone. He could see nothing amiss.

All day, he had sensed that he was being followed. In his twelve years of major and minor crimes, he never had felt so jittery. And the sense of doom lingered.

Granted, from Hamlet's viewpoint, he had been careless. He had allowed himself to be seen with José. There were witnesses—the bartender, the people in the bar, perhaps others.

Hamlet may have sent someone to San Antonio to keep tabs on him, to log his mistakes.

Henryk could hardly accept the probable fact that, after all his work, the decision had been made that he was to die.

But Carl's silence was most eloquent.

Henryk's orders had been to wait in his apartment.

And he *had* waited—longer than he would have under other circumstances.

But while he waited, he came to realize why Carl had ordered him to a certain place at a certain time.

The decision had been made to kill him.

So he had made his move.

He had survived too much to give up now.

As he approached the Post Oak Galleria, he felt easier. Maybe he was doing the right thing, for once. After Carl checked the apartment and found him gone, a cover would be put on the airports and bus terminals. His best bet would be to hide out for two or three days, then leave town.

He checked into the hotel attached to the shopping center. He showered, and sat for a time in his shorts, watching television. But the afternoon game shows were boring. Soon he was pacing the room in helpless desperation.

The thought came to him that perhaps his sanity was giving way at last. Certainly, he had every reason to expect that some day his mind would shatter. No one could endure more than forty years of mental abuse without some effect.

World War II may not have been staged for the sole purpose of harassing Henryk Mickiewicz, but for years he had harbored that impression. His father, a corporal in the Polish army, was killed in the first days of the war. Henryk realized he probably was fortunate in not knowing some of the things his mother did in order to survive.

Each night, she made certain that he still remembered the address of his aunt in Karnes County, Texas. The strange names were drilled into his brain. Throughout the early years of the war, she persisted in the delusion that someday her sister would be able to rescue them. Henryk's mother disappeared when he was eight.

Henryk himself had been bombed by one country or another until he was eleven—six years of dodging death, of fighting for survival. When he escaped from the Russian to the American zone after the war, and he was herded into a displaced persons camp, he doubtfully offered his aunt's name and address as a "sponsor."

Within weeks he was on his way to America.

Three months to the day after his thirteenth birthday, Henryk arrived in Texas, illiterate in every language, his speech a strange mixture of Polish, German, Czech, and Russian, along with a spattering of key English phrases such as "fuck you, Joe" and "son-of-a-bitch."

His bewildered aunt did not know what to do with Henryk. Her husband, a truck driver for a cattle company, could not stand the sight of him. For four miserable years, Henryk lived the life of a village idiot. English came slowly. School was endured until his sixteenth birthday. He then left the classrooms forever.

172

But when he at last fled Karnes County, a strange thing happened to Henryk. He found his wartime survival skills in demand. No matter that he still could not read or write well in any language. As a pimp, he was a Ph.D. He had passed the world's toughest exams in black marketing, smuggling, and fencing stolen goods.

The laws in his new country were different, but the methods of circumventing them remained the same. Henryk was an expert in a country filled with amateurs. His talents quickly came to light.

For a time, Henryk dealt in dope, mostly heroin and marijuana from across the Mexican border. Then came a big bust in Laredo. A pickup camper full of Mexican brown was seized. Henryk escaped charges. But all his money had been tied up in the load. Again, he had to change his line of operations.

That was when Carl first came to him with a simple job. Henryk was to move a sealed truck from a parking lot in Houston to a small suburban factory in New Jersey. Henryk had assumed that the truck was loaded either with dope or stolen goods. He felt better not knowing which. The pay was excellent. Henryk made several more trips. Other jobs came. Then, in a move he recognized as an advancement, he was hired as the go-between in securing the services of other people—burglars to steal specific merchandise, truck drivers who would follow orders without question. And, occasionally, there were assassinations.

He had engineered many deaths for Carl, and for whomever Carl represented. In one case, on Carl's orders, Henryk had eliminated the entire board of an oil company. He made arrangements for their private Beechcraft to disintegrate over Arizona, en route to a Los Angeles meeting.

A short time later, the oil company was acquired by a conglomerate.

There had been other, similar assignments. A Dallas banker died in a freeway collision. Cardiac arrest, suicide, and fatal illness had been arranged for a number of financial leaders and corporate executives.

173

Henryk did not dream up the plots. But he put them into execution.

After the publicity stemming from the Hamlet nuclear device in Santo Domingo, Henryk assumed that he had been working for Hamlet. When the assignment came to hire an assassination team for Johnson, he became certain.

And now, all the work he had done for Hamlet was arrayed against him.

He knew too much.

Henryk lay quietly, full length on the hotel bed, and attempted to calm himself.

But as the minutes crept by, he became convinced that he could not hide out for two or three days in the hotel.

Hamlet would find him. The organization had uncanny ways.

He had to travel far, and travel fast. The sooner he started, the better.

He could take a flight to Miami, then to South America. He would hide in some rural village.

There, with his fifty thousand dollars, he might have a chance.

In fact, the more he thought about it, the more he came to believe it to be his only chance.

Henryk dressed hurriedly. He did not bother to pack—not even a toothbrush. He would buy what he needed as he traveled. His briefcase would be enough to hold the money.

But as he headed toward the lobby exit, he saw a familiar face—the tall youth who had been standing outside the bank.

Henryk turned back into the lobby and quickened his pace. He had to find a crowd, fast.

The Galleria.

The large shopping mall, built in tiers around a central well that gave visitors a view of the ice rink on the lower level, was surrounded by shops that would be jammed on a Saturday afternoon.

He headed toward the central mall.

He glanced back.

The youth was still behind him, his head high, his eyes fixed on Henryk.

Henryk pushed his way to the left, headed into Neiman-Marcus, and sidestepped through the shoppers.

He trotted back onto the mall, toward an escalator and, shoving his way, moved past the other riders, reaching the lower floor just as the youth stepped onto the top steps. Mixing with the shoppers, he crossed the mall to the next escalator, and went up again, hoping to elude the youth.

He reached the top and, moving at almost a dead run, he hurried to a descending escalator. He went down the steps two at a time. At the next level, he looked up.

The youth was not in sight. Henryk had given him the slip, for the moment.

He was heading toward a street-level exit when he saw a sight that made him pull back abruptly, in a panic.

A phalanx of men was entering the Galleria.

He recognized the two in the lead. He would have known them anywhere, even without the large head bandage one of them was wearing. Their pictures had been in all the newspapers, on all television newscasts.

Loomis and Johnson had just entered the Galleria.

Henryk was certain that he was the reason they were there.

Chapter

15

"We have to take him alive," Loomis told the captain as they walked into the coolness of the air-conditioned mall.

"Loomis!" Grindstaff said, moving up beside them. "I'll handle this!"

Irritated, Loomis blocked Grindstaff's way. The time for secrecy, for procedural protocol, was long past. Yet, no one had told the Houston Police Department exactly what was happening. And through incredible bungling, matters were coming to a head in a shopping center, of all places. Loomis had never seen such rank, bureaucratic stupidity.

The Houston Police captain stopped, and turned to face Loomis. "I'll do my best here," he said. "But you people must understand that I'm not going to jeopardize my men, or any of these civilians."

Loomis held his temper. He would not help matters by making a delicate situation worse. He reached out and took the captain's arm in a firm grip.

Surprised, the captain jerked his arm by reflex in an effort to free it. Loomis held on, and bodily moved him to the rail near the escalators. He spoke low but intently.

"I don't know how much these federal numbnuts have told you about what's happening," he said. "But that man up there is key to a nuclear blackmail operation. If a thousand people have to die right here and now to keep him alive, we're still ahead."

"Loomis!" Grindstaff said loudly. "That is restricted information!"

Furious, Loomis turned on Grindstaff. "Listen, this man is in a supervisory capacity—of a police force we need. He has to make decisions. And he can't make the right decisions unless he has all the information."

Grindstaff's face was tight with anger. He stepped between Loomis and the captain. "If the police will just handle the civilians, our people will take all the risks," he said.

The captain was not intimidated. "This is my town," he told Grindstaff. "I think the rule is that you ask *me* to do the job. Politely."

Grindstaff and the captain stood glaring at each other.

Johnson came walking up. "Come on, for Christ's sake," he said. "Let's cut out this shit. Time's wasting."

"You can call my chief," the captain told Grindstaff quietly. "But he'll tell you the same thing I'm telling you."

Grindstaff hesitated. Loomis knew he was weighing the argument against loss of time.

"All right," he said. He turned to Loomis. "But you and Johnson are to stay out of sight. If you two are brought into it, no cover story we could devise would work."

The captain started for the escalator, with Loomis, Johnson, Grindstaff, several plainclothesmen, and a Galleria security guard close behind.

The moving crowds, the open shop fronts, the mingled music and noise, gave the mall a carnival atmosphere. Below, the ice rink was filled with skaters. All entrances to the Galleria were now covered, visually, by platoons of police and a sprinkling of Galleria security guards. Radio-equipped plainclothesmen were entering the upper floors, keeping Henryk in sight, alerting the entire force to his movements.

But there was no way Henryk could be separated from the swarms of shoppers.

As the phalanx of officialdom arrived at the top of the escalator, the captain unclipped the radio from his belt and spoke quietly into it for several seconds. An earpiece carried the reply directly to his ear. It was inaudible to Loomis, standing two feet away.

"He has moved onto the top level," the captain said quietly. "He keeps moving, constantly, in no set pattern. The feeling is that he recognized you when we walked in."

"Oh, shit," said Johnson.

Loomis shared his disappointment. With the element of surprise went the odds for taking Henryk alive. But maybe they were wrong. "What makes them think so?" Loomis asked.

"He was starting down, and reacted when we walked in. He stepped back from the escalator, then moved up a floor."

"We could wait," Grindstaff said. "He'll have to leave sometime, by some exit."

That would not work. Loomis explained why. "He would still be in the crowd. His best bet will be to try to walk out with a bunch of people."

The captain moved across the gallery floor to a storefront, still listening to the radio dialogue.

"He's sticking close to people," the captain said. "Right now, he's in the middle of a bunch of teen-agers at the central open court, on the second level, looking down at the skaters."

There had to be a way. "Maybe someone can get close enough to grab him," Loomis said.

"I'll go," Johnson said.

"He'd recognize you a block away," Grindstaff snapped.

"I've got some good men up there," the captain said. "We'll try it."

He spoke quietly into the radio. He waited for several seconds, listening.

"Brewer is strolling toward him now," he said. "Three more men are close."

He listened intently. "Goddamn," he said.

"What happened?" Grindstaff asked.

"He saw Brewer, and took off. He's moving fast across the top floor. He's wrecked our setup."

Loomis tried to put himself in Henryk's place, anticipating what he might do. "If he goes into a shop, we might seal him in," he said.

"He doesn't seem to be that dumb," the captain said. "He probably figures you people would burn a hostage or two, to get to him."

"We would," Grindstaff said.

The captain reached up and pushed the earpiece deeper into his ear, listening.

"This may be it," he said. "He's coming down."

His voice low, he spoke rapidly into the radio. "I'll call it from here. Carter, he's yours. Stay right where you are. When I give the word, step out and apprehend."

Across the open court, at the escalator, Loomis saw Carter nod his understanding. The captain moved back, motioning for Loomis, Johnson, and Grindstaff to get out of sight.

"Subject just stepped onto down escalator," the captain said into the radio. "Okay, now listen, Carter. Three teen-aged girls and two boys are on the steps in front of him. Three old ladies are right behind. Eight or ten others are on the ramp. He's halfway down, now. Remember, Carter. That escalator is going to keep dumping people right on top of you. Try to move him away from it, quick as you can. We're close. We'll be backing you up within seconds."

Carter's head nodded. Loomis could see two more plain-clothesmen approaching the escalator from behind Carter. But they were going to arrive too late to serve effectively as backup.

"Get set," the captain said. "He's two-thirds down. All positions unchanged. Carter, get between him and the teen-agers. Try not to take chances. Okay . . . Move!"

Carter's pistol came clear as he stepped out from behind the escalator railing. One of the teen-aged girls saw the gun and screamed. But instead of running out onto the floor, she retreated up the moving steps, still screaming. All six teen-agers backed up the escalator, creating a jam, with Henryk firmly pressed in the middle.

"Oh, shit!" Johnson yelled, breaking into a run toward the melee.

Loomis followed him. Although the action was only fifty feet away, the space was across an open well. The only way to get there was to go around.

Carter, gun still in hand, stepped onto the escalator. The knot of people was moving slowly away from him, backing up the escalator. The confusion grew as more bodies were fed into it from above.

The captain, running a few steps behind Loomis, yelled into the radio. "No! Carter! Back off!"

A dull boom reverberated throughout the Galleria. The echoes were drowned in screams from the crowd of shoppers. Carter turned away, took two hesitant steps, and collapsed.

"Dumb fucks!" Johnson yelled, now bearing down on the escalator.

"Carter's down! Subject going up the down escalator! Take him!" the captain shouted into the radio above the din.

The crowd, nurtured by a generation of television drama and assassination films, dropped flat on the floor. They lay in small clumps, heads down, awaiting the outcome.

Henryk fought his way to the top of the escalator, now emptying as it completed dumping its load.

Johnson, ahead of Loomis, jumped over the sprawled shoppers and took the steps three at a time. Loomis started up behind him.

"Alive!" he yelled at Johnson. "We want him alive!"

Johnson reached the next floor and disappeared from sight. By the time Loomis reached the top, Johnson was chasing Henryk toward the end of the mall. As Loomis watched, helpless, Henryk turned and fired. Johnson broke left, then right, and kept on running. Two uniformed policemen had their guns out but were waiting, the barrels pointed upward.

Running behind Johnson, Loomis saw movement in his peripheral vision. He looked up. A man stood on the next level, framed against the arched glass roof, aiming a rifle at Henryk. At first, Loomis assumed that the man was plainclothes, and would hold his fire, or else attempt to drop Henryk with a leg shot.

Then he knew.

"Henryk!" Loomis yelled. "Drop!"

And in that instant, Henryk saw the man, recognized him, and froze, staring.

Then the man fired.

Henryk dropped to the floor, spread-eagled, the top of his head missing.

The two policemen shifted their attention to the man with the rifle. The rifle swung in their direction.

"No!" Loomis yelled, attempting to stop the inevitable.

He was too late. Both policemen fired, and connected. The rifleman wheeled, dropped the gun, and stumbled crazily to the railing. He toppled over. His body made a graceful arc as it fell to a resounding splat on the ice on the bottom floor, narrowly missing a group of skaters who had stopped to watch the action.

Loomis walked over to the railing and looked down at the body.

There was no way the man could have lived.

Johnson came up to look, panting.

"Dumb fucks!" he said. "They blew it! But good!"

Loomis then walked back to look at Henryk's body. He stepped carefully around the scattered brains. The captain arrived with six detectives.

"Check that body out," the captain said, turning away.

The detectives found less than fifty dollars in cash, a hotel key, and a crumpled package of cigarettes.

"There's a bag or something under him," Johnson said.

A detective lifted the body by the belt, slid the small black bag free, and opened it.

"Jesus!" he said.

Loomis looked inside. The bag was full of hundred-dollar bills.

What he had feared would happen had happened. "I'll bet that's all we'll find," he said. "I'll bet the hotel room is clean."

"Probably," Johnson said. "Maybe we'll have better luck with that other fuck."

Chapter

16

Antonio Reale Giancarlo's position as Hamlet's philosopher was never questioned. Granted, others had contributed according to their own talents. Trane Thornsen was the acknowledged genius; he had provided the ambition, the perseverance, the nucleus, the techniques. Hampton perhaps had contributed the most actual work. The others were dedicated. But Giancarlo remained Hamlet's intellectual godfather.

In the beginning, Giancarlo had told the Hamlet Group: "We will need thirty years—a full generation. And by the end of the century, we will have the entire human race completely harnessed."

Giancarlo recalled that prophecy as his car crossed the Sûre at Pont Adolphe and maneuvered through the ancient streets of Luxembourg, turning northward on Côte d'Eisch, heading toward the Ardennes.

Hamlet now was ahead of his original schedule, by at least a decade.

Thornsen's mushrooming computer technology had helped immeasurably, of course. But mostly, Giancarlo reflected, the plan had progressed so well simply because the Hamlet Group had jelled into a team, functioning beautifully. Each member had contributed with strong, individual expertise. While each took full responsibility in a separate area of endeavor, none lost sight of the overall goal, coveted his own position, or felt resentment toward others. The long association, the long planning, had brought about a mutual trust and openness that was truly amazing.

And now the many years of planning, all the hard work, were about to bear fruit.

Beyond his animation, his excitement, Giancarlo felt most a strong sense of satisfaction.

He leaned back in the seat and relaxed as his driver slowed to begin the twisting, tortuous route through the incredibly green lushness of the Ardennes, following the banks of the Sûre.

Thirty kilometers beyond Luxembourg, Giancarlo's limousine slowed, made the final sharp turn to the left, then began the descent into the valley. In the distance, the castle stood silhouetted sharply against the trees.

Relatively modern, dating only from the early eighteenth century, and fully restored from its partial destruction during the Rundstedt Offensive of World War II, the castle had been owned through the 1950s by a Swiss banker. When he died in 1963, the distribution of his estate called for liquidation of all assets. The Hamlet Group, searching for such a place, had taken advantage of the bargain.

The castle had been a true stroke of luck.

As his limousine crossed the valley, Giancarlo studied the huge, rambling estate. There was nothing evident of the elaborate security facilities. By design, the entrance road curved in a gradual S across a carefully tended meadow, allowing ample time for the monitoring of visitors. Giancarlo knew that powerful zoom lenses, attached to closed television circuits, had followed his approach during the last two miles. The visual surveillance was activated by radar installations in the woods flanking the roads.

Two towers dating from the Middle Ages guarded the

approach at the rear. They were believed to be the only surviving structures from an earlier stronghold, built sometime in the twelfth century. In front of the castle, a six-foot native stone wall circled the grounds and extended into the distant trees. No casual observer would notice that the wall was electrically charged, and mined. Normally, the embedded wiring carried no current, and the explosives were safely hidden. But with the first hint of danger, the wires were charged with eighteen hundred volts, and the mines were activated. The rustic, pastoral fieldstone wall was far more effective than a moat.

The security system, staffed by experts gleaned from several countries, was not sufficient to hold off an army. But if necessary, the elaborate weaponry could delay an attacking force of several hundred men long enough for the Hamlet members to escape by predetermined routes.

The castle itself rose three stories above the paved courtyard. The shutters were not entirely decorative; they were half-inch steel, controlled by gears and motors to close on command from a central security desk. The roof was of fire-proof burnished copper. The four dormer windows jutting from the roof housed .50-caliber machine guns, which covered a full field of fire from the front of the building.

Giancarlo's driver slowed at the gate—a mere formality, for the car had been recognized and accepted several minutes earlier, or they would not have reached the house unchallenged. The entrance road also was heavily mined with explosives detonated by pressure devices activated from within the castle.

The gatekeeper, resplendent in period uniform, tipped his hat and waved them through. No one would suspect, from his formal demeanor, the vast armament he had at his disposal.

All of the security guards had been informed that the castle housed an advanced electronics research laboratory —one that reasonably could expect to be the target of raids by competing firms and, possibly, by foreign governments.

As Giancarlo's car circled into the parking area, Bernardo Perez came out the front of the castle to meet him.

"God, but I'm glad you're here," Bernardo said. "I'm worried sick about Trane. I just can't handle the full responsibility for him any longer."

Giancarlo felt a twinge of alarm. Thornsen was the key to the whole project. They could not allow anything to happen to him. Especially right now.

"Why?" he asked. "What's wrong?"

"He hasn't been upstairs for days. He hasn't shaved or taken a bath in a week. And he forgets to eat."

Giancarlo laughed, relieved. He poked Bernardo playfully in the soft overhang above his belt. "Come on. Trane's always been that way."

"Not like now," Bernardo insisted. "He won't even talk. When you say something to him, maybe he'll answer, maybe he'll wait five minutes. Sometimes he won't answer you at all. It's weird."

"He's got a lot on his mind," Giancarlo said.

"So have I. But I bother to answer people."

"Well, I'll have a talk with him, first thing," Giancarlo promised. "And you're right. We shouldn't put the full burden on you. He's learned your tactics. He has heard all of your lectures. Maybe he'll listen to me."

Despite Bernardo's warning, Giancarlo was shocked by Thornsen's complete dissipation. Always thin, he was now cadaverously emaciated, with deep hollows under his cheekbones. Unshaved, unwashed, he stared at Giancarlo with vacant, feverish eyes for a moment before recognition came.

"Hello, Giancarlo," he said. "Hail fellow well met."

In the old days, Thornsen and Giancarlo had made a sport of attempting to converse in Shakespearean phrases. Giancarlo grinned and slapped Thornsen affectionately on the shoulder by way of letting Thornsen know that he remembered. Then Giancarlo glanced around at the nerve center of the Hamlet network.

The computer room was filthy. The floors were awash in

computer paper, used cartridges from the high-speed printers, and other debris.

"Good Lord, Trane! What's happened to you?" Giancarlo asked.

Thornsen frowned, puzzled. "What do you mean?"

"You look like *hell*, that's what! Remember? I warned
you the last time I was here. Get some sleep! Eat! We need
you!"

Thornsen waved a hand at the mess. "The work," he
said absently. "It has to be done."

"Trane, listen to me," Giancarlo pleaded. "I've been
monitoring the logs. We're way ahead of schedule. And
with the Ultimatum, there'll be time to do things at our *own*
pace."

"No," Thornsen said, turning away. "You're wrong. We
can't lose our momentum now. Everything must be done in
the correct sequence, at the predetermined, precise moment. We can't let up, anywhere."

"All right," Giancarlo conceded. "We'll keep things moving. But we don't have to kill ourselves to do it. Come on,
Trane, we have years, decades, to do the things we need to
do."

"But that's just it!" Thornsen said, grabbing Giancarlo's
arm frantically. "There's not *enough* time. Each program in
each sequence needs its own command tree, feedback loops
for every eventuality, so the machine—the *machine!*—can
do its work. It has to be done!"

Giancarlo studied Thornsen's haggard face. Thornsen
would never allow anyone else to tamper with the machines. But clearly, he was now killing himself with work.

"Trane, can't we bring someone else in—a computer
person we can trust? Why couldn't we hire a whole platoon
of programmers, working under your direction? As I understand it, they wouldn't have to know the big picture. They
wouldn't know what was happening. They could take care
of some of the little details."

Thornsen shook his head emphatically. "No. That wouldn't
work. Don't you see? Every entry would have to be checked

anyway. Remember the Apollo missile that went off course just because someone at NASA left out a comma? That could happen to us. One comma or asterisk in a command string, one single error, could wreck us! And there are millions of possible errors. Every line has to be checked and triple-checked. It has to be perfect!" Thornsen's eyes had a feverish glint as he stared at the computers. "The machines simply do not permit human errors," he explained.

"Everything is going so wonderfully well," Giancarlo said. "But I tell you as a friend, Trane. If you keep this up, in six months you'll be dead. We can't afford that."

"Things have *not* gone so well," Trane said. He paused, his eyes focused on infinity, over Giancarlo's right shoulder. The silence lengthened. Either Thornsen's mind had strayed, or he was listening to something in the machines. Then he resumed talking as if there had been no interruption. "We've made errors. Santo Domingo, for instance. That bomb should have done what we wanted it to do."

"Still, we accomplished our purposes," Giancarlo argued.

"But we elicited only surprise—conventional response," Thornsen argued. "Not fear, not panic. So they now look upon us as just another terrorist group. They have measured us by their own half-bushel. Our other mistakes haven't helped. That clash with the CIA in Lisbon. And we failed to eliminate Loomis and Johnson."

Giancarlo nodded agreement. "True. But that was because we used third-rate people. We still haven't committed our best weapons—you, the machines. I think we're ready."

Thornsen looked at him intently. As he put a hand on Giancarlo's shoulder, Giancarlo could smell the Dane's strong body odor. When *had* he last taken a bath?

"Do you?" Thornsen asked. "Do you really think we're ready?"

"I've been monitoring your logs," Giancarlo said again. "I know your capabilities. And even if I had doubts, I would trust your judgment. If you say we're ready, we're ready."

Thornsen smiled. Thornsen had not been brushing his teeth, either.

Thornsen hugged Giancarlo with his bony arms. "You were always the one who pulled us back together when things went wrong. Can you do that now? Can you bring us all together, convince the others that we are ready? Bernardo is against it. I'm afraid he'll influence the others."

Giancarlo put an arm around Thornsen and led him toward the door. Maybe he could get him upstairs to eat, and to take a bath, and not necessarily in that order.

"Trane, don't worry about Bernardo and the others too much," he said soothingly. "You see, we're all different, and that is good. You, me, and Hamp were born with a wild hair on our ass. We get so wrapped up in what we're doing, what we're thinking, that sometimes we forget the real world. We *need* Bernardo and the others. They're the conventional thinkers. They worry. They remind us of things we might otherwise overlook. Let's listen to their worries. Then they'll listen to us. We have a wide spectrum of thinking in Hamlet. That's what makes us such a good team."

"I suppose you're right," Thornsen said.

"I am," Giancarlo said. He walked Thornsen up the steps to the castle. He patted Thornsen on the back. "We're simply the best," he said. "That's what makes us so dangerous."

After dinner, Giancarlo dismissed the servants. The seven members of Hamlet, carrying their brandies, filed into the huge baronial hall. Beneath the medieval armor and ancient trappings of war, Hamlet met to make a crucial decision.

Giancarlo had ordered a fire built in the huge hearth. With the lights turned low, the reflections of the soft flickering filled the room, providing an appropriate aura of warm camaraderie.

After all the planning, the years of expectation, the moment had arrived. Inevitably, the occasion brought with it a measure of sadness—and of trepidation. Clearly, they were entering a new phase—one wrought with uncertainties.

Seated at the long table, the group seemed unusually solemn.

Thornsen took the floor. Despite his pallor, Thornsen seemed to be in better shape. Giancarlo had cajoled him into eating a steak. He also had talked him into several hours of sleep. Fresh clothes helped. Thornsen now seemed more his old self.

He faced his friends with his slow, shy smile.

"I will bring you up to date," he said. "As you may recall from our last meeting, you gave me authorization to install Rapier, to be armed at my discretion. The job is now done, thanks to Hamp. Rapier is now armed and ready."

Thornsen then explained a number of minor but lengthy technical adjustments he had made recently to the Ultimatum. Changing conditions daily brought slight revisions to the program. But the basic plan remained the same. Giancarlo was thoroughly familiar with it, as was every member of Hamlet.

The first target was the United States.

Certain demands would be made. If they were ignored, Rapier would be fired. Thornsen estimated that 90 percent of the population downwind from the batteries would die —at least, maybe 30 million people.

In effect, the whole northeastern seaboard would be held hostage. If the United States did not cooperate fully with Hamlet, the hostages would be eliminated, and more seized. Other deadly mortars were ready. Sites were prepared near Chicago, Detroit, the Dallas–Fort Worth Metroplex, Houston, Denver, Phoenix, Los Angeles.

Yet, Hamlet's only demand would be that people do nothing. Hamlet would not demand money—nothing so crass and amateurish.

Hamlet would simply demand inaction while Hamlet's system worked.

Within weeks, the bulk of U.S. petroleum reserves and refineries would be absorbed by various dummy national and transnational corporations in mergers and acquisitions accomplished almost too rapidly for the eye to follow. The economic machinery was ready. The entire program of acquisition was stored in Thornsen's system, awaiting his keyboard command.

The petroleum takeover was only one of more than five hundred complex manipulations awaiting action.

The U.S. steel industry, the building industry, shipping, automobiles, and heavy machinery would be absorbed in carefully planned sequences. Controlled fluctuations in the economy would move U.S. gold reserves into various numbered accounts in Zurich and Bern, as further support for Hamlet's vast legerdemain.

After the United States, the rest would be easy.

Britain, Japan, and Germany would follow, along with France and the Scandinavian countries. They were integrated into a painstakingly considered plan of progression.

The Middle East, even Russia and China, eventually would be choked into economic submission.

After economic conquest, political takeover would be swift.

Hamlet's burgeoning computer banks would soon rule the world.

For the first time, all human life would be made 100 percent efficient. Eventually, Hamlet would issue routine directives to every individual on earth.

As Thornsen talked, Giancarlo studied the faces of the other five seated at the long table. He tried to guess how the voting would go. The group had agreed, long ago, that all major decisions would have to receive unanimous consent.

Three positive votes were certain: his own, Thornsen's, and Hampton's.

The other members of Hamlet were acting from various, deep-seated compulsions.

Giancarlo had spent long hours in studying his friends since that night, long ago, when they had pledged their lives to Hamlet. He knew the obsessions behind each member.

Trane Thornsen was driven by memories of the only close companionship he had ever known. In Hamlet, he had regained the family lost in early childhood. His parents had been heroes in the Danish Resistance, directing Allied bombers by flashlight to German military targets. After one raid, they did not come back. At ten Thornsen, hearing a name well known in Danish shipping, became the ward of various older aunts and uncles. Thornsen had worked himself almost literally to death seeking the acceptance, approval, that had been denied him in his boyhood. He doted on Hamlet's past, and forever made continual effort to rekindle, to relive, his most precious moments. Thornsen had a desperate need to show his friends, and the world, his genius. His fragile ego required constant reassurance. Hamlet's goals were deeply entwined with Thornsen's obsessions.

George Hampton's needs were much simpler. He was driven to prove himself better than his dead father, who had rejected him as unworthy of a place in a man's world.

The motivations of the other four were not so easily defined. To some extent, they had been trapped in the quicksand of Thornsen's strong emotions. He had worn down the resistance of other members by sheer persistence. Thornsen did not have the temperament for command. He wheedled his way over people. His ego required constant nourishment. No one could resist feeding that desperate hunger.

Through the years, Thornsen had moved from member to member, keeping the common dream alive. Giancarlo would have wagered that no member of Hamlet could say for certain exactly when he had become committed to the plan. Thornsen had kept talking the plan until all logic vanished, and nothing else seemed reasonable. Thornsen was both the wheedling child that continually must be pampered, and the guru-genius, a font for solutions to the problems of others. His hold on the members of Hamlet was complex, and immense.

In a sense, Thornsen served as the prototype, the psychiatric exaggeration of all Hamlet's members. Each had been born into a powerful and wealthy family. Each had experienced traumatic rejection. And each had felt challenged to excel beyond the wildest dreams of those who had shunted them to one side.

Each had been sent in the early 1960s to study at the University of Oklahoma. With the prescience of the truly wealthy, they had been assigned by family interests to study petroleum engineering in recognition of the role that energy was soon to play in the world's economy. The University of Oklahoma, at that time, had the best schools of petroleum engineering and geology in the world.

And there, in exile, alienated from campus life, the members of Hamlet inevitably drifted together.

They had much in common. To a man, they were the idle rich—intelligent, spoiled, social outcasts, unaccepted even by their own families.

One cold, snowy Christmas, with the campus virtually deserted, the seven were left alone in the big rooming house they shared. Under pressure of a weekend of marathon drinking, they mutually lamented their futures. They knew they faced a life of drudgery forced upon them by family expectations. To a man, they voiced strong rebellion. They, too, wanted the adventure, the sense of accomplishment experienced by their fathers and grandfathers.

In the drunken early-morning hours, as the talk had grown more animated, Thornsen in a blinding flash of inspiration had grasped a truth that previously had gone unnoticed. In that room in a boardinghouse in a small town in Oklahoma were gathered the heirs apparent to a large slice of the world's wealth.

Thornsen ignited two hours of unbridled excitement. With the fervor of youth, they made plans.

Each would return home and work himself into a position of power within the family structure. In ten years, twenty years, they would be ready to link their wealth, and assume control of a large portion of world economy.

Hamlet had succeeded even beyond those wild dreams.

Thornsen, the slide-rule freak, became the computer genius, the first to understand the leverage and power that computers eventually would command in the world.

And it was Thornsen who kept the dream alive, traveling, talking to other members, reminding them of the staggering possibilities.

Thornsen had organized Hamlet's early venture into computer technology. He assumed charge of product and development, concentrating on software more elaborate, effective, and economical than any offered by the competition.

And buried away in the millions of commands necessary to each program would be a sequence allowing Thornsen access to that entire system. This electronic trapdoor, a Trojan horse hidden away in the software sold to certain corporations, granted Thornsen use of any information in that system.

Thornsen also learned to tap other systems. Given enough time, he could find his way into any computer. But such painstaking work was not necessary. Disgruntled ex-employees, installers, and systems maintenance men would part with the necessary information, for a price. Tapped transmission lines could be monitored and analyzed.

Thornsen, the emotional child, the technological giant, had made Hamlet possible.

Now he stood before the members of Hamlet, smiling shyly, speaking with nervous urgency.

"I will never forget the night we dedicated our lives together," he said. "I knew then, on that wonderful night, that nothing could stop us. I want you to know now that I am ready to make any sacrifice. We still have problems. But working together, I know we can solve them."

He hesitated, hunting for words, overwhelmed by emotion.

Helpless for the moment, he motioned for Giancarlo to take the floor.

Giancarlo walked slowly to the head of the table. He turned and faced the members of Hamlet and stood for a moment, somewhat disturbed. Under the influence of Thornsen's emotional display, they were too somber. Now, at the point of action, they were hesitating. He would have to mesmerize them with his vision—with Thornsen's vision —as he had in the past.

He searched for common ground. He studied the four members of Hamlet he would have to work hardest to convince.

Bernardo Perez was frowning, fiddling nervously with a pen. Bernardo tended to vacillate in the face of every decision. An intellectual revolutionary in his teens, Bernardo had drifted with friends into the outlawed Aprista political party in his native Peru. In Hamlet, he found renewal of the political ambition he had experienced in his formative years. Yet, Bernardo retained a large portion of his basic, inherited conservatism. He would have to be convinced that the Ultimatum was the proper course.

Helmut Vogel had withdrawn into his aloof shell, his face expressionless. Helmut sought to recapture the glories of Nazi Germany he had witnessed in his childhood. He was convinced that Germany had lost the war only because of that peasant, Adolf Hitler. His family had supplied the world with arms for more than a century. Vogel would be cautious; he would not want Hamlet to lose.

Felix Zoff met Giancarlo's gaze with those cool, unwavering blue eyes. Felix viewed Hamlet as a world extension of his own orderly Swiss government, but one more effectively controlled and regulated. Zoff would have to be shown that the Ultimatum was the next logical step.

Ahmed Abdul Al-Turki sat staring into the fireplace. Ahmed's ambitions were simple: he wanted to rule the world. For some people, the planning of revenge became an end in itself. So it was with Ahmed. In a fit of temper he once had punched his crown prince in the nose. Only his family's position had saved him from worse than exile. Giancarlo would have to make Ahmed see that realization of a dream might be better than the dream.

"Thank you, Trane," Giancarlo said. "And allow me to say that, if it weren't for you, we wouldn't be here tonight, and we all know that."

Thornsen beamed. Led by Bernardo, the group broke

into applause. Giancarlo waited until the moment had subsided.

"But we *are* here," he said. "And we face our most crucial decision—probably the most crucial we will ever make. We must take a hard look at all probable consequences and responses. We must make absolutely certain we are taking the right course. And of course, as we agreed, we will take no action unless everyone here is fully behind our action."

Giancarlo paused, thinking ahead. He was not above using the advantage offered by his chairmanship. By presenting the pro views first, he might put matters in a more optimistic manner.

"Hamp, you've been closer to the scene than any of us. How do matters appear to you?" he asked.

George Hampton rose and walked to the end of the table. Giancarlo had not seen him in more than a year. He noticed that Hampton had gained some weight, especially around the middle. Big, beefy, and physical, there remained something of the country oaf about Hampton. For instance, although Hampton wore expensive suits, he never quite managed the style that Giancarlo felt he himself achieved with less money and effort. Instead of a simple club tie, or an elegant, understated pattern, Hampton tended to go for large, patterned flowers or racehorses. But what Hampton lacked in class, he more than replaced with aggressiveness. Hampton had become one of the most valuable members. He now turned to the membership with a disarming smile.

"My views may be somewhat biased," he said. "I've already burned my bridges. To my mind, there *is* no alternative. We *must* issue the Ultimatum now. We're ready. Trane tells me the economic programs are in the machines, waiting. The Rapier facilities are activated. Any delay at this point will be dangerous."

"In what way?" Giancarlo asked. He knew the answer. But he wanted Hampton to put it into words.

"Well, the longer we wait, the greater the likelihood that some connection will be made to us. Santo Domingo, Lisbon, Colorado, Barcelona—all of our past operations leave us vulnerable. All those activities are still under investigation. Any one may have left a fatal clue. Every agency in the Western world is hunting our identity. And there are other risks. Someone conceivably could stumble onto a Rapier site, or the radiation from the plutonium might show up on a National Reconnaissance Office satellite. And let's also remember: Trane has been fucking with the world's economy during the last few weeks. Eventually, someone is going to notice. If that happens, we will be placed on the defensive. The way I see it, we must keep on the offensive."

Giancarlo nodded as if he saw previously unnoticed wisdom in Hampton's words.

"Anyone else?" Giancarlo asked innocently.

Felix Zoff rose slowly to his feet and stood beside Hampton. Giancarlo could not help but compare the two. Zoff, the heir of a Swiss family banking firm hundreds of years old, bore solid aristocracy in his trim continental tailoring and in his tall, imposing build. He kept his Nordic eyes roving coolly from member to member as he talked.

"I'm not questioning our long-range goals," Zoff said. "My doubts lie only in the timing. Have we laid sufficient groundwork? When we deliver the Ultimatum, will they take us seriously? Let's look at the matter from Washington's viewpoint. The threat we pose may be beyond their immediate comprehension. Shouldn't we detonate another nuclear weapon somewhere, or in some other way demonstrate our capabilities? I certainly would prefer that the authorities in Washington take us seriously. If they do so, we would not have to use Rapier."

Hampton made an unintelligible noise deep in his throat.

"Felix, we've got to quit fucking around," he said heatedly. "That's where we've made our mistakes so far. They've underestimated us. What you say is true. They tend to think of us as just another band of terrorists, another Black September or Baader-Meinhof. Don't you see? If we set off another nuclear bomb, we'll *still* be relegated to that league.

196

The Ultimatum will show them they're up against something *new*."

Giancarlo sat studying Zoff. Of all the members, Zoff was the most elusive—the only true family man among the membership. For most members, wives and children seemed to be mere appendages. Zoff was the exception. He doted on his wife, his children.

Zoff now was attempting to put his doubts into words.

"You said that you've burned your bridges, George," Zoff said. "That's an apt phrase. That's exactly what we will be doing if we go ahead. Of all the actions we've taken, this is the most decisive. There'll be no turning back from this one. We will be committed."

Giancarlo sensed that the moment had arrived for him to intervene. "Felix, total commitment was a decision we made initially. That's what Hamlet is all about. We will only confuse ourselves by debating alternatives now past. We instructed Hamp to burn *his* bridges. It seems to me we now can only go forward."

"I think you're right," Thornsen said softly. "The machines will not run backward."

"And let me tell you something else," Hampton said to Zoff. "We *will* have to fire Rapier. We might as well accept that fact right now."

Giancarlo ardently wished that Hampton had not said that. But it was there. He had to pursue it. "What makes you think so?" he asked.

"The government of the United States won't believe us. They'll stall. We'll have to wipe out several million people before they'll believe what we're telling them. And frankly, gentlemen, I don't give a shit."

The Hamlet Group laughed, relieving the tension. Most were appalled, yet amused, by Hampton's flair for crudity.

Ahmed looked up at Giancarlo. His dark brown eyes reflected glints from the fireplace.

"Can we afford to do without the northeast part of the United States?" he asked Hampton. "From what I remember of geography, isn't that section heavy with manufacturing and wealth? I've wondered how you know that the region isn't essential to our plans."

"Trane?" Giancarlo said, tossing him the ball.

"I ran an extensive computer analysis on that," Thornsen explained. "The results were rather surprising. Actually, I found that New York and New England are expendable, from our standpoint. Oh, there are some negative aspects. We could make use of the heavy industry, shipping facilities, power production, and so forth. But population loss and the drop in the Gross National Product would tend to balance out. In fact, some of our principal sociological problems are concentrated in the East. All considered, the edge is in the direction of firing Rapier. For instance, there is a large segment of the population of New York that is nonproductive, a burden. From those aspects, we would be better off if we have to execute Rapier."

Zoff winced. "That's a rather cold way of looking at it."

Thornsen shrugged. "Well, that's the way the computers look at it."

"I thought we had long since crossed all our moral bridges," Giancarlo said.

Ahmed mumbled under his breath.

"Ahmed, was there something else?" Giancarlo asked.

"Why don't we fire Rapier, *then* issue the Ultimatum?"

Giancarlo laughed. He should have anticipated the Arab's viewpoint on the question.

Above all else, Ahmed did not want to lose.

"The psychology would be all wrong," Giancarlo explained patiently. "If we paralyze the country by eliminating a portion of it, we have lost all hope of dealing with it on a rational basis. We first must pose the threat. Then, if we are forced to show we are not bluffing, we merely pose another threat—to some other portion of the country. Maybe by that time they will listen."

"I always seem to be the dumb one," Bernardo said. "But I have to ask. Once we issue the Ultimatum, how do we know the United States won't find the Rapier sites, and destroy them?"

"Trane?" Giancarlo prompted.

"They *will* find them," Thornsen said. "We will *want* them to do so. But we will warn them: each site is booby-trapped with proximity devices. If they're tampered with in any way, they will fire. If the United States attempts to destroy them from the air, or by other means, the effect will be the same—complete pollution of the atmosphere."

"This is late in the day to ask," Zoff said quietly. "But if we have to fire Rapier, how widespread will be the effects? Could some of it drift across to Europe?"

"Trane?" Giancarlo said.

"Good question," Thornsen said. "Actually, we don't know. So much depends on factors we can't control, such as the prevailing winds. But in general, we know that plutonium particles will act just as any similar debris, falling to earth within a relatively short time. New York will bear the brunt. Downwind, Boston will have slightly fewer casualties. Montreal should escape, unless there is a perverse wind shift. Really, beyond Boston the casualty rate probably will drop rather rapidly. Iceland, England, Scandinavia, and northern Europe may have measurable increases in death rates. But probably not. It's a calculated hazard."

"Then Rapier could get *us!*" Zoff said.

Thornsen smiled shyly. "Very unlikely," he said. "Only a very eccentric wind situation would bring radiation here in significant amounts."

"But what *about* the wind pattern?" Zoff asked. "I remember, back at the beginning, that a problem existed because of prevailing winds. I've heard little about it since. Have you solved the problem?"

"Not entirely," Thornsen said. "The trick is to strike at the optimum moment, to achieve maximum results. Actually, this is a very good time of year, with numerous cold fronts coming down from Canada and drifting eastward. By using one of those great, natural wind machines, we can distribute the plutonium ash over a wide area very effectively."

"But what if the wind is *not* right?" Zoff insisted.

"Then we would fire the system anyway," Thornsen

said. "We would not achieve maximum results. But we have New York City ringed. The death toll will be spectacular, no matter what the situation."

"I've forgotten," Helmut Vogel said. "After we take over the United States, which country is next?"

"England," Trane said without hesitation.

"England? Who needs it?" Helmut quipped.

The Hamlet Group laughed.

A moment of anticipatory silence indicated to Giancarlo that the time had come.

"Do I hear a motion?" he asked.

Hampton raised his hand. "I move that the Hamlet Ultimatum be issued to the government of the United States."

"I second the motion," said Trane.

"All those in favor say aye," Giancarlo said.

The chorus of "aye" was prompt and strong..

"All opposed 'nay.' "

There was no opposing vote.

Chapter

17

"Somewhere, there's a link," Johnson insisted. "We're just too fucking dumb to see it."

Loomis walked to the front room of the small, two-bedroom motel suite. He stood for a moment, looking down at the vast array of police reports spread on the coffee table. Johnson was right. The clue probably was there in front of them, in plain sight, if only they could see it. He lowered himself onto the couch, reached for the material, and started through it again. He would simply examine every item.

The rifleman who had fallen to the ice had several aliases. His real name was Carl Bates. And he had no police record.

"What's the use?" Grindstaff asked behind him. "We've been through everything. His laundry lists. His shoes. His socks. His neckties. I know more about him than I know about myself. And we've got exactly nothing."

"There's a link," Johnson said again. "We've just got to find it."

"Maybe nothing's left for us to connect," Grindstaff said. "Maybe he memorized everything—the telephone numbers, addresses, all he needed. Maybe there *is* nothing on paper."

"We could take his brain apart," Johnson said. "There are approximately ten trillion bits of information in the human brain. Maybe we could look at them under a microscope, one by one. How long would that take?"

"Ten trillion bits?" Grindstaff said. "Is that a rough guess, or an accurate estimate?"

"Exact count," Johnson said. "Established by experts."

"Well I'll be damned," Grindstaff said. "How do you happen to know that?"

"You mean you didn't?" Johnson asked in mock surprise. "That's the kind of thing every intelligence officer is supposed to know. And if I know it, and you don't, how in hell did you get to be my immediate superior?"

Irritated, Loomis turned to glare at them. "Will you two shut up?" he said. He had patiently arranged the reports in categories, hunting a pattern. "Maybe we could go at it from his bank accounts," he suggested, thinking aloud. "We know he had no visible means of support—hadn't had for some time. Yet, he always had plenty of money. Deposits in cash or, in the past, from now-defunct business firms. How many were there, all together?"

"Checks? Or firms?" Johnson asked, flipping through his notes.

"Firms, damn it."

"Six. No, seven, all told."

"Those firms must have paid taxes," Loomis mused.

"Couldn't we ask Washington to run a computer scan on those old companies? Executives, owners, principal stockholders, board members, everything. We might find something in common."

"I suppose it'd be worth a try," Grindstaff agreed. He picked up the phone and dialed.

While Grindstaff talked, Loomis went on speculating aloud to Johnson.

"Let's look at what happened during the last few days. We can assume that Carl made a phone call, maybe several, to break some bad news. We can assume that he was the one who hired Henryk. We are certain Henryk hired José. So we've penetrated three levels—José, Henryk, Carl. Now, whoever Carl called must be high in the organization. He probably told Carl to kill Henryk. And I'll bet you a fifth of Jack Daniel's that whoever gave *that* order has already left town."

"Green label or black label?" Johnson asked.

"Take your choice."

"Done," Johnson said. "Reasoning?"

"Simple. We're bound to be getting close to that local honcho. We can assume he felt that things were getting too hot. If he has any sense at all, he at least left town until he learned how things went."

"That's a hell of a lot of assuming to do at one sitting," Johnson said.

Grindstaff hung up the phone. "They're putting some computer people on a scan," he said. "They say they'll have something within hours."

"Good," Loomis said. "Now, why don't we get a list of every business executive that has left town during the last two days?"

"In all Houston? Impossible!" Grindstaff said.

"And you CIA people are always bragging about all your electronic crap," Loomis pointed out. "Why in hell can't you do it?"

"Good Lord, man, this is a city of more than a million people," Grindstaff said. "You'll find that a surprising number of those people are engaged in the oil business. They come and they go—Alaska, South America, Middle East, North Sea. This also is the home of NASA. They travel a lot."

"And the Astros," Johnson said. "Don't forget the Astros."

"Suppose we *did* get a list," Grindstaff continued. "What would we have, except a bunch of names?"

"There should be one guy on that list who didn't go where he said he was going," Loomis insisted.

Johnson hooted. "One? I'll bet on at least a dozen. If we started checking that theory out, we'd sure be getting a lot of guys in trouble with their wives and bosses."

"All right. I still say it's a good idea. But if you're too lazy, forget it," Loomis said. "What about Carl's relatives, friends. Surely he had some. Read that bio sheet again, Johnson."

"Again?"

"Once more."

"I don't have to read it. I've got it memorized," Johnson said. "Carl Lynn Bates. Born in Dothan, Alabama, 1942. Father, itinerant carpenter turned itinerant corporal for the World War known as Two. Father killed in jeep accident in southern England in May 1944. Mother married John T. for Thomas Means, a merchant seaman. Many changes of addresses, schools. Completed high school Corpus Christi 1960, joined U.S. Army May 1961, served Vietnam 1962 and again in 1964. Discharged May 1965. Returned to Houston. Spent next five years Rice University. Completed master's in business administration. Worked for number of Houston-based firms, dealing in international products, import-export, what have you. All these firms now defunct. Records inaccessible. Diligent search of past city directories unable to locate employees of these firms, if indeed there were any."

"Best assessment is that there were not," Grindstaff said.

"Next seven years even more murky. Moved frequently,

from apartment to apartment. Managers and what neighbors we've been able to locate say the same thing, almost in the same words. He was quiet. He didn't talk much. He came and went at odd hours. He seemed cold, aloof, and a bit scary."

"Let's focus on the army," Loomis said.

"Essentially the same crap. A loner. Only one significant thing here from military. He was good in combat. Aggressive. He liked to kill. There was some feeling that he did more than was necessary."

"That could be said about a lot of people in those days," Loomis said.

"Present company excepted, of course," Johnson said. "Let's get into the things we don't have the answers to. What about his finances? Where'd he get all the fucking money?"

"He obviously was paid well for whatever he did," Grindstaff said.

"What'd the IRS have on him?" Loomis asked.

"Not much," Grindstaff said. "He apparently just reported enough each year to keep the wheels turning. Certainly, it wasn't enough to account for his present assets."

"So we're back to the defunct companies and the computer scan," Loomis said. "Any reason why we can't hunt more information ourselves? We've got the names of the companies. You've got the clout to open records and files. It'd give us something to do."

Grindstaff pondered the question a moment. "Oh, shit, we're already far beyond our charter," he said. "Why the hell not?"

So they went to work. Using the phones in adjoining rooms, they began assembling data from several states and foreign countries.

Within three hours, they had gathered enough material to detect a pattern.

Each company had fulfilled only the minimal requirements for existence. In most instances, the board members were the lawyer, a CPA, and perhaps a law associate. In every instance, none had actual contact with the firm, aside from its formation. Board meetings usually consisted of an exchange of notes, validated by "official" minutes.

Carl had controlled all the companies, virtually unaided.

After twelve hours of work, from a total list of forty-six names, only one duplication emerged.

Two of the earliest—and apparently more legitimate— firms listed a "George Hampton" as a corporate officer.

The detective who took the query from Loomis at the Houston Police Department did not need to check the files to give an impromptu preliminary report on Hampton's identity.

"He's one of our big rich," he said. "Hell, you've probably read about him. A recluse. Eccentric. String of wives. Not much known about him. But I'll get you what we have. I'll call you back."

Loomis left the phone, fighting elation. Everything fit.

He turned to Johnson and Grindstaff, and was surprised by the calmness of his voice.

"I think we've just scored," he said.

Chapter

18

Although more than five hundred full-time employees served on the staff at the Robertson White House, they worked from a single mood. At the beginning of each day, word filtered down from the Chief of Staff, the Private Secretary, or someone else in contact with the president: "The Old Man seems to be in rare spirits today." A casual, witty quip made by the president at breakfast was certain to be repeated dozens of times within the White House during the next two hours, and probably in the halls of Congress. Knowledge of the president's hourly disposition was considered to be a sure sign of position throughout Washington. Any indication of Robertson's frame of mind therefore was coveted and nurtured in the White House. His occasional shifts in temperament usually were reflected, minutes later, in the most remote office in the farthest reaches of the staff.

On Monday, the atmosphere was electric by the time most of the staff reported for work. Few knew exactly what was happening, but everyone knew that something was afoot. The signs of crisis were too evident. The circle of command had closed. The Chief of Staff, the Private Secretary, the Presidential Assistants, remained theatrically close-mouthed and grim. Yet, there was little speculation among White House staff members on the nature of the Administration crisis. Those who did *not* know could not admit they did not know. However, one startling bit of news soon filtered out: the president had just called an emergency meeting of the Security Council.

With unprecedented haste, the session was scheduled at 10 A.M.

Word also spread that the president was restless. That information was significant. Whenever President Robertson was worried, he literally paced the halls.

For forty-five minutes, Robertson walked about in the West Wing with that flat-footed gait the nation's nightclub comedians loved to imitate. Oblivious to his entourage of aides and Secret Service men, he went from office to office as if in a daze, nodding to some staff members at random, ignoring others.

He paused for a long moment in the entry of the Press Room, his deep-lined, habitual scowl and button-black eyes freezing the White House correspondents in their tracks. Before they recovered, he was gone. He wandered into the Rose Garden and stood for five minutes, contemplating the polished toe of his left shoe. Thirty minutes later, with his morning schedule hopelessly snarled, he was wandering aimlessly in the basement when his Chief of Staff, on the behalf of the Appointments Secretary and other members of the staff, took matters in hand and approached him.

"Mr. President," he said in a firm tone, stepping directly in the Chief Executive's path.

He waited until Robertson's eyes lost the glassy, vacant stare of intense concentration.

"Mr. President, there are some vital matters stacking up that perhaps should be taken care of before the Security session," he said, speaking as if to a child. The president often focused on the abstract so completely that he needed to be reintroduced, gently, to reality.

"What *are* these earth-shattering problems?" Robertson asked absently.

"Senator Walker insists on speaking with you personally, on the committee deadlock, concerning the new energy bill. He thinks he sees a way to maneuver, but he will have to make some concessions, and he wants your okay to do so because he knows it's your baby. State has received an enigmatic reply from the Arabs on our note, and they want to go over it with you. The UN Secretary General has sent a request, through channels, that he wishes to speak with you on a matter of greatest importance. And it's now nine thirty-two. We may need to gather some background material for the Security meeting."

Robertson rolled his cigar several times without speaking, calmly staring at his Chief of Staff, admiring his poise.

The man's devotion to administrative detail under the circumstances was commendable—and correct. No matter if the world were coming to an end, appearances should be preserved. Robertson put a hand on the aide's shoulder and started back toward the president's study, talking as he went.

At the moment, these routine crises seemed easily solved.

"Tell Senator Walker I trust his judgment. He knows those assholes on that committee better than I. Find out where he'll be about eight tonight, and if he's not in the sack with that assistant he's screwing, I'll call him. Tell State that's exactly what we could expect out of the Arabs —a reply evading the issue. We can play that game, too. Tell State to get the note over here. If it's what I think it is, we won't act on it immediately. After two days, they'll get nervous, and be ready to define their terms. Does the UN Secretary want a face-to-face?''

"No, sir. I gather he'd rather not, because of the attention his visit would receive. But he did mention something about security in reference to speaking with you."

"All right. See about a tight scrambler setup. Schedule a call about two fifteen. If that's too short a notice for a scrambler situation, we can make damned certain of the line. And this session coming up in the Cabinet Room. Let's tape it.''

The aide's eyebrows shot up.

Assuming that his Chief of Staff was remembering the mistakes of the Nixon Administration, he explained: "The trick lies in taping what you want, and keeping it to yourself. Granted, there are hazards. There are things that should not be preserved. Hell, Thomas Jefferson's secret instructions to Lewis and Clark probably would have got him hanged. But we may need to justify what we do today. Make damned certain we get it on tape. And it's for *my* files. Nobody else's.''

Thirty minutes later, Robertson entered the Cabinet Room. The full Security Council was present, along with selected heads of departments. A few aides and assistants were seated along the wall. In the light of what was to be discussed, Robertson's inclination was to ask them to leave. But he had second thoughts: the fact that he had tossed them out would make potential enemies of some bright young men.

"Hey, Mr. President," Vice-President Threadgill called. "What's the good word?"

Robertson moved toward his chair. Obviously, the vice-president was not yet aware of the situation. Nor was anyone present, judging from the expressions of anticipation and puzzlement around the table. In one sense, that was good. White House security remained solid at the highest levels. But Robertson had to set the tone of the council session abruptly. He turned to Vice-President Threadgill.

"Believe me, Hank. If I knew one good word, I'd tell you. I assure you that there *is* none today."

He solemnly examined the room, making certain of the identity of the aides and assistants along the far wall. The smiles of greeting faded. Robertson remained standing, wondering how best to say what he had to say. No tactful way came to him. He sensed that bluntness might serve his purpose best.

"We have no prepared agenda for today's meeting," he said. "All aides and assistants present may remain. But I want to stress at the onset that what is heard in this room today is not to be discussed, or speculated upon, in any way, after this meeting. Ordinarily, I would depend on your discretion and judgment. But the ramifications of what you are about to hear are so great that I feel this special appeal is necessary. And I promise you one thing: I will prosecute any offender to the fullest."

The Cabinet Room remained deadly silent. Robertson took his seat. The vice-president, who normally chaired the Security sessions, waved a hand in his direction.

"Obviously, the floor is yours, Mr. President."

Robertson nodded, wondering where to begin. He glanced at his watch.

"A little more than two hours ago, I received a strange document," he said. "It came in on a high-speed printer in the White House basement. The circumstances of that are being investigated. But for reasons I will outline, I believe the document is valid, that its message may be considered substantiated, and that it must be taken seriously."

He paused, giving the council time to absorb his words, before continuing.

"The message is couched in the form of an ultimatum. Briefly, the threat is this: New York City and the entire northeastern seaboard is ringed by several hundred special rockets and mortars which will loft a considerable amount of deadly plutonium ash into the atmosphere, unless we conform to certain demands.''

A low murmur of exclamation swept through the Cabinet Room.

Admiral Morgan, chairman of the Joint Chiefs of Staff, was the first to recover.

"That may not be much of a problem, Mr. President," he said. "We can overfly with a scanner, pinpoint the hot spots within minutes, and bomb them out of existence."

"I'm afraid it's not that simple, George," Robertson said. "You see, each site is equipped with proximity devices. If approached in any manner, by any object, the entire system will be fired automatically."

Robertson paused, unable for the moment to continue as he thought of the days, and weeks, that might lie ahead.

"Who is it? The Russians?" Admiral Morgan asked.

"The Ultimatum is simply signed, 'Hamlet,' " Robertson said.

"The Santo Domingo group?" asked Bob Thimble, Security Assistant.

"The group that *directed* the nuclear threat in Santo Domingo," Robertson corrected. "I'm afraid the press has given the world the erroneous impression that Hamlet was based in Santo Domingo, and that it was destroyed along with the bomb. I have suspected all along that Hamlet was based elsewhere—and survived."

The first practical question came from Defense Secretary Harlowe, as Robertson had anticipated.

"What do they want?" the Secretary asked.

"That's the interesting part," Robertson told him. "All they want is for us to do nothing."

"Nothing? What could they gain?" Harlowe asked.

Robertson hesitated. He shook his head in frustration. "The world, apparently."

He felt he should make an effort to convey the full extent of the threat. "This is not a sudden development," he added. "I should have seen it coming. There have been hints of it. And I certainly should have known something was afoot when Secretary Parker came to me a week or so ago and told me of some strange fluctuations his people had found in corporations, international currencies, and world trade."

"But what *is* the Ultimatum?" Admiral Morgan asked, still not understanding.

"Just what I've said, no more," Robertson explained patiently. "If the government acts in any way to impede certain events in American business, the devices will be fired."

"That doesn't make sense!" the admiral said.

"But I'm afraid it does, George," Robertson said. "And frankly, I don't see a fucking thing we can do about it."

Vice-President Threadgill was the first to comprehend the full import of the Ultimatum. A low moan of anguish came from his throat.

"My God, Travis! This is right out of a nightmare!"

"It *is* happening, and it's real, Hank," Robertson said quietly. "And it has caught us cold. As far as I know, there's not a single damned scrap of paper in our think-tank scenarios to alert us to this situation, or to tell us what to do about it. The entire commercial life of this country is being seized by a clandestine group for its own purposes. I don't know of a single precedent. There have been a few efforts to affect world trade—from the Jewish traders of Amsterdam two centuries ago to Prince Bernhard's Bilderbergers in the Netherlands, and David Rockefeller's Trilateral Council. But those were ostensibly overt movements. I doubt that a study of any existing parallels, no matter how slight, would help us in this situation."

"We might offer them a considerable sum of money," Defense Secretary Harlowe said. "Apparently that is what they're after."

"Not necessarily," Robertson said. "Power follows money. I believe that is what they really want—power.

They are out to seize this country. And our instructions are to sit back and to watch it happen."

"This plutonium threat," Harlowe said. "Exactly how bad is it?"

Robertson felt a chill of apprehension up his spine. Already, they were down to weighing the costs against lives.

"Thimble, you're the expert here," Robertson said. "You explain it."

Thimble's voice remained calm. "Plutonium burns, something like magnesium. The ash loses none of its deadly alpha radiation. In the atmosphere, with appropriate wind, distribution would be very effective over a wide region. Some people believe that plutonium is the most poisonous substance known to man. It's possible. A particle too small to see, if inhaled, theoretically would cause death within minutes from massive fibrosis of the lungs."

"Theoretically?" Threadgill asked.

"No one has ever done studies on it," Thimble explained. "But the subject did come up once, back when I was an aide to the Committee of Forty."

Robertson felt a glimmer of hope. He had forgotten about the committee. "What, exactly, do you remember?" he asked.

Thimble frowned in concentration. "That was a long time ago, Mr. President. I just have the vague recollection of the Forty Committee discussing the possibilities of a limited-area pollution by radioactivity. I only remember that plutonium was mentioned as a possible pollutant."

"Pollution by whom?" Robertson demanded.

"By us, Mr. President," Thimble said. "In Vietnam. A proposed operation was considered. Of course, it was never done. It was just one of many trial balloons shot down in the committee."

"Our chickens have come home to roost," Vice-President Threadgill said.

Robertson wondered briefly if a search of old records might be profitable. The Forty Committee, an informal, semisecret subcommittee of the Security Council, for a time supervised the clandestine operations of the CIA. But the group had been known by several titles through the years—the Special Group, the 54-12 Group, the 303 Committee, the Forty Committee. Meetings had been scheduled weekly. But the members were mostly the extremely busy, top-level officials from State, Defense, Joint Chiefs, the CIA and White House. Attendance had been spotty. The minutes, usually kept by the Assistant to the President for Security, were lax by design. Robertson doubted that the records would contain details, especially on a proposal never put into effect.

But he would have to make certain.

"Were any extensive projections done on potential effects?" he asked Thimble.

"No, sir. I'm positive of that."

"What do you remember of the proposed operation?" Robertson insisted. "How was it supposed to work? Why was it rejected?"

Thimble hesitated. "Mr. President, that was back in the mid-sixties. I was an assistant to the undersecretary of State. I never had the proposal actually in hand. But from the discussions I overheard, I gathered that the body-count factor was attractive, from the perspective of cost, but that the PR aspects negated implementation."

"PR?" asked Admiral Morgan, missing the context.

"Public relations," Thimble said. "World opinion. If you remember, there had been some flak about the effects of defoliants, accusations of germ warfare, and so forth. The committee simply decided that the heat wouldn't be worth the effects achieved."

"What *were* the arguments?" Robertson demanded. "The details?"

Thimble frowned for a moment. "Well, I remember it was argued that germ warfare was a two-way street. The germ is apt to come back on you. As someone said—joking of course—it could go around the world and sneak up on you from the other side. The argument *for* radiation pollution was that it was quiet, insidious, extremely cheap, and

213

very effective. On the negative aspects, there was talk of wind shifts, delayed response, and long-term hot sectors that would be of no military value. The point was made that with poor drainage, flushing of radiation would be minimal until the rainy season. The matter really wasn't seriously considered, as I recall—at least not up to the point of feasibility projections and scenarios."

"But the estimates made by the scientists, concerning possible effects, *were* examined and evaluated?" Robertson asked.

Thimble hesitated before replying. Then, his decision apparently made to be totally candid, he began speaking in a rush of frustration.

"Yes, sir. As I recall, the estimates on body count *were* validated. But from everything I've learned *since*, Mr. President, it seems to me that the disagreements among the scientists are moot. I mean, what does it matter if it takes one-thousandth of a gram of ploot to do you in, or one ten-thousandth? If you inhale a microscopic speck of it, all the mathematics in the world won't save you. That's why I really didn't pay much attention, Mr. President. The scientists can argue from now till doomsday whether sixteen ounces of ploot will kill one million, one billion, or nine billion people, but I don't see that it makes much difference, except to those scientists."

Robertson sighed. "I suppose you're right, Bob," he said. He posed his next question carefully. "You've spent almost two hours now, studying the Ultimatum. You've seen the details—you're one of the very few who have. Based on your experience in the committee, and on the considerable knowledge you have acquired since, tell us: what is your evaluation of the dangers posed in the Hamlet Ultimatum?"

Thimble looked at Robertson a long moment. He seemed to be searching for adequate words. Then he apparently remembered something. "Sir, one of the consulting scientists became furious when someone on the committee proposed a lengthy feasibility study. He said extensive experiments were not necessary. He told them, 'If you want to make a simple test, take a few plutonium shavings, put them in a plastic cup, tape it to a common flare, the kind that truck drivers use, take it to the top of the Empire State Building, and ignite the flare. I guarantee you at least fifty thousand people will die a death more horrible than you can imagine.' '' Thimble hesitated. ''If those rockets exist, Mr. President, and if they're fired, then I think twenty-five or thirty million Americans would be in serious trouble.''

''That many?'' Threadgill asked.

''At least,'' Thimble said. ''The total effect staggers the imagination.''

''That is close to Hamlet's estimate,'' Robertson told the council—and Thimble, who had looked up in surprise. Robertson explained. ''A brief, second message was sent for my eyes alone. Hamlet suggested that I compare the estimates of my advisers with those of Hamlet.''

''You mentioned the wind,'' Threadgill said. ''I gather that would be a considerable factor.''

''Yes, sir. The prevailing wind would have to be steady, and dependable for a certain length of time, for maximum effectiveness. But they claim the most populous regions are ringed. So the devastation would be widespread, no matter what the wind direction.''

''Why has there never been a projection made on anything like this?'' Robertson asked.

Thimble raised his hands in a helpless gesture. ''Apparently, we've just assumed that if any clandestine group did acquire high-grade plutonium, it would be used to make a bomb.''

''Well, I want some assessments made, and damned quick,'' Robertson said. ''The wind drift, what we can expect, the scientific consensus on plutonium radiation, a study of hot spots by the National Reconnaissance Office, and whatever we can assemble to verify the information contained in the Ultimatum. But for the moment, I think we *must* assume that the situation is *exactly* as Hamlet has defined it. The question before us now is, how do we respond to it?"

"Full-scale military alert," Admiral Morgan said. "That will let them know we mean business, and that we're ready for anything."

"Alert against what?" Robertson asked. "We don't even know what or who we're fighting."

"*That's* immaterial, for the moment," the admiral said. "If we can pinpoint the sites by overflight, I see no reason we can't bomb the piss out of them on a still day, and contain the radiation within a prescribed perimeter."

"Hamlet says that won't work," Robertson said. "They warn that if the sites are bombed, the rockets will be fired, and that in the long run the results would be essentially the same, give or take a few million lives."

"And if we try to go in on the ground they will fire," Thimble said. "What other alternative is there?"

Robertson carefully watched the men around the table, gauging their reactions as he spoke.

"We could accept the Ultimatum," he said quietly.

"Surrender?" said the admiral. "Unthinkable!"

"In my job, you often have to consider the unthinkable," Robertson told him. "We've been contemplating the unthinkable for the last two hours. At the moment, I'm convinced we have no alternative. If you gentlemen can find one, I would be damned happy to hear it."

"If we're going to so much as discuss surrender, you have my resignation, effective immediately," Admiral Morgan said.

Robertson stared levelly at the admiral for a long moment.

"Don't be a pig-headed fool, George," he said. "We are here to consider *all* our options. As a matter of fact, Hamlet has provided us with a scenario—or rather, two scenarios. One covers events through the next year if we accept the Ultimatum. The other covers events if we don't. Copies of the Ultimatum should be ready for you within the next few minutes. I want each of you to go over the entire text carefully, to see if there are any loopholes. But frankly, it seems to me they've covered all bases."

The admiral folded his arms and glowered.

Vice-President Threadgill had been listening quietly, making notes. He now moved to what Robertson felt was the heart of the issue, proving to Robertson once again that his vice-president, tacked onto the party ticket in a last-minute crunch, remained the most astute man on his administrative team.

"Travis, you mentioned that this thing came into the White House basement on a printer. What network was used?"

"We're not certain, Hank," Robertson said. "The printer is linked to several circuits, and fed from a memory store, on a priority basis. As I understand it, every keyboard that has access to that printer is encoded with an automatic identification number. But the Ultimatum, as received, bore no such number. It was fed into the memory bank with the highest priority. And that priority, gentlemen, is top secret, and reserved for very limited use."

"In other words, those sons-a-bitches are reading our mail," Threadgill said.

"They apparently *have* been for some time," Robertson said.

"Would that be possible?" the NASA director asked.

"Not only possible, but it has happened on occasion, I'm told," Robertson explained. "Mostly, previous electronic burglars have been harmless hackers, computer freaks just experimenting to see what they could do. But as you will see shortly, the Ultimatum contains detailed, top-secret information from every sector. In it are code names I've seen only on papers handled like the gold in Fort Knox— what there is left of it. They know everything, the way we operate, the bureaucratic setup, the personalities—it's all there. You'll see confidential information on our relationships with foreign governments, the names of our agents-in-place around the world, the locations of our subs at sea, the targeting of our fixed missile bases, operations orders of our Strategic Air Command—they haven't missed a trick. The entire Ultimatum runs one hundred and twelve pages, single-spaced. And I might add that it doesn't ramble. Every single paragraph is short and to the point. A tremendous amount of work went into its preparation. Obviously, they have access to every facet of our government. They have given us our course of action, in minute detail, for the next year."

Full comprehension came slowly around the Cabinet Room.

"You mean they're actually issuing orders? Telling *us* what to do?" Admiral Morgan demanded.

"The Ultimatum is couched more in the form of what *not* to do," Robertson said.

"It must be someone in the government," Admiral Morgan said. "This must be a takeover from within."

"My first assumption," Robertson said. "But then this thought came to me: nobody—no single office—has access to that much information. Not even the presidency. Yet, the most sensitive aspects of our entire government are tied up in one neat package. With all the bureaucratic infighting, gossip, and backstabbing prevalent in Washington, I doubt anyone here could accomplish this. I believe the Hamlet Group is everything it claims to be—a worldwide, highly professional organization. God knows how many members they must have. And until we know the identity of the Hamlet members, we are fighting in the dark."

"I have a suggestion," said Intelligence Director Wallaby. He lowered his voice. "We have at the agency, on the shelf, a special operations program we could initiate immediately, concentrating the efforts of our entire intelligence services. This plan calls for . . ."

"The Hamlet Ultimatum mentions that program," Robertson said. "We are ordered *specifically* not to put the program into effect—Code Name Collective, I believe the Ultimatum calls it."

Wallaby's mouth opened in amazement. "*Nobody* knows about that program," he said. "It was never presented to the Forty Committee, Net Assessment, Verification—anyone!"

"I'd never heard of it," Robertson agreed. "But correct me if Hamlet is wrong. Operation Collective would shift army, navy, and air force intelligence, the National Reconnaissance Office, and the Office of Defense Investigation from the Joint Chiefs to the wing of the Intelligence Director, for temporary duty. A total of one hundred and fifty-one thousand, two hundred, and fifty-six men, with an immediate, aggregate budget of more than sixty million dollars. The combined electronics facilities would be joined by an Interface Message Processor . . ."

"We've had a leak! Despite every precaution!"

"So has every other agency and department in the government," Robertson said. "That's what we've got to get through our heads. Our whole electronics system has become a sieve."

Vice-President Threadgill nodded his agreement. "I've been sitting here thinking of our limitations, Travis. We can't mobilize military, use our intelligence services, depend on our nuclear facilities—anything. Hell, we can't even discuss the problem with our department chiefs. If word got out, there would be absolute panic. And we have to assume that every electronics gizmo in Washington is working for Hamlet. Where does that put us? What can we do?"

"Nothing," Robertson said. "I've thought it out. I see no other way, at least for the moment. I believe the Hamlet Group will do exactly what it says it'll do—wipe out New York City and New England, just to make a point. We can go ahead with National Reconnaissance analysis of satellite data, simply because Hamlet gives us permission to do so. But beyond that, I think we should do nothing."

"You're surrendering!" the admiral said.

"History will judge us, George," Robertson said. "When a smart man gets in a bind, he analyzes his options, assesses his risks, and curbs his natural impulses. At the moment, we have no feasible options. The consequences of rash action are overwhelming. We must curb our knee-jerk inclinations.''

"What about contacting other governments through private, face-to-face meetings?'' the Secretary of State asked.

"We are ordered not to communicate with anyone,'' Robertson said. "I think we should comply. The risks would not be worth what little we might gain.''

"I understand you have been in contact with UN representatives on the Hamlet matter,'' said the Secretary of State.

"The Atomic Energy Agency only,'' Robertson said. "You can rest assured that I will sever contact immediately.''

"We still have one of their investigators in this country,'' Wallaby pointed out. "He will be a problem.''

Robertson nodded, wondering how to handle the matter. Loomis could not be expelled. He might know too much already, suspect even more. The entire search for Hamlet would have to be halted. And Loomis, the rebel, might not cooperate.

"All pursuit of Hamlet is to cease immediately,'' Robertson told Wallaby. "Keep Loomis under wraps.''

"He will not take orders from us,'' Wallaby predicted. "He will continue his own investigation.''

"Then do whatever is necessary,'' Robertson said. He met Wallaby's eyes.

The director nodded understanding.

Robertson's Chief of Staff entered the room, carrying eight copies of the Hamlet Ultimatum. He began the distribution around the table.

"I want each of you to read the Ultimatum thoroughly,'' Robertson said. "Report your findings and views direct to me, by military messenger. From this moment on, put no sensitive information into any machine linked to any communications network. Do not trust any phone line, or any messenger service, with other than routine material. Is there anything else?''

"I've been wondering all along . . .'' Vice-President

Threadgill said. "What are the facilities for replying to the Ultimatum? That might give us a clue to their identity."

"There are none," Robertson said.

Threadgill did not understand. "I beg your pardon?"

"There *are* no facilities for reply, Hank," Robertson explained patiently. "Hamlet assumes that we *will* comply. And while you're hunting clues, there may be one in that assumption. Anyone with the capability of destroying twenty to thirty million people can afford to be arrogant. Gentlemen, unless you can provide me with some feasible alternative, I intend to comply with the Hamlet Ultimatum, to the letter."

Admiral Morgan insisted on putting matters into plainer terms. "In other words, Mr. President, the United States of America has just surrendered to an unknown foreign power."

Robertson considered the remark carefully before replying.

"That's about the size of it," he said.

PART
THREE

PART
THREE

Chapter

19

Orgil Penfold, Sheila's second-best lover, found her body three days after the murder. Unable to reach her by phone, he used his own key to slip into her apartment. He was aware from the moment he entered the silent, frigid rooms that something was wrong. Against his better judgment, curiosity led him to push open the bedroom door. Sickened by the sight, Orgil in blind panic began a series of irrational acts that was to delay the murder investigation by almost a full day. In his initial anguish and confusion, Orgil called the police. A few minutes later the thought came to Orgil that he himself undoubtedly would be the prime suspect. He did not pause for a second thought, but fled the scene so rapidly that he collided with a parked car less than half a block away.

Off to this bad start, Orgil subsequently argued, pleaded, wept, and otherwise entertained homicide detectives more than six hours before he convinced them that he had nothing to do with Sheila's murder.

Orgil emerged from the experience a physical and mental wreck. Yet he made several valuable contributions to the investigation.

First, he helped to pinpoint the time of Sheila's death. Orgil had phoned her from Anchorage on Saturday, informing her he was heading back to Houston. When he phoned six hours later to tell her his exact time of arrival, she did not answer the phone. Even more odd, Orgil told police, was the fact that her automatic answering device had been disconnected. He explained that Sheila was on call twenty-four hours a day, seven days a week, to her boss, and she never left the phone untended.

The detectives theorized that Sheila was killed sometime between Orgil's first call and his second. This helped, for with the sixty-degree temperatures in the apartment, the medical examiner had been unable to establish the time of death with any exactitude.

Then, in direct response to a detective's question, Orgil made his most valuable contribution to the investigation.

"Who is her boss?" the detective asked.

Orgil hesitated only briefly.

"This is supposed to be a secret," he said. "I don't think hardly anyone knows. But she's dead, so what the hell. One night, when she was drunk, and pissed off at me, she bragged about it. She claimed she was sleeping with him. George Hampton. You know, the millionaire oil man."

The two detectives exchanged glances.

"You could have saved us all a hell of a lot of time if you'd mentioned that little tidbit in the beginning," the big detective said.

Loomis crossed the deep-piled carpet to the window behind George Hampton's desk, and looked out across downtown Houston toward the distant ship channel. He now regretted that he had agreed to coordinate his efforts with those of the CIA.

Clearly, the investigation was bogging down, right at the point where it should be picking up speed. The link to George Hampton had been the first major stroke of luck in the case. But one would never know, the way procedures were being handled.

Under the cover of the murder investigation, Hampton's

offices had been opened and thoroughly explored. True, the solid clues had been meager. But each bit of evidence had been relegated to a separate army of experts and carted off to some supersecret area of Washington for further study. No one seemed to have a grasp on the overall investigation. Thus far, all effort had gone into a division of the spoils.

Johnson and Grindstaff seemed accustomed to this bureaucratic compartmentalization. Loomis himself had forgotten the frustrations of the paperwork he had experienced in the early days of Vietnam. Now the governmental red tape was far worse. He knew he could never return to the bureaucratic life.

"We've got a preliminary report out of the electronics people," Johnson said, coming up behind him. "That gizmo here beside the desk was some sort of electronic scrambler, they think. They still don't know how it works. They'll have more in four or five days."

"Four or five days," Loomis said, shaking his head. He turned from the window and leaned against Hampton's huge oak desk. Johnson was carrying a clipboard. He was filling out some sort of form. "What are you doing?" Loomis asked.

"Filling out our requisition sheets," Johnson explained. "We do want copies on all this stuff, don't we?"

Loomis sighed. Johnson, one of the best field men in the business, was reduced to filling out forms.

"Doesn't all this strike you as idiotic?" Loomis asked him.

"What?" Johnson asked.

"Those fucking forms! Where's the head of this investigation? Who puts it all together? Who decides what to do next?"

Johnson looked at him, genuinely puzzled. "This is just the way it's done," he said. "There are assessment groups, evaluation groups, who assemble everything, try to make sense out of it. But that's not my department."

"Let's *make* it our department," Loomis said. "Where in hell is Grindstaff?"

They found him in the boardroom, also filling out forms. His were designed to accompany the various items of evidence to Washington.

Loomis explained the plan he had in mind.

"You and Johnson are supposed to be sharing information with me. Right? Now, why do we have to wait for your bureaucratic wheels to grind? Suppose I set up my own operation here—a special office of the United Nations International Atomic Energy Agency. When I say I need this or I need that, you and Johnson can get on the phone and get it direct from the agency involved in Washington. We can set up scrambler phones, or whatever you need. We would be hours, maybe days ahead of the investigation in Washington."

Grindstaff immediately saw the advantages of the plan. He nodded slowly, thinking it through. "It might work," he said. "And I'll tell you why. There's a presidential seal on your file. That would tend to intimidate anyone who might raise questions. And I'm working under verbal orders from the director—all very loose, but word has probably gotten around. Certainly, it's worth a try. We'll set up a code-name operation to give it class."

Within hours, Operation Strikeback was born.

The main portion of their work was concentrated on George Hampton.

"We need to know everything about him, his whole life history," Loomis said. "Something, somewhere, will give us the right lead."

Through investigations in the field, they also sought to trace his movements through the last few days.

By midnight, despite Hampton's elaborate use of false identities, they had pinpointed his flight to New York. This was not difficult. Any person who moves through banks, large buildings, and airline terminals will spend more time on camera in a single day than a TV talk-show regular does in a month. A time-lapse camera revealed Hampton's departure for Europe thirty-six hours later.

The delay was puzzling.

"Maybe he has a girl friend in New York," Grindstaff said. "It doesn't make sense, otherwise. He lands, he disappears. Thirty-six hours later, he's back at Kennedy, for his Icelandic flight to Luxembourg."

"I don't think it was a woman," Loomis said. "He

obviously had something to do before he left the country. He may have been picked up by someone. Or he may have taken a taxi or rented a car. If he did, we can assume it was under a cover name. So we're probably at a dead end on that. Let's concentrate on where he went. Do you people have much of a force in Luxembourg?"

"As I recall, not much," Grindstaff said. "It's a quiet post."

"But you do have someone there."

"Just someone attached to the U.S. Embassy staff, as I recall," Grindstaff said. "We can get him right on it."

"I think we also can assume Hampton is still in Luxembourg," Loomis said.

"Reasoning?" Grindstaff asked.

"Icelandic serves only Shannon and Luxembourg. If he wanted to go someplace else, some other city in Europe, he would have taken another airline. He flew Icelandic because it goes where he wanted to go. He's not the type to take a cheaper airline, just to save a few bucks."

"Maybe that's the way he got to be a millionaire," Johnson said.

Grindstaff offered a different theory. "Customs is a bit more relaxed in Luxembourg. And it's a part of the Benelux trade agreement. Maybe he wanted easy access to Belgium, or to the Netherlands. There's no customs check at the borders."

Loomis tended to doubt that possibility. He went back over the material they had assembled. "His papers apparently were in order," he pointed out. "He probably could have landed any place of his choice. He chose Luxembourg. I think that's significant. I suggest that we move our operations over there, immediately."

Johnson was looking at the map of Europe. "Luxembourg's not the biggest country in the world," he said. "If he's there, we ought to be able to find him."

"We need more on him before we go off half-cocked," Grindstaff insisted. "The more we know, the better we'll be equipped to deal with what we find over there. The Company and the National Security Agency combined have more than a hundred men at work. If we can wait six hours, we should have all we'll need.''

Loomis accepted Grindstaff's plan reluctantly. Although he was eager to get to Europe, to get into the field, he could see the logic in Grindstaff's argument. He soon was swept up in the search.

More than two dozen investigators were now fanned out over Houston, tracking down and interviewing everyone involved in Hampton's past life. Newspaper files, school records, federal profiles, and business-world biographies were researched. Ten NSA investigators flew to Norman, Oklahoma, to look into Hampton's college career. As Grindstaff had predicted, the material grew rapidly. Six hours later, they had assembled a detailed personal profile of George Hampton.

"There's a pattern here that easily could have contributed to personality disorders," Grindstaff said.

"The family, you mean?" Johnson asked.

"It's speculation," Grindstaff said. "But based on facts. The poor little rich boy syndrome. Papa was seldom home. He had women stashed away, here and there. So Sonny probably saw little of Papa. He no doubt was Mama's boy.''

"And she died," Johnson said.

"And she died," Grindstaff agreed. "After years of boozing and of ignoring poor George. Awkward for the old man, suddenly having full charge of a son he hardly knew. A hell of an interruption in his free-wheeling life. So Sonny was packed off to military schools.''

"Unloved and unwanted," Johnson said. "Of such material are terrorists made.''

"The rejections continued," Grindstaff said. "He was blackballed by the three fraternities of his choice. Apparently he had a surly attitude—everyone we interviewed mentioned it. The only social activity listed is membership in the Foreign Students' Association. Isn't that odd?''

"There may be something there," Loomis said. "Remember, the old man traveled constantly in his work. But at that time, the son had never been out of the country, as far as we know. Could it have been a desire to be like the old man?"

"That doesn't wash," Johnson said. "Maybe the foreign students, not able to speak English very well, just didn't know what a son-of-a-bitch he was."

"That association may be the key," Loomis insisted. "After he took over the family business, he still hadn't traveled. Yet, from the minute he took over the firm, he seemed to have solid overseas connections."

"That's natural in the oil business," Grindstaff said.

"Not to that extent," Loomis insisted. "Look at this stuff he was involved with—import and export, electronics, shipping. Oil men are too busy at their own game to mess with such time-consuming diversions."

"Then why did he get into it?" Grindstaff asked.

"If you find the answer to that, you may have the answer to Hamlet," Loomis told him.

"We have ordered a scan on his contacts in college," Grindstaff said. "We'll put our overseas operations on checking them out. By the time we get to Europe we should know something."

Loomis picked up a report Grindstaff had just assembled on the electronics gear in Hampton's office. The experts were puzzled. The terminal was straightforward enough. Utilizing telephone hookups, Hampton apparently signed into a computer system, somewhere. Backtracking on the long-distance telephone logs failed to yield any solid indication. Hampton's office made hundreds of long-distance phone calls each day.

One item on the electronics-gear report caught his eye.

"What did this black box turn out to be?" he asked Grindstaff.

"Some kind of an encoding device," Grindstaff explained. "Our experts were mystified by it. Hampton had smashed it with a fire axe. Reconstruction has been difficult. They're still working on it. Apparently a multiple substitution cipher is involved, the substitutions done by computer, with the substitution code varying moment to moment. Very complex."

"You have electronic experts working on it, but no cryptanalysts. Shouldn't there be one?"

Grindstaff thought for a minute. "You're probably right," he said. He moved toward a telephone. "I'll call Langley and get a couple of good men on the way down here. And while I'm at it, I'll make arrangements for us to move our operations to Europe."

Loomis agreed. There were some loose ends he needed to tie up, too, before leaving for Europe.

He went into his bedroom, sank into a chair, and dialed Maria Elena on the West Coast. The call was put straight through to her guest cottage.

He talked for a few minutes, filling her in on the investigation, giving her time to emerge from sleep. He then went straight to the point.

"Listen, I miss you, and I need you," he said. "I was thinking that maybe, if you came here and saw what was happening, you might feel different about it, about my work, about us."

"There's no way I would feel differently," Maria Elena said. "I am me, you are you. There are things you have to do. And I can't help the way I feel about them."

"Maybe we would feel the same way about those things if you saw them from my viewpoint," he said.

"No, this is basic," she said. "I don't know why you are driven to do those things."

"They have to be done," he told her.

"Even though you hate them?"

"Maria Elena, if you would come with us I could show you the necessity of all this. It isn't something I can talk about over the phone. But right now, it looks as if we will be moving to Europe. You could be of tremendous help. Can't you delay the film?"

She hesitated. "The film may be off," she said. "I don't know yet."

"Then there's nothing in the way."

"Let me think about it," she said.

"I've already done a lot of thinking about it," he said.

The line was silent for a moment. "So have I," Maria Elena said. "And I think I know why I feel the way I do."

"Then come here, and we can talk."

For a long moment, Loomis thought he had won. But Maria Elena remained hesitant.

"I need some time to think," she said. "Call me tomorrow."

Loomis hung up the phone, more disturbed than before. Maria Elena was a worrier.

If she had found some basic differences between them, and could find no solution, then there might not *be* a solution.

Loomis entered the front room just as Grindstaff returned from the phone. His face was pale, and his expression strange.

"We're ordered *not* to go to Europe," he said. "Operation Strikeback is canceled. We are to cease and desist. We are ordered to do nothing more on the case."

Loomis and Johnson looked at him for a moment in stunned silence. Johnson recovered first.

"Who the fuck says so?" he demanded.

"Langley passed the word to me," Grindstaff said. "But let me remind you that we have been functioning under direct supervision of the National Security Council. So cancellation would have to come either from the council, or from the president."

Loomis sat for a moment, trying to fathom the meaning behind the cancellation. "That order doesn't apply to me," he said. "I don't take orders from Langley."

"You were mentioned specifically," Grindstaff said. "I am to make certain you do nothing further. The word is that if you have any question, you are to call Sir Reginald."

Loomis stared at Grindstaff, trying to absorb this new state of affairs. Something was badly wrong. Not even Washington was capable of so abrupt a reversal in plans.

"There can only be one reason they've canceled," Loomis said. "There has been some kind of dramatic confrontation, concerning Hamlet. And Hamlet has them scared shitless."

"My thinking exactly," Johnson said.

"Well, I'm returning to Washington immediately," Grindstaff said. "I have some contacts. I'm goddamned sure going to find out exactly what's happening up there."

On his arrival at Dulles International Airport, Grindstaff walked straight from the plane to a bank of telephones in the concourse. He dialed a number he long ago had committed to memory. After several rings, the receiver came off the hook on the other end of the line. Grindstaff waited a moment to make certain his protégé would not break training, and speak.

The line remained silent.

"If you recognize my voice, don't say my name," Grindstaff said. "I need to see you, Mark."

The silence lengthened.

Grindstaff waited him out.

"I *can't* see you," Mark said.

"What do you mean, you can't? Of course you can," Grindstaff said heatedly. "And right now!"

"I'm not supposed to . . . say anything," Mark said. "I was warned."

"You're talking too much," Grindstaff said. "Just let me ask you one question. Where do your loyalties lie, man?"

"I'm . . . grateful to you," Mark said. "But this is something different. If you had been there, heard what was said, you wouldn't ask me to do this."

"I'm not asking you," Grindstaff said. "I'm telling you. And let's get the fuck off this phone. Remember the code we used to have for landmarks around here? Remember the name, 'Reclaim'?"

Mark hesitated only briefly. "I remember," he said. "Reclaim" once had been code for Washington National Airport, built on land reclaimed from the Potomac River.

"Well, just update Reclaim. Make it forty-five minutes. I'll be waiting."

"I don't think it'll do you any good," Mark said. "I don't think I should even see you."

"Just shut up, and be here," Grindstaff said. "And make goddamned sure you come alone."

"All right. But . . ."

Grindstaff slammed the receiver into its cradle.

After a hurried sandwich, he took up station behind one of the sloping buttresses. The position kept him out of traffic, yet gave him a complete view of the concourse.

Mark made the twenty-seven miles from Washington to Dulles in less than forty minutes. When Grindstaff saw him coming down the concourse, searching frantically, Grindstaff stepped up behind him and took him by the arm.

"Let's get out of here," he said. "Let's go to your car."

Mark had not changed. Short, thin, prematurely gray, and wearing heavy horn-rims, he was not the type one would suspect as a bureaucratic double agent. He left the terminal without protest. When they reached his green Pontiac in the parking area, he eased behind the wheel and opened the opposite door for Grindstaff.

"We'll talk here," Grindstaff said, latching the door. He turned to face Mark.

"Now. What in the hell is going on up here?"

"I told you! I can't talk about it!" Mark said. "If you'd heard the president! He said he'd personally prosecute anyone who leaked. And I swear to God. I think he was looking right at me when he said it."

Grindstaff felt a chill of apprehension up his spine. He forced himself back into the role he had determined to play.

"Bullshit," he said. "You work for *me*. That was understood when you were installed at Joint Chiefs. You're our ears over there. What the fuck good did it do me to work like hell and get you in there, if you turn turtle now?"

Mark put his hands on top of the steering wheel and lowered his head onto his arms.

"I don't know what to do," he said. "I mean, all right, I work for you. But this . . ."

"Look," Grindstaff said. "You're really not telling me anything. I know what happened. All I'm asking for is the details of that meeting."

Grindstaff was not prepared for what happened next.

Mark burst out sobbing.

"I don't know *what* to do," he said. "They've got to be stopped. But the government is helpless! What can we do?"

Grindstaff began to suspect that Loomis had been right. Hamlet had them by the balls.

But how?

"I sure as shit don't feel helpless," Grindstaff told Mark. "Come on, tell me about that meeting."

"You don't know . . ." Mark began. He stopped.

"I know that I've got some good men working with me," Grindstaff said. "Loomis and Johnson. They whipped Hamlet the first time. They can by God do it again."

"You are going to be ordered to kill Loomis," Mark said. "And maybe Johnson."

Grindstaff did not breathe for two full seconds.

"Who said?"

"The president."

Grindstaff hesitated. He had to make his next move carefully.

He put a hand on Mark's shoulder.

"Mark, you've known me a long time," he said. "And since those early days at the Farm, when I taught you everything I knew about tradecraft, have you ever had any reason at all to distrust my judgment, to doubt my word?"

Mark shook his head in the negative.

"This is the most important thing we'll ever do in our entire lives," Grindstaff said quietly. "It's important that we look at it from the right perspective. Sometimes the government—the administrative branch—is wrong. I can give you plenty of examples. Sometimes the Congress is wrong. Sometimes the judicial is wrong. But we have our checks and balances. That's why we have you as our mole at Joint Chiefs. You are a *part* of the checks and balances. The Intelligence Director is a political man. Sometimes he doesn't pass on to us things he should, out of political considerations. We're career men. We fought a cold war when half the government—and most of the American people—didn't know what the fuck was going on, or care.

236

We've got the expertise, the ways and means. And we've been there. *That's* the government I'm loyal to—the one that kept the night watch for twenty fucking years. That's the one you should be loyal to—the one that has put you in a certain position for a certain purpose. When you come right down to it, who in hell *is* the government?"

Mark nodded, sniffling. "I know," he said. "I know. But twenty to thirty million people . . ."

Grindstaff felt the chill return to his backbone.

"What twenty to thirty million people?"

Mark was sobbing so hard that Grindstaff had trouble understanding the words.

"The people Hamlet is holding hostage," Mark said.

Grindstaff dug his fingers into Mark's shoulder.

"Mark, I think the time has come for you to talk," he said.

Little by little, Mark talked. Grindstaff listened. He asked only occasional questions, making certain exactly what was said, the inflections put on key words spoken by members of the National Security Council.

A little more than an hour later, as dawn was breaking, he climbed, stiff and exhausted, from Mark's green Pontiac.

There was no doubt in his mind as to what he had to do.

He walked into the terminal, and bought a ticket on the first flight back to Houston.

Chapter
20

President Robertson, thoroughly exhausted after almost thirty-six hours without sleep, circled the Oval Office in an agony of indecision. On his desk were twenty-two proposed courses of action, submitted to him by various aides and agencies, the results of scores of long, heated conferences throughout Washington. He had been down each road a dozen times, examining all hopes and hazards.

He could not see sufficient merit in a single one to justify the terrible risks involved.

His muscles were aching from the long hours at his desk and at the conference table. Rising, he walked to the drapes behind his desk and looked out over the colonnade, the Rose Garden, to the peaceful, serene blue sky over Washington. Of all the vistas at his disposal, this was the only one that gave him comfort. He was surrounded by constant reminders of his awesome responsibility. That patch of blue was the only glimpse he had beyond the chains of office, his only link to normalcy.

He spoke loudly enough to be heard throughout the Oval Office. "I don't understand it," he said. "Of all the resources at our disposal, all our technicians, all our nuclear armaments, surely we should be able to do something. But we have nothing here that is new, nothing that is unexpected. Hamlet has analyzed our situation almost to the fillings in our teeth. We can do nothing."

Vice-President Threadgill pulled a side chair out from the desk and sprawled, flopping one long leg over the armrest.

"Travis, I'm in favor of doing *something*, even if it's the wrong thing," he said.

President Robertson turned to face him.

His relationship with his vice-president was unorthodox, perhaps unprecedented. Historically, a president and a vice-president by their very existence posed a mutual embarrassment. But Threadgill and Robertson had liked each other from the first, had shared many battles on the Hill, and had grown even closer under the pressures of office. Robertson knew that Threadgill's offhand ways and disarming rural demeanor hid one of the finest minds in Washington. In some respects, he valued Threadgill's advice more than that of any other man.

"Hank, what *would* you do if you were in my shoes?" he asked.

Threadgill grinned, shaking his head in dismay. "First, let me thank God I'm not," he said. "But since you ask, my option would be to plan to shoot down the communications satellites, and to sever all connections with Europe, including cable."

"That's mentioned in the Ultimatum," Robertson reminded him. "We are warned that if that happens, the sites will be fired automatically."

Threadgill nodded. "But prematurely, and on our action," he pointed out. "If we pick the right moment—like right now—with the wind blowing away from the most populated areas, we could cut losses drastically. In short, we would seize the initiative. And I think that counts for something."

Defense Secretary Harlowe and Bob Thimble, Assistant to the President for National Security, listened to the exchange in silence. The last session in the Cabinet Room, just concluded, had lasted twelve and a half hours. Their faces reflected the strain.

Robertson lowered himself into the high-backed chair and swiveled to face Threadgill. "We could cut our losses that way," he agreed. "Maybe we'd have no more than four or five million American citizens dead. New York and Long

Island are too close, Hank. I'm told that even without the assistance of surface wind, there's just no way we could avoid appalling loss of life."

"But we would cut Hamlet's water off," Threadgill pointed out. "All of Hamlet's computer links to the government, to all U.S. corporations, would be broken. We no longer would be completely helpless."

"With, at best, several million dead," Robertson repeated. He again tried to visualize such a calamity.

Burial alone would present a horrendous problem.

"We have to be realistic," Threadgill argued. "This situation is not so unusual, historically. Mankind has survived worse. Fifty million dead in World War Two. The flu epidemic during the First World War killed a half million people in this country alone, twenty million over the world. We could survive, Travis. There might even be some good come out of it—a nation united against a common enemy, that kind of thing."

The vice-president's argument revealed a toughness Robertson had sensed, but never had occasion to analyze. The president thoughtfully lit a cigar.

"Hank, we still wouldn't have Hamlet's identity. We still wouldn't have the smoking gun, to coin a phrase."

"We *would* be free to turn our spooks loose," Threadgill said. "We could *try* to find the Hamlet people."

Threadgill had stated the choice well. Any decision as to what course to take would have to be poised on the balance of loss versus possible gains.

Yet there was another consideration.

"On the whole, I'm inclined to agree with you," Robertson told his vice-president. "But I keep wondering." He pointed to the material on his desk, to the satellite photographs pinpointing the Rapier emplacements. "Hamlet claims this would be the first of a series of disasters, if we don't cooperate. I can't keep from speculating. If Hamlet was clever enough to come up with all this, what would they throw at us next?"

Threadgill nodded. "I suppose we *should* crank in that ball-numbing thought. How much more ploot do they have?"

"Rapier accounts for only a fraction," Robertson said. "We're still hunting the rest. I'm told that there are various ways of confounding radiation scanning."

"Does the weather picture look any better?" Threadgill asked.

"No," Robertson said. He spread the most recent satellite photo on his desk and pointed. "Our weather people say that once the front moves across the Rapier sites, Hamlet will have ten days to two weeks of highly favorable conditions. The sea breezes might protect a narrow strip along the coast. But we can't count on it."

Threadgill studied the overlay. "How long have we got before that happens?" he asked.

"About eighteen hours," Robertson said. "Maybe less."

"And we've already pissed away thirty-six hours."

"I know. I know," Robertson said. He rubbed his sandpapery eyes.

Constantly now in his mind were visions fueled by the data from his experts—and from his own imagination—of families at dinner, at play, in their homes, asleep, trapped in a horror beyond comprehension.

Parents would see their children die.

Children would see their parents helpless, writhing on the floor in death agony.

A whole population would be eliminated.

He tried to imagine what his own thoughts would be in such a moment—impotent rage, uncontrollable fear. Or would the pain consume all such emotions?

"We can't do it," he told his vice-president. "We simply can't take the risk."

Threadgill nodded. "You're right, of course," he said. "If we were computers, we could justify the loss. But fortunately or unfortunately, we are men. Our knowledge, our imagination, our feelings, overrule logic."

The decision made, Robertson leaned back in his chair, drained of energy. He was aware of a brief commotion at the door as Bob Thimble was summoned from the room. Robertson closed his eyes and a wave of darkness overwhelmed him. When he opened his eyes again, Thimble stood before his desk.

Robertson was momentarily confused, not certain how much time had elapsed.

"Excuse me, Mr. President," Thimble said. "But something strange has occurred."

Robertson brushed the sleep from his eyes. He forced himself to focus his attention. "Yes?" he said.

"When Herman Grindstaff was ordered to drop the case in Houston, he apparently ignored those instructions. He took the first plane to Washington. We believe he met with someone at or near Dulles last night. He returned to Houston on the next flight. He has now disappeared."

Robertson struggled to absorb all the ramifications. "Disappeared?" he asked, aware he must sound stupid. He was unable to stop himself. "He's not riding herd on Loomis and Johnson?"

Thimble inhaled and held a breath a moment before letting it go.

"Loomis and Johnson have disappeared, too," he said.

Robertson staggered to his feet, his mind racing. For a brief instant, hope flared.

Loomis and Johnson had turned the trick in Santo Domingo. Maybe they could do it again.

But rationality quickly returned.

Hamlet was simply too formidable for anyone. Hamlet had accomplished what no nation had managed to do in two hundred years.

If the most powerful nation on earth had been humbled, what could three men do?

"They'll bring the whole mess down on us!" Robertson said.

"How long have they been missing?" Threadgill asked.

"Four, five hours," Thimble said. "Langley is in an uproar. They're at a loss to explain it. Grindstaff has always been completely trustworthy. There's divided opinion. Some think Grindstaff is not the type to do something like this of his own volition.''

"They think he's been murdered?'' Threadgill asked.

"Or kidnapped," Thimble said. "But the majority opinion holds that Grindstaff's quick trip to Washington is proof that he has defected. He came alone. He was here less than two hours. And there was no sign of struggle—or even any untoward conversation—in the Houston safe house.''

"How do you know?'' Threadgill asked.

For all his expertise, the vice-president sometimes showed streaks of naïvete, Robertson observed.

"It was bugged," Thimble said. "Thoroughly."

Robertson's attention shifted to the Hamlet Ultimatum on his desk. The first command in the Ultimatum flatly stated that all efforts to identify the membership of Hamlet must cease immediately.

If that command were not obeyed, Rapier would be fired.

"Is there *any* indication who Grindstaff met at Dulles?" he asked.

"No, sir."

"Then there is a strong probability that someone leaked the Ultimatum to him," Robertson said.

"It's almost inconceivable," Thimble said. "But the remote possibility is being explored."

"Remote, shit," Robertson said. "You should know how Washington works by now. Infiltrate an aide into the top levels and you've stolen a march on all your competition. Grindstaff may be smarter than we thought."

Thimble shuffled his feet in confusion, thoroughly chastised. "I had not assumed that the Security Council might be compromised," he said. "We take every precaution. I know every individual well."

"Maybe not well enough," Robertson said. "Go back through past operations at Langley. Search for evidence that Grindstaff knew council decisions before they were passed down to his level. And I want a complete profile on everyone at the meeting when the Ultimatum was first discussed. Check every man's record for any contact with

Grindstaff during his career. If we have a plant at that level, the deal probably was made years ago.''

''I think we're hearing the voice of authority on the technique of political infiltration,'' Threadgill observed.

''The practice is far more common than generally supposed,'' Robertson said. ''In this case, the damage is done. But if we knew exactly what information was passed to Grindstaff, we might have a better chance of figuring out what he will do.''

''Assuming that he *has* defected,'' Threadgill mused. ''What would make him do such a thing? I've been thinking it over, and I can only come up with one reason. He's had a breakthrough in the case. Maybe we should let him play out his string.''

Robertson shook his head emphatically. ''If Langley knows about Grindstaff's trip and disappearance, there is danger that Hamlet may know, or soon find out.'' He looked up at Thimble, rolling his cigar, thinking it through, making certain that the extreme nature of his decision was as inevitable as it seemed.

It was. He could find no alternative.

''Loomis, Johnson, and Grindstaff absolutely must be stopped,'' he said. ''Tell Langley, every agency, to make it a full-scale operation. Tell them to use whatever means that are necessary.''

Chapter

21

"I still don't know what's in your fucking mind," Johnson said from the backseat. "What can *we* do?"

Grindstaff, driving, slowed as they neared the end of the Galveston Island Causeway.

"I don't know what we can do," he said. "I only know that we've got to do *something*."

Loomis, riding in the front seat with Grindstaff, was still attempting to absorb all the details he had just heard. He was jolted. But he was not surprised. There had been plenty of evidence that Hamlet possessed such capabilities. He was most disturbed that the U.S. government had knuckled under without at least attempting some defensive maneuver. He wondered if one were not being attempted, in a massive clandestine operation not revealed to Grindstaff.

"How good is your source on all this?" Loomis asked.

"My man was *there*. Right in the fucking Cabinet Room," Grindstaff said. "He heard everything. I got a complete report."

"And the president told the Security Council he intended to do nothing?"

Grindstaff slowed the car for an exit off Interstate 45. "Robertson's exact words were, 'Unless you can provide me with some feasible alternative.' According to my man, no one has done so."

"And you believe your man?"

Grindstaff looked away from the wheel to glance at Loomis. "I have no doubts whatsoever," he said. "I made several more phone calls up there. I do have contacts, you

245

know. Nobody is saying *anything*. Nobody *knows* anything. But everyone is aware that something big is going on. The atmosphere is so thick you could cut it with a knife. The whole fucking government is in shambles.''

"And all Hamlet wants is for everyone in Washington to stand around with his thumb up his ass,'' Johnson said.

"That's the general idea,'' Grindstaff said.

"Well, they're good at it,'' Johnson said.

Grindstaff began winding around the streets of Galveston, heading in the general direction of the beach.

For the first time in his life, Loomis felt completely helpless. If the United States, with its vast facilities, could not stop Hamlet, what could he do? At the moment, he had no weaponry of any description.

All he had was a tidbit of information.

"Did you tell anyone in Washington about Hampton's connection to Luxembourg?'' he asked Grindstaff.

Grindstaff turned onto a street and slowed, hunting the numbers on a row of beach cottages.

"Negative on that,'' he said. "I knew we had good, valuable information. But I could see that there was no one up there in any shape to handle it. They're scared shitless. One leak, and we would lose the one advantage we've got—surprise.''

Loomis found his estimation of Grindstaff growing. He liked the way Grindstaff had handled himself on returning to Houston. Driving from the airport straight to the motel, he had awakened Loomis and Johnson, his forefinger over his mouth to signal silence. He had motioned them outside, gesturing for them to leave their clothing and luggage.

"That place is wired like NBC,'' he had said outside. "Let's go for a drive.''

He had started south on the interstate, explaining that he was headed for a safe house on Galveston Island. En route, he had described his discoveries in Washington.

Grindstaff braked the car before a row of clapboard cottages. At number 325, he turned into a narrow, sandy drive and parked the car behind the building. "We'll go in the back door," he said.

The two-bedroom shack was spartan. The floors were bare, the furniture mostly wooden frame. The four large beds were comparatively clean, but unadorned.

"The guy that owns this keeps it for fishing parties," Grindstaff explained. "He rents it mostly to businessmen who bring broads down for a weekend of fun. The guy owes me. We'll be safe here for two or three hours. Then we'll have to get moving. But it'll give us time to decide what to do."

Johnson explored the place, checking the bedrooms. "You forgot the broads," he said.

"Sit down," Grindstaff said. "We've got some planning to do."

Loomis picked up a Texaco map of the United States that Grindstaff had found in the car. He spead it on the coffee table. "Do you know the location of the rocket sites?" he asked.

"Only in a general way," Grindstaff said. "But I think we can forget any hope of destroying them. If the government can't cope with them, precisely pinpointed from satellite readouts, I don't see how we can do any better."

"At least we now have some idea of what Hampton did during his layover in New York," Johnson said. "He must have traveled around the sites, for some reason."

"That's what I figure," Grindstaff said. "He was hooking them up, arming them in some way."

Loomis studied the map, unable to dismiss the rocket sites so lightly. At the moment, they were the one solid, physical evidence of Hamlet. "Don't you have any source that could give us the exact locations?" he asked Grindstaff.

Grindstaff considered the question for several seconds. "I can't think of anyone under the circumstances," he said. "No one trusts anybody. Besides, I'm probably considered a defector by now. There's rampant paranoia up there. I doubt that anyone would have anything to do with me."

"Is the Hamlet Ultimatum anywhere near general knowledge throughout the highest level of government?" Loomis asked.

"No. Definitely not," Grindstaff said. "There are all kinds of wild rumors afloat—the president has lost his marbles, the Russians have infiltrated Langley, the military-industrial complex has effected a coup. . . . One senator got wind of something, and was making noises about a congressional probe. But he shut up. So I assume certain people are being briefed."

"We can't attack the sites. We can't deal through Washington. What the fuck *can* we do?" Johnson asked.

"I don't know," Grindstaff said. "But I came back to Houston because it occurred to me that we may be the *only* hope. Nobody else is doing a goddamned thing."

"And we only have one clue—Luxembourg," Loomis said. "How can we develop that?"

"We know a guy who spent some time there during the war," Johnson said. "He still goes back every year or two. He might be of some help."

"Who?" Loomis asked.

"Dr. Burke," Johnson said. "He was a field surgeon in the Battle of the Bulge. He says Luxembourg is his favorite place in all Europe."

"Could we trust him?" Grindstaff asked. "Do you think he might be willing to help?"

"Sure."

"What makes you so certain?"

"We talked some, about government and such. He's got a—well, anger is the word, I suppose—about some things that are happening, the way people's lives are being manipulated."

"He doesn't have a corner on that," Grindstaff pointed out. "But most people seem to be willing to live with it. What makes you think he would act on it?"

"If you'd seen him save my ass in Colorado, you wouldn't ask that question," Johnson said. "He drove his jeep across that clearing, right at them, firing that old Lewis all the way. It was a beautiful sight, I'll tell you."

"Firing that old what?" Grindstaff asked.

"Lewis," Johnson explained. "He collects machine guns."

Loomis and Grindstaff exchanged glances. The idea apparently hit each at the same instant.

"Do you think he would throw in with us, on a hot operation?" Loomis asked.

"I know he would."

"Well, that's one," Loomis said to Grindstaff. "Me, you, and Johnson makes four. Who else?"

"Four for what?" Johnson asked.

"An assault team," Loomis said. "We've got about two hours to put one together."

"Wait a minute," Johnson protested. "Who the fuck said I was in?"

"Aren't you?" Loomis asked.

"You might at least give me a couple of seconds to think about it. I've a lot of time in. GS-16. You don't just blow a career on a whim, you know."

"Confidentially, Johnson, you blew it in Santo Domingo," Grindstaff said. "The only reason you're still on the payroll is the simple fact that they couldn't give you the shaft while the world was hanging medals on you."

"Well, in that case, all right," Johnson said. "But don't rush me into these things. A guy's got to consider his options. It's one thing for somebody like Loomis to go off on his own. But I've been star-spangled loyal almost twenty years. This takes some getting used to."

"If it's of any help, I agonized a bit on the plane back down here," Grindstaff said. "At first, I felt miserable—like a fucking traitor, a defector in my country's greatest hour of need, that sort of crap. Then, it came to me: it's the *agency* that has defected, given up, surrendered. Me? I'm still doing my job."

"I'm sure there'll be a letter of commendation in your file if we succeed," Johnson said.

"As soon as you two get your moral problems worked out, we've got work to do," Loomis said. "First of all, we'll need Tycoon."

Grindstaff went to his luggage, pulled out a briefcase, and returned to the couch. He shifted through some papers. "Can we count on him?" he asked. "Remember, we can't afford a single turndown. We have to be certain, before we ask. Otherwise, they might get misguided, patriotic ideas and blow the whistle on us."

"We need Tycoon," Loomis repeated. "We can't operate without him. He has the transportation. He has the contacts in Europe. And if we can't trust him, we can't trust anybody."

"Okay," Grindstaff said. "Who else?"

"There's Peter Rabbit," Johnson said. "He's nutty enough."

"Who?" Loomis asked.

"Our undercover dopehead in Europe," Johnson said. "Better known as Peter Rabbit."

"How times have changed," Loomis said.

"You knew him in Africa, one of those wars," Grindstaff told Loomis. "You knew him as Peter Welch. He told me he saw you there."

Loomis was amazed. "Pete? With the Company?" A thought came to him. "Was he then?"

Grindstaff was amused. "No. He wasn't sent to fulfill the contract on you. He came in later."

"Think he would do it?" Loomis asked.

"If we could convince him," Grindstaff said.

"That brings up a point," Johnson said. "How are we going to convince anybody? This is pretty heavy shit to lay on anyone, right out of the blue."

Loomis thought about it for a moment. "I can think of several people from the old days. But we can't take any risks. I don't know how we could get the point across, long-distance, after all these years. Somebody, somewhere, would query Langley, tip our hand."

"I know several," Grindstaff said. "Brad Jordan, station chief in Lisbon, code name Broadsword. You remember him. He has a good team. But I think you're right. We can't risk it."

"Let's face it," Loomis said. "If five men can't do it, chances are it can't be done with less than a company of Marines."

Grindstaff looked at Loomis, then at Johnson. "All right, we're in," he said.

Then, in high excitement, they began drafting plans, laying strategy. One by one, problems of personnel, weaponry, supplies, transportation, cover stories, and border problems were solved. And as the work progressed, they were seized by a euphoria best described by Johnson:

"My God, there's been nothing like this in all history!" he said. "Just think about it. We're setting out to save the whole fucking world!"

They piled hands, football-squad fashion, grinning like schoolboys.

Johnson phoned Tycoon while Loomis listened on the extension. Tycoon seemed puzzled and apprehensive.

"Hey, Tycoon, what you doing?" Johnson asked.

"I'm in bed with three Margaritas and two *señoritas*," Tycoon said. "Or maybe it's the other way around. What's up?"

"I hate to interrupt. But we got a little job for you," Johnson said.

The line was silent for a moment. "I'm still recovering from the last one," Tycoon said. "Things seem to happen when you and Loomis get together. He in this?"

"I'm in," Loomis said.

"Then it's trouble," Tycoon said. "Bad trouble. And I'm confused. I didn't know I fell under your assignments desk, Johnson."

"This isn't exactly what you might call a Company-oriented project," Johnson said.

"Oh, shit, I was afraid of that," Tycoon said. "What is it?"

"Our friends are at it again," Johnson said. "And this time they've won. Everything east of here is out of business."

Tycoon hesitated, absorbing the message. "You mean . . ."

"Everybody's knuckled under," Johnson said. "You're talking to the only game in town—maybe the whole fucking world. And we need you."

"I've heard some disturbing rumors within the last few hours," Tycoon said after a moment. "But this is worse. Are you certain on what's happening? What I'm saying, I'd hate to jeopardize my position just because you nuts got a screw loose."

Johnson lowered his voice. "Tycoon, I hate to put it into these terms, because of the shock value. But if our friends keep up their good work, they're going to take all of your toys away from you."

"That does it," Tycoon said. "You've talked me into it. When and where?"

They quickly agreed on plans: Tycoon would fly to Houston, landing just before dawn.

"But I'm going to finish my Margarita first," he said.

Johnson jarred Dr. Burke out of sound sleep at his home in Albuquerque.

"Doc, Johnson here. Do you remember telling me, once, that you could do some damage in anger?"

Loomis could hear Burke shifting the phone, apparently changing position in bed. "I remember," he said.

"Would you like the chance?"

"Depends," Burke said. "How's Michael?"

"He's doing fine, I'm told. Depends on what?"

"On what that chance is."

"The best. Your worst fears have been realized. Are you familiar with the expression, 'calf rope'?"

"I am."

"Well, the United States government has just yelled calf rope. You have been named to a very select team to see what can be done about it. I know, this is a lot to accept on such short notice. But you know us. You know what we've done on this job thus far. We're asking you to help us do more."

"We need you, Burke," Loomis said.

"And we need your hobby," Johnson added.

The line was silent for a moment. "All those items in my hobby are registered to me," he said. "If that makes any difference."

"Wouldn't matter," Johnson said. "Those registration papers have just been taken over by someone else."

"Oh, I see," Burke said. He then made his decision. "What is it you want me to do?" he asked.

"Load your stuff in a charter plane. Bring it to Houston tonight. We'll have transportation from here. Be prepared for a long trip back to your old stomping grounds. We'll fill you in when you get here."

"My God, I can't do that!" Burke said. "I've got surgery at eight in the morning."

"Our surgery is a bit more important," Loomis told him.

"You might say we've got to remove a massive malignancy," Johnson said.

"My old stomping grounds," Burke said. "Will I be back in four or five days?"

"If you come back at all," Loomis said.

"Loomis always tends to put the best face on things," Johnson said. "Look at it this way: if we fail, your medical practice is gone anyway, along with the rest of the country. So what the hell?"

The line was silent as Burke debated with himself. "I don't know how I can just walk away from my patients," he said. "Couldn't I send you the equipment?"

"We need *you*," Loomis said. "We need your knowledge of where we're going."

"And besides," Johnson stuck in, "you've already proved you have a secret yen to be a hero. Here's a real chance."

"All right," Burke said. "I'll plead sudden illness, and turn everything over to an associate. Believe me, when he finds out the mess I've left him, I'd *better* be out of town."

After they made arrangements for the rendezvous, Johnson hung up and glanced at his watch.

"That's it," Grindstaff said. "Let's get the hell out of here before the roof caves in."

Grindstaff and Johnson picked up gear and began moving toward the car. Loomis remained by the phone. Johnson looked back, questioningly.

"I've got one more call to make," Loomis said. "I'll be there in a minute."

He picked up the phone and started dialing.

Five men might be enough, if they were lucky.

But they also needed one good woman.

Chapter

22

"Remember how great it was, when it snowed?" Thornsen asked. "Remember? We used to walk over to Campus Corner and get a cheeseburger and a malt. Or sometimes, we would walk all the way down to the highway to that all-night drive-in. What was its name?"

Standing at the line printer, Hampton was only half listening. He did not have the tolerance of the other members of Hamlet for Thornsen's continual reminiscing about their college days. He could not work up the necessary concern for a drive-in he had not seen in twenty years.

Thornsen was looking at him with an uncomfortable intensity, awaiting an answer.

"I don't know," Hampton said, concentrating on the fast-flowing printout.

"It had a circular front," Thornsen insisted. "And you used to play the jukebox. Hank Williams, Eddy Arnold, Ernest Tubbs, Red Foley. Don't you remember that?"

"Vaguely," Hampton said. He pointed to the line printer. "What's this?" he asked.

Thornsen apparently had not missed as much as a comma

of the incoming data, despite his preoccupation with the past. "Not much," he said without bothering to look. "The National Reconnaissance Office has completed its satellite scan of the Rapier sites. The National Security Council has put out a cease-and-desist to the Houston operation, calling off the search for you. The council has been in almost constant session. But nothing much seems to be coming from it." He smiled. "Thus far, everything is going according to plan."

"What about the weather?" Hampton asked.

"Couldn't be shaping up better," Thornsen said. "A new front is well across the Lakes region, and pushing eastward. It should pass through the sites sometime tonight."

Hampton dug down through the folded computer paper, reviewing the data. Although he was not in Thornsen's league, he usually could determine the gist of the flow. Unlike the other members of Hamlet, Hampton was not content to leave all the electronic wizardry to Thornsen.

Hampton had no illusions: someday, Hamlet's unstructured camaraderie would come to an end. Under the pressure of running a world government, personal relationships would shatter. Someone would have to assume absolute control.

He intended to be that someone.

No other member was capable. Thornsen was too ineffectual in handling anything involving flesh and blood. Giancarlo was too soft, too easygoing. Bernardo lacked direction. Zoff was too conservative. Ahmed was an angry child. Vogel was a stuffed shirt.

At the moment, with their first real crisis coming to a head, the other members of Hamlet were upstairs in the castle, drinking and playing cards, awaiting developments. He alone was in the basement, smelling Thornsen's stench, worrying.

He monitored the machines almost two hours before he noticed. He then went back through the material, just to make certain he was not wrong.

Puzzled, he walked over to Thornsen, working at a terminal.

"There's nothing here about Houston. Doesn't that strike you as strange?"

Thornsen did not answer for a moment. After completing a sequence, he replayed Hampton's question in his mind.

"Not necessarily," he said. "I mean, they've stopped the Houston operation."

"But there should be something," Hampton insisted. "All these messages, orders, interoffice communications, neatly filed. And not a thing about Houston."

"I've only extracted the top-priority data," Thornsen explained. "Otherwise, we'd be swamped with garbage."

"Still, you'd think *something* would be there," Hampton insisted. "It seems to me all references are carefully being avoided."

Thornsen thought about it. He walked over to the table and flipped through the last few minutes of readout. "You might be right," he said. "Let's go to a lower priority extraction and see what we turn up. There should be some data filed—travel vouchers, work schedules, routine reports . . ."

"Isn't there some way you can extract references to Houston, without getting all the garbage?" Hampton asked.

Thornsen walked over to the terminal, thinking. "There might be a way," he said. "There's an originator extension. And an addressee encoder. . . ."

He began working at the keyboard. When he hit the execute key, the single word *Searching* appeared on the screen.

"It's working," Thornsen said, looking up at Hampton, his eyes seeking approval feedback.

Hampton nodded his appreciation of Thornsen's expertise. He watched the *Searching* signal, aware that during each second, the machines were going through hundreds, perhaps thousands of files, hunting each single reference to "Houston," and to the originator numbers and encoder phrases assigned to Houston.

Search Completed, the screen responded.

"Nothing," Thornsen said. "That *is* strange." He sat staring at the screen. "What do you think this means?"

Hampton had been projecting his own scenario. "They left Grindstaff in charge down there," he remembered. "You would think there would be some specific communication with him, in reference to Loomis or Johnson. To my way of thinking, that can only mean one thing. Grindstaff is no longer in Houston."

"But there would be something here if he were ordered out," Thornsen insisted. "They always file assignments. That's routine."

Thornsen was correct, Hampton realized. Another thought came to him.

"Maybe *they* don't know where Grindstaff is—or Loomis, or Johnson."

Thornsen looked up. "How could that be?"

Hampton continued to voice his speculations as they came to him. "Suppose . . . just suppose . . . Loomis found something in Houston. Some clue, maybe, maybe a connection to me. And suppose he got some hint of what was happening in Washington. Considering all we know about him, what do you think he'd do?"

"Cut loose from Washington," Thornsen said.

"Right. That would account for the silence. Washington doesn't know what has happened to him. And they don't want us to suspect that Loomis and his team are missing."

"But what could Loomis do?" Thornsen asked.

"I don't know," Hampton said, thinking ahead. "But we'd better prepare some options, just in case."

Felix Zoff, frightened out of his wits by the new developments, walked around the huge baronial hall, actually wringing his hands.

"The machines are automatic, aren't they?" he asked, his voice rising to a shrill falsetto. "So why can't we just leave, until it's all over? There's no reason to stay here and get shot!"

"No!" Thornsen shouted. "We can't leave the machines."

Hampton intervened. "The machines need tending," he told Zoff. "We need constant information, in order to make decisions. If anything goes wrong, we have to know."

"We can't leave the machines, Felix," Giancarlo agreed.

"But we can't just sit here and wait to be murdered!" Bernardo said.

Hampton turned away in disgust. He walked to the huge mantel. He allowed the argument to continue while he watched the burning logs, his anger building.

Then, unable to contain his fury any longer, he turned and shouted them down.

"Rulers of the world, shit!" he yelled. "Look at you! We work and plan twenty years. And at the first sign of trouble, you go to pieces! You want to cut and run! Well, go ahead! Run! Thornsen has put his entire life down the tube for you. I've cut myself off from everything, walked away from my entire life, thinking we were at last fully committed. I should have known!"

He walked over and slammed a fist onto the table. "To hell with all of you! I'm not leaving!"

He wheeled and walked back to the fireplace. Leaning against the huge fieldstones, he closed his eyes and awaited the reaction to his outburst.

Giancarlo was the first to speak.

"I suppose we had that coming, Hamp," he said. "You're right. We've tended to have our heads in the clouds, thinking only of the results. Maybe none of us has been prepared, mentally, to pay the price."

He hesitated. "What do you want us to do, Hamp?"

Hampton did not move. His face averted, he allowed himself a moment to exult over his victory.

He had just asserted himself as the leader of Hamlet.

And he had won without dissenting voice.

He waited until he was certain no evidence of gloat, of self-satisfaction, remained in his expression. He then turned to face Hamlet.

"If worst comes to worst, and Loomis, or anyone, should by some remote chance trace us here, there is an easy way to take the pressure off. The minute we even suspect we are in any personal danger, we fire the Rapier rockets."

Hampton allowed the members of Hamlet a moment of

painful introspection. They had planned Rapier for years. But as he suspected, to a man they were reluctant to use it, now that the time had arrived.

"That wouldn't save us, would it?" Zoff asked.

Hampton explained. "With Rapier fired, no one is going to worry about us for a while. They will have their hands full. We could make use of our escape routes, with plenty of time to organize the next step. We can do that from anywhere we can put Trane on a terminal. Italy, Japan, Argentina . . ."

"Any of our other centers would need more equipment," Thornsen said. "Line printers and such. But it could be done."

"What about the weather?" Bernardo asked.

"In a few more hours, conditions will be ideal," Hampton told them.

"What would be the next target?" Zoff asked.

"Chicago, the upper Midwest," Hampton said. "Some work remains to be done. But after Rapier, we will have plenty of time."

For a full minute, only the crackling of the logs in the fireplace averted complete silence as each member of Hamlet worked out his own rationale for what he was about to do.

Then Giancarlo reached for a wine bottle, and refilled his glass.

"All right, Hamp," he said. "I'm in."

And Hampton's proposal to remain at the castle was approved without further discussion.

Chapter

23

"I think we have the picture now, Mr. President," Thimble said. "It isn't good."

"At this point, I'd be surprised if it was," President Robertson said. "But tell me anyway."

His Assistant for National Security referred briefly to hurried notes. Waiting, Robertson noted that Thimble's eyes were red-rimmed and drawn. He had shed his customary jacket and vest. His white shirt seemed rumpled beyond redemption. Robertson wondered, idly, how many hours they now had worked without relief.

"Tycoon has left Mexico. Dr. Burke has left Albuquerque. A Lear jet was refueled before dawn this morning in Houston. The story was, it was an executive jet en route to a board meeting in Hartford. It was tracked in that direction."

"Let me guess," Robertson said. "No Lear jet of that description has landed in Hartford."

"No, sir. Right now, we don't know where it is. But we're searching flight data. That may yield something."

"Probably too little, too late," Robertson said.

Robertson was near collapse from fatigue. Thimble, Vice-President Threadgill, Admiral Morgan, all the other men in the room seemed distant, off in another, foggy world. Robertson did not trust his own judgment, and for him that was a new experience.

He leaned back in his chair and looked up at the oval

ceiling. "Assuming you were me, what would you do now, Hank?" he asked Threadgill.

Seated in a wing chair at the end of the desk, the vice-president groaned. "Travis, if you keep asking questions like that, I may reach the point where I won't even want your job." He paused for a moment. "Since you've asked, here's what I would recommend: list everything we know for certain. And number one, we can rest assured that the Hamlet Group is not in the northeastern portion of the United States."

Robertson lowered his head and stared at the vice-president.

"I'm getting blank looks from everybody," Threadgill complained. "But I'm only stating the obvious. The members of Hamlet wouldn't destroy themselves."

Robertson, too tired to speak, nodded his acceptance of the premise.

"Two, Loomis and his team apparently are bound for Hamlet's headquarters—or where they have *some* reason to assume that headquarters is located. They flew toward the Northeast. If they know of the ultimatum, they know of the proximity devices. Whatever else, Loomis and Johnson are reasonably intelligent. They will assume that if we cannot approach the plutonium rockets, with all of our electronic resources, they would not have a chance. So I think we can be certain that Loomis and his team are not moving against the Rapier sites."

Robertson nodded agreement.

"Now, if Loomis and his team are heading toward the Northeast, but not going to the Northeast, then they must be going *beyond* the Northeast. Right?"

"Europe," Thimble said.

"A reasonable guess," Threadgill said. "But that brings us down to the short rows. If we alert our forces in Europe, in an effort to stop Loomis, we could not help but inform Hamlet that Loomis is missing, and that he is out of our control."

261

"And they would fire the rockets," Thimble said.

Threadgill got up from his chair and began walking around the room. "They have promised to do so," he said. "But let's look at the alternative. If we keep silent, and the Hamlet people learn that Loomis and his team are en route, they will suspect collusion on our part—that we secretly have aided and abetted Loomis."

"And they would fire the rockets," Robertson said. "So we're damned if we do, damned if we don't."

"But there *is* a difference between the alternatives," Threadgill said.

Despite his mental exhaustion, Robertson understood. "Putting out the word to stop Loomis does at least have the face of cooperation," he said.

Threadgill stopped pacing. He turned and gave Robertson a long, searching look.

"But then Hamlet will know, for certain, that an assault team may be on the way. We will destroy Loomis's best weapon—surprise."

For a moment, Robertson allowed himself the luxury of hoping that Loomis and Johnson might find and destroy Hamlet.

But logic overwhelmed all hope.

"There is no other way, is there?" he asked Threadgill. "We've got to do it."

Threadgill shook his head sadly. "I've gone over it repeatedly. I can't see another way."

Robertson turned to Thimble.

"Put out the word to all our spooks in Europe—military intelligence, CIA, the works. Cover all of Tycoon's contacts, every conceivable route. Make it plain. Loomis, Johnson, Grindstaff are to be eliminated—shot—on sight."

Thimble hesitated.

"How will we make it known to the people in the field that we don't really mean it?"

"We *do* mean it," Robertson said patiently. "That's what we must make plain to Hamlet. Put it in all communications.

262

And file all the communications in those precious electronic storage units. Hamlet apparently reads our mail from information retrieval. Well, make certain they retrieve this."

After Thimble was gone, Threadgill reached for his coffee. He sipped, then made a face.

"I've always heard of the 'bitter dregs of defeat,' " he said. "I never knew they'd come with White House coffee."

Chapter

24

Once safely out over the Atlantic, Tycoon climbed for altitude. He had explained to his passengers that over the continental United States, the zone from 18,000 to 60,000 feet is designated Positive Control Airspace, rigidly monitored twenty-four hours a day. The layer from 14,500 to 18,000 feet also is restricted, but to a lesser degree. Only the air below 14,500 feet, in certain areas, is uncontrolled. So Tycoon had kept the Lear at low altitudes across the country, until they refueled at a small airfield near Boston. Then he had flown almost on the water until they were more than two hundred miles out to sea.

Loomis was riding in the copilot's seat. Dr. Burke and Grindstaff were napping just behind him. Johnson was sprawled across the two backseats, sound asleep.

Loomis watched the tops of the huge thunderheads sliding by, far below. The distance, the disassociation from the earth, tended to make all problems down there remote and unimportant. But Loomis knew that while the Lear wafted eastward at its most efficient cruising speed, much was happening. No doubt Langley had already missed Grindstaff, and had awakened to the fact that Johnson also had disappeared. Checks would be made. They would find Tycoon gone from Mexico, Dr. Burke from Albuquerque. Within hours, they would put it all together.

Loomis was certain that the government would make every effort to stop them.

He and his assault team had only one advantage: no one in Washington as yet would know their destination.

On the edge of the stratosphere, boosted along by the jet stream, the Lear had settled into routine flight. Tycoon had engaged the autopilot, and was now searching through his maps and charts.

Loomis studied his watch, calculating hours, speed, and distances.

Maria Elena would now be nearing the coast of Europe. And riding with her would be the failure or success of the mission.

Yet, there had been precious little time to brief her. Only a few minutes had separated her arrival and departure flights at Houston.

Loomis had taken her to one side of a waiting area where they stood, huddled against the wall, just two more people saying good-bye in the milling crowds at Hobby International.

There, in a few, brief, terse sentences, he had told her all they knew about Hamlet, about their situation, and how things were in Washington. Maria Elena had accepted it all without question, without comment. His face and tone must have helped him to convey the urgency. Only when he had finished did Maria Elena ask a question.

"What is it you want me to do?"

He told her, then, outlining it step by step, urging her to use caution, yet knowing full well the dangers.

"Make your phone call in Brussels as soon as possible," he told her. "Your contact is a friend of Tycoon. By the time you arrive, he should have the information you need. But Washington will be closing in on Tycoon's contacts. So you'll have to hurry."

Her flight was called even as he talked. And it was as

they were saying good-bye that she said something exceedingly odd. He continued to puzzle over it.

"I think I know now what is wrong between us—why I have such heavy qualms about your work, about the life you've led. . . ."

She grasped his arm. "Loomis, in your work, you only destroy. Granted, maybe it's an evil, like Hamlet, that needs to be destroyed. But there is nothing created, to take the place of what you destroy."

She frowned, struggling to put her thoughts into words. "I'll give you an example," she said. "I met a man in Hollywood who has spent his whole life trying to get the money to find a way to feed the world from the food that goes to waste in the oceans," she said. "Isn't that wonderful? Think what it would be like, to build, instead of to be wrecking things, tearing down. Think about that, Loomis."

His bafflement must have registered on his face.

"When this is over, we'll talk about it," she said. "I just wanted you to know what was in my head."

He did not escort her to the boarding gate. He assumed that all departure areas were being monitored. There had been time for only a brief, hurried kiss.

"You know, all things considered, this may turn out to be my greatest role," Maria Elena said.

And then she was gone.

Loomis knew his worry would not do her, or him, any good. He did not have time now to meditate over that perplexing remark she had made. They could sort out their lives later—if they lived.

There was too much work to be done.

He turned in his seat to face Tycoon.

"We better put what time we've got to use," he said. "Do you have a map of Luxembourg?"

"Only aeronautical charts," Tycoon said. "I don't know if they'll help much."

"I grabbed a handful of tourist material before I left home," Dr. Burke said behind him. "There are a few maps, and some photographs that might be useful."

Loomis leafed through the material. There was a great deal yet to absorb.

"Maybe we can all look them over before we land," Loomis said. "But could you just give us the basics?"

"Of course," Dr. Burke said.

"Kick Johnson," Loomis said to Grindstaff. "He should hear this."

Burke waited until he was certain Johnson was awake.

"Well, it's a small country, of course. Sixty miles or so at its longest, about thirty miles at the widest. The north portion is heavily wooded—the Ardennes. The south is more open. There are slightly more than three hundred thousand people—about the population of Albuquerque."

"Language?" Loomis asked.

"German, mostly, especially for business. French runs a close second, tending to be used on social occasions. The natives have their own language—Letzeburgesch—which is a real jawbreaker. English is taught in the schools, and since they tend to be trilingual to begin with, many people speak English well."

"Industry?" Grindstaff asked.

"Steel, I suppose," Burke said. "Mostly in the south. Very, very European, perhaps the most historically European place left in Europe. You feel like you're in the middle of a Metropolitan Opera set. And of course it's not much bigger."

"Government?" Loomis asked.

"Monarchy by democratic consent, I think is the correct terminology. They can trace the monarchy back more than a thousand years. They're not about to change. It's a strange place. Someone will be telling you something that happened, and you get the idea it happened yesterday. But when you ask, you find it was something that occurred in the thirteenth century."

Johnson sat up. He had been looking at some brochures. "I suppose that brings us to these old castles," he said.

"There are about two hundred scattered over the country. Many, especially the older ones, are in ruins. Some were restored in the eighteenth and nineteenth centuries. Some are open to the public. Some are privately owned, set back in the valleys, and virtually unknown to anyone but the natives of that region.''

"Military?" Loomis asked.

"Compulsory service until a few years ago. Now they have a professional army, with an authorized strength of five hundred and fifty."

"Five hundred and fifty what?" Johnson asked.

"Men.''

"Police?" Grindstaff asked.

"Here and there. They keep a low profile.''

Loomis found a fairly detailed map in the tourist brochures. "I wonder why Hamlet chose this little country," he said.

"We don't know that they did," Grindstaff reminded him. "If our guess is wrong, this may be the most costly wild-goose chase in the history of the world.''

"Just to put my mind at ease, let's assume our guess is right," Loomis said. "What is the economic setup?"

"Luxembourg City is smack-dab in the middle of the European federation," Burke said. "The Luxembourg people are fanatically independent. But they're not stupid. They've been allied with other European countries for years. They have a stock market—have had for half a century. They've wooed big business with tax incentives and other considerations. Goodyear makes the steel for tires there, and has put in a research and test center. DuPont, Mylar Polyester, Monsanto, several other big names have moved in.''

"That would tend to hide Hamlet's own business manipulations and communications," Loomis said.

"To an extent," Tycoon agreed. "But I think we can depend on Hamlet requiring at least two or three times the facilities needed by any other company.''

"Transportation?" Grindstaff asked.

"That's Tycoon's department," Johnson said.

"We've got a little problem in this area," Tycoon said.

"Five men. A private jet. A load of machine guns. We can't help but attract some attention. I'm aiming for a field just outside Brussels. That'll be our first step."

"What are our chances?" Grindstaff asked.

"Not too good," Tycoon admitted. "Here's the picture. Nine nations have an elaborate air-defense structure under NATO auspices. The last I heard, there were sixty-seven radar warning installations, and one hundred and fifteen other air-defense ground facilities on a north-south sweep, from Norway and Denmark through Germany, The Netherlands, Belgium, France, Italy, and Greece. And there are one hundred and eighteen missile sites."

He pointed. "Normally, nobody would pay too much attention to a single unidentified contact, not if we were to cross here, the route of most unchartered flights to Paris. But if U.S. forces in Europe, or the Hamlet team, are monitoring, we would certainly be picked up by radar. If Hamlet has penetrated U.S. computer systems, they're no doubt also into the NATO Integrated Communications System. The headquarters are in Brussels."

"What about flight control?" Loomis asked.

"All monitored by Eurocontrol, which now has some link with NATO Committee for European Airspace Coordination. All schedules and ETAs are cranked in. Hamlet may be reading their electronic mail."

"If they find us, can they stop us?" Johnson asked.

"One thirty-year-old Starfire with an obsolete Sidewinder missile would do the job nicely," Tycoon said.

They spent the next three hours in preparation. Burke uncrated the machine guns, one by one, and explained each individual weapon, its mode of operation, and peculiarities.

They would be armed well but strangely.

Hilarity rose as Dr. Burke demonstrated the old guns, showing how to load, how to fire. Loomis knelt beside him on the floor of the plane and examined the Model T era weapons. There was a 1917 .30-caliber Hotchkiss with an ungainly, awkward tripod mount. A 1916 Lewis in .303

caliber was equipped with a freaky, rotating ammunition pan. There was a .30-caliber Spandau Maxim aircraft gun that seemed tailor-made to go against Snoopy and his Sopwith Camel.

Dr. Burke took the high humor in stride.

"They may be old, but the workmanship, the quality, the dependability, outstrip almost anything being made today," he said. "Just look at this old French Chauchat. It may look weird. It should. It was introduced in World War One as the first true assault rifle."

Tycoon habitually kept six Ingram Model 10 .45-caliber submachine guns on board the Lear. Light in weight, limited to thirty-two-round magazines, the Ingrams came equipped with external silencers.

Johnson was unhappy with the armament.

"Antiques, and six peashooters," he fumed. "We're some assault force."

"Don't knock Doc's antiques," Loomis said. "A thirty-aught-six slug is a thirty-aught-six slug, no matter what kind of weapon fires it."

"And don't knock my Ingrams," Tycoon said. "They're beautiful little weapons. The change lever gives you selective fire for single shot, automatic at ninety-six rounds a minute, or cyclic at better than a thousand rounds a minute."

"With thirty-two rounds in the magazine. That's less than two seconds of sustained fire," Johnson argued.

"You don't need thirty-two forty-five slugs to kill a man," Tycoon said. "Leave it on selective fire."

"But doesn't that silencer limit the range?" Grindstaff asked.

"Absolutely not," Tycoon said. "The suppressor doesn't slow the bullet to subsonic, but conflicts the gas streams. Your target will still hear the crack of the bullet passing him, if you miss, but he won't be able to pick out the location of the gun."

From the travel brochures, they learned that electric trains ran from Brussels to Luxembourg almost hourly—covering

269

the one hundred and twenty-seven miles in just over two hours.

"I've taken that train," Burke said. "It crosses the border at Arlon. There are no customs and passport checks. Belgium and Luxembourg have mutual customs borders."

Through two hours of concentrated work, they completed preliminary plans.

Loomis and Tycoon would rent a car, load the machine guns, and head for Luxembourg.

Grindstaff, Johnson, and Dr. Burke would take the train, separately.

U.S. forces in Europe no doubt would be alerted to watch for five men, traveling together. By splitting up, they might increase their odds on getting through.

They would meet, outside Luxembourg City.

Loomis was gambling that by the time they reached the rendezvous, he would know their target.

As they neared the European coast, Tycoon took the Lear even higher, circling, constantly monitoring the radio. With a circular slide rule, he rechecked his figures.

"Something's off," he said. "I've missed my target. We may be in trouble."

Still monitoring the radio, he computed gas consumption against reserve.

"We've got to find my target in the next five or six minutes," he said. "If we don't, we'll just have to go in cold turkey."

Three minutes passed. Tycoon then broke into a broad grin.

"He's late," he said. "If the fix he just gave is right, we should see him in a minute or two."

They made two wide circles before Loomis caught the glint of sun on a wing above them.

"That's him," Tycoon said, advancing the throttles. "Thank God I souped-up this crate. Let's just hope our fuel holds out."

Tycoon climbed until the Lear was above, and slightly behind the Pan Am 747.

"He'll be letting down at Brussels," Tycoon said. "His transponder should hide us until then. We'll ride into Europe on his blip."

For the next hour, Tycoon concentrated on maintaining station above and behind the Pan Am flight. When the 747 began its steep descent over Ghent, Tycoon closed the gap, flying close on the unsuspecting Pan Am's tail. He held the position until the 747 started into the dogleg for its approach to Brussels National Airport.

Abruptly, Tycoon pulled away and put the Lear into a speed-building dive. At just over a thousand feet, he leveled off and made a sharp turn to the right.

"The seven forty-seven hid us to some extent," Tycoon said. "But you can pray that the people on the ground weren't paying much attention to their scopes." He banked slightly, and lowered the flaps.

"We're on our own, now," he said. "Let's just hope that everyone can make it to the rendezvous."

Chapter

25

Just beyond the Grand Ducal Palais, Maria Elena entered the Côte d'Eisch and drove the rented Fiat northward out of Luxembourg City, toward the Ardennes.

Dawn had come, cold and gray, and the pavement was wet from a gentle rain. Her plane had been late. She now was worried about time.

As the traffic thinned on the northern outskirts, Maria

Elena adjusted the rearview mirror to make a last-minute check of her face.

A brief glance, and she was satisfied. Through simple improvision, she could hardly hope to do better. She hardly recognized herself.

Her hair was pulled back severely into a bun, almost hiding beneath an inexpensive scarf. Round, tinted steel-rimmed glasses all but hid her eyes, and erased the natural symmetry of her features. She had used only a trace of makeup—to add a prim pallor to her mouth.

She was confident that she was in character, to all appearances, for the most important role in her career.

Mentally, she still had a long way to go. But she had studied an American tourist in Brussels, carefully memorizing her characteristics. As she drove northward, Maria Elena rehearsed her lines, planning her inflections, her every gesture.

She *had* to be ready.

Thirty kilometers north of Luxembourg, she came to terrain she recognized. Tycoon's Belgian friend had given her far more than the simple coordinates on a map. He apparently had excellent sources, who knew the countryside as well as they knew the communications facilities within Luxembourg. The landscape had been described accurately.

Slowing the Fiat, she pulled onto the shoulder of the road and came to a stop, leaving the motor running, the wipers softly clearing the windshield of mist.

Ahead, the road descended into the valley of the Sûre. In the distance, a castle stood almost lost amidst the forest around it. Maria Elena did not need the confirmation of her maps. The castle was as Tycoon's contact had described it. An entrance road curved through a long S across a well-tended meadow. Two ancient towers were visible behind the castle. The Ardennes encircled the castle on three sides, almost hiding it from view.

Tycoon's friend had ascertained from his well-placed

sources that this innocent-appearing castle housed the most elaborate telephone and microwave communications facilities in the region.

Stepping from the car, Maria Elena took two snaps with a Polaroid camera, patiently awaiting film development each time. Both were of adequate quality, providing an accurate view of the castle and its surroundings.

Loomis had said that any pictures she could obtain of the site would be a bonus. If the castle was indeed Hamlet's headquarters, Loomis had his bonus.

Returning to the car, she drove to the entrance road. As she neared the castle, she could see the shuttered turrets on the third floor more clearly. She picked up the camera and made a quick snap through the windshield.

Rounding a curve, she came unexpectedly upon a guard station, screened until the last moment by a stand of trees. Braking, Maria Elena stopped before the wooden barrier, and rolled down the glass as a costumed guard approached the car.

He was smiling pleasantly. He spoke to her in French. "Could I be of assistance, *mademoiselle?*"

The accent was German. His uniform was modified medieval —short, square-cut blue coat and clinging male trousers. The historic effect of his costume was dampened by a plastic cover protecting his hat from the mist.

"Excuse me," Maria Elena said in French, Americanizing her accent. "Would it be possible for me to see the castle?"

The guard was polite, but firm. "I'm sorry, *mademoiselle*. The castle is privately owned. There are no facilities for tourists."

"But I'm not a tourist!" Maria Elena explained with desperation as she fell solidly into her role. She fished in her purse for the pocket litter Tycoon's Belgian contact had furnished. "I have credentials! I am doing my dissertation on pre-Roman influences in medieval architecture. Those two old towers . . ."

"I'm sorry," the guard said again, ignoring the identification cards. "What you ask is not possible. The castle is never open to visitors. I'm sure you will find all the information you need in libraries. . . ."

"If I could only photograph the grounds," Maria Elena interrupted. "The towers. If I could study the mortar, the traces of tools in the stones. I wouldn't bother anyone. It's *very* important."

"I must insist, *mademoiselle*," the guard said.

Quickly, Maria Elena stepped from the car, camera in hand. "At least I can photograph from here," she said.

"Please!" the guard said, attempting to block her view.

But Maria Elena got the picture—the guard station, the road, the tree line, the front of the castle.

"You impose," the guard said, taking her arm. "You are trespassing on private ground, *mademoiselle*. You must leave immediately. I will have you escorted."

He turned and walked toward the station, calling out, "Herr Stoeller!"

The door opened. A tall blond man stepped out. Maria Elena had the impression of a European-cut business suit, but she was looking past him to the interior of the station. She caught a glimpse of a row of six or eight television screens.

The incongruity almost amounted to a time warp. A medieval castle with closed-circuit television monitors?

Maria Elena let the camera dangle by the neck cord. She held up her hands, palms out. "All right, all right," she said, backing toward the car. "I'll go." She stopped for one last effort. "But . . . please understand! I have traveled thousands of miles to examine these castles. I have put years of work, every cent of money I have, into it. Who can grant me permission?"

"I have explained to her that permission is never granted," the guard said to Stoeller.

Stoeller stepped forward. "*Mademoiselle*, whatever information you are seeking can be found in the libraries. Everything of value was recorded, long ago."

"If you don't have the authority to give me permission, then *please* tell me whom to ask," Maria Elena insisted.

"It would be futile," Stoeller said. "Permission is never granted."

"Well, thanks for nothing," Maria Elena said in English. She returned to the car, wheeled the Fiat around in a circle, and drove back to the main road. There she stopped briefly and examined the last picture.

It was perfect.

After numerous inquiries in a small village a few miles from Ettelbruck, Maria Elena found an elderly local historian thoroughly familiar with the castle.

"Oh, yes, I remember it well," he said. "When I was a boy, my father knew the family. I visited there, many times. The last time, I suppose, was before the second German occupation. The family was known for a fine light Pinot Blanc. Not as fine as some of the Moselle wines, of course. But very respectable."

"Who owns the castle now?" Maria Elena asked.

Returning to the present with difficulty, the old man seemed to be confused. "I don't know," he said. "The family died off. There was a Swiss nephew. . . ." He frowned. "I've heard that it is owned by an institution—a Swiss corporation. But I don't know. Somewhere, I have photographs of the castle as it used to be, and some information you are welcome to use."

Maria Elena spent the remainder of the afternoon and much of the evening photographing his records, and in making notes.

She then made one last effort.

"What is the castle being used for now?" she asked. "Why won't they allow visitors? Even professional people like myself, who need to examine it?"

The old man seemed vaguely uncomfortable. He shifted in his chair. "I don't know anything about it."

"But surely people talk," she insisted.

He shrugged. "Oh, there are rumors. But I don't know."

"What rumors?"

The old man took a deep breath and let it out slowly.

"They say a huge corporation is using the wine cellars as laboratories, producing secret materials, possibly even weaponry." He smiled. "That is what the villagers believe. But I don't know."

The wine cellars were detailed in Maria Elena's notes. Also, she had the prewar photographs.

Certain that she had all she needed, Maria Elena thanked the old man and left.

She was appalled when she discovered the time. She left Ettelbruck and drove the Fiat at top speed toward Hamm.

She was already late for the rendezvous.

And she was virtually certain that she had confirmation the old castle was the headquarters of Hamlet.

Chapter

26

Broadsword first saw the man with the goatee in Namur station as the Ostend-to-Luxembourg made a brief stop. The small, rotund man dashing to catch the train seemed vaguely familiar. Not until the man was aboard did Broadsword remember the fifth man on Loomis's team.

He signaled to Peter Rabbit, monitoring the crowd, three cars away. Broadsword hurriedly boarded the train. Peter Rabbit was close behind him. They conferred briefly.

"Dr. Burke is in the next car," Broadsword told him.

"Alone?" Peter Rabbit said, surprised.

"I figured all along they would split up," Broadsword said. "This will make it easier. They'll have to reassemble somewhere. All we have to do is follow the good doctor."

"Some of the others may be aboard," Peter Rabbit said. "Check out the whole train. But be careful. We don't want to spook them. I'll keep an eye on the doctor."

Entering the next car, Broadsword walked past the doctor to a vacant seat two rows back. Intent on tourist brochures, Burke did not look up. Broadsword leaned back in his seat and watched Burke through half-closed eyes.

There was a mystery about the man. Why had Loomis chosen this sixty-year-old man for his wild-hair junket?

In appearance, Burke certainly was unprepossessing. At the moment, no one would have guessed that he was other than a modestly successful American, touring Europe on vacation.

Watching Burke, Broadsword wished that some way existed to learn what was in the man's head.

Why had he thrown in with Loomis and Johnson on such a fools' mission?

Why had Grindstaff defected? And Tycoon, with so much to lose?

And why did Langley want them dead?

As the electric clicked away the miles, Broadsword puzzled over the whole affair. He knew that he did not have the whole story.

Yet, he would have to act on what he knew.

Solid reasons must exist for Langley's orders. According to scuttlebutt, all contracts now had to be cleared, at least verbally, with the White House.

Broadsword could not envision the scope of a problem that would require a full alert of all spooks in Europe, and the summary executions of five people.

What the hell was going on?

Broadsword wished he knew. He had been unable to learn anything from his contacts in Washington.

He dreaded what he had to do, for he had many good memories of Loomis, Johnson, and Tycoon, and even of Grindstaff.

He wondered what they could have done to bring such wrath down upon them from Langley.

Peter Rabbit returned and eased into the seat beside him.

"Grindstaff and Johnson are on separate cars, up front," he said.

"They make you?"

"I didn't give them the chance," Peter Rabbit said. "Besides, they've never seen me in a suit, with my hair cut. They probably wouldn't recognize me."

"No sign of Loomis and Tycoon?"

"I've been through the whole train," Peter Rabbit said. "They're not aboard."

Broadsword considered his next move.

It would have to be the right one.

"When we stop at Jemelle, you step off and contact Bowman. Have him airlift everyone into Luxembourg. That's bound to be where the action is."

"What's the plan?" Peter Rabbit asked.

"Just tell them to meet us in Luxembourg, and to follow wherever we go," Broadsword said. "I'm guessing that we're all heading to a rendezvous."

"And we'll take them all at the same time?"

"Less messy, that way," Broadsword said.

"Also be more dangerous," Peter Rabbit pointed out.

Chapter

27

"The woman was an American schoolteacher," Zoff insisted. "Stoeller said she spoke in French. But her accent, her dress, her mannerisms, were unmistakable."

Hampton examined the photograph of the woman. Something about her seemed familiar. But he could not place her. "What exactly did she want?" he asked.

"Something about doing her doctoral dissertation on pre-

Roman influences in medieval architecture," Zoff said. "She wanted to examine and photograph the old towers."

"That sounds legitimate," Giancarlo volunteered. "Celtic artifacts have been found on the grounds. The towers are incredibly old. Any authority on the subject would be intrigued by them."

Hampton was still holding the photograph. The woman would be extremely attractive if she made an effort, he noticed. Her build was hidden beneath an inexpensive cloth coat. But the cheekbones, the shape of the face could not be better. The mouth was too prim, the hair downplayed. Yet . . .

"I've seen this woman somewhere before," he said, surprising himself as well as the other members of Hamlet.

"Where?" Giancarlo asked. "Who is she?"

"I don't know," Hampton said. "It's just a feeling. What about the car?"

"It checks out—rented in Luxembourg this morning. Maybe we should look further. . . ."

Hampton was beginning to doubt his hunch. "I'm probably wrong," he said.

"Someone stops every few days," Zoff said. "American tourists, sometimes German, Danes. I don't think it's anything to get alarmed about. Stoeller wouldn't have mentioned it if she hadn't been so aggressive."

"Still, we're vulnerable," Hampton pointed out. "The longer the wait, the greater the risk. There's no doubt in my mind that Loomis has put together a team to search us out."

"What was the exact wording of the contract on Loomis?" Giancarlo asked Thornsen.

"It was phrased various ways, in various messages," Thornsen said. "The one filed as the order from Langley said Loomis and his team were operating independently, posing a threat to the security of the United States, and must be eliminated on sight."

"It could be a ruse," Hampton said.

"A ruse? How?" Giancarlo asked.

"I think there is a strong possibility that the U.S. government—or someone—has made the connection to me," Hampton said. "Somewhere, they may have found a clue.

They may have put together an assault team. They're afraid we'll get wind of it, so they've set up this diversion of a manhunt for Loomis.''

"It might be legitimate," Giancarlo pointed out. "If Loomis *is* off on his own, Washington has reason to worry."

"All beside the point," Hampton argued. "Either way, Loomis and his crew most certainly are in Europe, violating the conditions of the Ultimatum. What difference does it make whether Loomis has sanction or not? The effect is the same, and they let it happen. I think we should fire the Rapier rockets."

For a dozen heartbeats, no one spoke.

"What about the weather?" Giancarlo asked. "Has the wind shifted?"

"Along the western portions," Thornsen said. "But we need another hour or so for optimum conditions."

"I think we should wait, and make certain Loomis is headed this way," Bernardo said. "We may be acting prematurely."

"Tell them, Trane," Hampton said. "Tell them what you just learned."

"Well, there's some resistance building in Washington," Thornsen said. "The chairman of the Joint Chiefs, Admiral Morgan, is maneuvering behind the scenes for a military coup. He is spreading word among the brass, and the Ultimatum rapidly is becoming general knowledge."

"We now have absolutely no alternative," Hampton said. "We've got to nip that in the bud. Remember! We agreed that if there was any resistance at all, we would act. Well, here it is! There is nothing left for us to do but to fire the rockets."

The great baronial hall was silent. Hampton studied the face of each Hamlet member. No one offered a hint of protest.

"All right, Trane," Hampton said. "Fire Rapier as soon as the front passes the entire line of rockets."

"I'll set the machines to fire automatically," Thornsen said. "You see, there is that capability, built into the same circuit that monitors the proximity devices."

"Won't that negate the proximity devices?" Hampton asked.

Thornsen smiled. "Only for an instant," he said. "And after that, it won't matter."

Chapter

28

Loomis sat on the stone steps by the tomb of George S. Patton, Jr., and waited, worrying.

"She's late," he said. "Two hours overdue."

"We put a lot on her," Tycoon said. "Maybe we didn't allow her enough time."

Loomis looked out over the gently curving rows of white crosses toward the distant trees.

They had been unable to find Tycoon's friend in Brussels—the communications expert they hoped would be able to pinpoint Hamlet's location through his knowledge and contacts. As far as they knew, he was dead. And they had no way of knowing if Maria Elena had reached him first.

"If anything happened to her . . ." Loomis said.

"Let's not borrow trouble," Burke said. "We've enough as it is."

"There's no doubt that Langley's onto us," Grindstaff said. "We've got to face facts. They nailed Tycoon's Belgian contact."

"I thought maybe they would," Tycoon said. "It stands to reason that they'd put a cover on all my clandestine help. But he may be all right. Maybe he's just hiding out. We don't know that he's dead."

"Or that he got the information to Maria Elena," Loomis said.

"Well, there's nothing we can do but wait," Tycoon said. "If she has failed, then we have failed. It's as simple as that."

"You've failed," said a voice from the trees behind them.

Loomis rose slowly to his feet and turned, regretting that his Uzi was leaning against the monument, several feet away.

Broadsword emerged from the woods. He was carrying a 9-mm. Austrian Steyr submachine gun. He was flanked by three men, similarly armed.

"Hello, Broadsword," Loomis said. He thought he also recognized another one. "Pete, is that you?"

"It's me," Peter Rabbit said. "Looks like you've fucked up again, Loomis."

"This is a hell of a note," Tycoon said to Broadsword. "We discussed calling you, to invite you in on this caper. Now it looks like you're on the wrong side."

"I'm not on any side," Broadsword said. "I just tend to follow orders, until I have reason to do otherwise. From what I hear, that's more than I can say for you."

"Depends on the orders, the reasons," Loomis said.

"I think he's just pissed off because we didn't invite him in," Tycoon said. He glanced at his Uzi, resting beside Loomis's, two full steps away.

"It's Langley that's pissed," Broadsword said. "And highly. They want you dead. You've got maybe thirty seconds to tell me why."

Loomis let five of those seconds elapse while he framed an answer.

"Suppose you learned that the U.S. government had surrendered to a foreign power," he said. "And suppose you had a chance to wipe out that foreign power, even if Langley told you not to."

Broadsword hesitated.

"Pose him another riddle," Tycoon said. "Maybe he can't think and shoot at the same time."

"He needs to think," Loomis said. "He needs to think back. He needs to remember what we went through together. He needs to remember what he owes us. You, me, Johnson."

Broadsword started. "Where *is* Johnson?" he asked abruptly.

"Behind you," Johnson said. "And don't turn around. I'm holding an old Lewis on you. It may not be as cute as those little doodads you're carrying. But it's meaner. Just put those little things down in front of you."

Broadsword did not move. His three aides followed his lead.

"All right, then. Turn around," Johnson said. "I'm betting I can drop two of you before you drop me."

Broadsword slowly knelt, as if to put his weapon on the pavement. At the last moment, he wheeled, gun in hand.

Johnson fired, diving to the ground. Broadsword, Peter Rabbit, and their two companions were flattened by an awesome scythe of bullets from the Lewis. They did not get off a single round.

Neither did Loomis or Tycoon. By the time they reached their weapons, the battle was over.

Johnson slowly got to his feet.

"I'm even better than I thought I was," he said. He walked over and looked down at Broadsword's body.

"But this was some way to prove it," he added. "I always thought of Broadsword as a hell of a good friend."

"He must have grown fat and lazy in Lisbon," Tycoon said.

"I suppose so," Johnson said. "At least, he forgot how to count."

Chapter

29

Leaving the safety of the trees, Loomis crawled steadily across the meadow, dragging the tripod of the old machine gun, constantly watching the distant castle.

Along the entrance road, dimly lit, he could see the guards milling around their station. The castle itself was illuminated by floodlights set in the shrubbery.

"We've got to move left," Johnson whispered behind him. "Doc needs a full field of fire."

Loomis could see the problem. A grove of a dozen trees partially blocked the view of the castle. But there were other considerations.

"We don't want to put Doc too close to the guards," he pointed out.

"Fuck the guards," Johnson said. "They're Grindstaff's meat."

They had divided areas of responsibility. Grindstaff was to keep the guards at bay, moving along three machine guns. Burke was to concentrate on the castle itself, laying down heavy fire from the other three machine guns. Loomis and Johnson would advance on the castle, under supporting fire from Tycoon and Maria Elena.

They made three more trips across the open field, moving the heavy machine guns, the awkward tripods, and the varied ammunition into position.

Loomis carefully checked the traverse of each gun, making certain Grindstaff and Burke would have the entire entrance road and castle front covered.

Before dispersing according to plan, they huddled briefly.

"Johnson and I may need five minutes to find the back entrance," Loomis said. "Try to keep everything quiet until then. Wait until you hear us shoot. Then pour it on."

He turned to Maria Elena. "You've done your work," he said. "Don't try to show us up now. We don't want you hurt. Just make some noise with that thing, when the time comes."

They separated. Grindstaff and Burke crawled to the machine guns. Tycoon and Maria Elena, armed with the light Ingram M 10s, moved to the grove of trees that provided angle on the front door. Loomis and Johnson, weighted with extra clips for the Ingrams, began circling to the rear, where the prewar drawings and photographs showed an entrance to the wine caves.

Loomis assumed that would be Hamlet's escape route.

In near darkness, they approached the old stone towers. Loomis and Johnson were moving, virtually in silence, when Loomis heard a strange, metallic sound to his right.

"Down!" Johnson yelled.

The night exploded.

The seven members of Hamlet were at dinner in the great baronial hall when the castle was jarred by the blast.

"What was that?" Bernardo yelled, leaping to his feet, overturning his chair.

Hampton raised his hands, palms spread outward, signaling for silence. The other members of Hamlet froze. He listened carefully, but heard no further sounds.

"An animal may have tripped a mine," Giancarlo said. "It's happened before."

"Maybe," Hampton said. "But we can't take any chances." He tapped Vogel on the shoulder. "Come on, Helmut. We'll go get the machine guns set up, just in case. Ahmed, you and Bernardo go cover the escape tunnel. Zoff . . ."

"The securities," Zoff said. "I'd better get the securities."

"Damn it, we're not running," Hampton told him.

"But we'll need them if we *do* have to leave," Zoff insisted.

Hampton gave up. "All right. Go get the securities, then." He turned to Giancarlo. "You and Trane go stick with the machines."

Ahmed had moved to the arms case in the hall, and was dispensing Heckler and Koch MP54s and ammunition. Hampton reached out and took Thornsen by the arm.

"If anything happens, don't wait. Hit the manual override. Fire the Rapier rockets."

Thornsen attempted to explain something. "But the front . . ."

Hampton cut him off. "Fuck the front," he said. "Just fire them."

He turned and headed for the stairs. Ahead of him, he could hear the boots of the security guards as they raced for the machine guns on the third floor.

Stunned by the concussion, Loomis rolled to his knees. His night vision had been temporarily destroyed by the glare of the blast. He could hear Johnson moving beside him.

"Are you all right?" Loomis asked.

"I think so," Johnson said. "God, what was it?"

"A proximity mine, probably," Loomis said. "Or we may have tripped a wire."

"Wasn't a Claymore," Johnson said. "I didn't hear any slugs go by."

"Probably more of a warning device," Loomis said. "And it worked. The cat's out of the bag now." His night vision was returning. "Let's move," he said.

The area near the back entrance to the wine caves had been covered by vineyards in the old photographs Maria Elena found. The area was now a parking lot. A dozen or more large cars were clustered near the entrance, protected by a low shed projecting from the side of the hill. A uniformed guard stood at the door, looking off toward the site of the explosion. He was talking on a hand-held radio.

"We better take him quick," Johnson said. "You want to go left, or right?"

"Left," Loomis said.

He circled to the left, keeping low, hidden among the low shrubs bordering the parking lot. A few steps away, he stopped, fished on the ground, found a foot-long twig, and waited. When he had given Johnson enough time, he threw the twig past the guard, into the shadows behind the entrance.

The guard turned.

It was his last act on earth.

Johnson leaped from the shrubbery and throttled him.

Loomis checked the parking area to make certain that they were alone. He was approaching the door, to see if it was locked, when it burst open.

Loomis dropped flat. A stream of bullets from an automatic weapon went over him, slamming into the parked cars.

"Move!" Johnson yelled, opening up the door with the Ingram.

Loomis rolled to his feet and ran to the left, giving Johnson a field of fire. At the edge of the shed he knelt and waited, then began firing bursts into the open doorway as Johnson came up fast on the right.

Johnson did not slow down. He ran full tilt through the open door, taking up the firing as he went.

Loomis got to his feet and followed Johnson into the tunnel.

Johnson was kneeling, his Ingram trained on a curve in the tunnel twenty yards away.

Nothing moved.

Loomis squatted behind Johnson. There was no place to hide, no cover in sight. A single electrical wire along one side of the tunnel carried current to a string of naked bulbs. The floors of the tunnel, earthen in the old photographs, were now planked.

Up ahead, Loomis heard voices.

"No, Zoff! No!" someone yelled.

A black satchel jutted out from the curve of the tunnel, held chest high.

"We can make a deal!" the holder of the bag shouted, still not showing himself.

Loomis and Johnson waited. The bag holder walked into view—a tall, blond Nordic type, impeccably dressed in a soft gray three-piece pinstripe.

"Looks like a fucking banker," Johnson whispered.

"Zoff! I'm warning you!" the first voice yelled.

Zoff kept on coming. "Don't shoot," he called to Loomis and Johnson. "I have a fortune here. We can make a deal!"

He was still moving when the other figure came into view—a small Arab holding a Heckler and Koch MP54.

The Arab cut Zoff down with a burst of 9-mm. slugs.

Loomis shot the Arab. The Ingram was on cyclic. More than half a clip of .45 ACP bullets caught him high in the chest.

As the sounds of gunfire died, Loomis heard someone running on the plank floor. The sound of footsteps faded down the tunnel.

Loomis ran past Johnson. Stepping over Zoff and the Arab, he reached the curve.

The way was clear to a distant, closed door.

"Cover me," Loomis said.

Keeping to the left, to give Johnson a field of fire, he ran toward the door. It was big and heavy, and of solid oak.

He had just reached the door, and was wondering what to do, when there came the thunder of large-caliber weapons deep in the castle.

Loomis remembered the heavy third-floor shutters over the dormer windows. He had been concerned over what they might screen.

And now he knew.

Fifty-caliber machine guns.

Crouching on opposite sides of the computer room, Giancarlo and Bernardo kept their Hecklers trained on the closed door. Thornsen, oblivious to the danger, wandered from machine to machine, searching for signs of what was now happening on the East Coast of America.

"I tried to tell Hamp," Thornsen said, talking to himself. "You see, the atmospheric pressure switches are on the

288

same circuit as the proximity devices. Once you've relinquished control . . ."

"Shut up, Trane!" Giancarlo said in a stage whisper. He
called to Bernardo. "How many of them are there?"

Bernardo was still breathing hard, trembling. "I don't
know," he said. "It all happened so fast . . ."

"Think!" Giancarlo said. "Surely you have some idea."

"But I didn't see *anybody*," Bernardo said. "Like I told
you, Zoff went out, to make a deal. Ahmed shot him. They
shot Ahmed. I came back."

Giancarlo debated what to do. They could not abandon
the machines. Not now. Not unless . . .

"Fire the Rapier rockets!" he called to Thornsen. "Manual override!"

"That's what I've been trying to explain," Thornsen
said, now on the verge of tears. "We relinquished control
to the automatic system! There's no way to get it back! The
signal should come in, any second now. But until it does,
there's nothing I can do!"

The heavy machine guns at the front of the castle were
thundering again. Giancarlo felt an overwhelming urge to
retreat, to seek the comforting firepower of Hamp, Vogel,
and their men. Clearly, whoever was attacking the castle
knew about the security measures, the escape route.

Yet he could not bring himself to abandon the machines,
and twenty years of effort. He was still trying to decide
what to do when he heard the new sound.

Someone was using a fire axe, or a battering ram, on the
door.

Signaling frantically to Bernardo, Giancarlo braced himself against a line printer, took a firm, steady bead, his
finger tight on the trigger, and waited for the first sign of
movement through the door.

From his third-floor gun emplacement at the front of the
castle, George Hampton could find no targets, yet he kept
shooting. At least three of his security guards were dead,
and maybe more. The firepower from the darkness was of

unbelievable intensity—at least five or six large machine guns, scattered along the perimeter. First one would open up, then another. Their accuracy was remarkable. And he had heard gunfire off to the right, near the guards' hut. Maybe the guards there were dead, too.

"Hamp!" Vogel called from behind him.

Hampton ceased firing and dropped to the floor, accidentally putting a hand in a pool of blood from one of the slain guards. He wiped the hand on his trousers. Vogel was crawling toward him, keeping low.

"All of the guards are dead!" Vogel said.

Hampton was not surprised. He had always assumed that if a big crunch came, the security force would be worthless. That was the price they paid for secrecy; the security force was geared for industrial espionage and petty burglary, not for pitched battle.

And the .50-caliber guns were positioned to fire at two hundreds yards and beyond. They would not deflect low enough to reach the shrubbery where the assault machine guns were emplaced.

"I think it's time for us to get the hell out of here, Hamp," Vogel said.

Hampton laughed at him. "And leave all this? Twenty years' work?"

He rolled to the window, raised his head, and looked out. The floodlights illuminated the grounds for a hundred yards. Nothing moved.

"We can begin again," Vogel said. "All we need is Trane, and Zoff . . ."

Hampton was more mystified than frightened. "I don't understand it," he said. "There can't be many of them. If it was an army strike force, or even the CIA, they'd be all over the place by now."

"I heard shooting around back," Vogel said. "They seem to know what they're doing."

"Loomis and Johnson," Hampton said. "It must be them. But how did they find us? How did they get through the mine field? And where did they get those machine guns?"

"And how did they know about the back entance?" Vogel said. "You know, the others may all be dead back there. We may be all that's left of Hamlet."

"Not bloody likely," Hampton said. But he knew his voice lacked conviction.

He was well aware of the shortcomings of the other members of Hamlet. Zoff would run. Ahmed would do something hotheaded, foolish. Bernardo probably would go to pieces. Thornsen knew nothing but computers. And Giancarlo would hesitate, at exactly the wrong moment.

Vogel held up a hand, his head cocked, listening.

Hampton also heard the sound.

At first, he thought some of the security force might be returning to help.

Then he knew.

Someone had reached the third floor. Hampton reached for his Heckler.

"Maybe you're right," he said to Vogel. "Maybe it's time to go. Let's take care of these people, then we'll fight our fucking way out of here."

Grindstaff waited at the end of the hall on the third floor while Tycoon inched his way toward the first open door. Grindstaff could see him faintly silhouetted in the reflection from the outside floodlights.

The big guns had stopped. Grindstaff had no way of knowing why. Dr. Burke had poured hundreds of rounds into the four dormer windows on the third floor, but Grindstaff had to assume that at least some of the defenders remained alive.

Surprise had been the key—along with the knowledge of the castle layout, exterior and interior, supplied by Maria Elena.

Thus far, the entire operation had been easy. Grindstaff and Tycoon had eliminated the entire personnel of the guards' hut within minutes. Dr. Burke, covered by Maria Elena, had moved from gun to gun, keeping the assault fire continuous. The return fire had been high and ineffectual. Grindstaff had heard firing behind the castle; he assumed that Loomis and Johnson were also doing their work. Now, nothing remained but a mopping-up operation at the front of the castle.

The long, narrow hall had four doors opening to the left—apparently one for each dormer gun emplacement. The opposite wall seemed solid. Light from the front of the castle, entering through the windows, framed each doorway.

Down the hall, Tycoon signaled. Grindstaff left the safety of the stair landing and moved toward him. The carpet underfoot was thick, muffling his movement. As he neared the door, Tycoon nodded, then stepped abruptly into the light, his Ingram braced.

He did not fire. After surveying the room, he stepped beyond the door, motioning for Grindstaff to follow.

Cautiously, Grindstaff looked into the room. Two bodies lay sprawled near the machine gun. The blood spreading on the floor appeared black in the unnatural light.

Grindstaff moved past Tycoon and tapped his chest with a forefinger, indicating that he would take the next doorway. Tycoon grinned and shrugged. Crouching, Grindstaff approached the next opening. When he heard Tycoon coming up behind him, he stepped into the doorway, his Ingram at ready.

The room was almost identical to the first, except that the bodies were in worse condition.

Tycoon moved past him, tapped his chest, and grinned. He took the next room. Three men lay dead in that one.

Grindstaff moved to the final door. Some of his tension was gone. Maybe Dr. Burke had nailed them all with his ancient weapons.

He stepped into the doorway, and was puzzled for a moment by the abundance of bodies—six. Then realization came that at least one was alive, holding a weapon aimed at his chest.

Grindstaff fired, only vaguely aware of the barrage of slugs that came from the other gun. He felt his body slamming backward under a terrible weight, but he forced his concentration onto his own weapon, still firing.

As he hit the floor he heard Tycoon's gun open up, spraying the room. After a furious burst, silence returned.

"Oh, shit, Herman," Tycoon said, kneeling beside him.

Grindstaff looked up, trying to recall what it was he wanted to say. Then he remembered. The face. Hampton's. Just like the photographs.

But as Grindstaff opened his mouth to tell Tycoon, only a curious wetness came out.

He was still wondering about that as he sank into oblivion.

Loomis stood back, providing cover, as Johnson swung the fire axe. The door splintered, but did not collapse. Johnson swung the axe repeatedly, frantically, at arm's length, keeping his body well clear of the door.

As the axe penetrated, the shooting began. Two guns inside concentrated on the door, finishing the job the axe had started, shattering the heavy wood.

Johnson let the axe fall to the plank floor. The firing stopped.

Through the holes in the door, Loomis could see a large open room, filled with machinery.

Johnson picked up his Ingram, checked the load, and readied another clip. Loomis understood what he was planning to do.

"No!" he whispered.

But he was too late.

Johnson charged the door at a full run, one shoulder low.

The door shattered. Taking parts of it with him, Johnson sailed through the opening, dropping to the floor, rolling away.

Loomis fired into the room. At first, he had no target. But as he ran toward the door, he shifted his arm to the red wink of a muzzle blast.

He fell into the room, rolling, hearing Johnson's weapon firing.

Then Johnson was on his feet, gun ready, but silent.

"I think that's all of them, but one," he said. "And great gods and little fishes. Look at that!"

A tall, emaciated man stood in the middle of the room. His eyes were wide, feverish. He was dancing around, mumbling something unintelligible.

Loomis approached him, gun ready. Johnson moved out to flank him.

"You're too late!" the gaunt, pale scarecrow screamed, his voice breaking into falsetto. "It's been done!"

"What's done?" Loomis asked, knowing.

"It's automatic!" The apparition danced in glee. "The cold front is at the last station!" He cocked an ear. "Listen! When the signal comes through, you'll hear the switch close! And that will be it!"

Johnson fired.

For an instant, Loomis did not understand.

Then he did.

He joined Johnson, emptying clips into the banks of computers as fast as he could reload.

"No!" the scarecrow screamed as he dived, in a vain effort to protect the machinery with his body.

The stream of .45 slugs from Johnson's gun passed right through. The scarecrow crumpled to the floor and lay still.

Johnson and Loomis did not stop until all their ammunition was expended.

The machinery was in shambles. The Ingrams were burned-out hulls. Acrid smoke filled the air.

"I wonder if we stopped it," Loomis said.

"I didn't hear anything click," Johnson said.

"You couldn't have heard thunder," Loomis said.

Johnson agreed. "I owe Tycoon an apology. These little things sure can shoot."

All was quiet in the castle above.

Loomis was starting up the steps when Tycoon's voice came from above.

"Loomis? Don't shoot. It's me."

Loomis and Johnson went up the stairs. Maria Elena came to Loomis.

"Grindstaff bought it," Tycoon said. "He shot it out with Hampton and another guy. He got Hampton. I got the other guy."

"Burke?" Johnson asked.

"Flesh wound. That's his diagnosis. He's in a front room."

Johnson ran back into the tunnel to get the mysterious bag. Then they went upstairs and down the hall to a large room.

Burke was seated at a long table, securing a compress against his bloody leg.

"I've fixed hundreds of these," he said. "For the first time, I know how it feels." He grinned. "It hurts like hell."

Johnson put the bag on the table and started digging through it.

"These are all something called 'bearers' shares," he said. "What the hell does that mean?"

"It means we're rich," Tycoon said. "They're negotiable, just like money. Hamlet must have had that kind of a partnership. The guy that has the certificates owns them." He examined them carefully. "This looks like it might represent the entire Hamlet holdings, all over the world."

"And now *we* have them," Loomis said.

"Hey, here's a list of warehouses, marked *Pu*. Chicago, Denver, New Orleans, London . . ."

"Pu," Tycoon said. "Chemical shorthand for plutonium."

"Boy, will Langley be glad to get this stuff," Johnson said.

"Who said anything about giving it to Langley?" Loomis asked.

Johnson grinned. "What you got in mind?"

"There's an island in the Caribbean for sale," Loomis said. "I never thought I'd have the money. I could use some partners. What about it?"

"What the fuck would we do with an island?" Johnson asked.

Loomis was looking at Maria Elena. "Oh, I don't know. We might set up a research facility to extract food from the ocean, for one thing."

Johnson frowned, puzzled. "I suppose that's an idea that will make more sense after you think about it a while."

"What do you people say?" Loomis asked. "We're all in it."

"I'd say it's a good idea," Burke said. "It's about fifty years too late for me, but maybe not for you."

"Partners, I'd say we've got about five minutes to get the hell out of here," Tycoon said. "The local constabulary —and maybe worse—is bound to be on the way. I don't know about you folks, but I've always hated long explanations. My Lear is probably out of the question. But I know where we can lease a good Grumman Gulfstream that's a bit faster. It's also more expensive, but that shouldn't worry us now."

They started toward the door, helping Burke.

Johnson looked back at the huge baronial hall.

"Well, I guess that's the end of Hamlet," he said.

"What the hell are you talking about?" Loomis asked. "Now *we* are Hamlet. And I'll tell you one something else."

"What?" Johnson asked, on cue.

"Nobody's going to mess with us."